Ignite

Skye Malone

Ignite

Book Two of the Kindling Trilogy
Previously Published as The Children and the Blood Trilogy

Join Skye Malone's mailing list to hear about new releases!
www.skyemalone.com/mailinglist

For Avery

Prologue

Across the table in the greasy spoon diner, Harris watched the man who'd introduced himself as Brogan's employer. Lean-built and dressed in a well-tailored suit, Victor Jamison appeared to be nothing more than a middle-aged business man, and not the leader of a group waging a silent war.

But Harris remembered his first impression of Brogan. The giant had seemed the same, albeit while also appearing to be a human wall.

"What do you want?" Harris asked.

Jamison smiled, as if amused by the question. "Your help, of course."

Harris tried not to scowl. A month of searching, a million dead-end leads, and he'd gotten exactly nowhere toward finding Ashley, her sister or the boy they'd run away with. Or close to nowhere. He figured briefly catching the little girl and Cole scarcely counted, since with the help of others like Ashley, they'd only managed to escape again, leaving all his contacts with Brogan's people dead in their wake.

"Detective Harris, you *do* realize your capture of the boy and the little girl are the closest anyone has come to those children in eight years?" the man continued as though reading Harris' mind. "Add to that the fact the men who apprehended them with you are all dead and, well–" He smiled again. "–you can see how you possess information no one else does."

"What kind of information, Mr. Jamison?" Harris asked, resisting the urge to glance at his stack of essentially useless notes.

"Names, locations, places they might hide. You may not realize the extent of what you know, but any piece could be valuable. For example, the boy. Cole. Where was he living? Who were his keepers? Do you know where those keepers may go or whether he will seek to rejoin them?"

For a heartbeat, Harris didn't answer, trying to decide whether to trust the man. He claimed to be Brogan's employer, but words meant little. The giant never mentioned Victor Jamison. He never even mentioned having a boss. The man could be anybody.

But it didn't matter, Harris realized. He had to trust the man's word because he couldn't confirm Jamison's identity anyway, owing to the fact that, after hours of trying to reach him, Brogan had yet to answer the phone, and all his other contacts currently occupied the morgue.

He sighed. "The Smiths are gone. I'm not really sure if–"

"The Smiths?"

"Robert and Melissa Smith," Harris elaborated. "The boy's parents. They've taken off. Nobody's seen Melissa since yesterday, and Robert's been missing over a month."

A touch of hardness came into Jamison's eyes at Harris' words, but the man buried it swiftly. "And Cole?"

"He's disappeared. But I doubt he'll join back up with them

anyway. When I found him, he had a gun pointed at his mother."

Jamison paused. "Really?"

Harris hesitated before nodding. The man almost sounded pleased.

"And did Cole say anything when you had him with you?" Jamison continued. "Did he talk to you at all?"

Shaking his head, Harris eyed him curiously. "He was focused on the other car. The one with the little girl in it." He paused. "Why are you so interested in Cole, Mr. Jamison? I thought you and Brogan were trying to save the little girl and catch her sister?"

The man looked down as though deciding what to say. "Cole Jamison – or, as you know him, Cole *Smith*," he said the name like a curse, "is my son."

Training kept Harris' face straight despite his surprise.

"Eight years ago, the 'Smiths' and their associates stole him from me. Together with others of similar skill to the young lady responsible for nearly killing your partner, they kidnapped him and I have not seen him since." He grimaced. "Brogan and his men have scoured the country ceaselessly on my behalf, but these 'wizards', as they call themselves, have been damnably successful in keeping my son hidden."

Jamison paused. "And then an unknown young man turned up on a security video in the company of a child whose sister slaughtered over half a dozen people in a single night. And once I learned that young man was Cole, well…" His smile was cold. "For some things, one does not wait for word from others, no matter what the realities of the situation might be.

"I do not know what part my son has been forced to play in the wizards' game, Detective. But if I know him at all anymore, I can assure you it is not a willing role, whatever the news and the evidence might say. He may be confused and misled, but he is not one of them, and he does not possess the powers they do. He is in danger, as much as that child, and I need any information you have, no matter how seemingly insignificant, to help me find him before the wizards make him disappear again."

The undercurrent of iron in Jamison's voice made Harris pause. Studying the man's face briefly, he ran the conversation, and its ludicrous key points, back through his head.

"Why did they take him from you?"

"A disagreement," Jamison allowed after a moment. "In which they attempted to gain the upper hand by threatening my son. Wizards are not the nicest of people, Detective, as I am certain you are aware."

Harris didn't bother acknowledging the fact. "So how do Brogan and his group fit in? They're like these others? 'Wizards'?"

He struggled to keep his voice neutral, though he'd never expected to utter that word in a conversation in his life. In the past month, he couldn't say he'd become accustomed to living in this ridiculous new reality where people burst into flame or couldn't be seen by the human eye when it suited them. But it'd started to settle. Actually using words associated with fantasy creatures, on the other hand, was pushing it a bit far.

Jamison seemed to take it in stride, however, and simply shook his head with the same veiled intensity in his eyes. "Brogan and the others are not like them. Neither am I. We call ourselves the Blood, Detective Harris, owing to an unusual history with which I will not take your time. Suffice it to say, we possess comparable powers, but there the similarity ends."

Face tightening at the unsatisfactory answer, Harris didn't respond for a moment. "I don't have much else to tell you, Mr. Jamison," he said finally. "Last I saw your son, he was running into a forest with the younger girl in tow, while these 'wizards' and your men were blowing the hell out of each other with thin air. I attempted pursuit, but the aforementioned blasts of nothing slowed me down. By the time I reached the forest, they'd escaped."

"Do you know where they might have headed?"

Harris shook his head. "I–"

He cut off as a slender man with a ponytail of graying hair strode into the diner and headed for the table.

"My apologies," the man said, his attention focused solely on Jamison. "Isabella just called. It's Brogan. He's alive, but…"

"'*But*', Simeon?" Jamison prompted, his voice deadly.

The man grimaced. "It was Ashley, sir. He tried to apprehend her." Simeon paused. "She brought half a building down on him. Like I said, he's alive. But Isabella doesn't know how long she can keep him that way."

Harris couldn't see Jamison breathing. But then, he couldn't tell if he was either. He felt like ice water had replaced his bloodstream while the world had suddenly gone still. A screaming face burned beyond recognition rose before his eyes, bringing with it memories of all that followed.

He'd made himself believe Brogan when the man said finding the little girl would stop her older sister. He'd given so much time and energy to that task, despite his reservations, and despite how much he'd wanted to be out there catching the girl responsible for the mess his and Malden's lives had become.

And it didn't matter. He'd failed and she'd done it again. In the time it'd taken him to find – and lose – her sister, Ashley had ruthlessly eliminated another person who'd gotten in her way.

"You will have to excuse me, Detective," Jamison said with tight civility. "As you can see, there are matters to which I must attend."

Harris glanced between the men, briefly lost for words.

"But," Jamison continued, drawing a business card for the Rio Dulce Hotel from his pocket. "Your assistance is still crucial. Please be at this location at one o'clock."

He placed the card on the table.

"Good day, Detective."

Without another word, Jamison followed Simeon out of the diner. Harris stared after them, and saw the waitress glance around in confusion as the bell above the door clanged when the two men left.

He exhaled, pulling his gaze from the door. Over their plates of pancakes and hash browns, people were eyeing him surreptitiously with looks ranging from disgust to alarm.

Confusion flickered through him, and then he realized why.

Invisible wizards. Or Blood, or whatever. He cursed internally, but couldn't really find it in himself to care that, for the past ten minutes, he'd probably looked as though he'd been carrying on a rather elaborate conversation with the air.

Because she'd done it again.

Grimacing darkly, he shook his head. He'd had enough of chasing people several steps removed from the person responsible for this. He couldn't do it anymore. Because while he understood Jamison wanting to find his son, the girl who presented the real threat to Cole and everyone else in the world was still out there.

And now she'd nearly killed someone. Again.

His gaze dropped to the business card lying on the tabletop. He'd go hear what Jamison had to say, though he was fairly certain it would pertain to continuing pursuit of his son. On Jamison's list of priorities, Ashley was obviously a far second to Cole.

That was fine. Jamison could keep searching for the kid and the little girl. Harris didn't mind.

Shoving the card into a pocket, he glanced around the diner again. At his expression, the people at the other tables looked hastily away.

And that was fine too. Everything was absolutely fine.

Because he was going to stop Ashley.

No matter what it took.

Chapter One

Gravel skittering beneath her shoes, Ashe slid to a stop and then ducked behind a rusting dumpster. Bracing herself on the grimy metal, she tossed a quick glance to the blessedly empty rooftops, and then waited a heartbeat more before leaning around the garbage bin.

Three Taliesin wizards pounded up to the alley.

She jerked back. Voices shouted from across the street, revealing the presence of the wizards' allies, though their words were unclear. Heart pounding, she looked past the other dumpsters to the far end of the alley and then shifted her feet, getting ready to make a run for it.

More wizards rushed by. With a gasp, she retreated farther into the shadows.

She closed her eyes, clutching her gun despite how useless it'd probably be. The wizards were everywhere. On the street corners, on the rooftops. Every wizard who'd survived the apartment building and countless more besides.

And each one of them Taliesin.

Twenty minutes ago, they'd spotted her as she paused at a bus stop to get directions from the sun-bleached map on the wall. A shout had rung out, she'd looked up, and suddenly half a dozen Taliesin were chasing her.

They hadn't been interested in questions. She'd barely made it out of the bus stop before a blast of magic sent her flying and the tiny depot vanished in a shower of glass and metal shards. Scrambling to her feet, she'd taken off running and hadn't stopped since.

The wizards left the alley entrance behind, and as their footsteps faded, she let out the breath she'd been holding. Shifting her grip on the gun, she straightened slowly, checking in both directions before rising from the garbage bin's cover completely. With a final glance to the roof, she pushed away from the dumpster and headed toward the alley's far end.

Taxis and buses swept by on the busy street. People pushed past one another as they juggled coffee cups, cell phones and briefcases in their hands. In the distance, sirens still howled, attending to the bus stop explosion that she could only hope had been devoid of casualties.

The crowd parted as she walked, shifting to one side of her or the other with little notice of what they were doing. Scanning the road, she hurried toward the intersection. Clarkston Street had to be nearby. Back at the bus stop, she'd been only a few blocks away.

But she'd gotten turned around since then, and none of the street signs looked familiar.

Anxiety started to build despite her efforts to stay calm, and she ran a hand through her hair as she stared at the crowds. She needed to find Cornelius. To do as Carter asked. And to hide until the Taliesin wizards went away.

If they went away.

An apprehensive noise escaped her, though no one paid it any mind. Checking the rooftops again, she bit her lip, and then dropped the magic around her.

The crowd buffeted her, the jarring interspersed with rare apologies. With a gasp, she dodged a bicyclist weaving through the throng, and then grabbed the arm of the first person she saw.

"Where can I find Clarkston Street?" she yelled over the honking of a car horn.

Tugging out of her grip, the old woman gaped at her and then scurried away. Ashe swallowed hard and then reached out, calling the question again.

"Clarkston?" a man answered distractedly, barely glancing at her past the cell phone pressed to his ear. "Maybe five blocks that way."

"Thanks."

He'd already forgotten her. Magic rising again, she took off through the crowd. Cars slowed as she raced across the street and horns blared from the vehicles behind. On their leashes, a pack of dogs in the care of a professional walker suddenly went berserk, causing minor chaos for several yards around.

Her eyes widened at the sight and then magic was rushing at her. Throwing herself to the concrete, she covered her head with her arms as the window of the pet shop next to her shattered. Gasping, she scrambled for her feet while people screamed and every animal in the store went mad.

Two Taliesin stepped from a storefront door ahead. Two more raced at her from behind.

She looked from them to the animals, and then leapt the jagged window frame and ran into the store. Grabbing wildly at the nearby cages, she yanked them down behind her, sending the rodents inside scattering. Confused and panicking, the clerks hurried from behind the counter to stop the escapees.

The stockroom door slammed into the wall as she burst past it and raced for the rear exit. Shoving the fire door out of her way, she hit the alley and kept going. Tearing across streets and down alleys between office buildings, she barely noticed the horns blaring at her back. Mustard-toned street signs flashed past, noted and swiftly forgotten.

Clarkston caught her eye. She skidded to a halt, scanning the street for addresses and wizards equally.

A desperate laugh escaped her. The apartment building she needed was right across the road.

The laugh threatened to become hysterical, and she choked it back. It didn't matter. Nothing mattered. She was almost there.

She glanced around, and then darted across the street.

The wrought iron gate opened easily, its lock long since broken, and quickly she slipped through. A shadowed archway waited beyond and led to a courtyard at the heart of the apartment complex. Sticking close to the wall, she hurried along the tunnel and then paused at the end, eyeing the empty courtyard. A mosaic of tile crisscrossed the floor, its colors scuffed and faded by years of foot traffic, and ironwork fences ringed the galleries of the hallways above. A breeze twisted down from the open air roof, stirring the potted plants and carrying the faint sounds of daytime television.

Shaking with fading adrenaline, she glanced to the nearby apartment numbers and then headed for the stairs. Metal creaked beneath her feet as she climbed, sounding loud in the quiet. At the third floor she paused, catching sight of the apartment number at the end of the walkway.

Her hand lingered on the metal rail, and after a moment's hesitation, she forced herself to let it go. Gun clutched in her other hand, she started down the hall.

A door opened behind her and she spun, the weapon coming up instantly.

Oblivious to the gun-wielding girl only a couple feet from his doorstep, a scruffy young man with a backpack on his shoulder and a mug of coffee in his hand let the door slam as he left his apartment. Whistling inanely, he trotted down the steps and headed out of the courtyard.

Her hand shook as she lowered the gun. Drawing an unsteady breath, she watched the empty archway for a moment, and then turned back toward the end of the corridor. Gun still clenched in her grip, she strode to the door and knocked.

Silence answered her.

She trembled. Ordering herself to stop shaking, she knocked again. Nothing.

Her gaze dropped to the door handle. Hesitating briefly, she reached down and pressed it.

The door swung open at her touch.

She exhaled, her fingers adjusting themselves on the gun automatically. Still shivering, she slid through the opening.

The apartment was dark and a mottled cloth covered the lone sofa huddling in a corner. A fake tree stood by the door, with cobwebs hanging in dusty tendrils from its plastic leaves. Heavy curtains obscured the view of the street, creating deep shadows in which nothing moved.

Edging farther inside, she glanced into the single bedroom. A bare mattress occupied the room, with nothing else to keep it company. Through a narrow doorway, she could see an empty bathroom, the shower stripped of curtains behind which someone could hide.

She turned back to the main room, the hours of pent-up emotion rushing to fill the space adrenaline left behind. Cornelius wasn't here. From the look of it, he hadn't been for years.

Her brow twitched down spasmodically as she fought the tears that wanted to rise. She'd tried. She'd tried to do as Carter asked.

The last thing he ever asked.

Anguish rose, pressing hard against the carefully crafted barriers she'd built in the short time since Carter died. Tears burned and she cursed herself furiously, trying to stem the flow of grief with anger where everything else was failing. She wasn't a child and she wouldn't cry like one. So the wizards weren't here. They had to be somewhere. She'd find them.

She'd still do as Carter asked.

With a shuddering breath, she turned to leave.

The closet door behind her swung open. Four wizards rushed into the room, their magic blazing.

They were from Merlin. The thought registered amid her shock. The men and women took positions around her, their expressions changing swiftly from cold threat to veiled startlement and then settling into an inexplicable sort of recognition that set her racing heart pounding all the harder. Turning as she tried to watch them all, she tightened her grip on the gun and let her magic grow stronger. Nearly as one, their eyes narrowed as they felt the energy rise.

From the too-black shadows of the closet, another man emerged. Dark-skinned and tall, with a sable trench coat over his dress shirt and slacks, he stopped at the sight of her, ignoring the closet door as it swung closed behind him. Alarm rippled with lightning speed across his face as his gaze took in the bloodstains covering her clothes, the gash on her forehead, and the gun clutched in her hand. And then the shock vanished completely, as though it had never been.

"Secure the area," he ordered without looking away from her.

Anxiety fluttered in her as he spoke. Cornelius. She recognized his voice from the apartment. And like his voice, his face was familiar. Her brow twitched down, trying to place the memory dancing at the edge of reach.

Two wizards broke off from guarding her and headed for the far sides of the room. By the front door, one of them pushed away the leaves of the artificial tree and punched a few numbers into a keypad hidden behind the greenery, while the other strode to the window and tweaked back the curtain to check the street. Ignoring them, Cornelius crossed the distance to her, the air stirring as he moved.

Vanilla. Cedar. The scents brought back a rush of memory.

On a park bench down the road from an inferno, he'd held her hand as she cradled her baby sister. He'd waited with them as her father dealt with the aftermath of a freak explosion everyone said had been a gas main.

He'd watched over them the night the wizards' war began.

Deep inside, the quivering returned and she smashed it down.

"Are you alright?" he asked, his deep voice low as though to keep the others from hearing.

Her brow furrowed, as much from confusion at his concern as lack of any idea what to say.

"I am Cornelius Jones," he continued. "Third in line of authority on the Merlin Council and Representative of the Southern European Region. I promise we mean you no harm."

She stared at him, wondering what she was supposed to take from that. Blinking, she struggled to push aside her confusion and just focus. "Carter sent me to talk to you."

Traces of anger tightened his face at the mention of his cousin's name.

Coming back from the keypad by the front door, the wizard paused at Cornelius' side. "Several Taliesin nearby, sir," the woman told him quietly. Her gaze flicked to Ashe. "They may have been trailing her."

Cornelius' eyes narrowed slightly at the panicked look that flitted across Ashe's face, and then he nodded to the woman. "Find us a safe portal near the northern edge of town. We are returning to the Council immediately."

The woman bowed her head and then headed toward the closet, clicking on her cell phone as she went. Flipping through a few screens, she paused and then tucked the phone away. Ashe's brow drew down as the woman reached up and ran her fingers down the doorframe.

Electric blue letters appeared, glowing with light. Coalescing into words and then scattering too quickly to follow, they shimmered over the left side of the doorframe for several moments before fading into nothing. Ignoring the display, the woman pulled open the door.

The air pressure in the room dropped, and Ashe blanched. Darkness waited within the closet, and the impenetrable shadows gave a sense of distance they couldn't possibly have possessed. Wind stirred in the room, making the leaves of the artificial tree flutter.

With a short gesture, Cornelius ordered the wizards through the doorway. They stepped past the door and vanished into the darkness.

He stepped to one side, nodding to her. "This way."

Incredulous, Ashe looked between him and the impossible abyss. "You can't be–" She cut off as a beeping sounded from the alarm behind the fake tree. Cornelius made an irritated noise.

Before she could do more than register the fact he was moving, he reached across the distance between them and pulled her with him through the closet doorway.

Rushing air surrounded her. Blackness was everywhere, but not. Images seemed to blur around her so quickly, they became a streak of darkest gray. Bursts of sound accompanied them, rising and falling with impossible speed.

A city street appeared. A shop bell dinged. A subway train rushed past, vanishing almost instantly. For less time than it took to blink, she could see a playground filled with children.

And then she stumbled through a doorway.

Empty clothing racks filled the abandoned store and peeling sale posters covered the grimy windows. As the storage closet door swung closed behind them, Cornelius held her arm by his side with an iron grip.

Everything was swimming. Gasping, she reached out, attempting to catch herself on the wall as her legs wobbled.

Cornelius pulled her against his side tighter, forcibly keeping her upright. Struggling in his grasp, she tried to move the gun pinned between them, her efforts weak from nausea.

"Deep breaths," he ordered softly. "Eyes on the ground till the dizziness stops."

Unable to move, she hesitated and then complied.

The dizziness began to fade.

Swallowing hard, she tugged away from him, and no expression touched his face as he released her arm. Retreating, she scanned the shop. By the windows, the other wizards were checking the parking lots.

"Are we clear?" Cornelius called.

As the wizards nodded, he glanced back at her. A look of consideration flashed through his eyes, replaced almost instantly by fleeting irritation.

"We will take the cars," he ordered.

The other wizards hesitated as though confused, but after a heartbeat, they strode for the back door.

Shaking, she drew a deep breath and braced a hand on the wall beside her, the other still clutching her gun. His face impassive, Cornelius stepped closer, reaching to pull her away from the support. Instantly, her weapon twitched toward him.

He paused, his gaze flicking in the direction the wizards had gone.

"It is of the utmost importance you show no sign of how this is affecting you," he told her quietly. "Just remain calm and come with me. Say nothing. Do you understand?"

Incredulity struggled up out of her shock and her hand tightened on the gun. "What the–"

"That was a portal. A way of travelling which I will happily explain at a later time. But right now, we must get you to safety."

"Why–"

"Later," he interrupted calmly.

She backed along the wall as he started toward her again. Seeing her action, he stopped, frustration tightening his mouth. "I am trying to protect you."

A scoff escaped her and she shook her head, keeping the gun between them. "Why?" she repeated, clinging to the question.

He paused, old resentment playing across his face. "So Carter told you nothing?"

"Carter's *dead!*"

The exclamation burst from her before she could stop it, but at the words he froze. His eyes went to the stains covering her again.

Her fingers adjusted around the gun as she swallowed and then continued more softly. "A Blood wizard killed him trying to get to me. He died this morning. Just after he gave me this."

She drew out the scrap of paper, extending it to him cautiously. After a moment's hesitation, he took it.

"He wanted me to tell you about the Blood."

For a moment, Cornelius didn't answer, his eyes on the stains darkening the paper. With difficulty, he cleared his throat, and the reserved mask returned to his face, though it looked slightly more fractured than before. "We need to go," he said.

"But–"

"Please," he interrupted, his voice strained. "Do as I ask. And do not speak to the others till the Council has had the chance to talk to you first. Just… allow me to get you to safety. Please."

"What's going on?" she asked warily.

"The Council can best explain." He stepped away, clearing a path to the door. "I promise you, Ashley. We mean you no harm."

She paused. "Ashe," she said. A look of confusion moved through his eyes. "I go by Ashe. Not Ashley."

He bowed his head slightly in acknowledgement. Still watching him, she walked toward the door.

The mundane forms of two sedans waited in the service drive. Inside, the wizards sat, watching Cornelius as he crossed to the second vehicle and held open the door. Hesitating briefly, she joined him by the car and then slid into the back seat, half expecting when the driver turned the ignition that the vehicle would suddenly sprout wings and fly. But the car simply started, and a moment later, the two sedans rolled out onto the main roads.

Turning, she glanced through the rear window.

Skyscrapers towered in the distance over the urban sprawl. Billboards for shops and gas stations crowded the next strata of air below, and on the roads, cars were everywhere. In a few seconds, the portal had carried them for miles, right to the edge of the city and far from any wizards that might have been following her.

Unnerved, she turned back around. The fabric seats itched beneath her and she shifted uncomfortably. Glancing down, she caught sight of dust and cedar chips still flecking her jeans from the dash through the pet store.

A humored smile touched her face, dying almost instantly. She wondered if Bus and Spider had gotten out of town alright.

Pain rose at the question, and she tried to push the thought away. She'd see them again. Once this was done, once she'd finished what Carter asked, she'd head straight back to the Abbey or wherever the Hunters were staying. And the rest was nothing. Together or separate, those two were tougher than she'd ever hope to be.

They'd be fine.

With dirt-smudged hands, she brushed the dust from her legs as her gaze rose to the window. Up ahead, Cornelius quietly ordered the driver to take the next onramp and silently, the man complied. Cars swept around them, racing for the highway, and the two sedans accelerated, joining the throng. In the distance behind them, the skyscrapers faded into the smog.

Exhaling slowly, Ashe tucked the gun beneath her jacket and tried to remain calm as the cars sped northward, deep into wizard territory.

At one o'clock, the Rio Dulce hotel was solely occupied by those few travelers unlucky enough to have reserved more than a single night's stay, and the ostensible housekeeping staff, most of whom were taking a cigarette break by the building's side. Over the years, the hotel had changed hands so many times that locals had long since stopped keeping track of the current name, and from the look of the cheap vinyl sign covering the old marquis, even the present owners weren't holding out much hope for this incarnation's longevity.

Shoving his car door closed, Harris eyed the building skeptically. It didn't seem the kind of place a businessman like Jamison would choose for a meeting, but maybe that was the point. Ritzy hotels in better parts of town would have more traffic, and thus more chance for discovery.

But still, this place was a dump.

He strode across the parking lot and then pulled open the front door, trying to ignore the sticky palm prints coating the glass. At the desk, the young clerk barely looked up from her computer as the door announced his entrance with a sad ding. The reek of cleaning solution filled the air, though the stained carpets and grimy windows gave no evidence of where the substances had been used. Down an adjoining hallway, shrieking children with beach towels clutched in their chubby arms raced pell-mell for the pool area, while two bored-looking adults sauntered after them, occasionally shouting hypo-critical reprimands to stay quiet.

Grimacing at the noise, he glanced around. Beyond the sagging couches in the lobby, Simeon leaned against the wall, talking softly into his cell. A door waited beside him, the sign above it designating the space beyond as the hotel conference room. At the sight of Harris, the man nodded to the door before returning to his call.

Without a word, Harris walked past him.

Nearly two dozen people milled around inside, talking quietly. On the opposite end of the room, a chipped wooden podium faced the rows of metal folding chairs that filled the rest of the space. Obliquely, he watched the other people as he lowered himself onto a creaking seat, and then shifted uncomfortably as the uneven legs made the chair rock.

Only a few of the room's occupants glanced to him, their expressions almost uniformly wary, before returning to their hushed conversations.

Confusion moved through him. The suspicion shouldn't have been warranted. After all, Simeon had let him in here same as them. But then, he supposed they hadn't gotten this far in fighting Ashley's people by being instantly trusting.

He looked back to the front as another door opened, admitting Jamison into the room. Immediately, the others dropped whatever they'd been saying and took their seats while, with a face that could have been chipped from granite, Jamison approached the podium.

Harris' jaw tightened. From the man's expression, there seemed a good chance Brogan had died.

"Thank you for coming," Jamison said levelly. He flicked a switch to cue the ceiling projector and then glanced back at the screen on the wall. A picture appeared, grainy and oversaturated. Harris recognized it. He'd taken the shot with his cell only a couple days before.

"Cole Jamison," the man continued. "My son. As some of you know, Taliesin took him from me. Now we have the chance to take him back. Obviously, I wish him unharmed. The same goes for the little girl who may still be in his company. Any others may be killed if necessary, though bringing them in for questioning would be preferable. And, of course, the reward for his retrieval will be… considerable."

A low murmur of chuckles rose and fell around Harris at the man's words.

"He was most recently seen in Monfort two days ago with this child." The security camera photo of the little girl appeared. "His captors have gone by the name 'Smith', and he may also be using that name rather than his own…"

Harris struggled not to feel like an impatient schoolboy as Jamison's lecture went on, empty of any mention of Ashley, Brogan or anything else he didn't already know.

"Simeon has information on the specific areas I wish you to target," Jamison concluded. "Any questions can be directed to him."

Without another word, he headed for the door, while the others broke off into their groups as before. Incredulous, Harris rose and hurried toward the front.

"Mr. Jamison," he called.

The man paused, glancing back.

"Is that it?" Harris asked.

Impatience flickered beneath Jamison's emotionless visage, and he turned to the door again.

"Isn't there any word on Brogan?" Harris pressed. "Ashley? Anything?"

"Brogan's alive," Jamison told him shortly. "For now."

"And Ashley?"

Jamison's eyes went to Simeon, and the ponytailed man stepped between them. "You have your instructions," Jamison said.

Harris moved to avoid the other man. "I'm not going after your son."

With a hand on the doorknob, Jamison paused, and then his head turned back to Harris. His eyebrow rose eloquently.

"I've been thinking about something Brogan told me," Harris continued. "About the fact wizards don't know I can see them. They don't think I'm a threat, Mr. Jamison. But your son does. I didn't get a chance to explain anything to him in the car, and from his reaction, I'm pretty sure he thinks I'm one of the bad guys. I don't want to be a liability to you, but if I go after Cole, I guarantee you he'll run when he sees me."

Jamison watched him, his face unreadable, but Harris could feel the tension building in the man.

"But Ashley won't," Harris persisted. "She might remember me, but she won't run. Hell," he added, trying to keep the anger from his voice and only partly succeeding, "she probably won't even care I'm there. You've got this whole group going after Cole. But someone needs to stop Ashley too, before anybody else gets hurt. That's where I can do the most good right now."

Jamison said nothing, and Harris fought to keep his irritation down. He resented needing the man's permission, but as the morning progressed, he'd been forced to admit the reality of the situation. This man and his associates held the purse strings. Brogan had paid for his search for the kids after the police department had put him on leave, and wandering off the reservation without at least a nod in Jamison's direction would presumably bring his investigation to a rather bankrupt halt.

Even if it's what they wanted anyway. Even if it made the most sense. But this was a deeply personal issue to Jamison, for all that he acted like a paragon of impassivity, and Harris didn't want to bet on the man's understanding if he just left without an explanation. Not where Cole was concerned.

His mouth tightening, Jamison nodded and then glanced to Simeon. From his pocket, the ponytailed man took out a pen and business card, and scribbled something down before handing the latter to Harris.

"Her last known location," Jamison said. "And Simeon's phone number, in case you find anything. Not much is left, but one of her wizard associates inadvertently alerted us to the location by using their magic to travel there as we were passing by, so she may still be hiding in the vicinity."

Though it felt annoyingly submissive, Harris nodded. "Thank you, Mr. Jamison."

With a distracted gesture of acknowledgement, Jamison disappeared through the door, leaving Simeon to tend to the others still in the room.

Ignoring them all, Harris made a beeline for the exit. At the desk, the clerk glanced up and then gave him an odd look, as though questioning why he'd been in the conference room. Crossing the lobby quickly, he slipped past the door before she could speak.

The drive home flew by and he barely noticed when the front door slammed behind him as he headed for the bedroom. Yanking open the closet, he scanned the shelves and then tugged down his suitcase, coughing as a wave of dust descended with the luggage. Grimacing, he swung the bag onto the bed, and then tossed a few shirts over to join it.

With shirts and pants shoved haphazardly into the suitcase, he hauled the bag out to the living room and dropped it by the door while he surveyed the apartment to see if he was forgetting anything.

His eyes came to rest on the box from Brogan, left sitting on the table for the past month. Between the cardboard flaps, he could see the duplicate badge – a replacement for the one taken by the department – lying half-covered by packing peanuts, same as it had been since he first tossed the thing back after opening the box. Being paid as a private investigator was one thing. Overtly faking credentials he no longer possessed fell into a whole other category.

Absently, his hand moved to check his gun.

That was different. The gun meant protection for the innocent. It was a weapon, but he was trained and he had a permit. And as for everything else, he'd never explicitly told anyone he was still on active duty. But if he took the badge…

He grimaced. He was splitting hairs, possibly microscopically. Each was as bad as the other in its own right, and all the rational-ization in the world wouldn't make that change.

But then, maybe that wasn't the point. Like it or not, he'd need all the help he could get.

A few weeks ago, there'd been a time when he could still see the lines, and still believed that he could do this without irrevocably crossing them. And then a bunch of wizards turned an abandoned gas station into World War Three and a teenage girl brought a building down on a man twice her size. People with far more advantages than he could ever claim were fighting an invisible war in which he'd scarcely be noticed as a casualty, and not a single person in what he'd call the 'real world' would ever believe him enough to help him bring that war to an end.

He crossed the room. His hand wrapped around the badge.

It was illegal. Immoral too. He'd taken an oath to uphold the law, and this certainly wasn't it.

His life had never been black and white, but it'd also never been this gray.

And he'd need every bit of help he could get.

Shoving the badge into his pocket, he headed for the door. He snatched the suitcase from the ground, hefted it into the hall, and then pulled the door closed. Across the corridor, the door to the neighboring apartment swung back, and the old woman from number six stepped out.

"Oh, John," she said, startled. "Are you going somewhere?"

Harris nodded. "Something came up out east. Not sure how long I'll be gone, though. Would you mind keeping an eye on the place for me, Mrs. Pulaski?"

"Of course," she said pleasantly.

He lifted the bag and started down the hall.

"Have a safe trip," she called after him.

He didn't answer. With what he knew he was heading into, there wasn't much point.

Chapter Two

Exhaustion pulled at her as the hours crept by. Unmoving on the sedan's back seat, she watched farms and grasslands blur endlessly into billboards and nameless towns. Gray clouds drifted by, pierced by intermittent sunbeams. Ignored since the meager meal of canned food the night before, her stomach chewed itself and made her head throb in rhythm with the growl of the tires on the road.

In the passenger seat, Cornelius pulled out his cell, answering yet another call in a voice too low to hear. A sound of frustration escaped him this time, and numbly, she glanced toward the front.

He returned the phone to his coat pocket without a word.

Ashe's brow drew down. As she looked back to the window, she caught sight of the driver. With the build of a human mountain and a stone-like visage to match, he was watching her in the rearview mirror.

Uncomfortable, she turned away.

Silence fell back over the car. The sun slid along behind the overcast sky while gradually, office parks and automotive stores took the place of farmland again.

She wondered what she'd say when she saw the Council. They'd driven Carter out eight years before, ignoring his warnings about the Blood and writing him off as insane. As far as she knew, nothing had changed since, and the night Carter died, Cornelius had still dismissed everything he'd said as just fantasy.

But Carter had believed she could change their minds. As a wizard, and as someone whose family had died in an attack by the Blood, he seemed to have thought they'd listen to her where they never had to him.

And they could protect her. He'd said that too. Right before he called her his queen.

She grimaced, pushing the memory back into the morass of emotion and nightmare she was desperately trying to ignore. He'd been dying. In all the chaos, she'd probably just misunderstood that part.

Or something.

Exhaling, she forced her attention to the highway. Traffic was growing heavier, though the area around the sedan was still relatively clear. Overpasses swept by, bearing signs for roads whose abbreviations she couldn't understand, and concrete barriers closed in, obscuring all but the peaked rooftops of the houses behind them.

She looked ahead. Skyscrapers amassed like giants on the horizon, their spires turned misty blue by the smog. The concrete walls around the road vanished, giving way to an enormous steel bridge, and beyond the railing, the murky water blurred with the gray sky.

At an exit like any other, the two cars left the interstate. Houses clustered around them almost immediately, each building identical in shape with only the faded colors changed. In chain-link fenced yards, children played, while on street corners, teenagers watched the world go by.

They didn't seem to notice the sedans sliding past.

Neighborhoods surrendered to fast food restaurants and check cashing stores, and all the people on the sidewalks looked human, though she knew that didn't mean anything. Minutes passed, and gradually, the stores dwindled until, at a weathered road by a lonely gas station, the driver turned. Rolling hills swallowed the last vestiges of the city, and in only a few moments, the landscape returned to countryside.

Miles crept by and then the driver slowed to turn again at a gravel track nearly swallowed by weeds. The road climbed, and her eyes narrowed as they came over the rise.

In the distance, a warehouse complex sprawled across the land-scape, with an enormous factory towering up at its heart. She shifted on the seat, trying to get a better view. A chain-link fence topped with barbed wire protected the property, and behind the barrier, a field of scrub grass stretched for almost half a mile to a hodgepodge of concrete and aluminum-sided buildings. A pair of decaying security booths huddled by the fence, one inside the property and one out, and weathered signs flanked the gate, declaring in sun-bleached letters that the buildings beyond were condemned.

The cars pulled to a stop, and a wizard climbed from the first sedan to walk over to the security booth. At a small keypad mounted on the wall, he punched in a code and sent a small burst of magic into the device, and then headed back to the car as the gate rolled aside.

Ashe's brow drew down in alarm. For the barest blink of an eye, the air seemed to shiver and, though she hadn't noticed any fog, the view ahead suddenly became infinitesimally less hazy than before.

As though detecting her confusion, Cornelius glanced back with a cautioning look. Frustration rose in her and, as if seeing that too, his expression took on an edge of insistent request.

She looked away.

The cars pulled through the opening and rumbled down the path. Warehouses closed in around them, each gaping doorway revealing only shadows. At the end of the gravel track, the monolith of the factory waited, its white-painted walls chipping with age.

On the warehouse rooftops, wizards stepped into view, their gazes tracking the sedans.

Ashe glanced to Cornelius, but the man simply ignored them and then twitched his fingers to the automatic window controls when several more wizards emerged from behind the buildings to block the road. Weaponless, the men still managed to appear threatening as they walked toward the cars. Looking briefly into the first vehicle, they continued to the second, and then stopped when they spotted her in the back.

"Who–"

"You will let us pass," Cornelius interrupted calmly.

Snapping his mouth shut, the man's gaze went to Cornelius, and then he jerked his head in a stiff bow. Stepping back, he waved a hand and immediately, the wizards cleared the road.

Cornelius rolled up the window. "Go," he said to the driver.

His eyes locked on the path, the driver did as he was told.

Beyond the warehouses, an ocean of a parking lot surrounded the immense factory. Heavily overgrown and cracking, the concrete nevertheless showed faint remnants of orange lines where the parking spaces had once been. In spots halfway across the sprawl, the sedans came to a stop. Cornelius climbed from the vehicle and then turned, pulling her door open.

He glanced to the driver as Ashe got out of the car. "Go make certain the Council is ready," he ordered.

The man's eyes flicked from Cornelius to her and back again. Without a trace of expression, he nodded and then turned, striding toward the factory and motioning for the other wizards to accompany him.

Cornelius watched them go, waiting till they'd entered the massive building before glancing down at her. "Remember," he said, his voice barely breaking the stillness of the parking lot. "No sign. No reaction to anything." He paused. "Please."

Her brow drew down warily, but she gave a tiny nod.

Echoing the motion more firmly, he started for the building.

Spanning the width of several city blocks, at its heart the factory easily stood ten stories high. Smoke stacks towered from its core, dwarfing the shorter buildings edging the complex. Broken windows stared blindly from the entire height of the building, while the surviving glass reflected the gray sky. Weathered railings bordered the slope to a handicapped entrance, and at the metal door, Cornelius paused, glancing back again. Briefly, he studied her face, and then without a word, he pulled the door open and then held it so she could precede him inside.

Heavily, the door swung shut behind them, cutting off the dull sunlight. Deep shadows filled the hallway, broken only by hints of illumination from up ahead. Tarnished door handles glinted in the gloom, suggesting abandoned offices or storage areas lining the hall.

But unlike the parking lot, the corridor was anything but silent. A din of voices carried from deeper in the building, the noise distorted as it reverberated on the walls. Growing steadily warier, she followed Cornelius through the turns of the hallway, emerging finally at the factory floor.

Despite his request, she balked.

People were everywhere. Cots crammed the enormous concrete floor, divided one from another by curtains stretched across metal frames. Walkways encircled the expanse beneath a ceiling at least sixty feet high. Grimy skylights filtered light down onto the sea of humanity, all of whom seemed to be talking or crying or yelling at once.

And each of them was a wizard.

Unable to breathe, she forced her feet to keep moving as Cornelius didn't slow. Her gaze darted across the crowds, landing on faces and then flitting away, as she trailed him along the narrow path between the cots and curtains.

They were all Merlin.

She fought to take a breath. Of course they were all Merlin. What'd she expect? But the sheer scope of them all in one place was overwhelming.

People looked over as she passed and, in a slow wave, the din began to fade. Countless faces tracked her, their expressions ranging from nonexistent to fearful, and she saw some mothers turn their children away.

She struggled not to wince, realizing what she must look like, covered in bloodstains.

Striding to the far end of the massive room, Cornelius came to a halt at the base of a metal stairway. By the railing, the driver from the sedan stood, his eyes on the middle distance and his face like stone.

"Are they assembled?" Cornelius asked, glancing to the doors lining the walkway.

Staring straight ahead, the large man nodded.

Cornelius started up the stairs.

As she followed, the driver's gaze flicked down to her. With Cornelius gone, the man's impassive expression vanished, transforming into an almost predatory distrust. Quivering at the threat in his eyes, she watched him cautiously as she climbed after Cornelius up the metal steps and onto the walkway.

At a door several yards from the stairs, Cornelius stopped. He cast a glance to her again, as though confirming something she couldn't hope to understand, and then he headed inside.

Around the long conference table dominating the center of the room, a dozen wizards looked up, their conversation coming to a halt. With a motion somewhere between a nod and a bow, Cornelius stepped to one side, affording them a view of Ashe standing beyond the doorway.

To a person, they went still.

Her heart began pounding harder. With a glance to Cornelius, she walked into the room, turning slightly as he shut the door behind her. A small thread of his magic raced around the frame, silencing the noise from the factory floor.

None of the wizards said a word.

"Ladies and gentlemen," Cornelius said, turning back to face the room. "May I present Patrick's daughter, Ashley. Though," he amended, "she prefers to be called Ashe."

He glanced to her. "The Merlin Council."

The wizards stared, and with everything she had, she suddenly tried to follow Cornelius' request to not show any reaction. From the aristocratic woman with gold wireframe glasses, to the suit-clad man with oiled black hair, each of them studied her silently.

She felt like a lab specimen pinned to the wall.

At the head of the table, one of the wizards pushed to his feet, breaking the stillness. Though he was easily over seventy years old, his face was commanding beneath his silver hair and he carried his tall frame with a quiet authority that made Cornelius' pale in comparison. His eyes went to Cornelius briefly as he approached, and with a slight bow, Cornelius stepped farther aside.

Ashe's heart wanted to climb out of her chest.

The man's gaze flicked over her face and clothes, as though in a single heartbeat, he could take in everything about her, both inside and out. Barely breathing, she drove down the urge to let the magic around her become stronger as a defense.

He seemed to see the impulse anyway.

"You have nothing to fear from us," he said softly. "My name is Darius Greyson. It is an honor to finally meet you." He paused. "Queen Ashe."

Her breathing stopped.

A hint of sympathy touched the imperial cast of his face. "Come have a seat," he offered, stepping back and motioning to a chair at the end of the table.

Feeling paralyzed, she hesitated, but the only other option was to stand stupidly in front of a bunch of wizards who had yet to stop staring. Fighting to keep her face impassive, and barely succeeding, she crossed to the aging desk chair and lowered herself onto it carefully.

Circling the long table, Darius returned to his seat, with Cornelius taking the chair to his left. A sudden sense of isolation welled up in her, and she struggled to ignore it as she locked her eyes on the old man at the other end of the wooden expanse.

"I understand if you have questions," Darius said. "We do as well. But let me begin by apologizing for taking so long to find you. I cannot imagine what you must have endured this past month until now."

Cornelius' gaze dropped to the table, though no other reaction touched his face. Resisting the urge to shift in her chair, Ashe kept her eyes on Darius, uncertain what to say.

"You do not know us," Darius continued. "And, to a large degree, we do not know you. But each person in this room worked alongside the king for many years, trying to end the war."

He paused. "Did your father have the opportunity to tell you anything before he died? About Merlin or Taliesin, or the war in which we are currently engaged?"

She swallowed. "No," she said, her voice choked. "But the cripples did."

His brow twitched fractionally downward, while at his side, the suit-clad man with black hair gave her a look that nearly amounted to surprise.

"And did they tell you about your role in this?" Darius asked.

The sight of Carter dying returned, and ruthlessly, she shoved the memory away. "A bit," she managed.

He studied her face for a moment. "You are a direct descendant of Merlin," he said. "And with your father's death, you and your sister have become the last of the Merlin's Children, the sole survivors of a family that has ruled our people for five hundred years."

Ashe stared at him, and from deep inside, gibbering words rose like bees buzzing in her mind. Carter. He'd said… Carter'd known… he…

"As beneficiaries of this heritage," Darius continued. "You hold the key to ending the war. Unlike anyone short of the Taliesin king, you can take magic from your fellow wizards and use it, or bind it away from their use, as you choose. And thus, you possess the ability to reestablish the spell that bound all of Taliesin and kept our people safe for half a millennium.

"And this was why King Patrick was killed."

Barely breathing, she crushed down the shivers rippling from her core.

"By removing your father, and nearly removing you and your sister, Taliesin came close to securing sole possession of this ability, a situation which would have left our people in dire jeopardy. So far, the paradoxical saving grace of this war has been the fact that, while your father was unsuccessful in recreating the spell, the Taliesin king has been as well. But had Taliesin succeeded in killing you and your sister as they did your father, their king would have had time to rediscover the spell at his leisure, with no chance we could ever do the same. And the moment he finally did so, every man, woman and child of our people would have been stripped of the magical ability that protects them and makes us who we are.

"The Council has spent the past month contending with this possibility. And so, if you will forgive the melodrama, with your survival, we now have hope for our own restored."

For a moment, he fell silent, reflecting, and when he resumed speaking, the topic had been abandoned.

"But your father kept you ignorant of this. When the first Taliesin attack destroyed his own father and family, he took you far from our battles. He even changed your name. You were Ashley Carrington in those days, not the black-market identity he arranged for you later and kept secret even from us. But most importantly, he bound your abilities away from both you and your sister – a spell that held for eight years until his death. He wanted to keep you safe, to bury you away from the world and to prevent you from inadvertently drawing attention by using your magic if an enemy wizard ever passed by. Because while a bound wizard's magic might still be detectible to some degree, it is substantially subtler than one who is unbound. Were the worst to occur, it was his intention for you and your sister to hide till he or his guards could save you."

She swallowed, her jaw muscles cramping at the effort of keeping her face from giving anything away.

"Unfortunately," Darius said. "Matters did not go as planned. We've kept word of your father's death from the others for the past month, and due to the protections the king put in place for your sake, no one outside these four walls knows yet who you are. We told the guards only that you and your sister were persons of interest, to be captured alive at all cost, but nothing more. For all intents and purposes, you both ceased to exist eight years ago, and thus no one has connected the television newscasts with the Merlin royal family."

He paused. "And, for that, I must apologize. We may have found you sooner, had word of your father's death been spread, and you would have been spared tremendously. It was the decision of the Council, however, that we couldn't take the risk. To prevent a catastrophic loss of morale, we could not tell our people that the Merlin's Children may well have been destroyed. Your family is all that stands between us and annihilation by Taliesin's king, and our people know that. For them to learn you might all have been killed…" He shook his head. "Panic would have ensued. And amongst our soldiers, the loss of will to fight may well have cost us the war."

Darius met her eyes. "You are a symbol to our people, as much as anything. Your family represents hope against the incredible odds we face, and leadership in the midst of the chaos of war. Merlin and his Children have been the stabilizing force that has led our people through five hundred years of peace and two eras of bloody war. I cannot overstate the significance you and your sister have to us, which is why, once again, I can assure you that you both are indeed completely safe in this place."

She shivered as he stopped talking, and no matter how she tried, she couldn't stop the shaking. Her gaze left his, moving around the table. The other wizards were still watching her. They just wouldn't quit.

"Though," Darius began again, his tone careful. "From the news, it sounded as though you and your sister had become separated."

Her gaze snapped back to him. He glanced to Cornelius with a hint of question in his eyes, but Cornelius simply looked to her.

"Is this the case?" Darius asked.

She couldn't trust herself to speak. In a short, jerking motion, she shook her head.

"Then we will send out–"

He cut off as a hoarse noise escaped her. Wetting her lips, she tried again.

"Lily's dead."

The silence in the room became palpable.

"They…" She trailed off and then regrouped. "She died a month ago."

Because they only needed one of us.

She thought her bones would break from the shaking she was

fighting to hide.

For the first time, the wizards looked away. Her eyes tracked across them, watching the reactions breaking through the impassive masks they wore.

To a person, they appeared genuinely stunned.

But then, so was she.

Swallowing hard, she looked down. Merlin's Children. The Children. Cornelius had said that to Carter. And taking magic. She'd done that. She didn't know it at the time but she'd done it. And…

Queen.

And Carter'd known. Carter had known and he'd sent her here. Carter…

She forced herself to breathe as she returned her gaze to the wizards. "I have to talk to you," she said, her voice still rough to her own ears. "I… this isn't why I came."

Some of the wizards looked over, while others glanced to Cornelius questioningly.

"I–"

"Your majesty," Cornelius interrupted.

The words weren't anything but absurd, and at them she choked.

"There will be time for everything," he continued. "But at the moment, you've had a difficult night. A difficult month, in truth. You need food. Rest. Fresh clothing." He paused, meeting her eyes carefully. "It will do no one a dishonor to care for yourself as well."

Protests swelled up in her, but before they could emerge, Darius nodded. "Agreed," he said.

He motioned to the suit-clad wizard, and the man rose, circling the table to pull back her chair. "This way, your highness," the man said, gesturing toward the door.

"We will arrange for food to be brought to you," Darius told her. "And clothing as well."

The woman in the gold glasses nodded and stood to leave as he glanced to her.

Darius' expression hinted at a warm smile. "Welcome home, your majesty."

Ashe stared. The room was spinning and everyone was going too fast. Getting up, leaving, moving around like any of this was normal or sane. With quiet voices, the wizards had turned to confer among themselves, Cornelius included. Leaning over, he spoke quietly to a man with shoulder-length graying hair, and drew Darius' attention when his question could not be resolved.

And not a single one of them glanced at her again.

"Your highness?"

She blinked and then looked up at the man next to her. Dressed in a faintly reflective black suit with the light glistening from his oil-slicked hair, he regarded her with diplomatic politeness as he waited.

Her gaze returned to the wizards. It would be so easy to just say the Blood were real. To tell them the Blood killed Lily. Her father. Carter. So many others. She could just yell the words and then get out of here.

Because these people were crazy.

Cornelius glanced up, meeting her gaze across the length of the table. Her brow furrowed at the look in his eyes.

Behind her, the man cleared his throat and she flinched, turning back to him. He gestured toward the door again.

Feeling vaguely lost, she followed him.

On the factory floor, people glanced up as she emerged from the conference room. Her eyes darted from them and locked on the grated metal walkway. The man strode ahead of her, turning down a narrow passage that bisected the sheer wall. The ceiling overhead felt far away, while the walls felt too close, and shadows crowded out the air. Struggling to breathe, she hurried after him when he turned down a wider corridor.

At a door several yards down the hall, he stopped. Glancing around, he checked that no one else was near, and then pushed it wide. Watching him warily, she stepped into the room.

In years past, the space had been an office. Or perhaps two, if the girder running down the center of the ceiling was any indication. But now a four-post bed was against the far wall and an oak cabinet stood nearby, its doors open and hangers waiting for clothes inside. Matching nightstands were positioned on either end of the headboard, and a dense rug lay by the bedside.

"The royal suite, your majesty," the man said, his voice perfunctory.

Ashe glanced back. "The…"

"Such as it is," he amended, a touch of sarcasm emerging, and then he explained. "This was your late father's room."

She trembled.

"Once we announce your presence, it will be easy to arrange servants for you. Until that time, should you need anything, my name is Sebastian Monroe, second in line of authority on the Merlin Council and Representative of the Eastern States Region. I will be happy to assist you."

He paused, waiting for a response.

Her head managed a nod, though the motion felt alien.

"Katherine should be in shortly with food and clothing," he continued. "Until then, if there's nothing else…?"

Jerkily, she shook her head.

With a fractional bow, he stepped back and closed the door behind him as he left.

Slowly, she turned, her gaze straying to the bed. The nightstands. The cabinet.

She jumped as a knock sounded on the door. Heart pounding, she blinked in numbed confusion at the noise.

The knock came again, and the right response returned to her.

"C-come in," she said, trying to keep her voice steady.

The door swung open, admitting the woman from the Council. Balancing a stack of clothes in her arms, she nudged the door closed with her foot. Over the rims of the gold glasses perched on her nose, she regarded Ashe.

"Katherine de Vila, my lady," she said by way of introduction, cool precision in her tone. "Fourth in line of authority on the Merlin Council, Representative of the Western Canadian Region, and lead healer to your people." Her gaze dropped briefly to the clothes. "These are for you."

Crossing to the bed, she placed the stack on the edge of the mattress and then turned back expectantly. Ashe hesitated, and then walked over and glanced down at the clothes.

Jeans. T-shirts. Everything she could need, down to socks and underwear. She looked at Katherine. "Thank you."

The woman nodded, and then her eyes scanned Ashe's face. "If you would permit me, I would heal that cut for you."

Ashe tensed and Katherine's eyebrow lifted at the reaction.

"Unless you prefer I not?"

"It's okay..."

"I will not hurt you."

Ashe hesitated. "Alright," she said uncertainly.

Katherine's lips tightened, but she raised a hand, her slim fingers coming to rest lightly on Ashe's forehead. Barely breathing, Ashe struggled not to flinch away.

Powerful but brief, a surge of magic licked across her skin, its focus so narrow it felt like a laser. In spite of herself, Ashe recoiled, but the magic was already gone.

Katherine stepped away, her hand brushing an imaginary piece of her auburn hair toward her tightly styled bun. Watching her warily, Ashe reached up, touching the place where the gash had been.

Smooth skin met her fingertips, without any trace of bruising or scar.

"Do you have any other injuries to be addressed?" Katherine asked.

Ashe shook her head.

"Then I will return once you've had the opportunity to change."

The woman left the room.

Ashe's gaze dropped back to the clothing, and after a heartbeat, she hesitantly unzipped her jacket and pulled it off. The holster straps and gun followed, and then her jeans and shirt. From the pile, she drew out the closest matches to her old clothing she could find.

It felt better that way.

Smoothing the shirt down, she glanced to the holster and weapon, trying to determine how to wear them now that the jacket would probably be taken away.

A knock came on the door. "Come in," Ashe said.

Katherine walked back inside, her clinical gaze taking in Ashe and her new clothes before catching at the sight of the gun. Her eyes flicked to Ashe, and a new expression touched her cool face, almost considering in tone.

"You will not need that here, your majesty," she said carefully.

Ashe didn't answer, and after a moment, Katherine bowed her head.

"As you wish."

Carrying a tray of food, a man approached the door, hesitating as he saw Katherine. His gaze on the ground, he waited until the woman made a small noise of approval before coming in. Without looking up, he edged around Ashe, placed the tray on the nightstand, and then disappeared back out of the room.

Katherine waited till the door shut before speaking.

"You *do* realize you are safe here?" she hazarded. When no answer came, she continued. "There are people who can protect you now. Anyone who dares threaten you will have hundreds of wizards to contend with. Wizards who would willingly give their lives for you."

Ashe couldn't find the words to reply, but at her silence, the quiet insistence in Katherine's voice became stronger.

"You are home, your majesty."

Pausing, Katherine watched her, but whatever response she'd been seeking didn't seem to be in Ashe's face. Consternation flickered through her eyes as she bowed her head again.

"Call if you need anything," Katherine said.

Still appearing slightly perturbed, the woman gathered Ashe's old clothes and then left.

Silence settled on the room.

Ashe sank onto the bed, her hand finding the gun.

Safe. Home.

Images played back through her mind, and her fingers tightened around the weapon as she pushed the memories away.

Home died a month ago. And no matter what Katherine said, she'd long since learned there wasn't any such thing as safe.

------- ♦ -------

The little yellow house on Pine wasn't more than a few days dead, but the neighborhood teenagers had already taken to it as a canvas by the time Harris reached the ruins. Graffiti covered the charred beams, and beer cans littered the yard beyond the cordons of crime scene tape. As he left his rental car, Harris could feel the eyes of the kids across the street on him, though when he glanced back, they were predictably looking elsewhere.

Climbing the steps from the curb, he surveyed the house. Forensics had already been over the place, as had any detectives in the area. According to the newspapers, they hadn't found much in the way of leads, but Harris wasn't concerned.

It wasn't the first time the cops thought Ashley'd left no evidence behind.

He'd headed here after learning that Jamison's men had already screened the apartment wreckage for clues to her whereabouts. They'd gathered little information from the debris, though. Whoever had been staying inside had apparently set up an extensive network of explosives that'd destroyed their computers and records in the building's final moments. The location was a complete wash, and it was currently too early in the morning to follow his other leads. But no one had looked back at the house since Ashley had left.

From what he'd read in the paper, the property had been one of those relics sometimes found in less-than-pleasant areas: a quaint cottage owned by the same old lady and her late husband since the neighborhood's happier times. In the moments before the blast, however, a neighbor had called the police to say that the woman had been taken hostage by a handful of people, including the black-haired girl wanted for murder in Montana. The police had hurried to the scene.

Then the house blew up. The old woman hadn't been found in the ruins, but she also hadn't been seen since. Given how Ashley generally treated those who got in her way, it all tracked.

And left slim odds that the old lady was still alive.

Shaking his head, he nudged a piece of drywall aside with his foot, revealing the half-burnt photograph of a smiling couple in a charred frame. Sighing, he left the picture alone and moved on.

He wondered what Ashley had wanted with the old woman. Was it just a place to stay, or had she known the lady somehow? And if she hadn't, why come here of all places? The elderly were vulnerable, he knew, but the girl had a whole country of potential spots in which to hide.

Picking his way through the wreckage, he moved farther into the yard. Glass crunched beneath his shoes and blackened bits of plaster covered the ground like grimy snow. Chunks of wall and ceiling had been tossed haphazardly into the shrubbery, and from the boards covering the windows of neighboring homes, he guessed some of the debris had made it into there too.

"Hey you."

Harris glanced back. Beyond what remained of the chain-link fence, a boy stood, an artfully patched backpack slung over his shoulder and an expression of cultivated boredom on his face. A thick swath of purple hair flopped in front of his kohl-lined eyes, and his jeans were tighter than any Harris had seen since the seventies.

Looking as he did, Harris found himself wondering if the kid got beat up a lot, living in a neighborhood like this.

"What're you doing?" the boy continued, tossing the question out like an accusation.

"Did you know the old lady who lived here?" Harris asked, backtracking across the yard.

The boy's eyes narrowed. "You a cop?"

Harris paused. "Not anymore."

The answer seemed to please the kid, and a wry grin twisted his face. "You get booted or something?"

"Or something."

The grin spread. Half-glancing toward the wreckage, the kid gave a nod. "Yeah, I knew her. Total freak. Never left her house."

"Did you see what happened a few days ago?"

A casual shrug answered him. "It was weird. Never seen the old lady have visitors before. And then a day later the house blows up? Totally wild."

"You saw her visitors?"

A semi-bored nod.

"What'd they look like?"

Shrugging again, the boy kicked at a piece of explosion-warped chain-link fence near his foot. "Two guys and two girls who really didn't seem the types to be visiting her. She never let anyone in besides that old guy down the street. And even he–"

"Old guy?"

"Norman or Norton or something. Lived about three houses that way. But he moved out in a real hurry about a day ago."

Harris' gaze moved in the direction the kid pointed. "And the others?"

The boy shrugged as though it was his default action before answering. "An old white man and a black guy who looked like, I don't know, maybe fifty? The blonde girl with the dreads was pretty freaky looking, but the other might've been cute. I couldn't see much of her though. She tucked up under a hood real quick when she got out of their van." The shrug returned. "Dark-haired white girl. That's all I saw."

The last would have been Ashley then. And as for the others…

"Did you see what happened to them after this place blew up?"

"Nah. My friends and I were inside my place when it happened. Shook the whole house though. Thought the walls were going to come down."

Harris nodded. He could imagine. "Thanks," he told the boy.

The kid shrugged.

Ignoring the motion, Harris headed for his car, glancing to his watch as he went. It was still early, but the hour would have to do, because the kid's descriptions had corroborated one thing. Just as in Monfort, she'd been on the run with a middle-aged African-American man.

And according to the paper, a body matching that description, found only a few blocks from the apartment fire, was lying in the city morgue right now.

Cranking the engine, he checked the street swiftly and then sped off, leaving the ruins of the little yellow house behind.

Chapter Three

He'd originally intended to reach the morgue at a reasonable hour, and thereby appear more credible, but from the look the mortician had given him the moment he entered the door, Harris was glad he hadn't bothered.

"You're from where, again?"

"Monfort, Utah."

"And why do you want to see the body?"

Harris suppressed a scowl. He'd answered the question twice, and was starting to suspect the mortician had a mental disability of some kind. "Because it may be related to a case."

"And you're a cop?"

"Yes."

"Where's your badge?"

"In my pocket."

This met with a suspicious look. Harris forced his face to remain calm.

"So what's the case?" the mortician persisted.

"Homicide."

"And you think this guy might be involved?"

"Yes."

"Why?"

"Because I do," Harris snapped. "Now, are you going to let me in, or do I need to report you for hindering a murder investigation?"

The mortician blinked, his already pale skin going snowy in alarm. "I'm not supposed to let anyone down here without an escort," he sputtered defensively. "We got in major trouble last year because–"

"I don't care," Harris retorted, relieved that the aggressive approach was working. After twenty minutes of repetitive questioning, laying into the ghoulish little man was cathartic to say the least. "Either you let me in to see this body, or I start making phone calls, understand?"

For a moment, the man considered the words, and then he gave Harris a resentful look. "Well, you're still going to have to sign in," he sniped. "*And* I'll need to see your ID."

Harris couldn't stop himself from grimacing. Even if the badge *was* in his pocket, he'd still hoped not to have to bring it out.

The damn thing felt like it weighed a hundred pounds.

Turning the expression into an impatient glare at the mortician, he tugged out the badge and showed it to the man. Still glaring, he crossed to the logbook and scrawled something resembling a signature.

"Happy?"

The man looked as though he wouldn't ever have considered using that word. Mouth twisted sourly, he led the way back to the heart of the morgue.

Over the years, Harris had often wondered if morticians sent out special for the lights that glowed radioactively in every morgue he'd set foot inside. This one was no different, and the almost imperceptible, rapid-fire flicker of the bulbs sent familiar pain shooting through his head within seconds of stepping past the swinging doors.

Immune to the obnoxious lighting and looking more ghoulish than ever, the mortician wove by the covered bodies on the autopsy tables to the steel doors lining the wall. Tugging the latch, he yanked the door open and then rolled out a tray. Tossing Harris a last scowl for good measure, he twitched aside the sheet and then waited with obvious displeasure.

Ignoring him, Harris looked down.

He hadn't been looking directly at the camera when Harris had seen his picture, but nevertheless, he was still recognizable. A bloodless, dark bullet hole now pierced his chest, along with thick black stitches from the autopsy. But his face was the same.

Harris sighed. He wished he could believe the loss of one of her allies would slow her down, but he knew he was just kidding himself. A bunch of people engaged in a war would be used to casualties by now, and wouldn't stop killing just because of one more.

"Well?"

The little man's snide voice snapped him out of his thoughts. Affecting a considering expression, Harris made a noncommittal noise.

"Did he have anything on him when he was brought in?"

Mouth twisting again, the man said, "Gun, cell phone, nothing else. Cops bagged it for evidence."

Harris buried a grimace. Of course they did. Protocol.

"So is he the one you're looking for?" the mortician asked impatiently.

Thinking for a moment, Harris pretended he hadn't heard the question. "The people I'm after have something of a pattern. They don't just kill one in an area. It's usually more. Any other murders get brought in over the past few days?"

His pasty face tightening further, the mortician hesitated. "Yeah," he admitted. "There was that mob hit on Jefferson."

Harris nodded. Ridiculous as it was, the papers were claiming the destruction of the apartment building had been some kind of mob hit, despite its location at the heart of the state college's campus. Of course, the building had been wired like crazy, which gave a bit of credence to the theory. And it'd also possessed enough computers to take over a small country.

But still, blaming the *mob* seemed a bit of a stretch.

"And then someone torched a homeless guy in an alley off Van Elliot."

At this, Harris looked up.

"They haven't reported it yet," the mortician said, flustered by Harris' expression. "They're trying to get an ID, notify the family, that sort of thing. It's procedure."

"Anything to tie him to this guy?"

The mortician blinked. "Why would there be?"

Harris gave him a look.

"Well, not that anyone's told me."

"How many died in the apartment fire?" Harris asked, returning his attention to the body. From the brief interchange he'd had with Simeon, there hadn't been any discussion of fatalities, just mention that they hadn't found anything and then a click as the call came to an abrupt end.

After talking to the man, he'd been reminded why he was grateful to have mostly dealt with Brogan and Jamison thus far. For some of the wizard converts to Jamison's cause, their prejudices against 'regular' humans obviously hadn't been left behind.

"Ten," the mortician said. At Harris' raised eyebrow, he grudgingly gestured to the bodies on the autopsy tables. "Six burned and four shot. But the burned ones show minimal traces of smoke inhalation, and no bullet wounds or other injuries, so we're checking for drugs to see if they were unconscious before they were set on fire."

Pausing, the man studied the bodies. "It's sort of sick, if you think about it."

Harris stared at him and the man's pale skin flushed a splotchy pink. "Well, I mean… I mean, obviously or whatever, but–"

"Thanks for the help," Harris said, cutting him off. He cast a last glance to the body on the tray.

"So is he the one you're looking for?" the mortician asked again.

Harris shook his head. "Not quite."

Without another word, he left the morgue.

Shutting the car door behind him, he closed his eyes and then wrapped his hands around the steering wheel. Ten bodies. Eleven, counting the homeless guy who might have been one of Brogan's men.

Or maybe he hadn't. Maybe he'd just been some poor schmuck, sleeping off his last beer or whatever.

And then he'd gotten in the way.

Harris looked out the window. Cars slid past and people strolled along the sidewalk. The spring weather was drifting toward summer, and pedestrians were gladly taking advantage of the renewed warmth. Fluffy white clouds dotted the blue sky and in all ways, it was a postcard perfect day.

It took effort to force himself to breathe.

There was a chance she'd left the city already. He had to admit it to himself. But there was an equal chance she hadn't, and until he'd exhausted every lead, he couldn't abandon the search. And meanwhile, she had one less ally. He knew it wouldn't slow her down but, on some level, it was still comforting.

Turning the key, he glanced back at the street. She'd come here for a reason, taken the old lady hostage for a reason, and burned that building for one too. There was a purpose to this place, to Monfort, to everything she'd done. And no matter what, he'd figure it out.

He had to.

------- ◆ -------

Grimacing, Ashe opened her eyes.

She was still in the same room. Soft pillows supported her head, and the gun remained clutched in her fist. A few lights glowed in the drop ceiling of the converted office, and the thick blanket beneath her felt uncomfortably warm.

But nothing had changed. Despite what she wanted, nothing had turned out to be a dream.

Same as always.

Pushing away from the pillows, she sighed. She'd only lain down for a moment after Katherine left, just to process the chaos spinning through her head, and then… morning.

Or several hours into the morning, she realized, glancing at the bedside table and the small clock perched there. But in spite of the time, a tray of steaming food sat waiting on the nightstand.

She looked to the door. They'd slipped in and out of the room while she slept, replacing the food without her waking. And despite their words, repeated over and over about her safety, the knowledge they'd been so close when she was sleeping sent shivers running over her skin.

Drawing a breath, she tried to stay calm as she eyed the tray. Wisps of steam rose from the bowl of oatmeal and moisture dripped from the tiny carafe of cream nearby. A flask of orange juice sat next to the meal, beside a crystal glass. Carefully setting her gun aside, she reached up, tipping a small amount of the cream into the bowl and then drawing the dish down from the table. Vaguely sweet and deliciously warm, the oatmeal nevertheless hit her stomach like lead, though her body seemed determined to accept even lead as welcome at the moment. She kept eating, and in only a few minutes, returned the empty bowl to the tray.

Her head cleared as the food settled, and she ran a hand through her hair, tugging at the mess of tangles. They'd be waiting out there. The wizards, with their talk of royalty, former identities, and binding spells. They'd want to speak further, and carry on like she had any intention of staying in this place, all while continuing to stare at her like a bug on display.

She closed her eyes. It didn't matter. Everything Darius said yesterday was psychotic, certifiable, and all otherwise insane. She couldn't let it affect her.

It wasn't why she was here.

Exhaling resolutely, she rose and, after a moment's thought, tucked the gun into the back of her jeans. Crossing the room, she opened the door, and then came to a sharp stop at the sight of Cornelius waiting outside.

"Good morning," he said impassively. "May I speak with you?"

Hesitating briefly, she nodded and let the door shut behind her. Displeasure crossed his face at their location in the hall, but he buried it swiftly.

"I came to ask you not to discuss the so-called 'Blood' with the Council."

Her brow drew down. "Why?"

"The Blood were Josiah's creation. They do not exist."

A choked scoff escaped her at the bluntness of his tone. "Yes they do. I saw them."

"What did you see?" he asked, as though he already knew the answer. "A human? Perhaps one who was nearby when magic was done? Perhaps even one *so* nearby that it almost appeared the magic originated from them?"

When she started to shake her head, he grimaced. "Please. Do not bring this up again. That Josiah is known to be insane is enough. But dredging up these fantasies… it will accomplish nothing but to further shame the memory of a man who served your family with unwavering loyalty for twenty years, and who would have continued to do so had he not lost his mind to the ravages of war."

She stared at him, uncertain whether to be offended, outraged, or just both. "He wasn't crazy."

Cornelius' face darkened. "Yes, he was. And he spent the better part of eight years proving–"

He cut off as Katherine and another man rounded the corner. With a measure of difficulty, he reasserted his composure and then nodded coolly as the others walked up.

Ashe glanced over, struggling to bring her expression back to something that wouldn't raise questions she wasn't ready to answer.

"Good morning," said the man at Katherine's side. He gave Ashe a small bow, and she tried not to shift uncomfortably. "Elias de Vila, your majesty. Fifth in line of authority on the Merlin Council and Representative of the Eastern Canadian Region."

He smiled as her eyes went from him to Katherine. "I believe you've already met my wife. Did you sleep well?"

"Fine," she managed, though the word felt like a lie, since collapsing where she sat probably didn't count. She glanced between them again, struggling not to appear rude. The man was a perfect foil of his wife, as friendly as she was cold. His wavy hair hung loose to his shoulders, with gray interspersing the brown, and his ageless face belied any years the color might have tried to ascribe.

"I think they're ready," Elias said.

Ashe looked to Cornelius in confusion, but the man simply nodded again. He motioned for the others to precede them, and then looked back at her as Elias and Katherine walked away.

"After you," he said.

"What's going on?"

"A presentation in your honor," he replied, stiff propriety settled firmly back in his tone.

Her eyebrows rose. "What?"

"You will see," he said, gesturing to the hall. "It is nothing to be concerned over."

When she didn't move, the barest hint of insistence entered his voice. "They are waiting, your majesty."

"Don't call me that," she snapped, letting anger cover the fact the words made her skin crawl.

"It is your title."

"No, Ashe is my title. It's my name. And as for the rest..." she made an impatient motion, "I don't care. I'm going to talk to the Council and I'm going to make them understand the Blood are real, because whatever you say, I know Carter wasn't crazy." She paused. "And I know what I saw."

Aggravation touched his gaze, though the rest of his face remained still. "As you wish," he said with tight neutrality. He motioned to the hallway again. "Now, if you will please…?"

Eyeing him cautiously, she started down the hall. Her brow lowered as she rounded the corner, a sense of something wrong hitting her. Resisting the urge to look back, she continued through the corridor and out onto the walkway.

Her feet came to a stop.

The factory floor was empty. Cots and curtain frames still stood where they'd been, but not a single person remained. The silence was deafening in the cavernous room, and as Cornelius strode up behind her, his quiet voice carried in the stillness.

"This way," he said.

Slipping around her, he took to the stairs, leaving her to follow. Swallowing nervously, she gripped the metal rail as the steps clunked beneath her feet. The vast space stretched before her as she reached the concrete floor, seeming even larger than yesterday for the lack of occupants. In the distance, she could hear voices, strangely loud and yet indistinguishable. Biting her lip, she continued after him across the room. At the far side, he turned, swiftly climbing a narrow stairway to a metal door set high in the wall. He waited till she joined him, and then bowed his head.

"Remember," he said. "No reactions."

Before she could speak, he took her arm, opened the door, and then pulled her outside.

They were on the roof of one of the lower parts of the factory. Up ahead, the Council formed a line, their backs to her as they looked out on the parking lot several stories below. In the center, Darius was speaking, his hands on a microphone attached to an impromptu podium.

"…I give you Her Royal Highness, Ashley Rebecca Carrington, Queen of Merlin," he announced.

Darius turned, extending his hand to her, and Cornelius' arm carried her forward even as confusion chased itself around her face.

And then the expression melted as the hundreds of wizards filling the parking lot came into view.

For a heartbeat, their eyes locked on her.

The rooftop shook from their cheers.

Her legs were like water and she wanted to fall through the floor. To hide. To grab her gun and run like the wind to escape the hordes of people suddenly convinced she was something she could not possibly be.

Queen. Royalty. And her father had been a freelancer. A researcher. The others were farmhands. They'd been wizards, and they'd died because of the war, but this was insane.

Absolutely insane.

"Breathe…" Cornelius murmured, his voice barely audible above the roar.

Air forced itself into her lungs in response to the command, and nausea followed on its heels. In a blur of words, Darius concluded his speech, and below her, the crowd poured into the building like a flood breaking through a levee. Gripping her arm, Cornelius nodded to the Council as they flowed past and returned to the door.

"The guards will protect you," Cornelius told her quietly. "They will keep the crowd at bay. Your only responsibility is to walk forward. Keep your eyes straight ahead. Show nothing of your emotions or fear. Do you understand?"

She looked up at him, words escaping her.

"You can do this."

"But…"

"You are their queen. Whether you believe it or not. And you have to show them strength. Confidence. Someone worthy of the fight it has taken for our people to survive." He paused. "They need this, Ashe. For your father's sake, do not disappoint them."

She swallowed hard. "But…"

He gripped her arm. Her feet worked where her mind could not, obeying the pressure to move as he led her back to the door.

The factory floor was crammed.

Smashed up to the walls and shoved against the barrier of guards lining the narrow space through the center of the throng, people filled every inch of the room. By the bottom of the stairway, the Council waited, and as she reached the steps, Cornelius dropped his arm from hers.

"Walk forward," he said again, his words a low murmur.

Her feet obeyed.

On legs held up by motion alone, she reached the base of the stairs. At the landing, the Council stepped aside, clearing her path. She faltered and fought frantically to keep her face as emotionless as possible as she looked to Darius in alarm.

The barest tinge of sympathy showed past the regal expression on his face. His gaze slid to the side, motioning her along.

She walked forward.

Standing shoulder to shoulder, guards walled a straight path through the crowd, their impassive eyes gazing out at the middle distance while behind them, the mass of wizard humanity stared.

"Long live Merlin! Long live the queen!"

She flinched and, an instant later, the shout reverberated off the walls as the crowd picked up the cheer. Her knees wanted to buckle at the din, but her eyes locked on the stairway, clinging to it as a lifeline. With each step it drew closer, and it took every shred of willpower she possessed to keep from breaking into a run.

The guards at the stairs bowed and then stepped aside as she approached. Gripping the banister, she climbed the steps, finally reaching the walkway.

"To the left, your majesty," Darius said behind her.

She followed the direction, and turned when he quietly said the word.

The chanting died into expectant silence.

Her heart scrambled into her throat, choking her completely.

"Nod, my lady," Darius murmured, his lips motionless.

Her head dipped toward the crowd. The roar of cheering returned, even stronger than before. Darius and the other councilmembers echoed her motion, and then he gestured for her to exit via the hall.

Fighting the urge to bolt, she turned and walked into the narrow corridor as behind her, Darius began speaking about coronation ceremonies and other such lunacy to the throng. Beyond the corner, the next hall was blessedly empty and without hesitation, her feet picked up speed, rushing her back to her room.

The door slammed behind her. Heart pounding, she started forward and then stumbled, her legs unwilling to carry her farther. Her knees met the ground with a painful jolt as her arms wrapped around her middle in desperate attempt to stop the trembling.

This couldn't be happening. This was stupid. This was insane. This was…

A dry sob choked her. Twenty-four hours ago, she'd watched Carter die. Thirty-six hours ago, she'd killed a wizard to save Spider's life. Three days ago, she'd been living at the Abbey.

One month ago, she'd been a farm kid in Montana, putting up pinwheels with her eight-year-old sister while planning what kind of cake to have for her seventeenth birthday.

Her hand hit the floor to keep her from falling, and her fingers pressed into the concrete.

This wasn't real.

She had to get out of here.

This was psychotic and insane and–

The door opened and she spun, terrified.

Cornelius stared. Carefully, he eased the door shut behind him, never looking away from her. "Your majesty…?"

A gasping noise escaped her, and she shook her head. "Don't call me that."

He paused.

"Don't…" she continued, holding a hand up to stave off the words as her gaze dropped to the ground. "Don't…"

"It is who you are," he said slowly.

"No, it's not!"

Fire rushed out of her, bursting against his defenses before fading as quickly as it had come.

Choking on her own air, she crushed the magic down, staring at the floor.

"I'm just me," she whispered. "I'm not… I'm just…"

Warily, he lowered the barrier of energy surrounding him as she trailed off. For a moment, he remained motionless, and then slowly, he crossed the room and sank down onto the bedside.

"Your father never wanted to be king either, you know," he said softly.

Trembling, she glanced up at him.

A touch of a rueful smile ghosted over his lips. "He was second in line to the throne," Cornelius continued. "And he was happy to keep it that way. Your uncle, Alexander… now he wanted to be king. He'd been born to it. At least, that's what your father used to say."

He looked down at her, seeing the questions in her eyes.

"My family has been close to the throne for generations," he explained. "And as a result, every so often, your father confided in me. He trusted me." A pensive look crossed his face. "Most of the time."

He drew a breath. "I do not know if you remember," he said. "I know what happened to you at the start of the war. But I was there the night most of the royal family died. I stayed with you and your sister."

She nodded faintly. "I remember," she whispered.

"It scared your father, what happened to you. That much magic, ripping through a young child… it left your sister stripped of everything but a shadow of her power, and you nearly a vegetable. For hours, he refused to leave your side, even to address the needs of his people, suddenly embroiled in a war. In the end, he had twenty of us stand guard that night, though I was the only one out in the open."

Her brow drifted down. "'That much magic'?" she repeated.

"The spell. Or truly, the backlash of it. God knows how much magic, hundreds of years old, released in a single moment when the Taliesin king shattered the spell. The binding that held their magic was tied to your line, carried on specifically by those who remained part of the royal family itself. And in a moment, most of them were gone. The effects rebounded through the survivors, almost incapacitating

Patrick and sending you into a short-lived coma.

"He thought you were dead. And I do not think he was ever as relieved as in the moment when you woke, even in the midst of everything else occurring at the time."

Cornelius fell silent, remembering, and Ashe looked away.

"Must've been convenient…" she whispered after a moment.

His brow drew down in confusion and she gestured distractedly to herself.

"You mean what happened to your memories," he said, only partly asking.

She didn't answer. For a few seconds, he was quiet.

"Yes," he replied. She glanced at him. "But not for the reasons you think. Darius was not entirely correct in his description of why your father kept you from the war. It's true a bound wizard is not as noticeable as an unbound one, and that some part of the emergency plan consisted of you and your sister hiding till help could arrive.

"But that was not his true purpose.

"Your father hated what happened to you. It tortured him inside. But it gave him the chance to protect you in a way that otherwise would never have been possible. The king believed that if he helped you remember what it was to be part of our world – and if you had access to all you could do – sooner or later you would insist on being involved in the war. You would want to help him. And that meant watching you fight. Kill. And possibly lose your life.

"He couldn't stand the thought of you or your sister being part of this, because you were his children more than just heirs to his throne. He was protecting you, not out of disrespect, but love. So yes, he used what happened to you, but he believed that more than being to his advantage, it was to yours.

"His plan had always been to end the war, and then restore your magic to you. He wanted to introduce you to our world at peace, and teach you what you needed to know to rule. But until that could happen, his goal was to give you the best life possible, far from violence and bloodshed, even if he could not be there to share it with you."

She looked away, remembering. Stress from his job had carved new lines on his face whenever he came home, and most nights found him pacing his room while clutching the phone.

Work calls, she thought distantly. Right.

"I don't believe this," she whispered. Her gaze darted around the room as though to encompass everything. "Any of it. It's crazy. Crazier than wizards and cripples and I just… I don't… "

He paused. "You do not have a choice."

She closed her eyes, wanting to tell him she did. She could leave. Run right now and just forget any of this ever happened.

Even though she knew it wasn't really true.

"So what am I supposed to do?" she asked softly.

"Become the leader your father would have wanted you to be."

A scoff escaped her.

"I mean it, Ashe."

She looked up at him, seeing the quiet insistence in his eyes.

And she turned away, wishing more than anything for it to be the day before yesterday, when the world had still sucked, but not like this.

"You are not alone here," Cornelius said. "You have the Council. Almost as much as the royal family, we have guided our people through the past five hundred years. We are your allies. We can teach you what you need to know."

She didn't answer, knowing he wouldn't understand anything she wanted to say. The whole mess of their world was psychotic, and acknowledging even a fraction of it just meant agreeing on some level that any of it was sane.

And that'd never been why she'd come here.

She took a breath, focusing back on the one measure of stability left in the world. "I'm still telling them about the Blood."

"Your majesty–"

"Carter told me to," she interrupted. "And yes, they're real. They're out there right now and you have to let me tell people the truth." She paused. "They killed my dad, Cornelius."

He closed his eyes. "It will not go well."

She watched him. "But will you try to stop me?"

A heartbeat passed. "No."

She hesitated at the reluctance in his voice. "Then when can I meet with them?"

Cornelius sighed. "Most of the Council will continue to participate in the festivities for a few more hours," he allowed. "If you would like, I can arrange for them to meet you after that time."

She nodded.

"As you wish, your majesty," he said, rising to his feet.

At the title, she grimaced.

He glanced back when he reached the door, catching sight of the expression. "It is who you are, Ashe," he repeated.

The door closed as he left the room.

She shook her head. "No," she whispered assuredly. "It's not."

Chapter Four

With an arm curled beneath her head and her body propped up by a pile of pillows, she waited. The gun lay behind her, and through the walls, the distant noises of revelry filtered, the sounds occasionally drowned beneath a faint hum every time the air conditioner kicked on.

And finally, a knock came.

She pushed to her feet, and tucked the weapon into the back of her jeans as she crossed to the door. Cornelius stood outside.

"They are ready."

She followed him down the hall.

Guards bowed as she passed, their murmured 'your majesties' trailing her. Partiers still filled the factory floor, and scattered cheers rose as she emerged onto the walkway. With her eyes locked on Cornelius' back, she forced herself to keep breathing as she strode after him into the conference room.

Stepping to one side, he waited as she entered and then closed the door, his magic sealing out the sound from the factory.

The Council watched her.

"You wished to speak with us, your majesty?" Darius asked.

Her gaze darted to the side as Cornelius slipped around her and circled the table to take his seat to the left of Darius. Keeping her face solidly expressionless, she nodded once and then took a chair as well.

"I wanted to talk to you about why I'm here," she said.

A few people glanced to Cornelius in confusion, but he'd long since locked his eyes on a spot somewhere beyond the tabletop and didn't look away.

"The Taliesin weren't responsible for my father's death," she continued. "Or Lily's. Not entirely. The man who ordered their deaths didn't look like a Merlin wizard, or a Taliesin. And he didn't have an absence of magic inside him like a cripple. He was something else. He looked human, but he had magic too.

"He was from a group that calls themselves the Blood."

Around the table, grimaces twisted the faces of several council-members. At Darius' side, Sebastian looked away, nearly rolling his eyes with impatient disbelief.

Cornelius didn't take his gaze from the table.

"I know you've heard of them before," she said. "Josiah Carter tried to tell you about them eight years ago. But I'm here to confirm that they're real. I've seen them. This man, Mason Brogan; he attacked me with magic two nights ago. And he nearly killed me with it before I took it from him.

"The cripples saw him for what he was. They recognized those like him from crowds that just seemed like regular people to me."

She glanced at Cornelius, but he didn't look up.

"Carter and the others weren't lying. They weren't delusional or insane. I've seen ferals. Wizards. Cripples. And I'm telling you, these monsters are something else. They hunted down my father and sister, and even though Brogan's gone… the rest are still out there. They're killing people with almost no chance of being stopped because the wizards who could help fight them don't believe they're real.

"So I'm here to ask you to change that. Go back to the cripples and work with them to stop these monsters. The Blood aren't just a threat to the cripples; they're a threat to all of us. But with your help, they don't have to be anymore."

Exhaling slowly, she fell silent, watching the Council for their reactions.

For a minor eternity, none came. Gazes darted from one side of the table to the other, and beneath their imperious masks, hints of expressions surfaced too quickly to be identified. But no one said a word.

And then Katherine cleared her throat. "Your majesty…" she started delicately. "As you say, this information is not new. But… it is not quite as you describe."

Ashe waited, barely breathing.

"Since the start of the war, there have been rumors. Weapons, designed by Taliesin, to aid those without magic in wielding powers like our own. It is understandable, given their binding for so many years, that wizards of Taliesin's breed would have attempted such a thing." She hesitated. "But it came to nothing, your majesty. What you describe cannot be done."

Ashe shook her head. "I'm not saying they had weapons, and I'm not saying they were human. I'm saying they had magic. That they glow to the cripples. Visibly. Unmistakably. And they were leading Taliesin wizards, not working for them."

Katherine grimaced, but before she could speak, another council-member interrupted. "Your highness," the portly man said in a tone edging toward condescension. "We know one another as wizards because we possess magical skill. Cripples have none, and thus are fortunate to be aware of us at all. Given the facts, it makes no sense for them to be able to perceive anything of magic that we cannot."

"I watched them do it."

"You watched them do something," Sebastian cut in. "And most likely that thing was manipulate you."

"Excuse me?"

From his position at Darius' right hand, the suit-clad man glanced to the other councilors and then gave her a look tinged with pity. "With all due respect, your majesty, you're young. Inexperienced. Your father bound your magic at age eight, and you haven't grown up in this world. Everyone at this table knows the cripples could have told you any number of stories, and you would have had no reason to disbelieve them, because everything here is new to you anyway." He shook his head at her. "You were an easy target, your highness. They saw a chance to convince a naïve young wizard to attack random humans on the street in an effort to corroborate their fantasies, and they took it. I'm not saying it's your fault, but try to be reasonable now."

She stared at him. "That's not what happened."

"That's what they wanted you to believe," he countered. "They're *broken*, your majesty. And not simply because they don't have magic. They want to be part of a world they can never have, and each one of them is more than willing to lie, cheat, and manipulate their way into it, if necessary. I'm sure they made themselves sound like victims. They always do. The whole world is after them, to their mind, when in reality, all the world wants is for them to accept their place." He scoffed at her enraged expression. "And yet you still want to defend them as innocent. But did they tell you how they murder our kind too? Or did they justify it to you, with their imaginary crimes and vigilante heroes? Did you actually meet *Carter* and his little–"

"The Hunters?" she snapped. "Yeah, I met them. Who do you think kept me alive this past month?"

Breathing hard, she stared around the table. "Do you all even know what's going on out there? Ferals are butchering people in the streets – the very people who can see the Blood wizards and help you take them out. There's a whole other war going on, and while you were writing it off as rumor and mocking the cripples for their 'fantasies', it went out and killed my family!"

Sebastian gave her a wry look. "No disrespect, your majesty," he said, his voice twisting the last word perilously close to an insult. "But in your one entire *month* of suffering from this war, I don't believe you've earned the right to speak to the years of loss we've had to endure. And before you let a bunch of *defectives* convince you how to see the world, perhaps you'll heed the advice of wizards who've been leading their people since before you were in diapers, and who actually know what wielding magic means."

She blinked, struck speechless. Around the table, councilmembers shifted, their expressions lost in a gradient of meticulous impassivity and discomfited agreement.

"That," Darius said, razors edging his tone. "Will be *quite* enough, Councilman Monroe."

Disgustedly, Sebastian looked away.

"My apologies, your highness," Darius continued, glancing at the rest of the Council before returning to Sebastian with a look that could have pierced steel. "For the opinions of some of our members. I assure you they are not shared by all."

For a moment longer, he pinned the other man with his gaze, and then turned back to her as though dismissing Sebastian from relevance. "Will the cripples listen to you?" he continued.

She paused and then nodded, still shaking with residual fury.

Darius echoed the motion thoughtfully, his eyes moving occasionally to the wizards nearby. "Then you have done better than us."

Her brow drew down.

"It is true that eight years ago, Josiah tried to tell us the same information you're passing along now. And it is true that, at the time, we refused to believe him. It could even be said that we were, as you put it, mocking. But that disagreement sent Josiah from our midst, and we have not seen him since that day. He gathered his people and fled to the far corners of the country, and if we heard of him at all, it was only from the bodies he and his 'Hunters' left behind.

"I apologize that remnants of the bad feelings left by those realities have come back to show you such unparalleled disrespect."

She said nothing.

"And yet," he continued, "regardless of what happened later, I cannot help but wonder what it would have cost us to simply have verified Josiah's story. Perhaps it would have proved to be nothing. Or perhaps…" His jaw tightened briefly. "Perhaps King Patrick, your sister, and who knows how many others would still be alive."

He fell silent. From the corners of her eyes, she could see the rest of the Council, their gazes on the table with clear expressions of unwillingness to speak.

Darius drew a breath. "So I propose we do as you suggest. We invite the cripples back. We form a joint task force comprised of carefully selected wizards who will be open to what we're asking–" His gaze landed sharply on Sebastian. "–and who will work alongside the cripples. If these 'Blood wizards' you describe prove to be fantasy, so be it. But if not…"

He met her eyes across the length of the table. "You may be young," he said solemnly, "and you may have lived a life till recently that would leave some jealous. But that does not give us the right to deride your information or assume that, because you have not had the same experiences as us, you must be wrong." He paused, regret flickering over his face. "We've burned enough bridges in this war."

Darius glanced to the Council. "I would take this to a vote," he said, a touch coldly. "But as sole remaining heir of Merlin and ruler by right of the laws we have dedicated our lives to uphold, Queen Ashe unquestionably has the final word. If she asks this of us, we *will* see it done."

He looked back at her and raised an eyebrow.

Ashe's heart quivered, the ludicrous authority Darius was handing her suddenly hitting her in full force. Everything Carter wanted, and with a single command, it would begin. Incredulity burbled up inside and she swallowed, trying to appear calm. "I do," she managed.

He nodded. "Then I have only one thing to ask in return. If we do this, if we send out wizards to fight these invisible monsters you describe… you do not go with them."

Her brow twitched downward.

"You are the last of the royal family, your highness," he explained, a hint of gentleness in his tone. "You are all that stands between us and the loss of our magic to the Taliesin king, and you are quite literally our only hope of uncovering the spell to bind our enemies again. For you to be lost to us in a battle or even just an accident…" He shook his head. "It is unthinkable. We need you here as a symbol to our people, to give them hope and courage so *they* can go out and fight the enemies that have plagued us for so long. They need you here so they can know that, even if they die, hope for their families and loved ones remains.

"This does not mean you will be doing nothing," he continued at the protests in her eyes. "Not remotely. Your father's work is unfinished. We can train you in magic, teach you what we know, but only you can learn how to reinstate the spell to bind Taliesin."

Darius paused. "Please do not see this as less important, your majesty," he insisted. "I cannot understate what it will mean to end this war. We can negotiate with Taliesin as we have no chance of doing now. We can deliver war criminals to justice, if the stories you bring from the cripples are true. And once there is peace, your Blood wizards will have infinitely more difficulty trying to hide. With the first one we capture, you will be able to extend the binding spell through them to all on their side, rendering them incapable of harming anyone ever again.

"That is the extent of your power, your highness, should the spell be reclaimed. And that is why you *must* remain safely here. So… do we have an agreement?"

With everything in her, she wanted to say no. A breath away from emerging, the word hovered on her lips. But her gaze tracked around the table, watching the unwilling expressions strengthen, and she could already hear the arguments that would follow if she disagreed. Everything would shatter. Carter's plan and everything he'd asked her to do would just fall to pieces, because the only thing stopping them from dismissing every word she'd just said was the fact Darius was on her side.

But to stay here… to hide as others fought the ones who'd killed her family…

She swallowed, protests pushing so hard against her chest it hurt to breathe. But she'd come this far. She couldn't back down now. Not when, with this one sacrifice, everything Carter wanted would be realized.

It killed her. But she couldn't let that destroy Carter's dream. "Yes."

Darius nodded gratefully. "Then we will gather wizards to assist us and, with your blessing, we will send them out to find the cripples. Given how they have hidden from us and the distrust they have for our kind, it may take time. But," he added, "it is also a royal order. And we have the good faith you built with their so-called Hunters to aid us. No matter what it takes, we *will* see it done."

Air escaped her. "Thank you."

He bowed his head in return.

She glanced around the table. Cornelius didn't look up, and Sebastian seemed ready to explode. But the others were expressionless and no one said a word.

"Well, if there is nothing else," Darius continued after a moment. "Then I suggest we adjourn."

At his words, the others rose, disappearing from the room in near silence. Sebastian was the first out the door. Ashe watched him go, and when Cornelius circled the table to her side, it took a moment for her to turn around.

"If you would come with me, your majesty," he said with rigid decorum.

She stood, her gaze slipping over the room again and catching on

Darius.

Incrementally, he nodded, giving her a tiny smile.

Drawing a breath, she echoed the motion and then turned, following Cornelius from the conference room. On the factory floor, she could see Sebastian snapping at a few wizards as he marched past, and swiftly, they hurried after him. She grimaced darkly and kept walking.

Winding deeper into the building, Cornelius led her through corridors she'd had yet to see, and along walkways that stretched past areas easily as large as the one they'd left behind. Doors opened along the walls below her, admitting wizards toting boxes of produce and bread through abyssal portals that made her cringe. Rows of crates were arrayed in front of the doors, the stenciled names of various foods on their sides, while tangled piles of metal and plastic lay in a jumble at the far end of the room. She eyed the mess in confusion till she realized the scrap heap contained the remnants of whatever machinery had once filled the factory.

Ignoring the organized chaos, Cornelius continued onward, never looking back to see if she was still with him.

"Where are we going?" she called, speeding up to keep pace with his long legs.

"Library."

She blinked at his sharp tone. Reaching the far side of the walkway, he yanked open a door and then headed inside without pause. Scowling, she broke into a jog, trying to catch the door before it slammed shut and she lost sight of him completely.

A panicked cry brought her up short.

With a bleeding wizard supported on his shoulder, a man rushed from a portal below her. Dropping their boxes of produce to the ground, the other wizards ran to help as more people came through the opening, some under their own power and others leaning heavily on their companions. From deeper in the building, she could hear shouts, along with the drum of footsteps running in her direction.

"Ashe."

She flinched. Cornelius had reappeared behind her.

"Go back to your room," he said, his gaze locked on the wizards coming through the portal.

"What–"

"Do it now."

"Cornelius–"

He glanced over to her and she blanched at the look in his eyes. At a loss for what to do, she backed away and then started for the hall, still watching the factory floor. Behind her, Cornelius strode down the metal stairs and then grabbed the nearest wizard for information.

Guards rushed from the hallway and, startled, she stumbled back against the wall to stay out of their path. On the factory floor, more people were being carried in. Suspended between two wizards, a woman without an arm screamed, the bandages on her shoulder soaked and dripping red. Howling for his mother, a toddler flailed in the grip of a man whose head was wrapped in his own t-shirt and whose back bore viciously seeping burns.

And others didn't move at all.

Trembling, her hands braced themselves against the wall.

"Your highness?"

Catching himself as he ran from the hall, Elias looked at her in alarm. Barely giving either of them a passing glance, Katherine kept going, a dozen wizards carrying bundles of medical supplies coming after her. "What're you doing here?" he asked.

"C-Cornelius was…" she started, her gaze still on the wounded and the dying. She faltered, forgetting her response. "What happened?"

Elias grimaced, glancing to the factory floor. "You shouldn't be here."

"What *happened?*"

"We're not sure yet. Ambush at another safe house, probably."

Her brow drew down tremulously as a tiny body wrapped in a purple fleece blanket came through the portal in the arms of a larger wizard.

The look on the man's face told her all she needed to know.

"Please go back to your room, your highness," Elias said, gentleness struggling to cover the urgency in his tone. His gaze darted between her and the factory floor, and he reached over to guide her back toward the hallway. "There isn't any need for you to see this."

She shrugged off his hand, watching as the man set the little body down on a crate. A bloodied hand slipped from beneath the fleece. A pink bracelet dangled from the wrist and the glitter inside caught on the bright factory lights. Heavily, the man sank to the floor, and as he buried his face in his hands, his shoulders began to shake.

Ashe headed for the stairs.

"Your majesty!" Elias called, rushing to catch up with her. "Please, this isn't–"

She ignored him, making a beeline for the man. Pulling his tear-stained face from his hands, he looked up as she stopped by the body of the child.

Her fingers shaking, she pulled back the blanket. Confusion clouded the man's face as he looked from her to Elias.

"Who…?" the man asked, his voice thick with pain.

"Her Royal Highness," Elias explained quietly. "Queen Ashe."

The man stared at her. She barely noticed.

With her dark lashes resting on her pale skin, the girl could have been sleeping, but for the blood staining her little green t-shirt above the blanket's hem. Feathery strands of auburn hair lay across her face, above freckled cheeks still touched with pink.

Gently, Ashe brushed the hair from the child's face and then looked down at the man.

"I'm so sorry," she whispered.

Grief tugged at his expression. Wordlessly, he managed to nod.

Ashe turned. More people rushed down the steps to help, while others carried the injured farther away. Children wailed for their parents, the sobs mingling with the moans and cries of the wounded. Healers shouted for bandages as their magic flared, treating what could be quickly fixed and staunching the blood of what could not. The less injured leaned against crates at the edge of the chaos, their eyes glazed with residual horror. At the center of it all, Katherine stood, calling orders to her army of healers and pouring her magic into the worst of the injured brought her way.

Across the room, Ashe spotted Cornelius heading for a portal, a handful of guards at his back. She started toward them, only to come to a sharp stop as they disappeared through the opening and the shadows vanished in their wake, leaving only an empty doorway.

"You should go, your highness," Elias insisted, stepping aside as two healers rushed past.

Ashe ignored him and took off toward Katherine. "What can I do to help?" she called, raising her voice over the din.

Katherine cut off in mid-command, irritation flashing across her face before she realized who had spoken.

"Your majesty, you shouldn't–"

"What can I do to help!" Ashe yelled furiously.

Katherine paused. "Ermengarde!" she shouted at a rotund woman bustling past with an enormous bundle of bandages in her arms. "Take her highness with you."

Ermengarde's eyes went wide as she looked from Katherine to Ashe. Swallowing, she nodded and then motioned with a nervous tilt of her head for Ashe to come with her.

"You don't have to–" the round woman protested as Ashe reached her and immediately moved to take the bandages from her arms.

At the look in Ashe's eyes, she fell silent and relinquished the wrappings.

"Now what?"

Blinking rapidly, Ermengarde faltered at the question. Jerkily, she nodded toward a healer nearby and then obeyed her own direction and hurried his way.

Gripping the bandages, Ashe followed.

The healer barely glanced up from his wounded charge as they came closer. "One of you hold her and the other clean this up," he ordered. "I can hardly see what I'm doing here."

With an anxious glance to Ashe, Ermengarde dropped to her knees, ignoring the wet ground as she moved to hold the woman's wound closed. Ashe set the bandages on a nearby crate and then grabbed two bundles before crouching down.

"Go on," the healer snapped.

Biting her lip, she obeyed. Blood soaked the woman's torso and dripped from the tatters of her shirt. In her abdomen, a ragged wound with blackened edges gaped and dark lines traced the veins radiating from the hole, as though the tiny capillaries had been burnt to charcoal. Magic raced around the perimeter of the wound, knitting the skin beneath the healer's intent stare.

Swallowing hard, Ashe reached down and tried to wipe the blood from the edges of the wound.

"Hurry up, dammit," the healer muttered at Ashe.

She worked faster. Skin knit beside her hands as she sopped the blood away and the woman gasped for air. His face tightening, the healer cursed and poured more magic into the wound.

Skin merged over the woman's abdomen. The magic spread wider, covering her chest, her head, her arms and legs.

And then her breathing eased.

The healer sighed as the woman slipped into sleep. Without a word, he rose and headed for the next wounded person he could see.

Ermengarde took a breath and then gestured to two wizards watching from nearby. As they came to lift the woman between them, she gathered the clean bandages into her arms and then glanced over, catching sight of Ashe still crouched on the ground.

"My lady?"

Dryly, Ashe swallowed and dropped the soaking cloths. Trembling, she rose to her feet as shock raced in on adrenaline's heels. Carefully keeping her bloodied hands away from her sides, she closed her eyes, struggling to drive away the memories clamoring at the edge of her control.

"You don't—" Ermengarde started.

Ashe looked over at her and the woman blanched. Licking her lips, Ermengarde hesitated and then gave an uncomfortable nod before hurrying after the healer. Ashe followed right behind.

Hours passed. After a while, she barely noticed the time. The day became divided into who survived and who didn't; a series of snapshots that eventually began to blur. Bloodstains and sweat were inter-changeable, and she soon stopped paying attention to either. Only the person she was helping mattered and the shouts and screams were just background noise, filtered for what was relevant to the moment, and otherwise ignored.

And then, it was over.

She sat back on her heels as the wizards carried away the boy she'd been helping, his eyes closed in sleep below the bandage she'd wrapped around his head. At her side, the healer blinked tiredly, and then sighed. Glancing over, he bowed his head to her with a smile.

"Thank you, my lady."

Rising, he headed for the stairs.

She watched him go and then looked to the rest of the factory floor.

The room was quieter since she'd last noticed it, and the majority of the wounded had been taken elsewhere. A few wizards moved through the space, cleaning up the blood and mess, while others helped the remaining injured toward the cots that had taken up residence against the far wall.

Stiffly, she rose and then hoisted herself onto one of the crates. Ermengarde was nowhere to be seen; she'd lost track of the woman an unknown amount of time before. Katherine was likewise gone, and she could only assume both women were attending to the worst of the wounded in other parts of the factory.

Two wizards moved by, bearing a young man on a litter between them. Vague memories rose at the sight; she'd helped hold him as they bandaged his legs. Now he slept, soothed by the magic of the healers on either side.

"Thank you, your highness," the women murmured, bowing

their heads as they passed.

Her gaze tracked them, and then she closed her eyes, resisting the urge to rub her temples due to the dirt and blood on her hands. Aching muscles took the opportunity to make themselves heard now that the chaos had passed, and her stomach staged a conspiracy with her head to form a throbbing ache at the base of her skull. Images from the past hours crept through her exhaustion, interspersed with flashes of memories from the days before.

"Here."

She opened her eyes to see Elias standing beside her. With a lifted eyebrow, he proffered a glass of water. Hesitating briefly, she took it from him and then watched as he lifted himself onto the crate by her side.

"Go on," he said with a jerk of his chin toward the water. "You could use it."

She eyed him a moment longer, and then drained the glass.

"Thank you for what you did today," he said as she finished. "Turns out most of the wounded came from my region, and I can't tell you what it meant to them, having you here to help. What it meant to us all, honestly."

Uncomfortable, Ashe looked away. "I should get cleaned up," she said, slipping off the crate and avoiding the blood still on the floor.

"It's strange to you, isn't it?"

She glanced back to find him regarding her thoughtfully. Her brow drew down in cautious questioning.

"Being queen," he elaborated. "You just see yourself as a regular girl. Or close to, anyway." He paused. "Right?"

Warily, she gave a small shrug. His lip twitched in a smile.

"But then, you only learned of this… what? A little bit ago?"

She watched him a moment before answering. "Yesterday."

His eyebrows rose. "And the wizard thing was just last month?"

She nodded.

He whistled softly and then gestured back toward the crate. A heartbeat passed, and then she returned and hoisted herself back up beside him.

"You're taking it pretty well," he commented.

Her gaze dropped to the floor. He seemed to read the silence.

"Well, it seems that way to me."

She glanced up. He gave her another small smile.

"Everyone here lives a double life, your majesty," he continued with a look to the wizards across the room. "Or, at least, they did till the war. On the one hand, they were regular folks who had jobs, paid their taxes, voted in elections and whatnot. On the other, they're wizards, with a royal family to whom they pay allegiance, magical powers they hide and all that entails. It's never been easy being a part of our world. It's complicated, keeping one foot with the humans and one foot here. More so when you go from regular girl to royalty-who-can-save-us-all in the space of a month."

At her silence, he turned back to her.

"You're doing really well, all things considered."

She paused, uncertain what to feel. "Thanks."

He shrugged.

From the corner of her eye, she studied him. Leaning back with his hands braced on the wooden crate, he looked as though he should have been sitting in a hayloft, calmly watching the sunset. Only the blood on his clothes told a different story.

"Elias?"

He glanced over.

She hesitated. "The wounded were from your region?"

"Yeah," he said. "Survivors of an attack on their hideout in Montreal. They were heading here when the Taliesin caught up with them."

She nodded awkwardly. "Okay, no, I just…"

His eyebrow twitched up curiously.

"What's a region?" she asked quietly. "I mean, when you say that… and the others…"

The second eyebrow rose to join the first. "Oh," he said, understanding. "Right. Of course. A region is an area that a council-member presides over. We're elected by the wizards who live there, and we serve as representatives for them to the king. The regions are divided by things like population, family ties, all sorts of reasons. There are twelve regions, so there are twelve members on the Council, though it's pretty rare for spouses to serve concurrently like Katherine and I do."

Elias watched her for a moment. "Anything else you'd like to know?"

She hesitated. He gave a small look to the rest of the room.

"I won't tell anyone you asked, your highness," he continued softly.

Silent, she regarded him, trying to decide whether she trusted what he said. No pressure or impatience was in his eyes as he waited for her answer, just a tinge of humor that never seemed to leave.

"Okay," she said. Licking her lips uneasily, she glanced from him to the room and back. "Um… this queen thing. Why does everyone *care* so much? I mean…"

"You mean why did they care you were here?"

"Or any of it."

He shrugged amicably. "You're queen."

She looked away in exasperation.

"Seriously," he said. "You heard Darius. You're as much a symbol to them as anything. You represent hope for the war to end. That's a big deal to folks who haven't had an easy night's sleep in eight years."

Ashe grimaced.

"And it's more than that. You represent the continuation of a part of their identity as the people of Merlin. They know what your presentation means. King Patrick is dead. But while they mourn that, the fact you're still here means the royal line will go on."

A heartbeat passed, and then incredulity and discomfort twisted her face as the implications of his last statement settled over her. He chuckled at her expression.

"No worries," he assured her amusedly. "They're not thinking like that just yet."

Mortified, she locked her gaze on the ground, wishing she could melt through it.

"But," Elias continued, "they're also not thinking that the new Queen of Merlin would rush to get herself covered in blood and sweat, just to aid the wounded of a people she barely knows. Your father helped us, yes. He did what he could between his efforts to restore the spell. But you grew up outside this war and just got here yesterday. They have no idea who you are or what you're about. To be honest, none of us do. But you just marched down here and de-manded to help people you'd never met, despite the 'recommendations' of a quarter of your council. So yeah, even more than before… now they *really* care."

Still feeling awkward, she couldn't bring herself to look back up from the floor. "But…" she tried, faintly desperate.

"You're just a regular girl?"

She made a noise of agreement.

"Not to them."

Ashe looked away. On the far end of the room, healers moved among the wounded, most of whom seemed to finally be asleep. Closer by, several wizards cleaned up the boxes of food knocked over in the earlier chaos, discarding what was damaged and keeping what could be salvaged.

"So anything else?" Elias asked.

She blinked, pulling her gaze back to him. Hesitating, she floundered through the plethora of questions she'd amassed over the past day. "'Line of authority'?"

He chuckled. "Hierarchy. Basically how the power goes if one of us falls."

She bit her lip. "So Sebastian takes control if Darius dies?"

"Unfortunately," he murmured dryly. He glanced at her askance. "Let's make sure that doesn't happen, eh?"

She met his gaze. The humor in his eyes strengthened.

"But how did *he* end up...?" Her face twisted expressively.

"Good connections. Knowing the right people." Elias shrugged. "It's politics."

Ashe grimaced, and then looked back up as another thought occurred to her. "And Katherine outranks you?"

"Yep."

Noticing her watching him, Elias shrugged again. "She's been at this a bit longer. Seniority matters too."

Ashe didn't say anything.

Pushing a broom ahead of him, a wizard came by, and the two of them pulled up their feet to stay out of the man's way. Murmuring an apology, the sweeper bowed as he passed, driving the dirty bandages along. With a twitch of his head, Elias motioned for her to jump down, joining her a moment later. Side by side, they began walking back toward the stairs.

"That all you wanted to know?" he asked when the sweeper was out of earshot.

"What are those blue lights on the doors? The ones that appear sometimes near a portal?"

"Wizard writing," he answered. "Which is a ridiculously self-important name, if you ask me. Basically, it's magic writing humans can't see. There's some scientific explanation for why it's blue and not some other color, but that doesn't really matter. These days, it's mostly just used for certain types of portals. Some portals can be set up ahead of time and given variable destinations, so the wizard writing really helps distinguish…"

He fell silent when her hand twitched up.

Coming to a stop at the base of the stairway, she glanced at him. "*Variable* destinations?" she asked, trying to ignore the quiver in her stomach at the words.

"Right. Sorry, my lady. Variable destinations means–"

"Elias?"

One hand on the banister, he looked over at her.

"Could you just call me Ashe?"

He paused. "Never going to happen, your majesty," he said assuredly. "My apologies."

Bowing slightly, he gave her a small grin and then started up the stairs.

"Variable destinations," he continued as though she hadn't interrupted, "means that a wizard can attach the portal to more than one endpoint, typically selected by options written on the door itself and accessible through a variant of the basic portal spell. Portals themselves are just a rather unique twist of magic that uses magical resonance to create an effect far stronger than any one wizard could achieve on their own, which means that ultimately, portals possess a tremendous amount of energy and that even a fairly weak wizard can make one…"

She watched him as he climbed the steps. A mystified look drifted over her face, and she shook her head to drive it away. Gripping the banister, she hurried up the steps. He glanced over as she joined him, barely pausing before continuing his explanation.

"So, more recently, we've managed to connect technology to these variable destination portals, as you might've seen with cell phones. It's all just magic, whether it's tied to a phone, a doorframe, or some stereotypical staff with a big jewel on top. But regardless, the cell phones and the wizard writing serve the function of confirming the selected destination's viability…"

A bemused expression on her face, Ashe followed him away from the factory floor.

Chapter Five

"**...a**nd two cousins," Elias concluded.

"Two?" Ashe repeated.

"On your mother's side," he clarified. "On your dad's side, you only had one."

Her temple resting on her hand, Ashe's brow furrowed as she traced the wood grain of the table with a fingertip. Isolated in an office in an infrequently trafficked part of the factory, they'd spent the past hour running the gamut of every question she could think to ask, coming at last to the touchy subject of her family history that no one back home had ever wanted to discuss.

"What were their names?" she asked, still studying the table.

"Peter and Olivia were your cousins on your mom's side. They were about…" He thought for a second. "Maybe two and four years older than you, respectively? Madelyn was on your dad's side. She was three when she died."

Ashe paused in her tracing and glanced up at Elias. He shrugged, a sympathetic look in his eyes.

"And my uncle?" she asked after a moment, returning her gaze to the tabletop. "Cornelius said my dad had an older brother."

"Alexander," Elias confirmed. "His wife was Yvonne. On your mom's side, Rebecca had an older sister named Lily, for whom your sister was named. Her husband was Michael, who was a cripple, actually."

She glanced up again.

Elias nodded. "They met when Michael was in college and Lily was… auditing classes," he said with a grin. "After a fashion, anyway. Your maternal grandmother, Imogene, wasn't too fond of the match, but as I remember her, your aunt was nothing if not headstrong. She–"

He cut off as the office door opened. Ashe turned, irritation surging at the interruption.

Cornelius glanced into the office and then stopped at the sight of her. Expressions chased themselves across his face so fast she almost couldn't catch them, racing past surprise and alarm and then vanishing behind the mask of meticulous propriety she was starting to suspect he wore nearly all the time.

"Your highness," he said tightly. "Councilman de Vila."

With a small nod toward them both, he stepped into the room and let the door shut behind him. "I've been looking for you, my lady."

Elias glanced to her. "Perhaps we can continue our discussions later, your majesty." Pushing his chair away from the table, he rose. "Did you catch the Taliesin?" he asked Cornelius.

"No, they had already fled by the time we arrived. Discussions?"

"Her highness and I discovered we had acquaintances in common from my region," Elias answered easily. "Among the cripples, that is. We were just sharing stories, reminding me of home."

Cornelius paused. "Ah."

Elias eyed him briefly, curiosity flickering through his gaze at the man's tone. With another look to Ashe, he grinned, though the comfortable humor was missing from his eyes.

"Take care of yourself, highness," he said.

He gave her a small nod, glanced to Cornelius again, and then left.

Cornelius waited for the door to close. "I asked you to return to your room."

She didn't respond, uncertain what she was supposed to say.

He grimaced slightly. "I was concerned," he continued more softly.

"I'm fine."

"I can see that."

She watched him as his gaze ran over her.

"You were helping the wounded," he said.

Ashe nodded, assuming it was obvious. Engrossed in talking with Elias, she hadn't paused for much more than washing the blood and dirt from her hands.

"You should get cleaned up," he said with a look to the door. "People should not see you like this."

"Elias said it just makes them think better of the monarchy," she commented dryly.

"It also scares them."

His tone made answering difficult, and after a moment, she pushed away from the table and stood. He stepped out of her way as she crossed to the door.

"Once you're clean," he said. "Come to the conference room."

"Why?"

"Because we have an agreement, and your part needs to begin as soon as possible."

She hesitated, remembering Darius' request. Stay here. Find the spell. Let others do the fighting. With effort, she kept from scowling. In the midst of talking with Elias, she'd managed to forget.

Cornelius' face darkened when she didn't answer, and her irritation rose again. "So you've already got people out finding the cripples then?" she asked. "Because that was part of the agreement too."

"Those were your orders, highness."

The irritation strengthened at the tone. The title. All of it. Moving past him, she stalked out the door.

Fresh clothes and a hot shower later, she reluctantly headed for the conference room. On the factory floor, most people were already asleep, while overhead, the lights were dimmed to a fraction of their normal brilliance.

Cornelius looked up as the door shut behind her. A scattering of papers lay on the table before him, which he gathered swiftly and returned to a folder. Rising, he walked past her to the door.

"Where are we going?" she asked. "I thought you wanted to meet here?"

"Only to meet. Not to stay."

Eyeing him with suspicion, she followed when he left the room. Striding ahead of her, Cornelius turned at the hall and continued farther into the building, barely pausing to see if she was coming. Winding through the corridors, he emerged onto the walkway over-looking the cots of the wounded.

Biting her lip, she glanced to the sleeping wizards, not wanting to wake them with the questions bubbling up inside. Hurrying after Cornelius to the end of the walkway, she slipped through the door after him and then sped up, trying to catch him as he climbed the stairs.

"What's going on, Cornelius?" she asked as they left the stairwell. The hallway was empty and each of the office doors lining the corridor was shut. Exit signs lit either end, casting a red glow along the length of the dusty linoleum floor. "Is this about the deal Darius made?"

He stopped, but didn't turn around. A humorless look crossed her face.

"I'll take that as a yes," she said dryly. At his silence, she continued. "So what? No one can even *try* to see if Carter wasn't crazy? Is that it?"

Cornelius looked back at her. She raised an eyebrow.

"Of course not," he said.

He started down the hallway again.

"Then what?" she called.

Turning the corner, he kept going.

"Cornelius!"

Scowling, she jogged after him. By a door like any other, he paused, pulling a ring of keys from his pocket.

"*What?*" she asked again.

With a key in the lock, he paused. "No good will come of this, highness," he said quietly. At her expression, he cut in before she could speak. "Darius is kind to you. Listening because you are queen and because he does not want to alienate you moments after you walked in the door. But he doesn't believe. None of them believe. You ask me if it's so hard to simply show that Josiah wasn't insane? I wonder that you think I wouldn't have tried that before."

He moved to unlock the door and she reached over, putting a hand to the bolt. "What do you mean?" she asked.

Cornelius closed his eyes. "He was my cousin, highness. And

nearly a brother, for all that. Of course I tried to prove he wasn't insane, even after the Council dismissed him with barely a word."

"What'd you do?"

"I went into the city with him, despite the war, despite the fact people were being killed in the streets. I spent hours searching with him, following every person he said glowed, even testing them by tossing a bit of magic their way. I did everything I could, short of attacking them outright." He shook his head. "And nothing happened. They saw Josiah. Gave him strange looks for staring at them so hard. And then they moved on. They never even noticed I was there."

"They were pretending," she said.

"Josiah swore they were," he agreed. "Each time one of them walked off, or came up and asked him what the problem was, he was emphatic that they were only preserving their cover. But it went on all day, your highness, and it never changed. He became more and more agitated, wanted me to believe him despite the evidence of my own eyes, but… it never changed."

She hesitated. "And so what did you do then?"

"What could I do? Lie to the Council? Tell them I witnessed something I had not, just so they'd send even more wizards in search of enemies that didn't exist? People were *dying*, your majesty. Families, children… I could not let the forces we needed to fight the *real* war go off on some fairytale mission just to please Josiah."

Cornelius fell silent.

She dropped her hand from the lock. "It wasn't," she said flatly.

"It always has been," he replied. "Josiah was a good man, your majesty. A loyalist to the monarchy and a respected leader to his people. But when the Council refused to believe him – when *I* refused to believe him – he abandoned one in failed service to the other, and so destroyed them both.

"My cousin is known as a murderer, your highness, and most of the wizards here are fairly certain the world is better off with him dead. He left a trail of bodies eight years long, each one of which he swore was justified. But you try telling that to the friends and families of his victims, all of whom see him as a madman and will *never* believe their loved ones could do the things he claimed. His delusions ruined him, Ashe. Him, and every one of his people who bought into them." Cornelius paused. "I do not want to see them ruin you and the legacy of the Merlin's Children as well."

She shook her head. "I know what I saw, Cornelius. And what I felt. The man who murdered my dad used magic. I know; I took it from him. I killed him with it."

At the last, he glanced over, and discomfort hit her at the alarm in his expression.

"Brogan looked human," she insisted, pushing past the feeling. "They all did."

For a long moment, he said nothing. And then he closed his eyes. "Taliesin has many tricks, your highness."

"It wasn't Taliesin!"

"Are you sure?"

Without another word, he turned away, sending a thread of magic into the lock as he twisted the key. Pushing open the door, he headed into the darkened room beyond.

She stared after him. Despite the ostensible question, nothing but cold certainty had been in his tone, cemented by years of resigning himself to belief in Carter's supposed insanity.

And he couldn't let it change.

Watching Cornelius, she followed him inside. In the dim light coming from the hall, she could see a filing cabinet near the door. Reaching behind it, Cornelius flipped an unseen switch and, with a garish flicker, utility lights overhead buzzed to life.

Gray surrounded them. From the gray walls to the gray carpet, and all across the gray utility table in the center of the room, the color dominated the space. Above the filing cabinets lining the walls, metal shelves stretched to the ceiling. Each level was stacked high with papers, folders and cheap plastic binders that provided the only deviation from the monochrome of the room, though even they were faded with age. More files spilled across the table, coating the metal surface in chaotically scattered piles. On the only wall devoid of shelving, a narrow window shared space with an enormous corkboard, the latter of which was speckled with thumb tacks and almost completely obscured by further layers of paper.

"What is this place?" she asked guardedly, looking around.

"Your father called it the library."

She glanced over at him.

"It's everything we have on Merlin, the spell, and our history."

Her eyebrows twitched up in surprise, and her gaze returned to the piles of paper, suddenly seeing them as a whole lot smaller than before. "This…"

"Used to be much greater, yes," he said, reading the tone. "As was everything else. We had so much more than a factory once, your highness. But in war, everything is a target. Monuments and places of beauty most of all.

"Taliesin killed our historians," he continued. "They attacked our archives in the first days of the war and destroyed everything and everyone in sight. This was all we could salvage. Notes. Photocopies.

Reproductions from family collections."

He looked around with a wry expression. "It's ironic, really. Considering they need this information just as much as we do. Yet they still attempted to destroy it. One wonders if they even knew what they were burning."

She studied him for a moment and then came farther into the room. No organization separated the mess atop the table, but after a heartbeat, she paused. Familiar handwriting crowded the margins of nearly every page.

"He intended to come back after his visit to you," Cornelius said quietly. "He asked us not to touch anything until then."

Ashe's gaze traced the letters, the words. Fragments of sentences drifted past, nonsensical.

"He was in the middle of something?" she asked distantly.

A hint of old irony touched Cornelius' tone. "He always was."

She glanced up.

"Your father didn't share much," he explained. "Especially in the past few years. His research was circular as much as anything, and new discoveries often only led to further questions he had not yet considered. In the end, I think he'd begun to despair of sharing information, simply because it raised our hopes and then so often went nowhere."

Cornelius paused. "I do not know where he'd gotten to before he died."

Her gaze tracked across the shelves, taking in the books and binders that so alternately appeared overwhelming and yet not sufficient at all. "But… what am I supposed to do?"

"Read. Study. Use what you know of your gifts to find the answers to Merlin's spell." He glanced down at the table. "Follow the breadcrumbs your father left to fulfill your part of the bargain Darius made."

"But I don't even–" She caught herself, reluctant to admit any weakness to him. The binders and notes stared back at her, and she suppressed a scowl, knowing she had to continue.

"I don't know *anything* about magic, Cornelius."

He paused. "I know." At her expression, he held up a hand. "But not everyone here does. And it is not important. You will."

She watched him cautiously.

"Your father wanted to shelter you," Cornelius said. "To keep you from needing to become the kind of wizard he had to be. But…" A grimace surfaced briefly. "The world is what it is. And that is not possible anymore. Thus, anything of magic we know, I will teach you. Anything I can do to assist you, it will be done. I swear."

She looked back at the papers, saying nothing. She didn't want to bring up Carter again. It wouldn't help and the conversation wouldn't go any differently than it had five minutes before.

And at the moment, it wasn't the point.

A vague sense of helplessness pressed down on her as she brushed her fingertips across the papers. "I'm just not sure I–"

"Ashe," he interrupted quietly.

She glanced over at him.

"What you saw today. The attack. Your people need this. More than they need you bandaging wounds, more than your presence or support. They need you to fix this. You are the only one who can."

She shifted uncomfortably. "But where do I start?"

His gaze went to the aging desk chair at the head of the table. "How about here?"

Hesitating a moment, she circled the table and then sank into the creaking chair. The scattered paper before her seemed to stretch out infinitely.

"Read what you can tonight," Cornelius said. "And then get some sleep. We will start in earnest tomorrow morning."

He crossed to the door and then paused, looking back at her. "You can do this, your highness."

The door shut. Silence echoed in the room.

She closed her eyes. Study. Read books while others did the only thing that really mattered to her. It was infuriating. And yet, if it meant the Blood were destroyed, people like the dying kids today were spared, and Carter was proved sane at the same time…

Ashe sighed. She'd always liked to read.

Grimacing, she opened her eyes. Scanning the sea of papers before her, she selected a small stack at random. Placing it atop the piles in front of her, she drew a tired breath and then set herself to piecing together the clues her father had left behind.

Chapter Six

"You aren't concentrating!" Cornelius snapped from his post by the wall of the massive storage building.

Gritting her teeth, Ashe extinguished the fire around her hands. "I'm trying," she growled.

"Try harder," he retorted. "That last attack would have hurt you if the guard hadn't pulled it in time."

Furious, she turned away, swiping the sweat from her eyes and resisting the urge to strike out at the infernal man. Around her, dozens of makeshift targets smoldered, victims of her offensive training.

Four weeks had passed since she'd come to the Merlin hideout on the edge of Croftsburg, and each moment had been nearly as unproductive as possible in regards to anything she cared to be doing. For starters, there had been the trouble with locating the cripples. No one had expected to find any in the city itself, of course; so many wizards in the area had long since driven the cripples far from Croftsburg. But days upon days had gone by, and for each message Darius sent to every wizard within a thousand miles, he'd received nothing remotely helpful in reply. Most hadn't seen a cripple in years. A trio of Merlin in southern Indiana finally found a few hiding in an abandoned barn, but the wizards had barely had time to ask for help on behalf of their queen before the cripples had taken off running. No matter what the wizards said, they couldn't stop them fleeing, and their attempts to follow had been met with guns.

Nothing had changed since.

And meanwhile, the fruitless search was taking its toll. Already infinitesimal, the Council's patience for 'her' Blood wizards was dwindling rapidly toward nonexistence. Of them all, only Darius maintained any determination to do as she'd asked, though lately even he'd begun to look concerned. Her attempts to initiate discussions of her going out to help had been resounding failures, however. They'd made a deal. And she was needed here.

So the days crept by. In the morning, she studied her father's files, pouring through years of handwritten notes and cross-references. In short order, she'd discovered that when Cornelius said the library consisted of remnants, he'd made the understatement of the century. Even her father's journals lamented the lack of information he'd constantly encountered. Pages ended in midsentence, with the next page nowhere to be found, and countless records mentioned other books no one could remember seeing.

It was maddening.

By early afternoon, Cornelius rescued her from the stacks of notebooks, though only to deliver her to their training area and then drive her till she thought she'd scream. Initially, it hadn't been so bad. Basic defensive techniques, baby steps, and talk of how magic worked dominated their time. But soon, he'd started her on offensive tactics, insisting she learn to accomplish by design what she'd thus far pulled off only by instinct. Hours of maneuvering through physically and magically demanding obstacle courses followed, as well as entire sessions spent trying to bind more than one wizard simultaneously. The guards were her guinea pigs, and their avowed trust in her ability to unbind them once finished was only occasionally belied by the hints of anxiety she saw in their eyes.

She'd struggled at the start, trying to remember how she'd taken Brogan's magic away. The whole night was a blur, and recreating what she'd done meant revisiting memories she'd rather forget. But slowly, it came back to her, and now Cornelius steadily worked more and more wizard attackers into their sessions, expecting her to bind them without fail every single time.

It was good training, she supposed. But it helped nothing toward the spell. No matter how hard she pushed herself or what she read, taking magic from multiple wizards at the exact same time remained beyond her reach. She could bind one, and then another and another, and keep them all bound till she wanted to let them go, or even take the magic of one and use it against another, but simultaneous binding required more strength than she knew how to find.

And that was the problem really, though she hadn't discussed it with Cornelius. Strong she might be – likely stronger than most of the wizards here, if her father's notes on her general family history were any indication – but even for her there remained a point she couldn't exceed.

She'd discovered it soon after they started their lessons. At the beginning, the practice had been so liberating. Their training building was a massive concrete-walled space with only a semblance of a roof to worry about, and for their part, the guards and Cornelius were so accustomed to defending against magical assaults that, for the first time, she could let the fire go and trust that everyone would be okay. But as the intensity of their practice escalated, things changed. One moment, she'd been pushing herself harder and harder, trying desperately to snare the magic of two wizards at once, and the next she'd been on her knees, gasping as her magic faltered at the edge of a great cavernous gulf in her mind.

In the days that followed, she'd taken to calling it the black hole, though 'abyss' would have been equally fitting. Like a cliff at the end of the world, the void demarcated the nonnegotiable point beyond which her magic absolutely could not go.

From her father's journals, she'd pieced together information, learning what she could of the 'limit' he occasionally described. The human body only possessed so much capacity for magic, he wrote, beyond which the mind would simply break. Most wizards never came close to this, but with her family's history of strength, for them the situation was not the same. At the start of the war, he'd tried to push beyond it for the sake of the spell, but the attempts left him unconscious for days and frightened the Council into thinking he'd been permanently incapacitated. Eventually, when months of trying left the limit unchanged, he'd given up and clung to the hope that strength alone had not been the sole factor in what Merlin had done.

She'd danced close to the edge since reading his words, but never pushed past it. Sooner or later, she knew she probably would, but until her skill with magic improved, she wasn't sure it would go particularly well. At best, she'd be knocked unconscious. At worst, she'd be a vegetable.

And thus, she kept training. No matter how infuriating Cornelius could be.

"Go again," he called. At his command, the guards scattered to search for hiding places. Scorch marks covered the maze of cinderblock barricades and showed in multilayered swaths across the walls. Of the fabric and hay dummies, only piles of smoldering ash remained.

"No flames this time," he told her. "Only force. Stop resorting to pyromachy just because it makes you the most comfortable."

She scowled and then turned away to give the guards a chance to hide.

"Go!"

Sometimes, the hours among the books almost seemed appealing.

The sun rested heavily on the horizon when Cornelius finally signaled the end of their training and ordered the guards back to the factory. Sinking down onto a pile of cinder blocks, Ashe released their magic with a twist of her power and then dropped her head into her hands as the men filed out of the building.

Every muscle in her body ached. She wondered if she'd be able to move tomorrow.

"Not bad," Cornelius said, lowering himself down beside her.

She didn't bother to look up.

"I have asked Elias to begin teaching you about portals this evening," he continued. "They are his forte, and thus he is best suited to teach them to you. He should be here soon."

Her gaze went to him incredulously. "I'm about to fall over, Cornelius. Can it wait?"

The man grimaced.

"Please?" she tried.

"As you wish, your majesty."

She drew a breath and then let it out in a sigh. Over the past weeks, she'd often marveled at the bizarrely mixed role of dictator and subordinate Cornelius played. In matters of training, he drove her mercilessly, only to switch back to unflappable deference the moment their lessons were done. If she hadn't known better, she'd almost have thought he *was* insane.

The storage building door swung open and she looked over tiredly as Elias walked in. Surveying the damage, the familiar hint of humor twitched his expression.

"Love what you've done with the place, your highness," he commented.

She gave him a flat look before focusing her attention on stretching her cramping shoulder.

"Her majesty wishes to start portal training tomorrow," Cornelius said.

"That's fine," Elias replied as he crossed the room. "I actually just came to let you know we've found a few cripples."

Freezing in mid-motion, Ashe stared at him.

"They're willing to help us," he continued, "and claim to have encountered your Blood wizards as well. They're on their way here now."

She hesitated. "Did you get their names?"

He shook his head. "Sorry, no. But I can take you to meet them, if you'd like. Provided you're both done, that is?"

Cornelius nodded, but she'd already risen to her feet.

"Where?" she asked.

"The old loading bays."

Elias had to hurry to catch her.

The loading bay entrance was opening as she reached the top of the stairs leading from the factory to the bay floor. Eyes locked on the door, she stopped, her hands gripping the metal guardrail.

Led by two wizards, an old woman and a teenage boy edged into the room. Watching the area around them nervously, the cripples clung to each other and hung back from the wizards.

The door closed.

"Are those the only ones?" Ashe asked, her voice tight.

"Yeah," Elias said. He glanced to her. "You okay?"

She didn't answer, not taking her eyes from the unfamiliar pair. Swallowing dryly, she pushed away from the guardrail and headed down the stairs.

The caution on the cripples' faces grew as she approached them over the length of the loading bay. Stepping to either side of the pair, the guards regarded the empty space in front of them and bowed their heads as she came near.

She ignored them.

"Hi," she said to the cripples, trying to appear nonthreatening. "I'm Ashe."

Behind her, Elias coughed.

An urge to scowl hit her and she fought it, not wanting to frighten the old woman and boy just because the wizards were uncomfortable with the familiarity she was showing.

"The Queen of Merlin," Elias amended politely.

The old woman blinked.

"I just wanted to thank you for coming," Ashe pressed on.

Cagily, the woman studied her. "They said you believed us about the Blood."

Ashe nodded. "They killed my family."

The teenager looked to the old woman, desperate hope in his eyes, while the woman's hand tightened on the boy's own, caution still in her gaze.

"They didn't mention that," the old woman allowed.

Ashe kept from looking at the others. "They don't like to spread it around."

"We had to take the chance," the woman continued, her tone almost daring Ashe to challenge her. "We had to try to stop them. They killed his mother. My daughter. Like she was nothing. So we just… we needed to…"

She trailed off, unable to go farther.

"We will," Ashe said.

Nodding angrily, the old woman looked away, resolve steeling her expression.

"We have some space set aside for you," Elias said after a moment passed. "Away from the wizards."

Her expression unchanged, the old woman nodded again. Her gaze went back to Ashe. "Thank you."

Uncertain what to say, Ashe nodded as well. "You too."

She watched as the guards led the pair toward the steps.

"You want to go out there with them, don't you?" Elias asked.

She didn't answer.

"It's not safe, your majesty. If–"

"I know," she said sharply. Grimacing, she forced the frustration down. They were here. It was a beginning.

And that had to be enough.

"I know," she repeated more quietly.

Taking a breath, she turned and walked away.

— ◆ —

He'd dug through leads to come up with nothing, and poured over newspaper articles with equal lack of success. He'd talked to reporters who'd eventually stopped answering his calls, and surfed the internet till he thought his laptop would break.

And four weeks after his visit to the morgue to see the body of her accomplice, he still had nothing to show for his efforts.

Harris wished he could convince himself that after so long of searching for Ashley and her sister, he'd become accustomed to the frustration, but he knew it would ring a lie. The dearth of progress was infuriating, and when it finally became shoot something for the hell of it or move on, he'd decided to do what all good detectives did when the trail ran cold.

Go back to the beginning.

He'd avoided Monfort, and all of Utah for good measure, on his journey back. There weren't any answers there, but there were plenty of people with questions he didn't care to engage. In her typical, conscientious way, Malden's wife, Rhianne, had kept him apprised of everything, though he'd yet to answer a single one of her emails. Scott was due to start physical therapy soon, and the plastic surgeons were hopeful they could restore at least a semblance of normalcy to his face. The kids were doing well, all things considered, though Nicole's grades were suffering and Andrew had gotten in a few fights. Meanwhile, the department kept checking to see if she'd heard from Harris, as they'd received word he'd taken some new work during his leave and they wanted to follow up with him about it.

She put it so mildly, but he could read between the lines. And stay the hell away as a result.

Annoying as it was, though, the department being after him didn't really matter. He didn't need to go back to Monfort because, as many lives as Ashley had destroyed there, that city was only part of the story. Everything was only part of the story.

This was the beginning.

The weeks hadn't been kind to the ruins of the farmhouse. Soaked by rain and baked by the sun, the blackened boards were warped and yellow tatters of crime scene tape still hung in several places, fluttering in the early summer breeze. A hole gaped near the edge of the ruins, marking where the firemen had extracted the bodies from the basement, such as they were. Charred corpses without a shred of identification, not much of use was found on anything or anyone inside the wreckage.

And the same could be said for the whole situation, really. Since arriving in the state a few days before, he'd practically lived in libraries and county clerk's offices, digging through everything from musty paper records to electronically scanned files, with little to show for it. Paid for in full eight years ago by a small company that'd since gone bankrupt, the house's bills had been accounted for by automated transactions from a network of shell accounts, more small companies, and general confusion. The deed and utilities all listed people of whom he could find no trace, and who – he was starting to suspect – never had existed at all.

He grimaced. Like everything else with this girl, the mere concept of a discernible trail was starting to seem like a joke. There was no pattern, no thread connecting anything. Each location in which she'd left her mark was as unrelated to the others as kangaroos were to cowboys.

A clink sounded by his foot and he glanced down to see the sun-faded pipes of a broken wind chime lying in the grass. His mouth tightened as he nudged them with his shoe. If he was honest, he hadn't really expected to find some grand clue to her whereabouts in the ruins of her farmhouse. He'd just wanted to see the place, rather than merely look at photos online. And if, somewhere inside himself, he'd hoped the sight of the girls' home would bring him closer to understanding what'd prompted a teenager to massacre her whole family... well, that was forgivable.

Even if he knew that when it came to homicidal maniacs, sometimes the opportunity was reason enough, and the high they got from the experience was its own justification.

His brow drew down thoughtfully.

"Come to cry?"

He turned at the weedy voice, and then tried not to stare at the woman several feet behind him. Her hair looked as though her daily styling ritual included sticking her finger in a light socket, and her eyes were freakishly bright in her narrow, wrinkled face. At least a dozen cats swirled around her ankles, though an exact count was hard to come by since the animals never stopped moving.

"Excuse me?"

"Why are you here, then? Little flower and the rest were all taken away by the firemen, and someone besides us should cry."

He blinked, not knowing where to begin with the gibberish she'd just said. "Did you know the family who lived here?" he tried.

She looked at him as though he was the one babbling.

"Did you know Ashley?" Harris reiterated.

The woman hesitated, a mistrustful expression creeping onto her face.

"Ashley?" he repeated. "The girl who lived in this house?"

The expression strengthened.

"Why *are* you here?" the woman asked warily. "Are you trying to get me to talk about Elvis? Because I already told her and I'm not telling anybody else."

He considered his answer, and then decided the direct approach was probably best. "I'm trying to find out why Ashley killed her family. I want to stop her before she hurts anyone else."

Shock washed away her caution with theatrical speed, leaving her gaping in horror.

"*Killed* them?" she gasped.

Her gaze darted around the countryside before returning to him. "You're a bad man," she said, shaking her head. Hands raised in front of her, she backed up as though expecting him to attack. "You're very bad. You say bad things. You…"

She kept retreating till she reached the top of the rise, and then she pulled up her skirts and took off, her spindly legs churning madly as she dashed away.

He stared after her, and for more reasons than he could name, anger suddenly made it impossible to breathe. He was a bad man? *Him?* For the love of God, he was the one trying to stop this! He was the one trying to protect people! He was the one who'd spent every waking hour working to keep that girl from murdering one more innocent, destroying one more life, wreaking hell on one more city. And Ashley…

His gaze dropped to the wind chimes near his feet.

Ashley just kept killing. And killing, and killing, and…

Maybe that was the answer.

He paused. His brow drew down as he nudged the chimes again, listening to them clink lifelessly.

She wouldn't stop. And he couldn't stop her. Not now. Not proactively, as he'd spent weeks trying to do. She was too elusive, and there were too many places she could hide.

But that didn't mean he didn't have a lead. That didn't mean there wasn't something he could follow. He'd thought she left no trail and that there was nothing to track, but that wasn't exactly true.

He looked up at the farmhouse decaying in the sunlight.

She left bodies.

And she never stopped at just one.

Chapter Seven

<hr>

Three months later

"Hey, Paul! You fed the hogs yet?"

Cole looked up at the sound of Ben's voice from the far side of the paddock. "Yeah," he called, setting the manure shovel to one side and then stepping out of the barn into the early morning sunlight. "That one you got from Jesse still seems to be having trouble though."

Leaning on the wooden fence, the middle-aged man shook his head with frustration. "Alright, I'll go take a look at her." Still looking exasperated, he turned and headed down the dirt lane.

Cole watched him go and then returned to the barn. Pulling his gloves a little tighter on his hands, he reached for the manure shovel again.

"You missed a spot."

He glanced back with a raised eyebrow at the little girl sitting on a hay bale, her arms cradling a sleeping tabby kitten. A grin pulled at Lily's mouth.

"You want to get over here and help?" he asked.

With an innocently baffled expression, she gave a look to the kitten as though to ask how she was supposed to do that. He shook his head as he went back to work, trying not to let her see his smile. It'd only encourage her.

More than three months had passed since they'd found their way to Sweet Summers Farm. In the first few days after they parted ways with Travis, they'd headed west, travelling on the basis of Robert's rants about wizards living in the eastern portions of the country. Spending the night in supermarket and truck stop parking lots, they'd wandered from town to town, just trying to think of a plan and stay a step ahead of anyone looking for them. Of the wizards, they hadn't seen much, though they'd had a few close calls with human security guards wondering why two children were sleeping in a truck and not their own home. After the third narrow escape from an over-interested patrol officer, Cole had taken to parking in whatever abandoned barn or overgrown back road he could find. Their system had worked beautifully for weeks, though neither of them slept very well and their tempers had run short with ferocious consistency. But they'd kept moving, and by the time they'd reached the farmlands of central Washington, they'd had their routine for scouting potential sleeping locations down, even if having enough money to simultaneously afford food and gas had been starting to present a problem.

But then everything went wrong.

The barn looked as abandoned as any he'd seen, and with their usual practice of leaving long before sunrise, he hadn't expected much trouble. But when the pounding on the truck window came at four in the morning and the first thing he'd seen in the darkness was a man with a shotgun, Cole thought their luck had finally run out.

An escapee from Washington State Penitentiary was rumored to be in the area, and Ben Summers wasn't apt to take any chances with an unfamiliar truck sitting in his old barn. The discovery of two kids inside startled him, however, and stepping away from the door, he'd waited cautiously to hear what their explanation for sleeping on his property might be.

Keeping Lily behind him, Cole'd climbed from the truck, squinting in the glare of the man's flashlight. Over the past weeks, they'd concocted cover stories for their alter egos, Paul and Hannah Wood, as they'd been so named by the identification cards Robert bought a lifetime ago. One hand on Lily and the other raised placatingly, Cole'd launched into their story, tensing at every slight move the man made.

The two of them were siblings, he said. Their parents had been killed in a car accident, for which he'd not been present, but which Hannah had barely survived. In the aftermath, the Department of Children and Family Services had stepped in to care for the newly orphaned kids, but their plan included splitting up the siblings and placing Hannah in a group home. The trauma she'd experienced had left Hannah nearly mute, and the caseworkers and psychologists determined supervised care was her best option, even if it meant taking her from the only relative she still had. Desperate to protect his sister, and determined not to let the remnants of his family be destroyed, he'd gathered what money he could and they'd run.

It might have been the way Lily clung to him, or the protectiveness Cole couldn't hide, but as the story ended, Ben Summers paused, and then lowered the flashlight.

They looked starved, Ben said, and from the thinness they'd acquired over the past few weeks, Cole couldn't argue. After inviting them to his house for food, Ben told them to follow in their truck, and then turned around and walked away.

Cole glanced to Lily, but the little girl just shook her head. Neither glowing to him, nor appearing as a wizard or cripple to her, Ben Summers showed all probability of being just a regular man. Hungry enough to take their chances, they'd climbed back into the truck, and cautiously trailed him away from the barn.

Life at Sweet Summers Farm revolved around the white, two-story farmhouse at the end of a long gravel lane a mile from the dilapidated barn. In the front yard, a massive oak tree shaded the house, and beyond the home's shingled roof, there rose an enormous newer barn. Sunrise lit the sprawling orchard to the right of the driveway and past the wooden fence to their left, cattle roamed.

Eyes wide, Lily stared as they drove up the gravel track in the early morning light. Wishing he could share some of her wonder, Cole'd glanced at the rearview mirror, internally sweating the growing distance to the main road that was their only route of escape should things go wrong.

Pulling his truck over by the house, Ben had climbed out and then waited as Cole and Lily cautiously joined him. Still looking torn about his decision to bring the kids back to his home, the man nevertheless headed for the door and then called to his wife as they came inside.

Sue Summers was a big-boned woman whose family went back five generations in the central Washington area. At the sight of them, she'd given a pointedly questioning look to her husband, but at his brief explanation, she'd turned an abrupt about-face and called over her shoulder for them to follow as she marched to the kitchen to make food.

Over orange juice and scrambled eggs, Cole'd repeated their story, while watching the unreadable looks passing between the couple.

When he and Lily finished their meal, the couple excused themselves, and he heard the low sounds of their voices as they retreated to the living room.

And softly, he'd told Lily to get ready to run.

Fear in her eyes, the little girl inched from her barstool. His gaze locked on the entryway to the living room, he'd slid off the seat and started toward the door when Ben called to him. Motioning Lily to stay near the back door, he'd walked to the entryway.

Still wary, the couple regarded him for a moment before Ben spoke. The two kids could stay through the night if they wanted, which would at least give Paul and his sister a chance to get a few decent meals. The guest room upstairs was empty and they both looked like they could use a good night's sleep anyhow. Ben and Sue didn't want any trouble from DCFS, but if nothing else, feeding the kids for a day seemed the right thing to do.

Cole glanced to Lily, raising an eyebrow. At the girl's incremental nod, he'd looked back at the couple and carefully agreed to a single night's stay.

The Summers didn't call the authorities as he'd feared. And with plentiful food and soft beds to draw them, Lily and Cole found themselves lingering until, at Sue's invitation, they'd stayed overnight again. Two nights became three, and then more, and though Sue and Ben remained cagey about the two kids without much more than their own word as to their history, the couple never questioned too deeply. For a while, Cole saw the older man scouring the web for corroboration of their story on his shaky internet connection, but nothing seemed to come of his search. Whether they remembered the newscasts from earlier in the year, neither of them seemed to connect shy little Hannah clinging to her brother's side

with Lily, the multiple homicide survivor and victim of sex traf-
ficking the news had portrayed.

And so the days went by. Lily swiftly became the darling of the
farm, her position cemented the first time she'd cautiously asked Sue
if she could make some crafts from the scraps of cloth and paper the
woman's own creations left behind. By the second week, Ben offered
to let Cole work on the property, as extra hands were always welcome
on the small organic farm. Though they were isolated to some degree
by the rural countryside, Sweet Summers nevertheless faithfully
served what customers they could with free-range meat by special
order, as well as fresh fruits and vegetables as the season allowed. The
work was harder than anything Cole had ever tried, but as time
passed, he found it wasn't as bad as he'd feared.

That it got him in better shape than any other time in his life
didn't hurt either.

But weeks crept into months and despite the fact they both felt
reasonably safe for the first time in recent memory, he couldn't ever
relax. The wizards were still out there. They'd still be looking for the
two of them.

They'd still killed all the family he and Lily had known.

And he had no idea why.

He tried not to show how much that reality upset him. Lily had
enough trouble with the nightmares that woke her screaming almost
every night and her fear of the magic they both knew she possessed.
Sue worried about the girl, and Ben did too, and the last thing either
of them needed was to know he'd give almost anything to be back
out there, tracking down the fantasy creatures he believed responsible for the mess he and Lily were in.

But the situation was slowly driving him insane.

He hated to admit how often he thought of just leaving. The girl was safe. Ben and Sue weren't a threat and the farm was so isolated, it might as well have been on the moon. But he knew how that story went too. Lily's dad had probably thought the same thing, right up until the Blood and their henchmen shot him and burned his house to the ground.

And so they stayed, while he tried to tell himself it would only be a matter of time. Something would change. Or the hours he spent on the internet would yield a clue. Or he'd see something on the television.

Or he'd finally lose his mind for lack of anything else to do.

Grimacing, he pushed the frustration aside as he set the shovel against the wall. The stall was done enough and Ben would be satisfied. Everything else could wait, and mostly needed to. Glancing to Lily, he headed for the door, trying to escape his own thoughts more than anything. Curling the kitten tighter into her arms, the little girl climbed down from the hay bale and followed him into the sunshine.

"What'd you name that one?" he asked, working to sound more cheerful than he felt. Soon after arriving, Lily had taken it upon herself to name every one of the multitude of interchangeable tabbies roaming the farm, and now most of the cats were wandering around with titles ranging from Apple to Zigzag.

With a considering look to the kitten, she shook her head. "I haven't decided yet," she answered. "He's a tough one."

In spite of himself, he smiled as he kept walking.

"Paul, is that you?" Sue called from the kitchen as he opened the screen door.

"Yeah," he called back, watching Lily set the kitten on the wicker porch chair. Blinking blearily, the little animal checked its surroundings for a heartbeat, and then promptly went back to sleep.

Holding the door, he waited till Lily came in and then started for the kitchen. Inside, Sue had the week's orders laid out across the table and countertops. By this point of the summer, business was at its peak and her face showed it. With a harried expression, she glanced up as they walked through the door.

"Oh." She checked around as though to remind herself what she'd wanted. "Right. Could you run an order out?"

At the reluctance in his eyes, she grimaced. "Please, Paul? Ben normally does this one, but he's tied up with that blasted pig Jesse sold us. He's not sure what's wrong, but the vet is coming and Ben's got to meet–"

"Sure," Cole said, holding his hands up to stave off more explanation. She didn't know why he'd rather not go where wizards or who knew what else could see them, but his ostensible wish to steer clear of DCFS wouldn't explain not helping with a simple food delivery.

She gave him a tired smile. "Bless you." Turning to the counter, she hefted a large box stuffed with wrapped beef, as well as bags of fruits and vegetables.

He blinked and then took the heavy box from her.

"Address and directions are on the tag," she said with a jerk of her chin to the paper stapled to one of the bags. "And thank you."

Nodding, he turned and waited for Lily to rush ahead of him to the door. Shifting the box awkwardly, he made his way down the porch steps and then shoved the box into the narrow back seat of the truck. Hurrying to the other side, Lily hopped in and then fastened her belt.

He glanced at the address before climbing into the driver's seat. The house was practically on the Canadian border by the look of it, though far from the main roads if the lengthy directions were any indication. It'd probably take most of the day to reach it and get back again. Joining Lily inside, he tugged the door shut and then punched the address into the GPS.

Nothing. On the GPS system's version of the planet, no such location existed. Sighing, he started the engine.

Miles later, as trees in parts of the state far hillier than those they'd left behind closed in around them, he reached back and tugged the directions from the bag. When it came to aiding navigation, back roads left much to be desired for anyone who wasn't a local. Grimacing as they passed another nameless path winding off into the trees, he checked the scrap of paper and shook his head.

Minutes passed. Approximately two seconds before he finally admitted they'd taken a wrong turn and needed to go back, he saw the first of the landmarks mentioned on the note. Feeling vaguely relieved, he kept driving, following the gravel road on its serpentine path. Blind turns succeeded one another rapidly, and warily he slowed down.

And then he slammed on the brakes. Lily gasped, turning from her study of the forest outside the passenger window. He exhaled, grateful not to have been going faster when he'd rounded the turn.

Towering a dozen feet high, an ornate black fence blocked the road only a couple yards beyond the truck. Security cameras mounted on the gate swung lazy half-circles in surveillance of the road and forest, only to turn back sharply as they spotted his pickup. A speaker box was affixed to a decorative pole near the fence and, without any other option, he crept the truck up next to it. He rolled down the window and then reached out to press the call button, doing his best to keep his face from view.

"Yes?" came a crackly voice.

"I've got a delivery for… Mr. Geoffrey Redmond?" he said, checking the name on the tag again.

A long pause answered and then the gate began to move. Creaking back on its hinges, it swung barely wide enough to admit the truck.

He frowned and then rolled up the window before putting the truck back into gear and pulling forward. Dense walls of pine trees lined the gravel path, complete with further security cameras bolted high in their branches. The little black shapes tracked the truck as it rolled past, and he grimaced, turning his face aside. A minute passed on the narrow road and then the trees finally gave way, revealing a wide grassy lawn.

Cole's eyebrows rose. The house ahead of them was huge, even compared to what he'd seen in the richer neighborhoods of Monfort. Constructed of enormous blocks of living space, each standing shoulder-to-shoulder as though in military formation, the brick edifice dominated the forest surrounding it. Rows of narrow windows glared out at the trees, their reflective glass giving no hint as to what lay beyond their surface. Tightly squared evergreen bushes lined the dark flagstone path from the driveway to the door, and precisely placed lampposts circled the property, as though marking off the territory upon which the massive house had come to land.

But there was no one to be seen. The yard was empty of life, from birds to squirrels, and there wasn't even a footprint on the grass. His frown returning, he kept driving.

Lily gasped. A headache flared in his temples and he spun, looking back.

A man stepped onto the road.

Cole swore. His hand went for the gearshift as his foot hit the brake, and then the truck was in reverse.

Excruciating nothingness slammed them, sending the truck sideways. Cole hauled on the wheel, fighting to get the vehicle back on the road. The man flung himself from their path as they roared by and, for a blessed moment, the pain went away.

But only for a moment.

The truck left the road. The ground and anything near it. Down became up as Lily screamed and gravity abruptly changed its mind.

And then came the tree.

———◆———

Cole muttered a curse as he opened his eyes. Dirt swirled before him, gradually coalescing into a floor. Aches throbbed through his body and he winced as he looked up.

He was alive. That in itself was shocking. And he was in a shed, which couldn't be good. A light bulb dangled from the low ceiling and tools hung from hooks in the pegboard sheets on the walls. Planks of wood lay to one side, and the odor of sawdust was heavy in the air. On the far end of the room, sunlight filtered through gaps around a small door.

Shifting around, he tried to stand, only to find that his hands were bound. An unsteady wooden chair wobbled beneath him, to which his ankles were likewise tied.

Drawing a breath and ordering himself to stay calm, he turned his head, searching for Lily.

She was curled near a pile of wood behind him, unmoving. Ropes circled her hands and ankles, while her arms were wrapped around her head protectively.

And her clothes were splattered with blood.

"Lily!" he hissed in panic.

Sniffling, she pulled her head from her arms, tear-streaked dirt smudging her cheeks. At the sight of him, she gasped and scrambled up to shuffle over and bury herself against his side.

"Are you okay?" he asked, scanning her for injuries and seeing nothing.

"Uh-huh."

"What happened?"

"The truck crashed."

He started to nod and then regretted the motion. "Yeah, I guessed that," he said, wincing. "But then what?"

She sniffled again, her brow furrowing tightly as she fought the urge to start crying again. "The wizards did something. Made us better. You were really hurt and the blood just wouldn't stop and…"

"It's okay," he managed hoarsely when she trailed off.

She didn't look like she believed him. Closing her eyes, she tucked her head back against his shoulder.

"Lily."

The little girl nodded jerkily. "They dragged us behind the house. I tried to fight them but they… they just…" She cut off, breathing hard. "You don't think they're with the bad men, do you? The ones who hurt my dad?"

Cole hesitated. "I don't know," he admitted. "Do you know what kind of wizards they are?"

"Merlin."

He grimaced, uncertain how to take the information. It meant they probably wouldn't ship him off to the Taliesin, but said nothing for any other plans the bastards had in mind.

"How long have we been here?" he asked, changing the subject.

She shrugged, and then her face crumpled when he gave her an insistent look. "Maybe half an hour?"

He glanced back at the door. Not long enough for Sue or Ben to start wondering, then. But long enough that the Merlin could have called any number of people to have them begin coming this way. He grimaced again as a shadow blocked the sunlight around the door, only to move away a moment later.

And there were guards. Great.

"Listen," he said. "Can you untie these ropes behind me?"

"They told me they'd shoot us if I did that."

"Lily, please."

Fearfully, her eyes darted between him and the door.

"I need to be able to move."

"But they… they have guns. And they showed me how they'd… how they'd…"

His gaze slid to the door furiously as she choked on a sob again.

"Lily," he said, forcing his voice to be calm as he dragged his attention back to her. "It's okay. They're not going to shoot us. If they wanted us dead, they wouldn't have made us better. Now come on. I need you to help me here."

Swallowing hard, she glanced up at him.

"Please," he said, meeting her eyes.

A heartbeat passed, and then she nodded. Shuffling on her knees, she crept around behind him, and a moment later, he felt her pulling at the knots holding his wrists.

He looked at the walls, trying to focus. Everything else aside, he needed a plan. The chisels or the hammer on the pegboard would make good weapons, and if the guard was armed and he could take the man by surprise, they'd be able to secure a gun. The Merlin had to have cars around here somewhere, and if he could find one with keys, it'd be a matter of moments till the two of them were gone.

Perfect. Great plan.

Until reality got involved anyway.

He grimaced and twisted around to see how Lily was faring.

The door lock clanked and they both froze. Breathing hard, Lily dropped her hands from the ropes, tears brimming in her eyes.

Sunlight poured into the shed as the door swung open. A man with dark eyes stepped in, followed a moment later by another nearly twice his weight. Both took up positions on opposite sides of the room, though their cold gazes didn't leave Cole or Lily.

Cole watched them, trying to tug the ropes from his wrists without letting on.

Bowing his head beneath the low doorframe, another man came into the shed. Older by far than the men around him, he nevertheless straightened to a height above them both. His gray hair was cut tightly above his sharp features, and though his face was wrinkled, even the creases had a way of appearing precise. For a long moment, he regarded the sniffling girl, and then his eyes flicked to Cole.

"A cripple and a human," he commented. "Fascinating. What purpose did you have in bringing her along? Allay our suspicions, perhaps?"

Cole glanced between the men, trying to judge the best answer before finally settling on playing dumb. "Look," he said placatingly. "We're not here to–"

"Who sent you to find us?" the man interrupted with disgust.

"No one. We were just trying to make a delivery for–"

"Who are you working for?"

"Ben Summers!"

A scowl tightened the man's face. "Answer the question, cripple."

"I did! Look, I swear, okay? We don't want any trouble. We don't have a clue who you are, and we don't care, alright? We just–"

"I am Magnus Carnegean," the man said scornfully. "As though you didn't know."

Cole blinked, momentarily thrown. He knew the name. He'd grown up hearing the name. But the man may as well have called himself the Wizard of Oz, because the name belonged to a children's story his mother had told him every night till she'd died.

Magnus Carnegean, and all the Carnegeans, had been regular features in Clara Jamison's bedtime stories. The arch nemeses of her heroic woodland creatures, the Carnegean family of bears had viewed themselves as supreme in the forested world Clara imagined for her son. Cole had spent his childhood dreaming of the adventures her heroes had stopping the Carnegeans' plots or escaping their clutches.

And now a man claiming that name was standing right in front of him. On any other day, Cole thought he might've laughed.

Instead, he just fought desperately to keep his face from giving anything away.

The man's contemptuous expression only increased, however. "I thought so. Now, we healed you and your human for information, not so you could waste our time. So, unless you wish us to return you to your former condition, I suggest you tell us everything, including who informed you of our location. Understand?"

Magic filtered into the room.

"No one did," he told the man, gritting his teeth against the pain.

"We're just here on a delivery for Ben Summers. You can call and ask him."

"Hmm."

The sound was lost somewhere between disbelief and disdain, but at the noise, Cole's headache spiked, making his hands jerk at the ropes. "I swear! We're not involved in this!"

"Yet you knew my name," Magnus said.

The man came closer and the pain came with him. Lily recoiled, whimpering.

"It's not like that!"

"How is it, then?"

The pain increased. Blackness throbbed at the edges of his vision and his head felt like it wanted to explode.

"Stop it!" Lily cried.

Magnus ignored her. The pain grew stronger.

"Damn you!" Cole snarled through clenched teeth. "My mother told me stories about a Magnus Carnegean. That's all!"

The man stopped. The magic in the room faded as swiftly as it had come. Breathing hard against the retreating pain, Cole looked up.

"Your mother," Magnus stated, his tone level.

"Yes. I swear we didn't know you were here."

The man regarded him. "And who is your mother?"

Cole hesitated, the idea of making up a name flitting through his head. But while the man's expression was mostly unreadable, there was something about the intensity of his eyes that made lying seem the riskier option. "Clara Jamison."

Though already immobile, the man seemed to become ice. "Clara… Jamison."

His skull throbbing, Cole nodded.

"Clara Jamison is dead," Magnus said.

"Yeah, I know."

"And who are you?"

"Cole," he said and then paused. He hadn't said his full name in years. At least, not the real one. But that same intense look remained in the man's eyes, making truth seem bizarrely safer than a lie. "Cole Jamison."

"You lie."

Incredulous, Cole stared. "Why would I lie about that?" he asked, knowing there were a million reasons, none of which hopefully had anything to do with a bunch of Merlin in the middle of nowhere.

"How did Clara Jamison die?" Magnus retorted instead.

"Why do you care?"

"Answer the question, cripple!"

Magic pervaded the air, making him wince. Fury darkened Magnus' face, threatening more pain if he didn't answer.

"She was shot in a robbery," Cole growled. "Or killed by Taliesin wizards. Depends on who you believe."

The magic vanished. For a moment, Magnus regarded him, and then he glanced back at the other men. "Geoffrey, call Ben Summers. Ask him if he sent a delivery boy here today, and get an exact description if he did." He looked back at Cole. "Tell him we haven't seen anyone, and we are concerned."

Nodding briefly, the dark-eyed wizard started out of the shed.

Cole's gaze darted between them, his heart rate spiking. "H-he doesn't know my name is Cole," he called to the man.

Geoffrey paused.

"He thinks my name is Paul Wood," Cole finished uncomfortably.

Magnus scoffed as Geoffrey left the room. "And you ask why we would think you a liar, when the man you claim as your employer doesn't even know your name?"

"It's not like that."

"Hmm."

Silence fell between them, broken a minute later when Geoffrey returned.

"Sue Summers was reluctant, but she did finally confirm that a young man has been staying at their farm for the past three months. She sent him and his little sister on a delivery today." He glanced to Cole and Lily. "She asks us to call the minute we see them."

"Did she give descriptions?"

"They match."

Magnus looked back over at them, and his eyes narrowed. "Your sister?"

Cole said nothing.

Mouth tightening, Magnus glanced to Geoffrey. "And there was nothing in the truck?"

"Bernhard couldn't find anything but the food the cripple claims he was delivering." Geoffrey paused. "He still has to be lying about her, either way."

Cole's brow furrowed.

Magnus was silent, muscles working beneath the skin of his jaw, and then he shook his head. "We have to be sure. Bring the boy to the house and get rid of the human. Make it look like he lost control of the truck."

"What?" Cole sputtered, shocked.

Lily gasped, scrambling backward while, at Geoffrey's motion, the overweight wizard started toward her. The ropes tore at Cole's wrists as he twisted, trying to get between the girl and the enormous man. With a shove, the wizard sent the chair sideways, tossing Cole to the floor, and then he bent over Lily, ignoring her scream as he hefted her from the woodpile.

"Get your hands off her!" Cole yelled.

Thrashing in the wizard's grip, Lily clawed at the man, her nails leaving red marks anywhere her fingers could reach. With a snarl, the wizard slapped her hard, sending her head snapping to one side, and for a heartbeat, she went limp.

Rage stole Cole's words. Blood slicked his fingers as he yanked at the ropes. Flopping the girl around, the enormous wizard gripped the back of her shirt and then dragged her through the door.

Paying no attention to them, Geoffrey sliced the ropes holding Cole's ankles. Instantly, Cole kicked at him, but the man blocked the motion and then slammed his fist into Cole's face.

Red lights blinded him as Geoffrey hauled him up and then propelled him toward the door. Stumbling, Cole blinked hard, searching for Lily as the wizard shoved him outside. Her shrieks drew his attention. Thirty feet away, the other man was towing her toward the driveway.

"You can't do this!" Cole snarled, planting his heels into the turf to stop the wizard from dragging him farther. "She's a kid, dammit! You can't just–"

"Shut up," Geoffrey ordered.

Inarticulate with rage, Cole ignored him. Throwing his weight to one side, he fought to break the man's grip.

Geoffrey faltered, and then jerked the ropes hard, sending pain shooting up Cole's arms. Whipping Cole around, he looked back toward the shed.

Magnus stood by the shed door. The older man gave a short nod.

"Fine," Geoffrey growled. "You can keep your pet a bit longer." He raised his voice. "Alfred! Just bring the human with us for now. The kid's panicking that we're taking his toy."

Wordlessly, the large man diverted toward the house. Breathing hard and torn between relief and adrenaline, Cole let Geoffrey haul him after them, his gaze locked on Lily. The little girl twisted in the wizard's grip, tears shining above the livid mark across her cheek. Cole nodded as he met her eyes, trying desperately to look reassuring.

Wrestling Lily to one side, Alfred yanked open the French doors beyond the marble patio and then dragged the girl with him as he headed in. Scowling, Geoffrey pulled Cole after them. With a warning glare for them both, the men came to a stop inside the door and then glanced back, waiting for Magnus.

Cole ignored them, casting another look to Lily. The little girl didn't lift her gaze from the carpet. Shaking with fury, he turned to the enormous room.

The lavish parlor would've made the Smithsonian green with envy. Glass cases were everywhere, filled with ridiculously ornate antiques. Dark mahogany tables were scattered throughout the spacious room, each topped with further displays, and on the alabaster walls, paintings hung between imposing bookcases. Past the archways on two sides of the parlor, more rooms stretched back through the house, their walls blockaded by an army of bookcases extending from the distant ceiling to the dense carpet. Identical to the parlor in nearly every way, more display cases occupied each room, though the closest possessed the addition of a bored-looking older woman idly dusting.

At a large, Victorian-era writing desk on the far end of the parlor, another woman glanced up as they entered. Perfectly coiffed gray hair sat in rigid waves above her glistening reading glasses and, at the sight of the two wizards, she set aside the leather-bound book she'd been examining and rose to her feet.

"What do you mean by bringing them in here?" she demanded.

Her gaze raked over him and Lily as though taking in every smudge of dirt and sawdust, and when her eyes came to rest on the blood falling from Cole's wrists, her brows shot up in indignation.

"Louise!" she cried, her voice rising to a near shriek.

The woman in the next room looked over and then set down her feather duster resignedly before trudging toward the parlor. As she came closer, Cole could see the resemblance between her and the other woman, despite the boredom that seemed permanently etched onto her face. "Yes?" she sighed.

"Get bandages and stop that cripple boy from dripping blood on the Persian!"

Without any change of expression, Louise walked away.

"I do *not* know what you were thinking, Geoffrey. Bringing those two in here. Look at the dirt that human is dragging in. Honestly! You couldn't keep them outside?"

Making an irritated noise, the woman turned away and retrieved her book, carrying it farther into the house as though to hide it from ballistic drops of blood or dirt that might suddenly hurl themselves through space. Paying no attention to the retreating sounds of annoyance, Louise returned with a box of bandages under one arm.

"Try anything and your pet is back out the door," Geoffrey told Cole calmly.

At Cole's silence, the man smirked and then spun him around. Pain tingled through Cole's hands and arms as the ropes were sliced away. Gritting his teeth, he looked over at the two wizards as Louise set half-heartedly to bandaging his wounds.

"Untie her too," Cole growled.

With a sneer to mirror Geoffrey's own, Alfred released his grip on Lily and instantly the girl plummeted to the floor. The overwhelming urge to punch the man welled up in Cole, but his eyes went to Lily, watching as she scooted away from the massive wizard. Strolling through the open French door, Magnus glanced around at the tableau.

"Go ahead and untie the human as well," he ordered dismissively.

Reluctantly, Geoffrey jerked his chin at Alfred, and the man bent to cut the ropes. Scrambling away the moment her wrists and ankles were free, Lily rushed to Cole and clung to him, her fingers digging into his side.

"Watch it, brat," Louise snapped as the girl jostled her work.

Wrapping his free arm around Lily, Cole gripped her tightly. With an aggrieved sigh, Louise tied off the last bandage and straightened. Muttering imprecations about cripples, she plodded back to her dusting.

"Have a seat," Magnus instructed.

Cole didn't move. "What the hell do you people want with me?"

"Yes, Magnus," the other woman said imperially, returning to the room. "What in the *world* do you mean by bringing a filthy cripple and human into my house?"

The man glanced to her as she crossed to his side. Regarding him over the length of her severely pointed nose, she waited for his response.

"Florence, I would like you to meet Cole…" Magnus paused.

"Jamison."

The arch expression faded, though her lifted eyebrow didn't drop from its height. Glacially, her gaze slid over to Cole and Lily again.

"Surely not," she stated.

"He says so."

Eyes narrowing, her icy stare grated over Cole.

"What's going on here?" Cole demanded. "Why are you looking at me like that?"

"And he's a *cripple*," Florence said, ignoring him. She sniffed. "How predictable."

"Hey! I asked you a question!"

"How can you be certain?" she asked Magnus.

The man paused, his mouth tightening. "Boy, answer me this. The woman you claim was your mother–"

"Clara Jamison *was* my–"

"*Clarinda!*"

Cole blinked at the near-rabid snarl. Trembling rage briefly suffused Florence's face before being smothered by rigid propriety.

"What was her favorite color?" Magnus continued as if the exchange hadn't happened.

"Why do you need to–"

"Answer the question."

He looked between them. Obviously psychotic, they still possessed an implacable cast to their expressions that made them seem even more dangerous than they were insane. At his side, he could feel Lily shaking as she clutched him. "Indigo blue."

"And her favorite food?"

"What does this have–" He cut off at the look that flashed through Magnus' eyes. "Pineapple and mushroom pizza," he allowed tightly. "I think. But I was only ten when she died so, you know, it's a bit fuzzy."

Magnus glanced to Florence, who sniffed again. "Well, regardless, it's not like we have room for anyone else," she said acerbically.

"Hang on, what?"

"We will just have to make do," Magnus told the woman. "It's not like he's given us much choice."

"Hey!" Cole interrupted, stepping forward only to have Geoffrey snag his shoulder. "We're not staying."

"Yes, you are," Magnus replied. "We are not going to risk letting you back into the world with what you know."

"'What I know'?"

"You know where we are."

"We're not planning on telling anyone!"

"And that's very noble," Magnus said. "But you're a cripple. By nature, you lack the capacity to uphold that intention if a wizard wished to take the information from you. And she is a human, so she isn't even a viable part of the equation."

He stared at them, torn between anger and incredulity, and briefly lost for words. But at his expression, a condescending look came over Florence's face.

"Oh, *do* spare us your righteous indignation," she sneered. "Honestly. It's so tiring."

"Who the hell do you think–"

"We are the premier historians of Merlin, so we have authority on the situation," Magnus interrupted, and then he paused, as though deciding whether to acknowledge his next words with actual speech. "And we are your grandparents, so you'll do as we say."

Florence looked as though she'd tasted something sour and

turned away.

Cole stared, his anger screeching to a nearly speechless halt. "*What?*"

The woman made a disgusted noise, but Magnus just sighed. "We will take care of you, now that you're here. You haven't given us much choice, showing up like this."

"We didn't know you were here!"

Magnus gave a dismissive wave. "Irrelevant. Now that you are here, you have to stay. You're too much of a liability to our work for us to jeopardize it by letting you roam free."

Cole scoffed, his disbelief momentarily joining forces with his anger, though both were making it hard to breathe. "Your… your *work?*" He shook his head, trying to regroup. "I don't give a shit about your work! You're my–" He choked on the word. "And you're going to take *care* of me? You left me out there to rot! You left my…" He fought for air. "You sick *freaks*, what the hell–"

Florence's gasp cut him off. "How dare you, you disrespectful little *throwback*! Do you have *no* understanding of who we are? What we do? We are the guardians of the very lifeblood of our people! We protect their *history*! We secreted away each one of these artifacts at tremendous personal risk at the beginning of this little uprising, and you want to… to what? To endanger our sacrifice by running back out there, where the first Taliesin miscreant who found you would instantly torture you to death for that information? You uncultured *savage*, do you have any *idea* of the catastrophe you would cause?"

Cole stared as the woman spun away, her chest heaving with horrified fury. For a moment, he wondered if she seriously believed the knowledge of their location would be tattooed across his forehead, or if she was just that narcissistically paranoid.

And then he realized it was probably both.

"You *abandoned* us," he told her. "You left while Taliesin—"

"Oh, please," Florence replied disgustedly. "We abandoned no one."

"Taliesin is only worthy of consideration if they learn our location," Magnus explained. "And Merlin can easily attend to any 'threat' those upstarts may try to pose without the placation of knowing our whereabouts."

Cole wanted to laugh, though he wasn't sure why. "Wait, *Merlin* doesn't even know where you are?"

"Our location is immaterial to them," Magnus said calmly. "King Patrick has this little uprising well in hand, for all that those fools would like to call this some kind of 'war'. It is only a matter of time till our forces subdue the troublemakers. And in the interim, we've simply taken steps to ensure that any Taliesin reprobates who desire to endanger our invaluable history will believe the records destroyed – a falsification we are determined to keep in place. After all, we have a duty to uphold."

"This nonsense was a foregone conclusion before it even began," Florence added derisively. "There's no need to risk irreplaceable artifacts simply because some Taliesin nitwits actually thought they could win a war against *Merlin*."

She scoffed, shaking her head.

He blinked, trying to put words to his rage. "You... those 'nitwits' killed your *daughter*! They left her bleeding to death all alone and you just—"

"She brought that on herself!" Florence hissed furiously.

He stopped, struck speechless by the hate staring him in the face.

"Clarinda was always headstrong," Magnus continued for his wife.

"Never listening. Never respecting the duty we held. Even as a teenager, she sullied her legacy, obstinately involving herself in everything from Taliesin reconciliation programs to cripple aid projects. She never appreciated that, as the preeminent minds of our people, our responsibility has always been to uphold the purity and honor of Merlin. Her brothers understood that and tried to stop her. We all tried to stop her. It only stands to reason that her poor choices ended her in the position that they did."

Magnus glanced to Florence as the woman made an inarticulate noise.

"He called himself a *king*," she sneered, spite twisting through her expression like a snake. "King of *Taliesin*, as though that's anything to advertise. And she married him anyway. Took her heritage and just ground it into the mud. And look what it got her. Murdered like a common human, and where were her dear king's guards? Guess he wasn't so royal after all. And her only child was a cripple. Though that last was practically predictable. You can't expect a mutt not to have difficulties."

Magnus shrugged his eyebrows, agreeing.

Cole stared. His heart was pounding. He couldn't remember the last time he'd drawn a breath. Muscles jumped in his arms and he wasn't sure what he'd say even if he could speak.

"Oh, you act all indignant," Florence told him. "But you know nothing of the sacrifices we've made. These conditions are nothing short of reprehensible for the priceless works we're laboring to pre-serve, and without our constant attention, any number could be lost forever."

"People are dying," Cole whispered, barely able to keep from smashing his fist through the nearest case. "And you sit here in your *palace–*"

"It is *hardly* that," Florence said, affronted.

"History is filled with sacrifices for the greater good," Magnus explained. "But jeopardizing the memory of those sacrifices by losing the records that they ever occurred is simply unconscionable."

"We think of more than the mutable present," Florence added superciliously. "Perhaps you should do the same, if you possess the capability."

Cole drew a ragged breath. "We're leaving," he said, glancing to the doors. Three wizards stood on the patio, watching the lawn and the house equally.

"No," Florence corrected. "You are staying. And if you wish us to allow you to keep that–" She gestured to Lily as though motioning to a mess on the floor. "–you will do so graciously. We will provide less sullied clothing–" She sniffed at their bloodstained clothes. "–though I expect you to do better in keeping the replacements clean. Your uncles will have charge of watching you, and you will be given quarters on the top floor where you'll run the least risk of disturbing our work. Understand?"

Confusion hit him and then she gestured to the men behind him.

"Geoffrey and Alfred," the woman explained. "Your mother's brothers. I believe your uncle Bernhard is storing what remains of your truck in the garage. Also, your mother's cousins help us in our work, as does her aunt, Louise. You will stay out of their way unless instructed."

"And you will call your employer, Mr. Summers," Magnus added. "Tell him you quit."

"The hell I will."

Magic flickered around the older man. "Or the human is gone.

Which would you prefer?"

At Cole's silence, Magnus gestured to the two men. Geoffrey grabbed his shoulder and Alfred sneered at the warning look Cole gave him as the man reached for Lily.

"Relax, nephew," Alfred said sarcastically. "We're not taking your pet. Yet."

"Do keep it confined to your room, though," Florence said. "I won't have some human running around, putting its filthy hands on–"

Cole couldn't take any more. Pulling Lily with him, he shrugged off Geoffrey's grip and started for the patio, only to be brought up short by Alfred's smirking face.

Magic crackled around Geoffrey as the man snagged his shoulder again. "Nice try, brat."

Forcibly, he wrenched Cole's arm behind his back and then he shoved him around. Alfred bent, grabbing the little girl and hefting her up.

"What're you–" Cole started.

"Shut it," Geoffrey ordered. With a push, he drove Cole after Alfred toward the rest of the house.

Endless rooms filled with books surrounded them till, a small eternity later, they finally reached a stairway. Thick railings of polished wood swept down on either side of the massive staircase and dense carpet absorbed their footsteps as they climbed. Wide halls stretched away from the landings they passed, and dozens of closed doors blocked access to the rooms beyond. On the fifth floor, Alfred turned, taking Lily and leaving Geoffrey to follow.

By a door at the end of the hall, Alfred released Lily and then smirked as the girl rushed immediately to Cole. Ignoring the display,

Geoffrey shoved Cole aside and then tugged a keychain from his pocket. Swiftly, he flipped through the keys and then inserted one into the lock.

Crates filled the room. As with the rest of the house, paintings covered the walls, though these were clearly not as loved as those downstairs. A gray patina of dust coated the frames and stained pictures. Gesturing sharply, Geoffrey stepped back to let them enter the room.

Expressionless, Cole eyed the man before walking inside. "Where are we supposed to sleep?" he asked, glancing around the crowded space.

"Louise will bring blankets. In the meantime…" Geoffrey pulled Cole's cell phone from his pocket. "Call your boss."

Watching the two wizards, Cole reached for the phone.

Geoffrey pulled it back. "And if you even *try* to hint for him to come up here…" He glanced to Lily illustratively.

Cole took the cell. His eyes still on Geoffrey, he thumbed the number and then raised the phone to his ear. "Hey, Ben," he said flatly. "It's Paul."

Alfred scoffed.

"Paul? Where are you? Redmond called to say he hadn't seen you yet. Are you alright?"

"Yeah, we're fine."

He fell silent.

"Paul? You still there?"

"I'm here. Look… turns out Redmond's a relative."

Geoffrey's eyes went wide and he lunged for the phone. Stepping back swiftly, Cole talked faster. "We're fine. We'll be back when we can."

He hung up.

"You little son of a—"

"He wouldn't believe I'd just quit. He'd have been up here himself to find out why."

Snatching the phone back, Geoffrey glared. "You'll pay for that."

The man glanced to Lily, who shrank behind Cole.

"You want him up here poking around," Cole argued, "by all means, make me quit. He thinks we want to stay at the farm as long as possible, so if I just bail on him out of nowhere, he'll know something's up." He paused. "I'm saving you trouble."

Geoffrey studied him for a heartbeat. "I so much as see a truck I don't recognize on that road, your pet is dead, you get me?"

With a final dark look to them both, he motioned to Alfred and then stalked away as the other man slammed the door.

Closing his eyes briefly, Cole sighed. He glanced down at Lily and then grimaced at the sight of her cheek. "You okay?"

She shrugged half-heartedly.

"Here, let me see that."

He reached over, taking her chin gently and turning her face to one side. Alfred's hand had caught her straight across the cheekbone and the redness still hadn't faded.

"You're one tough kid," he told her.

She gave him a small smile "You too," she said, motioning shyly to the bruise he could feel forming on his own face. She blushed. "Or… I mean… not a kid, but… you know."

Cole tried to grin in response, though the expression felt mostly fake and died within a second of being formed. Tough wasn't the word he'd use to describe himself right now, given that they were stuck here and he hadn't been able to stop the wizards from almost taking Lily. Countless other words came to mind, however, none of which were fit for a kid's ears. Struggling to cover his discomfort, he turned away, studying the room again.

"What're we going to do?" Lily asked quietly.

He didn't answer. His gaze was locked on one of the paintings, seeing the picture clearly now that the wizards weren't breathing down their necks.

It was an image of Merlin.

No one had described the man to him, but it didn't matter. The godlike aspect of the subject was enough indication. Holding a glowing staff aloft, the radiant figure stood on a cliff and gazed into the heavens like a latter day Moses, while below him hordes of grotesque Taliesin cowered and scrambled over one another to escape his sight. A pair of regal-looking wizards kneeled at his flanks, their upturned faces bathed in rapturous awe and their hands raised in worship of their triumphant wizard king.

Cole thought he was going to be sick.

They believed they were gods, that much was clear. All of them, Merlin and Taliesin alike. And the Carnegeans…

He couldn't think past the anger that came roaring up inside. They'd run. They'd left him. His family. His mother. And they didn't even care. They sat here in their mansion, blathering on about sacrifice and suffering and…

"Cole…" Lily said worriedly.

He realized he couldn't feel his fingers for clenching his fists so hard. Closing his eyes again, he forced himself to breathe, working to calm down when all he wanted was to rip the painting in front of him into confetti. Their image of their god, made so they could worship their supposed superiority and their victory over…

Dad.

His thoughts came to a stop at the memory of Florence's acidic words. King. King of Taliesin. Victor told Clara he was king of Taliesin.

And the Council had taken Cole after killing them both in cold blood.

Shaking, he sank down onto one of the crates.

His parents had lived in a rundown apartment on the edge of a neighborhood most folks avoided after dark. They'd barely been making it, though they'd done the best they could. He'd known his parents' families had disowned them out of disapproval of their marriage, but that'd been the end of it.

And his father had been king of Taliesin.

The Council murdered their own king.

"Cole?" Lily asked again.

His father had been a king of wizards.

Apprehensively, Lily reached over, putting a hand on his arm. Inhaling sharply, he glanced down at the girl.

"What're we going to do?" she repeated.

Releasing a breath, he tried to focus. She was right. They needed a plan. Or something. Pushing away from the crate, he crossed to the narrow window and looked down at the lawn.

Wizards patrolled the yard. Between the branches of the trees, he could see several of the plethora of security cameras surrounding the property, their small black forms turning in lazy arcs as they surveyed every square inch of the grounds. Of his truck, there was no sign, though it was probably destroyed and Florence said Bernhard had taken it anyway. But if there were other vehicles nearby, they weren't anywhere he could see.

Frustration welled up in him again, and he fought it back down. It wasn't helpful and it wouldn't get them out of here.

He turned away from the window, knowing there was only one answer he could give.

"We're leaving," he said. "First chance we get."

Chapter Eight

A she leaned away from the notebook, her head throbbing in time to her heartbeat. The words were burned on the backs of her eyelids, flickering in unintelligible patterns of light every time she blinked. It didn't matter if she couldn't see them clearly. She already knew them by heart.

Four months of research and training. More like four decades. She could scarcely believe that less than half a year ago, she'd been living on a farm, without words like portals and bindings and magical transference as a part of her daily vocabulary. Now every day was comprised of waking up to the prospect of more studying and training, all under the guise of ending a war she hadn't known existed a year prior.

And ostensibly ruling the people on one side of that war, though the idea of being a queen still felt like a bad joke.

She saw this room in her dreams now, more than the nightmares of Lily and her father dying, more than the memories of Carter bleeding to death in an alley. The worst were the nights she dreamt she'd found the answer, and the binding spell to hold all of Taliesin and the Blood was finally in her grasp. The elation at the thought she could finally end this was almost too wonderful to bear, and she'd wake with a smile on her face, only to realize none of it'd been real.

It was hardest to drag herself out of bed those days. To make herself face this cold, gray, storage-locker of a room with the knowledge she was no closer to stopping the war than she'd been the day prior. Weeks of studying had yielded precious little beyond allusions to other books not in the wizards' archives. Mentions of Merlin's possessions, his staff, and all manner of tools he might've used to supplement his power only left her fuming for days at the hopelessness of it all, and the plethora of magical techniques she'd learned invariably proved useless toward taking the magic from multiple wizards at once.

And meanwhile, the war ground on.

More cripples had come in the past months, slowly at first and then in increasing numbers. In short order, the wizards had gotten significantly better at working with them, since within two weeks of the first cripples arriving, a Blood wizard had been found. The cripples spotted him on a street on the opposite side of town and, in an act of blatant frustration at years of not being believed, one of them resorted to simply firing a gun at the man.

The Blood panicked and blocked the shot. Everything she and Carter and all the others had said was confirmed in that moment.

She'd wanted to cry when Darius brought her the news, though by then it had become practically habit not to show weakness. And as leader of the Council, he'd gone out on a limb enough for her as it was, standing up to the others and insisting they fight the invisible monsters no one believed were real. He didn't need to see her crumble. Burying the emotions down deep, she'd just nodded as he told her how the Blood wizard died, and then returned to searching for Merlin's binding spell.

No one stopped by the library the next day, and thus she was spared any comments about her red-rimmed eyes.

Galvanized by their discovery of invisible enemies, the Merlin spread the word swiftly, and more wizards came to join the hunt. Teamed with cripples, they fanned out through the cities to guard hideouts and safe houses against the possibility of Blood attacks.

And everything seemed to finally be turning around.

Yet, with their identities uncovered, the Blood changed their strategy. Within days of the Merlin discovering them, all trace of Blood wizards disappeared from the streets. Driving them underground would have been comforting, if not for the fact that the Merlin learned quickly that they'd been half right all along. The Blood had innumerable supporters lurking in the ranks of Taliesin, and every one of them was only too ready to defend their absent allies.

Dozens of cripples died.

The old woman and her grandson had been among the first, taken out by Taliesin covering a Blood wizard as he ran. But word of their sacrifice brought more cripples to help, and soon after, the number of those coming to fight almost equaled the number Taliesin and the Blood managed to kill.

Though the reality left her aching inside.

She'd stopped going to the loading bay to meet the new arrivals after the first few weeks. Facing them when she knew what they were in for, and how she was stuck here unable to help, was more than she could stand. She wasn't certain anymore, if Spider or Bus or the others finally showed up, what she'd even say to them. They knew the score, what the obstacles were, but the idea of explaining how she had to stay here, safely ensconced from danger like some medieval princess in a tower, left her nauseated every time the thought crossed her mind.

At first, Darius had pushed her to go down to the dock. They'd made an agreement for her to study, but people still needed to see her. It was her duty to meet with those going into battle. To let the cripples know that even the Queen of Merlin was on their side. She was, to more than just the Merlin now, their symbol of hope for peace.

But in the end, when he saw how it was affecting her, even he left her alone.

In her heart, she knew recreating Merlin's spell would be useful, despite the fact it left her trapped in a room with books while others fought a war. If the stories were to be believed, as one of the Merlin's Children, she only needed one of her enemies at hand, and she could bind everyone associated with them, no matter where their allies were hiding. The war would end in a heartbeat. All the Blood and Taliesin would be rendered harmless.

And nobody else would have to die.

With every passing battle, with every new stream of wounded pouring through the door, she was reminded of that fact, till now it had become nearly an obsession. Merlin's binding spell could be the answer to everything. It was the one thing she could do to truly help everyone.

Provided she could ever learn how it worked.

Drawing a breath, she pushed away from the table and rose to her feet. Scrubbing a hand through her tangled hair, she drove down the urge to torch something out of sheer frustration as she paced the perimeter of the table.

The door opened behind her. "What's wrong?" Cornelius asked, his tone sharp.

Ashe didn't turn around. "Nothing. Just taking a break."

She could feel the displeasure radiating off of him in waves, but she didn't care.

"Any progress?" he asked in the same tone.

Turning, she gave him a flat look.

Meeting her gaze expressionlessly, he let the door swing shut behind him. "A few refugees came in from Ann Arbor; survivors of a Taliesin attack on the apartment where they'd been staying." He gave a glance to the book in his hands. "They didn't have much, but they brought this with them when they fled."

Eyebrow rising, she crossed to his side and took the book. Swiftly, she flipped it open, scanning the first few pages.

Her hope faded. She closed the book and handed it back to him. "What?"

"It's Megilio's history of the war," she sighed, walking back to the table and leaning against it. She gestured absently to the racks of shelving behind her. "We already have the photocopies of an earlier edition in one of the binders over there."

"There could be additions."

She shook her head and then rubbed her eyes. "Dad discounted most of the historicity of Megilio's account. The guy got most of the facts about the human world in Merlin's era jumbled. Said Elizabeth the First had been queen of Scotland, not England, and that Magellan sailed for King Charles of Portugal, not Spain. Dad thought it left everything else he said suspect too, and Prillson's records from the same century dismiss the man entirely."

A sour expression crossed his face. "There still might be something–"

"I already checked, Cornelius."

For a moment, he looked ready to continue pressing the issue, and her expression darkened. Grimacing slightly, he set the book on the file cabinet near the door.

"How are you progressing with the spells you learned from Vanschauser's books?"

"They're great for portals. Nothing else. And Elias said Dad had him look into them six years ago."

"I thought it was a permutation of the spell."

She shook her head. "Original. The variation was what Dad gave him three years ago."

"Well, have you compared the two? There might–"

"Cornelius."

The frown on his face grew deeper and she tried not to scowl. In the past months, she'd done countless hours of comparison between all manner of spells. But he knew that.

"You should get back to work," he said after a moment.

"How's it going out there?"

His mouth tightened.

"I've hardly left this room for a week, Cornelius," she persisted. "How's it going?"

"Fine."

She could tell he was lying, even through the cold mask he wore.

"Cornelius."

"It is not your concern. Keep your focus here." Turning, he started to leave, and then paused with his hand on the handle. "I will have someone bring you lunch in a while."

Without another word, he disappeared out the door.

Staring after him, she exhaled as she fought the impulse to throw something. Every conversation with the man went that way these days. Short. Sharp. Vaguely accusatory in his implicit reminders of the responsibility she bore.

And how she was failing.

Leaning on her clenched fist, she drew slow breaths as she tried to calm down. It wasn't just about the spell, she knew. It was about the Blood. For months, he'd been silent on the topic, save for curt answers to direct questions and an increasingly icy silence owing, she supposed, to Carter having been right and him wrong.

At first, she'd understood. His cousin was dead. It hurt. She got that. But now, with every exchange degenerating into single syllable answers that told her nothing, her frustration was steadily over-whelming any compassion she'd had.

Muttering a few of Spider's favorite curses, she shoved away from the table and began to pace, her temper refusing to fade. She hadn't been exaggerating to say she hadn't left here in a week. It was probably more. But for bathroom breaks and the occasional shower, she'd lived in this room for damn near half a year, and the sight of the cold gray walls was starting to drive her insane.

But she couldn't quit. They were counting on her. Every person dying out there right now was hoping that, before their friends and family had to suffer their same fate, she'd stop failing and uncover the method to recreate the spell to bring the war to an end.

As Cornelius so often reminded her.

She could feel her heart pounding and furious tears stung her eyes. More than anything in the world, she wanted to set the binders on fire, if only to stop them from being there every time she opened her eyes. She needed a new book to study. A new file to research. Anything besides the shelves full of useless scraps of history she knew by heart.

Familiar rage rose at the thought, searing her as it came. Her father had stayed in this room for years. He'd spent every day pouring over these books, and here she was, cracking after only a few months. It was stupid. Weak. Self-indulgent. Childish.

Tears splashed on her hands, and she swore at herself for crying. She wasn't looking hard enough. There had to be an answer. It was here. Somewhere.

It was never going to be here.

It *would*. She just had to–

Her heart beat faster. She couldn't breathe.

She had to get out of this room.

Panic thundered through her as she glanced to the door. Cornelius would be out there, though. Or the guards. Or any of the numerous wizards roaming the building, all of whom recognized her by now. And they'd all want to know why she wasn't in here, pouring over the stupid, pointless stacks of flame-worthy material they'd hoarded like obsessive-compulsive squirrels from hell.

Her gaze darted to the closet and, before she even finished registering the impulse, she was already pouring her magic into making a portal. Blue light raced around the doorframe, charging the air with electricity and dropping the air pressure with ear-popping speed. Darting across the room, she yanked open the door and then ran into the darkness.

She skidded to a stop as her feet hit the dirt floor of the training warehouse. Piles of cinder blocks and charred dummies lay scattered around the massive room. A cool breeze twisted down through the open roof and white tendrils of cloud drifted below the overcast sky. In the doorway behind her, the darkness of the portal faded into gray daylight.

The blessed quiet of the empty outdoors surrounded her. Heart slowing, she walked unsteadily to one of the cinder-block mounds and sank down onto the rough surface. Propping her elbows on her knees, she dropped her head into her hands. Tears soaked past her fingers to splash on her jeans.

It would be so much easier to be out there, fighting. She knew how to do that, at least.

Minutes crept past in the silence and finally her tears slowed. Straightening tiredly, she sniffled as she swiped the moisture from her eyes. Whether or not she could leave here, Spider and the others would've joined up with the wizards by now. They'd be thoroughly engaged in taking care of the Blood, Taliesin and everything else she couldn't do. And they'd know Carter's dream had finally come true, though for her part, it didn't mean she'd get to see them again anytime soon.

On some level, though, that had to be enough.

Or so she tried to remind herself.

Running a hand through her hair, she struggled to shove away the old hurt as she glanced around the empty room. She'd never really wondered what going stir-crazy felt like, but her reaction in the library had probably been an example. And the fact that, in the midst of her panic, she'd managed to form a portal was nothing short of incredible. Even on a good day, she wasn't exceptional at them. Elias' instruction left nothing to be desired, and she understood the theory of using her magic to link stationary landmarks to guide her along, but the thought of crossing distances by way of magical tunnels through space and time always left her shaking. The fact that even masters like Elias could only reach a distance of about ten miles –

and anyone who'd tried to push beyond that had gotten lost in an oblivion from which they never emerged – just added to the paralyzing lack of appeal the traveling method held.

Which just went to show she needed to freak out in order to successfully pull one off.

Grimacing ruefully, she glanced back through the doorway. Anyone near the library would've felt that portal, small though it had been. And Cornelius would send someone with food shortly. Either way, they'd be looking for her. As a respite went, this couldn't last long.

For a moment, she contemplated using a portal to go back to the library, and thus avoid their questions, and then abandoned the idea when her stomach quivered at the thought. It was just a simple unidirectional spell, and it wasn't like she was going to tie her magic to something stupid like a box, and thus risk her landmarks moving, breaking the portal spell, and catapulting her into the lovely void Elias warned her about. But the idea of traveling a quarter mile over and ten stories up in little more than two heartbeats still made her knees weak.

Elias assured her she'd get used to it. Cornelius insisted she do so. But she didn't figure two people who'd spent their lives traveling by magical expressway could understand the reservations of someone who hadn't. Pushing away from the pile of cinder blocks, she resigned herself to hiking back to the factory, and to answering their furious questions when she finally arrived.

Despite the time of year, the glowering clouds lent the air a chill it otherwise wouldn't have possessed. The bone-white walls of the factory were stark against the iron sky while, like golems at the edge of a concrete sea, the warehouses crouched at the border of the parking lot, gaping emptily.

Eyeing the monolithic factory, she hesitated. The entrance across the parking lot would dump her straight onto the factory floor, and thus into a crowd of Merlin who'd all wonder why their queen was down among them, instead of up in the library where she belonged. The loading dock would have the same result, only from whatever cripple-and-wizard teams happened to be back from their hideouts in the city. The Council would deeply not appreciate either scenario, and would probably have a number of chastising things to say in each case.

But the fire escape on the rear of the factory would take her to the roof of the outlying buildings, and from there to the halls in the heart of the complex. A humorless grin tweaking her lip, she began winding her way through the warehouses toward the far side of the factory.

Just because she didn't want to use a portal didn't mean she had to throw herself into the lion's den.

Gravel crunched beneath her feet, the sound loud in the quiet. With this many wizards in close proximity, the skies were empty of birds for nearly a mile around. The stirring of loose tarps over the warehouse windows carried eerily through the silence, and she could hear her own breathing as she walked.

The sound of an engine in the distance brought her up short. Tires growled across the gravel, coming closer by the second. She glanced around, and through a gap between two warehouses, she caught sight of a white-sided delivery truck rolling toward the factory's rear door.

She exhaled, rolling her eyes at her own nervousness. It was just one of the trucks the cripples and wizards used to get around. With their vulnerabilities to magic, cripples couldn't travel by portal. That much power in close proximity shattered the strange shell around them, killing them instantly even if the wizard tried to hold the effects back with a shield. To compensate, the Merlin had picked up a few windowless trucks, and now most of the teams went around town under the cover of being delivery drivers.

But since the truck was pulling to a stop by the rear entrance, they were now squarely between her and the fire escape.

Biting her lip in consternation, she glanced around and then crept to the end of the line of warehouses, trying to keep the gravel from making too much noise beneath her. She could wait till they were inside and then skirt around to the stairs. With the rear door and the truck in clear view only a few yards away, it wouldn't be hard to tell when they'd gone.

Two wizards climbed from the front of the truck, heading for the back. The rolling rear door squealed as they tugged it up and their footsteps clunked heavily as they climbed inside. Muffled sounds followed. Wary confusion threaded through her. And then the factory door swung open.

A cocksure smile on his face, Sebastian sauntered down the steps and waited for the wizards to emerge.

"Well," he commented. "You didn't get far."

Her confusion grew.

The wizards hauled two people from the truck, dumping them at Sebastian's feet. On their knees with their clothes in tatters, the teenage boy and girl clung to each other tightly.

Ashe's heart started to pound as her mind tried to make sense of what she was seeing. The kids were cripples. But they were terrified.

"Where are the others?" Sebastian asked them.

At their silence, he gave them a reproving look. "Come now. You let your friends out, and after I went to so much trouble to catch them, too. You must have had a plan. Where were you headed?" He grinned. "Where are those hideouts you cripples are so fond of?"

"Go to hell," the boy spat.

Sebastian sighed. "So rude."

The boy said nothing, while the girl just buried her head in his side. Bending down, Sebastian took her chin in his hand, tilting her face up toward him.

"Hush, child," he said tenderly. "We're not going to hurt you."

His magic lashed out.

The girl's chin slid from his grasp as both teenagers slumped to the ground.

Sebastian straightened, rolling his neck languorously as the shards of light around the kids faded into him.

"Find the others," he ordered, and then motioned to the bodies. "Get rid of those."

He turned and walked back into the factory, leaving the guards to stuff the corpses into the truck and then drive away.

Ashe stared. She couldn't feel her hands or feet. Everything had gone numb. Screams bounced around inside, trying to find the way out, but she couldn't remember how to make a sound.

Ferals. They…

Oh God…

Her gaze went to the building.

Sebastian… Sebastian was a feral.

She shook her head, uncomprehending. How *could* he? How could *anyone* who knew the Blood existed murder the only people who could see them?

Unless…

His bigoted words from the Council meeting so many months ago came back and her blood went cold. She'd watched him storm across the factory floor. She'd watched him grab a few wizards on his way out.

He'd been planning this all along.

And there wasn't any reason to think the Blood didn't have allies among the Merlin as well.

Air forced its way into her lungs.

The Council didn't know. They couldn't. They didn't know he was killing while they were trying to build a bridge, and he was going to destroy everything they'd worked for if…

She ran for the factory. Yanking open the door, she darted through the dark hallways and hit the hospital wing at full speed. People stared as she raced past, and the guards called questions as she tore up the stairs. Whipping around the corner, she bolted onto the walkway and then skidded to a stop at the conference room door.

Someone had to be here. They always were. And as long as that someone wasn't Sebastian, she stood a chance of explaining before she went off and set one of the Council on fire.

Shoving open the door, she choked in relief as Darius glanced up from his notes.

"My God, your majesty," he gasped at the sight of her. Rising swiftly, he rounded the table and then gripped her arms to steady her. "Are you alright? What happened?"

She shook her head. Breathing hard, she closed her eyes briefly and forced the words out. "Sebastian, he…" She swallowed. "Cripples. Outside. He killed them. Darius, he's a feral. I think he's working for the Blood."

The man blinked, his normally unflappable expression fracturing into genuine shock. "Are… are you *certain?*"

She nodded.

Clearly struggling to maintain his calm, he turned away. "I always knew he had *prejudices*, but I never…" Darius' brow furrowed as he looked back at her. "Is it possible they were spies? We had word Taliesin–"

"They were *kids*, Darius."

A hint of nausea broke past his composure. "Ah."

He exhaled, absorbing the information as he tried to regroup. "Sebastian will be coming in shortly. Returning from addressing a threat in town… or so he told me." His expression tightened and then he glanced to her again, reading her anger. "And perhaps you shouldn't be here when he–"

The door swung open. "Darius," Sebastian said as he strolled in. "I–"

He cut off at the sight of her. Confusion and caution flashed over his face as his gaze darted between her and Darius. Carefully, he pushed the door closed, his wariness growing as he saw the fury in her eyes.

"What's going on?" he asked, his tone attempting to be casual, and failing.

"I saw you," she whispered, trembling with rage. He looked so calm. A bit intimidated by them staring him down, but not like someone who'd just committed murder less than three minutes before.

His gaze flicked between her and Darius again, and he chuckled bewilderedly. "Well, I *am* standing in front of you, your majesty. So–"

"I saw you kill them."

Sebastian blinked. He tried another baffled chuckle.

Her hands began to shimmer with heat.

"Your highness," Darius protested. "Please. We need to handle this appropriately. You cannot–"

"Okay," she agreed coldly, not taking her eyes from Sebastian. She jerked her chin at the door. "Let's handle it."

Anxiety increasing, Sebastian looked between them. "Darius, this is crazy. What is she–"

Flames flared from her clenched fists, and he cut off at the sight.

"Go," she ordered. "Out there. I want everyone to know what you've done."

Sebastian tore his gaze from the flames, looking to Darius.

And the fear melted from his face, leaving only loathing.

"So that's it, then," he said to the man. "You hang me out to dry."

Confusion cut through her rage, and she looked between the two councilmen.

"You are *such* a fool, you know that?" Sebastian told her. "You think he's such a strong wizard because he was just born that way?"

Darius' magic lashed across the room like a whip, crackling powerfully from Sebastian's shields. The two men stared at one another, icy and sneering in turn.

Suddenly trembling, Ashe backed away from Darius.

"It was a great plan, really," Sebastian continued. "Hundreds of cripples answer the call of their trusted ally, Queen Ashe, to stop the bogeymen that terrify them so. The queen stays in her tower, finding us the spell to bind Taliesin. And we get fuel to fight the war. Brilliant."

"Your lies will not save you, Councilman Monroe," Darius said quietly.

The man choked on a laugh. "*My* lies?" He glanced to Ashe. "Where've you been, your majesty? What've you heard? That we found your Blood wizards? That they're running scared? That cripple-and-wizard teams are roaming the city from their hideouts so conveniently located elsewhere, while they fight the good fight to save us all?" Sebastian couldn't stop his laughter this time. "Yet no one said a word about your little 'war', did they? No one said anything at all. But Darius… Oh, he told you all about how Taliesin killed your precious cripples, and how your 'Blood wizards' died. And he let you stay away from the cripples when all their noble sacrifices became too hard for you to bear." His eyes went to Darius. "How thoughtful."

"I will *not* let you speak like this further, Councilman," Darius warned darkly, electricity crackling from his fingertips.

Sebastian ignored him. "You'll be happy to know we've made good progress in turning the tide against Taliesin, by the way. Though I think lately they might have resorted to taking power from cripples too, since our forces have become so much stronger."

"If you value your *life*, Councilman Monroe, you will cease these lies at once!"

Sebastian scoffed, shrugging as though it was all the same to him, but she felt the magic around him grow stronger. She looked to Darius.

"Tell me he's lying," she said.

Darius turned to her, alarm beneath the tension in his eyes. "Highness, I *swear* he is."

She paused, her gaze not leaving him. "And take me to where the cripples are staying."

"Of course. I will prepare—"

"No. Right now."

His brow drew down. "Your majesty, it is not safe. We must–"

"Darius," she pressed, desperation tingeing her voice.

"Come on, Darius," Sebastian chimed in. "That won't be a problem, right? Taking her there this instant, before you can threaten to kill any cripple who says a word to her?"

At his silence, she began to tremble harder. "Darius… please."

His eyes met hers. Thoughts raced behind them too fast to read.

And then he sighed.

"You will pay for this," he said to Sebastian.

"I'm sure," the man retorted sarcastically.

She couldn't breathe. Her hands shaking, she reached behind her, clinging to a chair.

"We all make sacrifices, your highness," Darius said quietly. "Some more than others."

The air felt denser than stone. Her head shook back and forth of its own accord.

"We all do what we have to," he told her.

"Y-you *killed* them?" she heard herself say, her voice small in the sudden immensity of the room.

"Through their deaths, cripples make our forces stronger than they ever would have been otherwise. Their sacrifices save lives."

"But–"

"The 'Blood' do not exist, your majesty," he said, and the kindness in his voice felt clammy on her skin. "And we have more than enough real enemies in this war."

"You said you found them," she protested. "You said… you said you were stopping them."

Tears wanted to emerge, but she was too shocked to cry.

"Yes, well," he allowed, a touch regretfully. "You would have had trouble focusing where you were needed otherwise."

She choked on the air she attempted to draw into her lungs.

"You *killed* them," she said again. "You let me believe…"

More waves of horror rolled over her.

"And you told them… you told them…"

Her grip tightened on the chair as she tried not to fall. Spider. Bus. Samson. Magnolia. Jericho. Oh God.

He'd sent word to the cripples in her name.

"Dear me," Sebastian chuckled. "I don't think her royal majesty is taking the news too well, Darius."

"Silence," the man ordered. He looked back at her. "There is nothing I can say to make this better for you, your highness. I realize that. But I also know that *you* realize sacrifice is never easy, even when it is necessary. And I can assure you. No one suffered any pain."

Flames burst from her, slamming Darius' shields. Instantly, Sebastian struck out at her, and she swiftly diverted magic to block his attack.

The conference room door crashed open as guards rushed in. At the sight of the three of them, confusion brought the men up short.

"Her highness ordered surrender to Taliesin and attempted to harm herself when we begged her to reconsider," Darius announced, disconcertment and propriety suddenly in his voice. "For her sake, she must be taken to the cells to be kept under watch till she calms down."

The guards' eyes widened. They started toward her.

"*What?*" she protested, retreating. "No, you have to arrest these two! They've gone feral. They're killing cripples to make themselves stronger."

The guards looked between her and Darius, and then the closest held up his hands placatingly. "Please, your highness," he said, his magic rising around him protectively as he approached. "Just come with us. Everything will be fine."

Behind his shields, Sebastian smirked.

"No decision needs to be made today, your highness," Darius persisted. "I'm certain matters will seem clearer once you've had some time to think."

Her gaze darted between them as the guards came closer. Around the room, shields strengthened.

Swiftly, she ripped the magic from the nearest guard and threw it at them all. The blast tossed the soldiers into the walls and sent the councilmen stumbling as it cleared a path to the door.

She raced out of the room.

Metal grating clanked as she ran across the walkway, heading for the stairs. From the factory floor, people stared as she dashed down the steps and into the crowd.

"Stop her!" Darius shouted from the doorway.

Guards rushed from the crowd to block her path. She skidded and then spun only to find more guards emerging from the halls, cutting off any retreat. Bafflement on their faces, they looked between her and Darius as the councilman walked down the stairs.

"Please, your highness," he called to her. "You cannot surrender to Taliesin! For your people's sake, listen to reason!"

"Stop lying!" she yelled as gasps rose from the crowd. "I never said that!"

"Please!" Darius pleaded over her words. "I understand what the loss of your family has done to you, but this is not the answer!"

"Stop *lying*!" she shouted again. She looked to the guards. "Get out of my way!"

Warily, the guards tightened their circle around her, tossing uncomfortable glances to one another. She backed up, trying to keep away from them as her gaze darted to the throng beyond the soldiers. Fear and horror were everywhere.

Coming to the edge of the wall of guards, Darius placed a hand on one of their shoulders, motioning the man aside. Worriedly, the soldier hesitated, and then moved enough to allow the councilman to pass.

Her hands burst into flame as Darius came toward her, and he shook his head sorrowfully at the sight.

"Stay away from me," she warned.

Near-theatrical pity moved through his eyes. Flames licked his defenses as he stopped only inches from her.

"Look around, your highness," Darius murmured. "Look at the children. See the terror in their eyes. And think, your majesty. I can assuage their concern, tell them the surrender was a misunderstanding. But if you attack me now, or if you burn these innocent guards alive, everything I've made them fear of you will be proved true."

Her stomach clenched as he met her gaze. "What will you choose, your highness? Will you become the monster of these children's nightmares?"

Barely breathing, she didn't look away from him. Tears stung her eyes, impotent and furious. She could feel the pressure of the crowd, staring at her in horror.

And she let the flames on her hands grow higher.

His face tightened, suggestions of anger moving beneath the surface. "Then consider this," he whispered. He bent his head closer to hers and she twitched away. "The cripples we captured are not all dead. But they could be. And if you do not surrender, or if you try to escape, one will die for every day you oppose me."

She could feel his breath on her cheek. Her hands shook with the desire to let the fire rise. Her gaze slid back to meet his, and caught on Sebastian standing in the crowd.

He winked at her, dark assurance in his eyes.

Trembling, she looked around him. Fear marked so many faces.

But not all.

The air slipped from her.

And she let the flames die.

"Good girl," Darius said softly.

Motioning to the guards, he stepped aside as they rushed forward. Grabbing her shoulders, they spun her around to guide her back the way she had come. The crowd parted hurriedly before them, clearing a path.

She looked back over her shoulder, meeting Darius' gaze.

Decorous gratitude on his face, he bowed his head as they led her away.

Chapter Nine

nside a storage room in the basement of the factory, she paced. Cement walls surrounded her, and a cot huddled beside a small utility table in one corner. Outside the metal door, four guards waited. An additional pair flanked the inside, each the size of a linebacker. Clearly discomfited by their duty, they nonetheless sat in unquestioning silence.

Though it was late summer, the basement room was freezing. Worried for her comfort despite the fact her magic and anger were keeping her quite warm, the previous shift of guards had brought extra blankets when they put her here, though Darius had forced them to remove the coverings again.

The queen had already tried to hurt herself once, he reminded them. He'd hate to imagine the guilt they'd suffer if she tried to use the blankets to commit suicide.

With expressions made all the more determined by their uncertainty at their task, the latest pair of guards watched her, the knowledge she could rip their magic from them at any moment clear in their eyes.

"Perhaps you could sit down, your majesty?" one of them offered. As the slightly smaller of the two, his nervousness was easily twice that of his partner, and for the better part of his shift, he'd been watching her like she was a rabid tiger with whom he was sharing a cage. "Maybe rest will do you well?"

Her gaze darted to him as she paused in her pacing, and she could see the man swallow. They'd alternated with variations of the same suggestion throughout the past few hours, though at her glance, the man looked as though he wished he'd skipped his turn. For his part, the larger guard simply locked his gaze on the wall and tried not to breathe.

It'd taken her a bit to recognize the larger man, all these months later, as the driver from the day she arrived. The predatory threat in his eyes was gone, after all, leaving only a sort of paralysis that made him look like he was trying to merge with the wall. From his expression, though, every one of his earlier suspicions of her had been confirmed, and now he just hoped to live long enough to tell his cronies he'd been right.

"Did you know Darius was killing cripples?" she replied.

The smaller guard shifted awkwardly. "Councilman Greyson wouldn't do that, your highness. Please? You could get some sleep? No one's going to hurt you. You're safe with us."

Pinning him with her gaze a moment longer, she could read the thoughts behind his pacifying expression. She was safe. They weren't. And they believed every word Darius had said.

"You know," she told them for what felt like the hundredth time, "I never tried to commit suicide. And I never ordered anyone to surrender. The words never came out of my mouth."

"Things'll seem clearer when you've had rest, your highness."

Rolling her eyes, she returned to pacing. Upon delivering her to the cells, Darius briefed the guards on her supposed madness. Through the air vent above the door, she heard him describe the regrettable instability she suffered, and how he and Sebastian, as leaders of the Council, had attempted to keep it from view for so long. Her highness became confused about what had been said, and suffered from delusions of persecution from invisible enemies, to the point of even accusing the Council of committing crimes against their people. For a time, they'd thought perhaps it was simply stress, but eventually were forced to admit that the horror of seeing her family killed must have damaged her somehow.

They'd tried to play along, hoping the fantasies would work themselves out. But today, alarming news had come to light that changed everything. In her confusion, the queen had begun taking counsel from cripples who, they learned, were secretly allied to Taliesin. This led to her compulsion to surrender, owing to her trust in cripples above her own kind. After all, the cripples had been the first to find her, wandering the streets after her family had died. In retrospect, it only made sense that she would have fixated on them.

The queen commanded Darius and Sebastian to stand down the Merlin forces and surrender to the superior might of Taliesin. Shocked, the men refused and, in her deranged state, the queen attempted suicide right in front of them, nearly succeeding despite their efforts to stop her.

He was determined to find a treatment, Darius assured them. Now that the truth was out, he was going to speak with Katherine about what could be done for the queen. In the meantime, he trusted them to keep her safe – from herself most of all.

"How can you just believe him so blindly?"

She tossed the question to the guards reflexively.

"Councilman Greyson is a good man, your highness," the smaller guard said. "He's led our people for years. I mean, not led. No more than yourself, that is. Or the Children. I mean…"

His gaze twitched nervously to his colleague as he trailed off.

She eyed him briefly, and then shook her head, resuming her pacing. And that was the point right there. Councilman Greyson led them. He had all along. The Council ruled the people.

While the Merlin's Children stayed locked in the library.

She should have realized it, months ago when she first came to the factory. The shock of Carter's death and discovering she was some kind of magical wizard queen had blocked everything but the immediate from her notice, but she should've picked up on it nonetheless. He'd motioned her away from her own 'presentation to the people' – a grace at the time, but suspect anyway. His words ended Council meetings. His words started them.

For that matter, she hadn't been to a Council meeting in months. At the time, she hadn't cared. It wasn't like she wanted to be queen.

Cursing herself silently, she shook her head again. So blind. So myopic. She'd been so focused on finding Merlin's spell, she hadn't seen the problem right in front of her. And with his constant status reports on the 'war' against the Blood, Darius had left her no reason to think of the world outside.

Just like it'd probably been with her father.

Anger boiled at the thought of Darius deceiving her dad the same way. He'd stayed in the library day and night, Cornelius had told her. Did he ever wonder what was going on elsewhere?

Or had Darius kept him 'updated' too?

Her hands clenched, the desire to release even a trace of fire almost overwhelming. From the corner of her eye, she saw the guards shift and, trembling, she forced her fists to relax.

Darius didn't need her help in convincing anyone she was insane.

Grimacing darkly, she kept striding across the six paces of the cell. Early on, she'd thought about taking down the door, Darius' threats be damned. With the training Cornelius and Elias had given her, she was fairly certain she could buy herself a few minutes before Darius realized she was gone, though there was little she could do for the cripples still in his possession during that time. But the stairs would just dump her into the midst of the Merlin, and even if she used a portal to bypass that issue, she'd still have to find a way past the magical barriers securing the factory property. And she'd have to hurt the guards. Stupidly obedient they might be, but they were just doing their job.

She glanced at them again, her jaw muscles jumping. Of course, right now their job was getting people killed.

The thought brought with it images of her friends, and brutally, she shoved the memories aside. She couldn't think about them. About what might've happened. She'd fall apart if she did and she couldn't afford that right now. Elias or Cornelius would come soon and she'd get out of here. She'd make Darius and Sebastian pay for what they'd done and she'd save the people they were holding captive.

Then she'd worry about Spider, Bus and the others.

If they were still alive.

The guards tensed as she came to a stop, fighting to keep from shattering as her nails dug into her palms.

Pounding sounded against the door. She looked up, the immediacy of the noise driving the emotions back. With a cautious glance to his smaller compatriot, the larger guard rose as the men on the other side unbolted the door.

Cornelius strode into the room. Coldly, his gaze took in the two guards, and then he motioned sharply for them to leave.

"Sir, it isn't safe–"

"Get out."

Hesitating briefly, the guards nodded and then left, tugging the door shut behind them. Glancing to the vent, Cornelius sent a small amount of magic up to the grate, blocking all sound.

"Are you alright?" he asked without turning her way.

"They're killing cripples, Cornelius. No, I'm not alright. When can I get out of here?"

He paused, not answering for a moment. "What happened?"

Her brow furrowed. He wasn't looking at her. It was starting to make her nervous.

"I saw Sebastian kill two teenagers. I tried to tell Darius and the bastard turned out to be a feral who'd orchestrated the whole thing."

Silent, he studied the ground. Her heart began pounding harder. "Cornelius…"

"They were Taliesin spies," he said with difficulty.

"No, they weren't! Or if they were, who gives a damn? Sebastian killed those kids and he enjoyed it!"

"Your majesty…"

"What? Spies or not, don't you people have trials for something like that?"

"Yes, but–"

"But what?"

"It's not the point."

She stared at him, flabbergasted.

"This situation is… bad, your highness," he said quietly, floundering for a moment before settling on the generic term. "The people are frightened. They are uncertain what to believe. The soldiers do not know for whom they've been fighting and they're worried now that Darius' accusations are true. For the monarchy to betray us like this–"

"You can't seriously believe I ordered a surrender to Taliesin!"

"No, but my beliefs are not the ones that matter at the moment," he said pointedly. "We have to fix this. Quickly. I do not know what was said; what perhaps Darius misunderstood. But our people cannot afford to doubt their leaders. Not now."

"He didn't misunderstand anything, Cornelius! He made it up! He just wanted to distract from the fact he and Sebastian are murdering the cripples who're coming here thinking they're going to fight the Blood!"

Cornelius was silent.

She watched him. "You don't believe me, do you? You don't believe he's a feral."

"I have known Darius Greyson for thirty years, Ashe. And these allegations are…"

He struggled again to find a word and fell silent when his efforts failed. Turning away, he sank onto one of the chairs the guards had left. Resting his elbows on his knees, he clasped his hands in front of him as he studied the ground.

"I can help you fix this," he said carefully, nodding to himself. "Darius' claims of your attempted suicide have frightened the Council, and most of them favor keeping you here in custody for your own protection. But I can talk to them. Tell them it was a misunderstanding. That you had an argument, and Darius perhaps doesn't know your personality as well as he might like–"

"I'm sorry, *what?*"

His gaze met hers sharply. "This is an extremely tenuous situation, your majesty. Darius is speaking of injunctions to remove your right to rule, something that hasn't been done in ten generations. That you're the only one of the Children left makes this even more serious, as there is no one of the royal family to take your place. You have to restore the people's faith in your ability to lead, and in the cohesive bond between the Council and the monarchy. That your disagreement with Darius–"

"Disagreement?"

"–escalated to the point of being seen by our people is a breach of protocol that is going to take months or even years to repair. The Council is the voice of the people. The monarchy is their protection. To have those sides at odds with each other is disastrous. And now that word of your credence in the cripple theory of the Blood has come out, the people are at a loss to know what to believe."

"The cripple *theory* of the Blood?"

"They found nothing, your majesty."

"Were they looking?"

Cornelius gave her an exasperated look.

"*Were* they?" she repeated. "Did you see them go searching? Or the places the cripples were supposedly hiding? Do you know if anything Darius said *actually* happened, or are you just trusting his word that it did?"

He didn't answer.

"Why are you here, Cornelius?" she asked after a moment of silence went by.

"To reason with you," he said, a tinge of entreaty in his voice. She scoffed.

"You nearly set fire to a councilmember in full view of your people, Ashe. If you hadn't calmed down in time–"

"*Calmed down?* Cornelius, he threatened to kill a cripple for every day I opposed him!"

He blinked, looking down again as he worked to process the statement. Seething, she watched him as the seconds ticked by.

"Why didn't you say anything?" she demanded. "All those months where they apparently found nothing, and you just …" She shook her head. "Do you even know the stories Darius was telling me?"

Cornelius glanced away. All expression fell from her face.

"It was determined," he said with difficulty. "That, to keep your attention where it was needed, Darius would allay your concerns. Yes."

She stared at him.

"You would have tried to go out there," he continued, as though attempting to explain to himself as much as her. "You would have wanted to prove Josiah right, despite the danger and the increase of Taliesin forces in recent weeks–"

"The increase of forces," she repeated flatly, her derision clear.

He glanced up. "The war has gotten worse, Ashe. That part wasn't untrue."

She said nothing.

"So yes, I kept it from you." Cornelius paused. "I was trying to protect you."

"What about them?"

He looked away. "The cripples made their choices," he said, clearly struggling to make himself believe the words. "They believed Josiah and–"

"The Blood are real, Cornelius!"

"No," he countered sharply. "No, they are not."

"You–"

"Let it *go*, Ashe! For the sake of your family and their legacy… for the sake of our ability to win this war… I beg you. Let it go. Make peace with Darius. Just for now," he added swiftly, holding up a hand to stop her protests. "I will have people investigate what you're saying about the cripples, and what Darius may have done. We can do all that, but through the Council and the channels that have kept our people together for half a millennium. Please."

She regarded him. "You just can't let it be true, can you? You can't bear the thought Carter might have–"

"This is not about *Carter!*"

Closing his eyes, he drew a breath, forcing his composure back into place. "This is about Merlin. It has always been."

He turned, pounding his fist on the door.

The lock clanked, and then the door swung open. "Think about what I've said," he told her with a tight bow.

And then he walked away.

She stared after him, hurt and anger fighting for precedence and leaving only shock resonating inside. It stung, the way he'd yelled Carter's name. The way he'd called him Carter, and not Josiah as he'd always done. The way he'd looked at her.

The way he'd lied. Looked her straight in the face day after day.

And just lied.

Numbly, she sank onto the bed.

He couldn't let it be real. She knew that, no matter what he claimed. He had to believe everything he'd been told, because the alternative risked the idea that Carter might have died when Cornelius could have helped him, and that his cousin might have been right all along.

And she was just a child in his eyes. What did she know?

Quietly, the guards slipped back into the room, sharing grateful looks as they saw her sitting on the bed. She ignored them. They didn't matter anyway.

Cornelius just wanted her back at the books. Back at the mission they'd set her to months before. And to hell with the cripples. To hell with the dead. She had no purpose but binding their enemies, and when it was done, they'd all go back to ruling while ostensibly calling her queen.

To hell with them.

Her gaze flicked up, burning into the door as rage seethed inside. She'd been sent here with a purpose, ordered to come here by someone she respected more than everyone in this building combined. And while part of that purpose had come to an end, she still had a job to do.

Find the Blood. Take them out. And save anyone she could at the same time.

Her gaze moved to the guards, who shifted worriedly at the look in her eyes. She didn't bother telling them she wasn't insane. They'd believe whatever they wanted anyhow. But she let an apology flicker over her face as she prepared to rip their magic away.

"Oh, did I miss Cornelius?"

The faux-innocence of Sebastian's voice in the hall hit her like ice water.

"Sir, I'm not certain you should bring–"

"Just open the door, peon. Opinions don't suit you."

The lock clanked. Nervously, the guards eyed her as she rose, her body trembling with fury. With a creak, the door swung wide, admitting Sebastian, who glanced to the guards and then waved a hand, dismissing them from the room and his attention simultaneously.

"Good afternoon, your highness," he said as the other men left. "You miss me?"

She didn't answer, her jaw muscles jumping.

At her silence, he grinned. Tapping a finger to his chin thoughtfully, he began to stroll around the cell.

"You should know," he commented, "that I don't take kindly to people accusing me of heinous crimes, draining the life out of so-called innocents and the like. I don't appreciate it. I'm nothing if not forgiving, however. So I thought, now that our meetings about your 'condition' are over and you've had a chat with dear, loyal Cornelius… well, I'd see if maybe you'd settled into the new way things are going to be."

"Go to hell," she muttered as he circled past her.

"Or not," he amended, still smiling. "But as a symbol of good faith, honesty, trust, et cetera… I wanted to give you the gift of meeting someone you *could* blame for your situation. Someone besides me and your precious fantasies."

He motioned to a pair of new guards outside the door. Reaching past the doorframe, the men drew a woman with them as they came into the room. Straight blonde hair hung past the woman's shoulders, extending from darker roots several inches long. Specks of diamond jewelry dotted her ears and neck, the gems glittering too brightly to be real. In her pale fingers, she clutched a yellow plastic food tray, and beneath lashes coated in thick layers of mascara, she glared daggers at the floor.

Ashe's brow twitched down in wary lack of recognition.

"Your highness," Sebastian said. "I'd like you to meet Tanya, the wife of Howard Bartlow, the man who sold your family's location to Taliesin and got them killed."

Ashe froze.

Shrugging off the guards' hold, Tanya turned her baleful gaze on Sebastian.

"Oh, come now, Tanya," he chided at the woman's silence. "I'm sure, as a fellow prisoner, the queen wants to say hi."

The woman glanced to her, the hate in her eyes joined by a flash of satisfaction so strong it made Ashe's blood go cold.

"I mean, after all, your highness," Sebastian continued, shrugging charitably. "If you're going to have delusions of persecution, they might as well be directed at the appropriate people."

Trembling, Ashe looked at Sebastian. Beneath the pseudo-naïve expression, a grin hovered on his lips. His eyes scanned her face, devouring her shock and anticipating the pain that would surface afterward.

And amid her hurt, cold thoughts rose, giving her focus. There was no reason to believe Sebastian. She remembered Howard. He'd been Lily's doctor for years. And, even if he *had* betrayed her family, there was nothing to say he'd done it alone. Darius could've been behind it. Or someone else on the Council. And whichever it was, they would pay. But right now, the man in front of her was craving her pain, so much she could almost see him salivating at the idea of seeing her shout or cry. He'd do whatever he could to make her suffer, knowing that if she tried to hurt him in return, she'd just prove everything Darius said right.

Icy resolution settled in her veins.

He wanted to see pain.

She'd show him the queen her father would have wanted her to be.

Drawing a breath, she forced herself to hold her voice steady as she pushed the words past the choked feeling in her throat. "Is that true?" she asked the woman carefully, ignoring Sebastian.

Flicking her gaze away from the floor, Tanya gave her a look that told her where to put the question in no uncertain terms. Trembling at the expression, Ashe drew another breath, fighting to keep her hands from bursting into flame.

Because she'd be damned if she gave Sebastian the satisfaction.

"Tell me," she ordered, her voice quivering slightly.

Tanya glanced up again. "Why do you care?"

"Was he working for them?" Ashe asked with a jerk of her chin to Sebastian.

The woman's snort was answer enough. Ashe paused, uncertain whether to be glad.

"Oh, honestly, your majesty," Sebastian scoffed. "What do you take us for? The *mafia*? You think we ordered a hit on your daddy? Howard betrayed them on his own, and it's not like it matters why. He did it. He gave up sweet Lily, all your strong and loyal bodyguards, and your beloved father. He just handed them over to the fun of the Taliesin. I mean, for all he knew, they could have raped you and that precious little girl before they blew her head off or–"

"Shut up!" Ashe snapped.

A smile of pure enjoyment twisted around his mouth, belatedly suppressed. He chuckled as he continued ingenuously. "I'm not trying to upset you, your majesty. I just thought surely you'd want to know why everyone in your family is dead?"

Rage pounded through her, keeping time with her racing heartbeat. In the back of her mind, she could hear herself screaming. See herself running through the house with her dad, and leading her sister out to the yard where they'd watch their father die.

Ashe drove a breath into her lungs. She had one weapon, short of blowing them all to hell.

It had to be enough.

"Tell me why," she said to Tanya, her voice rigid with control.

"He made a deal with Taliesin, your majesty!" Sebastian exclaimed. "I mean, it must've seemed perfect to him. As Lily's doctor, he had to care for her even while she was in hiding. After all, the poor thing was so damaged after the start of the war – though no more than yourself, I suppose, with your little amnesia problem and all. But he was one of the only people on the planet who knew where you were hiding, except maybe Tanya, since I can't imagine he'd keep that secret from his wife."

Sebastian sighed. "And to think he turned out to be a cold-hearted murderer who callously offered up your family to the slaughter."

"That is *not true*."

His eyebrows twitched up as Tanya's growl pounded the words as though nailing them to the wall. "Oh, really?" he asked.

"He had to have been protecting us," Tanya snarled. "Howard would never–"

"Tanya, Tanya," Sebastian sighed. "Not this again. 'Protecting you'. Honestly. And how do you explain him sneaking away from the bodyguards we gave you all, only to show up on the royal family's property *just* as they wound up dead? Besides yourself, your majesty," he added conscientiously. "You obviously managed to survive even if your father and little sister didn't."

With everything she had, Ashe ignored him. "Why do you think that?" she asked Tanya.

The woman rolled her eyes, not answering.

"Why!"

Sebastian choked on a laugh, but Tanya just scowled.

"Because he wouldn't have," the woman stated as though it was obvious.

Ashe swallowed, hearing an implication in the words.

"And you?" she pressed quietly. Sebastian's snickers were making her hands grow warm and she couldn't stop it.

The woman's eyebrows rose sarcastically. "What? You want me to admit something? Give you an excuse to leave my daughter an orphan and prove this 'noble compassion' crap you're trying is just an act?"

"Now, Tanya," Sebastian chided.

"Screw you, Councilman," the woman snapped. The guards shifted warningly and she glared at them too. "You all think you're so good. Better than Howard, blindly loyal as he was, and better than me. Well, Howard would've died for us, so if he's dead then that's what he did. And you can go to hell for thinking otherwise." She ran her gaze up and down Ashe. "All of you."

Ashe flinched as, with a resounding crack, Tanya slammed the tray down, splattering cream corn and mashed potatoes over the concrete floor. Turning sharply, the woman stormed across the room, only to be brought up short by the guards.

Seething, Tanya spun. "I'm sick of this, you bastard!" she shouted at Sebastian, her voice breaking. "You have nothing! No proof! Nothing but my husband's dead body at her goddamn house and you've locked us up for months over it! And what? Her family is dead? So *what*? So is mine! You lost a little sister? Well, I've got a five-year-old who can't figure out why everyone hates daddy all of a sudden. And while you've had countless lackeys kissing your feet in your sorrow, your *highness*, we've been the only ones mourning an innocent man!"

Sebastian's enjoyment was almost too much for him to contain. Tears shone on Tanya's red face and her hair quivered with the ferocity of her trembling. Ashe could hear the staccato snickers bursting from the councilman, while his guards stared impassively at the wall.

Magic coursed through her veins, begging to be released. And it hurt. Oh, it hurt to breathe. To stay calm, if only on the surface. Somewhere inside, she wanted to smile at the knowledge Howard was dead. To rejoice that someone who even *might* have endangered her family wasn't still alive. She wanted to punch the woman for mocking Lily, her father, or anyone else she loved as being less important, simply because she remained here to mourn.

But Sebastian brought Tanya here for a reason.

And any reaction would mean he'd won.

Drawing a careful breath, she forced herself to meet the woman's gaze.

"I'm sorry for your loss," she whispered.

Tanya stared. Rage and confusion chased themselves across her face and her hands balled into fists as magic rose around her. Muffling his chuckles tightly, Sebastian darted glances between them.

The air around Tanya crackled with electricity. By the door, the guards backed away, eyeing the councilman questioningly.

Ashe didn't move.

Overhead, the lights buzzed, the ambient charge making them burn brighter till one of the bulbs burst in a shower of sparks.

And then the magic faded.

Gritting her teeth, the woman glared. "I could have," she growled.

At Ashe's silence, she snarled wordlessly and spun, shoving past the guards as she fled the room.

Not breathing, Ashe slid her gaze to Sebastian, meeting his eyes.

He gave another chuckle, the sound forced. For a heartbeat, he hesitated, as though trying to think of something to say, and then he turned, striding out the door with the guards on his heels.

Silence settled over the cell.

Magic churned through her, roiling above aching rage and fighting desperately for a place to go. Her gaze dropped to the floor as her body remained standing, paralyzed.

A breath escaped her, loud amid the quiet.

Nervous as always, the smaller guard inched back into the room. At the sight of her, he paused, gripping the doorframe with a bloodless hand. Nausea flickered over his face and, swallowing hard, he shoved away from the door and darted down the hall, chasing Sebastian with requests that someone take his place. Cagily, the larger guard walked in, forcing himself to do what his companion could not, though he only made it a few paces before he also stopped and glanced back to the door.

His gaze locked on the empty space for a moment.

And then slowly, he turned and crossed the room.

Rigid with tension, she watched as he stopped before her, his bulk towering more than a foot higher than her own form. His eyes met hers, every trace of fear gone.

He sank to one knee before the splattered food at her feet. With a napkin from his pocket, he carefully cleaned the edges of the plate and then straightened, placing the tray on the small table nearby. Glancing to her briefly, he tore a piece from the hard-crusted roll lying half-submerged in cream corn and then dipped it into everything else on the plate. His gaze went to the door, noting the absence of anyone there.

And thoughtfully, he ate the bite of bread whole before looking back her way.

"To be certain," he whispered.

She stared, uncomprehending, and then she blinked. Poison. Her brow flickered down.

"You are not alone, your highness," he continued, his voice so low she could barely hear him. "Just hang on."

Infinitesimally, he bowed his head before meeting her eyes again. Speechless, she watched him return to his chair by the door. Dread and nervousness dropped back over his face like a mask, indistinguishable from before.

White with terror, the smaller guard stumbled back into the room, looking between his companion and their prisoner as though shocked the man remained alive. With a shaking hand, he found his chair and lowered himself down. The guards from the hall returned and, glancing into the cell, they gave disparaging looks to the others for leaving the exit open in their own fear.

A clunk sounded as the metal door settled back into its frame.

She sank onto the cot. Numbly, she reached up, pausing a moment before wrapping her fingers around the roll.

Her gaze flicked to the larger guard, curious and cautious at the same time.

And then she looked away.

Rage and hurt still pulsed somewhere inside, emanating from emotions scoured raw. Sebastian's words hovered at the edge of memory, accompanied by images of the night her family died.

But the pain wasn't as strong as before.

Because she'd won.

And now she just had to hang on.

She figured it was getting late when the lights of her cell dimmed. The fluorescent bulbs flickered down to a ghost of their former glow and, for the thousandth time, the tired guards hinted that she might want to sleep, though she could tell by their tones they'd long since stopped expecting the suggestion to accomplish anything. From the hallway, she hadn't heard a sound since Sebastian left, and through the air vent, she could see the corridor lights lower as well.

Briefly, she toyed with the idea of letting her hands catch flame just to make more light, but with how tense the pathologically frightened smaller guard had become over the past day, she wasn't certain he wouldn't just blow up the room at the first hint of magic. Pushing the temptation aside, she shifted position on the cot, and then regretted it when the man flinched.

She buried a grimace. Every second hurt. People were in trouble out there. And if she could escape this cell and force the feral bastards to give her the cripples' location, she might be able to do something about it.

Instead, she was waiting.

Her gaze twitched to the larger guard. Questions burned inside her, becoming more intolerable as the hours crept by. The man hadn't said a word beyond suggestions of sleep ever since Sebastian left and, on some level, she'd started wondering if his whole display earlier had just been some kind of tactic to keep her in Darius' custody. The claim of possible poison could have been solely for her benefit, and the guard never even said what she was supposed to be hanging on for.

Like everything else, it could be just another trick.

Every light in the cell went black.

In the darkness, a muffled shout rang out, followed by a heavy thud. Ashe scrambled to her feet, flames rushing up her arms.

"Your majesty, wait!" the guard cried, holding up his hands in the firelight.

The smaller man lay in a heap on the floor. The guard opened his mouth to speak when a clunk from the door interrupted him. Keeping one eye to her, he pulled open the door.

Ashe blinked. "Elias?"

"Are you alright?" he asked as he hurried inside, leaving three men waiting in the hall behind him.

She nodded, looking between the councilman and the guards.

"I'm sorry about the delay," Elias said. "We've come to get you out of here."

Relief hit her, followed almost instantly by caution. Darius had lied to her for months. Cornelius had betrayed her for the sake of the monarchy. Sebastian had just wanted an excuse to hurt her more. By all reports, the Council thought she was insane.

And Elias wanted to defy them all by helping her escape.

She'd had enough of trusting anyone blindly.

"Why?" she asked as she glanced through the doorway, evaluating her chances of fighting past the wizards before they raised the alarm.

"Your majesty, we need to go."

She scoffed, not moving. At the sound, the large guard shifted uncomfortably.

Elias exhaled. "Because this is madness," he stated. "I don't know what happened today, but I know you. I've worked with you for months. You're not crazy and you're not a traitor. But this afternoon

I heard a man I've known for years suddenly propose we undermine the monarchy and put the Council in control. He's charging you with high treason, and the kangaroo court he's set up is already planning what they'll do once they find you guilty.

"Everything's falling apart," he continued. "And the only reason people are going along with it is because they're scared. But this is insanity, and I refuse to risk that it could get the last member of the royal family killed."

Ashe hesitated, eyeing the wizards again.

"Please, your majesty," the large guard urged quietly.

She glanced to him, caution still in her gaze.

"Nathaniel was one of your father's personal bodyguards," Elias told her. "As were the others with me. You can trust them."

"And Darius was his friend," she replied.

Elias grimaced. "Give me some credit in who I chose to have watch out for you."

She hesitated a moment longer and then nodded.

"Alright," Elias said. "Katherine and the others are waiting. I can get us out of here if–"

"We can't leave yet," she interrupted.

He stared at her.

"Darius is holding a bunch of people hostage. I don't know where. But if I leave, he said he'd kill them." She paused. "We need Sebastian."

"Your highness–"

"Can you get a portal close to his room?"

Elias hesitated. "Yes," he allowed. "But it's going to attract attention."

"Do it."

His mouth tightened, and then he sighed. "This side of the door," he said to the three men in the hall. He glanced to the large guard. "Nathaniel–"

"I stay with the queen," the man finished, any alternative negated by his tone.

A grateful smile pulled at Elias' mouth, though it didn't reach his eyes before it died. He took a deep breath as the others came into the cell and then he extended his hand toward the exit.

The doorframe sizzled with electricity, the air pressure in the room plummeted, and then the view of the hallway was dragged into a vortex of gray smoke.

"Go," Elias ordered.

She followed the guards through the portal.

Dim light surrounded them as they stepped from the stairwell doorway. The three guards hurried ahead of her, leading the way to Sebastian's room, while Nathaniel fell in by her side. At the door, the men paused, looking back at her and then to Elias coming up behind.

She nodded.

They shoved the door open and Ashe followed them in.

Sebastian sat up sharply in his bed, and then his magic was gone. The guards rushed him and swiftly, one drove magic into Sebastian's mouth, silencing him completely while the other two hauled him from the bed.

"You miss me?" she asked as they dragged him past her.

The hate in his eyes was answer enough. Struggling to shout past the gag, he thrashed in the guards' grip as they headed for the door.

She hesitated, her gaze flicking in the direction of her bedroom. Her gun was back there. Of everything here, it was the only thing she didn't want to leave behind.

Shouts rose from deeper in the building. Lights came up in the corridor and she could feel the air pressure drop from portals forming nearby. At the door, Elias raised his hands, and the view of the hall vanished into shadow.

"Your majesty?" he called.

She cursed internally, hurt swelling though there was nothing to be done. Drawing a sharp breath, she raced after the others through the portal.

The moist, concrete wall of the subbasement brought her to a halt.

"What took so – wait, why is he here?"

The flustered voice greeted her and she glanced over to see Katherine staring at them in the darkness, the red light of a distant exit sign reflecting from her gold glasses.

"Her majesty insisted," Elias explained as the five wizards with Katherine joined the others in dragging Sebastian down the hall.

Katherine's gaze flicked over her. "You are unharmed?" the woman asked, the words equal parts question and statement of what would be, regardless.

Ashe nodded. Katherine echoed the motion distractedly, turning to watch Elias follow the guards.

"This way," the woman said.

By the doorway of a storage room at the end of the hall, Elias tugged out his cell, swiftly checking the locations he'd set his portal to reach. A grimace twisted his expression. "They've already prepped the main gate. Twelve guards. More than normal. Other access points for the shield aren't any better."

He glanced to Ashe, and she nodded at the question in his eyes.

Drawing a breath, he turned, running a hand over the door. The blue glow of wizard writing raced down the frame, sorting destinations faster than she could read. Ignoring the display, he yanked the handle and then stepped back. "Go."

Guards blocked the chain-link gate beneath the irradiating glow of a security light. Eyes going wide, they tensed as Ashe and the others came through the booth doorway.

Like dominoes, she sent their magic cascading through their neighbors, toppling them all to the ground.

"Nice," Elias said behind her. "They alive?"

She nodded, eyeing the faint haze of the factory's defenses. As one massive security system, the barrier was tissue-thin and almost undetectable, though that didn't stop it from being formidable. Wizards couldn't pass it, nor could any other living thing, and a single trace of magic nearby was reported instantly to the guards monitoring it in the main building.

If he hadn't known she was here already, Darius would now.

She glanced back as Elias yanked open the security box mounted to the booth wall. The keypad beeped rapidly beneath his jabs, and he gave a humorless grin to the gate as it began to roll back and the shield flickered enough to let them by.

"Council override," he told her. "Run."

The guards hefted Sebastian between them as they rushed toward the security booth on the other side. Darting after them, Ashe tossed a glance over her shoulder. In the darkness, a portal was churning. Her breath catching, she skidded to a stop beyond the barrier.

"Elias, hurry!" she yelled over her shoulder.

Cornelius rushed out, with Darius only a step behind.

"Your highness, wait!" Cornelius called.

Around the gag, Sebastian yelled as he fought the wizards' grip. Energy surged around Darius, lashing out at the brief weakness in the shield, only to fizzle to nothing as it passed the barrier. At his back, his guards stabbed codes into the keypad.

Elias wove his magic through the booth doorway.

"Ashe, please!" Cornelius shouted. "Don't do this!"

Magic surged behind him, radiating from Darius' hands. The barrier flickered, the key commands taking effect.

She spun, racing after the others as the barrier around the gate vanished, Darius' magic rushed her, and the darkness of the portal swallowed everything.

Chapter Ten

Puddles splashed beneath her feet as she came to a stop in the alley. Neon lights reflected from the rippling water and cast strange shadows into the doorways of the brick buildings nearby. From behind a dumpster, a cat fled, eager to escape the wizards' proximity.

"Where are we?" Ashe asked, turning to Elias.

"South side of town. I'm not taking this bastard anywhere near a safe house, so if there's something you want from him, now's the time to get it."

She nodded and then glanced to Sebastian, ignoring his attempt at a smirk despite the magic muffling him.

"Where are they?" she demanded.

His expression turned condescending and she jerked her chin at the guards. They let the magic blocking his mouth dispel.

He spat at her. A guard's fist slammed into his face, knocking his head sideways.

Ashe wiped the spittle from her cheek and dried her hand on her jeans. "Where are they?" she repeated.

"Darius will know you're going—"

"Then it won't matter if you tell us."

The contempt in his eyes couldn't hide the sadistic anticipation peaked by her words.

"Where are they?"

He glanced to the guards and then gave a dry laugh. Shaking his head, he worked his jaw around. "Layton Marina," he said finally.

She looked to Elias. "You know where that is?"

He nodded.

"Take us there."

———— ◆ ————

After the first few weeks in Croftsburg, Harris had taken to driving the streets at night, hoping to catch sight of things no one else could see. The body count was high enough around here to justify the effort, though the cops attributed it all to serial killers, drug deals and gang crime. The populace was worried and most people stayed in after dark, except for those with agendas and those too burnt out on life to care.

And wizards.

Or so he hoped.

The news made him shake his head these days. Serial killers. Gang wars. They had it half right. They just made the mistake of assuming all killers were human.

But then, everyone always did.

Jamison's people sent him reports of unidentified murder victims from all over the nation these days, feeding him whatever information he required for his part of their mission. After an initial reluctance, the man seemed to understand Harris' strategy, though he still left the detective working alone.

But that was alright. After what happened to Malden, Harris preferred it that way.

Shifting his grip on the steering wheel, he grimaced at the red light glaring in his eyes. By one in the morning, most stoplights in the better parts of town had switched to flashing in both directions. But on fringe streets like the marina road, such ground-breaking technology had yet to make an impression. And regardless of the fact he was probably the only car for a mile around, for the past minute and a half the light had perversely insisted on remaining red, while determinedly casting its green glow down an empty frontage road.

He hated Croftsburg.

For a long time, he'd wandered from city to city, kept afloat by funds from Jamison's coffers and chasing one empty lead after another. But of all the cities east of the Mississippi, this sprawling metropolis had the most unidentified bodies, a statistic that hadn't diminished as the weeks ground on. Some of the corpses were written up as outright homicides, while others were allegedly the victims of drug deals or overdoses. A few had been chalked up to suicide, while the others were filed under causes unknown.

None were burned, but it didn't matter. Harris suspected her involvement in them all.

Some nights, when the streets were empty and even the criminals had gone to bed, he could almost picture himself catching her. With his car parked on the deserted stretches of dark city roads, he'd imagine seeing her again, the innocent victim act fallen from her face and the true intent finally revealed underneath. And he'd know what he'd done was right.

He'd have to call Jamison's men to take her in; he knew that. Against so many of them, she'd have less chance to set anyone aflame. And they wouldn't take her for any trial he'd be accustomed to, but he wasn't certain anymore if that was the point. He'd have captured her. She couldn't hurt anyone ever again.

The rest was immaterial.

Overhead, the infernal light finally deigned to become green, and with a sigh, he took a left turn. Past his window, the glimmering lake shone beneath the full moon, silhouetting the hulking storage buildings of the abandoned marina and the rotting boats dying slowly nearby. Yellow security lights dotted several buildings in an attempt to dissuade the local teenagers from using the harbor as a hangout, though the graffiti scrawled across the walls proved how ineffective the measures had been. He regarded the mess dryly as the rough pavement grumbled beneath his tires and potholes set the car lurching every few yards.

A group of people emerged from one of the warehouse doors. Instinctively, Harris' mind ran a swift count, noting the ten men too large to be teenagers, the one body suspended between them, and the narrow forms of two women at the center.

The buttery light caught their faces as they glanced around.

His car nearly went off the road.

Turning, the group headed deeper into the marina, hauling the body with them. Heart pounding, Harris guided the vehicle to the shoulder by instinct, his eyes locked on the people disappearing between the buildings. Fumbling with the seatbelt latch, he shoved the car door open and then clambered outside.

It was her. Months of searching. Months of nothing. Months and months and…

He drew a breath and tugged out his cell phone.

"Layton Marina. Southeast Croftsburg. Get here. She's inside."

Before anyone could speak, he hung up and shoved the phone into his pocket. Dryly, he licked his lips, ordering himself to concentrate.

Jamison's men would be coming. They were better equipped to handle her. But she had a victim with her right now.

There wasn't any time.

He couldn't let it happen again.

Harris drew his gun.

———— ◆ ————

She could hear the water lapping the lakeshore as they emerged from the portal at the edge of the marina. Overhead, a security light glared, turning the corrugated sides of the warehouses to gold. Gravel crunched as Elias and the others arrived, but she didn't turn.

Her eyes were locked on the graffiti scrawled on the metal siding.

"Your majesty?"

A breath entered her lungs sharply, and she looked back.

"What is it?" Elias asked, concerned.

"Nothing," she answered, her voice more choked than she'd have liked. Blinking, she turned to Sebastian, unable to keep the fury from her eyes.

He smirked vaguely, seeming confused by her expression, and his gaze twitched to the wall curiously.

Her heart jumped. "Where?" she demanded, letting her anger cover everything else.

For a moment more, he looked between her and the markings,

and then he jerked his chin toward the heart of the marina. "Dry storage. End of the row."

"Go," she ordered the others.

They hauled Sebastian with them as they headed away from the security lights into the deeper shadows of the yard.

Her gaze returned to the three large scribbles of graffiti amid the common vandalism coating the building.

Trap. Run.

The last symbol was unfinished.

Swallowing hard, she turned and followed the others.

The sound of the water grew louder as they moved toward the end of the gravel drive. Stenciled numbers in chipping paint differentiated the identical buildings, most of which gaped emptily in the darkness. At the final building on the row, Sebastian grumbled instructions to stop.

"That one."

Drawing a rough breath, she started for the entrance, when Nathaniel grabbed her arm. With a warning glance, he shook his head and then moved ahead of her toward the rusting metal door. Despite their weathered appearance, the hinges made no sound as he pulled the door wide.

The smell hit them before anything else.

Ashe's hands flared to life, and the shadows fell back. Nathaniel turned quickly to block her path.

"Your majesty–"

"Move."

Nathaniel hesitated, but at her expression, he just turned and led the way inside.

Not breathing, she followed. Behind her, one of the guards

fumbled for a light switch.

"Oh sweet God," she heard Katherine whisper.

They'd tried to make it look like an argument gone too far. She could see it in the way the bodies were laid. Six people, arrayed as though trying to escape the seventh, the latter of which held a gun. Murder-suicide. So neat. So easily dismissed by the police.

She was trembling so hard the ground felt like it was shaking, but somehow her feet still carried her past the empty boat racks and across the room. Behind her, the others followed, and she could hear them dragging Sebastian with them over the rough floor.

Numbly, she stopped at the edge of the circle of bodies and looked down, nausea twisting her insides. The pools of blood had mostly dried on the concrete. Ragged holes peppered the backs of those staged as fleeing, and the seventh was missing part of his skull. Their eyes were glassy, empty and cold.

She didn't recognize them.

The thought was distant, and she questioned it absently. Had they been at the Abbey? Had she just not noticed them? Could they have known Carter, and that'd been why they came?

Seven more cripples, killed because the wizards sent word on her behalf.

A short burst of chuckling broke out behind her, silenced almost instantly by the sound of a fist hitting flesh. "What the hell is this?" she heard Elias snarl at Sebastian.

Her gaze slid back as the man scoffed again, refusing to answer.

"The cripple forces," she told them. "The ones who came to fight the Blood."

Bafflement colored Elias' face as he looked between her and the bodies. "They sent them home," he protested. "The cripples didn't find anything and they…"

His words caught up with his eyes and he looked over at his wife in desperation.

Ashe ignored them, watching Sebastian. "Darius did this?"

"Probably the minute you found out about him, my *lady*."

Air scraped her lungs, carrying the rank stench of the room. She choked and then swallowed hard. "Are there others? Other locations?"

He seemed to weigh whether to answer. Her hand caught fire again before she could stop it.

His theatrical expression melted into disdain. "No," he grudged. "We've been short supplied for awhile now. Even had to start culling some of our informants. Your precious cripples got smarter, you see. Stopped coming in such large numbers when their buddies didn't answer calls anymore."

She looked away.

"I've got to say, though," Sebastian continued conversationally. "That could change, especially if you keep treating me like this. Darius was well aware you knew more than you let on. Heaven knows what you gave up without realizing. You let me go, maybe we can make a deal. Otherwise…"

Her gaze darted to him as he trailed off meaningfully.

"You know," he said as though she'd asked him to explain. "Like hiding places. Some of their darling 'Hunter' secrets. You always were so transparent. Like back by the–"

He cut off as she crossed the distance between them swiftly. "What does he know?" she demanded.

"What makes you think I'll–"

Her hand wrapped around his throat. Gasping, he tried to recoil as, beneath her fingers, his flesh began to burn.

The guards didn't let him move.

"What does he know?" she whispered.

"Nothing," Sebastian spat hoarsely. "Just rumors. He was going to set something up to get you to tell him more."

Her hand grew hotter. Skin sizzled as smoke curled up from his neck. "Is that true?"

"You little cripple-loving–" he snarled and then cut off as the guards jerked him in her grip. "Yes! Yes, damn you–"

She released his throat, leaving a blistered and bleeding imprint of her hand. She stepped away, her gaze returning to the cripples lying dead on the floor.

"You… you stupid, fire-flinging *bitch*!" Sebastian cried, struggling to break the guards' hold. "How *dare* you hurt me! You think you're anything? You pathetic little *infant*, you get someone over here to fix this! Do you hear me? Get that healer over here!"

Ashe looked back expressionlessly.

Fury and impotence twisted his face as he read her response. Quivering with rage, he looked down, his gaze searching the ground and then catching on the blood staining his shirt. The shaking strengthened. His lips twitched into a snarl.

"No one hurts me," Sebastian whispered. "*No one*, do you understand?"

His gaze rose to meet hers. In spite of herself, Ashe tensed at the look in his eyes.

He chuckled. "Some of the cripples tried to hurt me too, you know? Those tough guys and that blonde bitch." He smiled. "You really liked them, didn't you? The 'Hunters'. Carter's little crew of misfits. Were you friends? Did they trust you?" His smile deepened.

"Want to know what it felt like to crush them? To see the agony in their eyes before they died? To watch the horrible, gut-wrenching realization that their precious Ashe had—"

She didn't even feel the fire as it left her body and set him aflame. With a shout, the guards stumbled back, unburned and staring.

The charred corpse fell to the floor.

Choking, Ashe spun away, suffocating the fire inside. Hot tears ran down her cheeks as she squeezed her eyes shut and tried to keep from screaming.

And then the world exploded.

———— ◆ ————

Harris crept toward the storage building, careful to stay out of the light spilling from the doorway. Unintelligible voices muttered inside, rising and falling in the rhythm of an argument.

Dryly, he swallowed and shifted his grip on the gun. If they were arguing, the hostage could still be alive. Taking a breath, he inched to the door and leaned his head around the frame.

Rigid control kept him from cursing, aided by a fair measure of shock.

A heavy stench hung in the air. Bodies lay on the floor. And Ashley was standing beside them all.

She looked back to the captive, who seemed to be cursing her roundly. Over the distance the angry words were indecipherable, though the cold expression with which she met them was clear. On either side of the kneeling prisoner, two men stood, while at their backs, several others were surveying the room.

He ducked out of sight as a few of her accomplices glanced toward the door, and waited a cluster of heartbeats before edging his gaze around the frame again.

The captive fell silent for a moment. He muttered something to Ashley.

And without a trace of expression on her face, she burned him alive.

Harris gasped. Her accomplices stumbled backward. Swiftly, Ashley turned to the rest of the dead sprawled across the floor while behind her, the blackened corpse lay smoking.

Choking down a breath, Harris raised his gun.

He didn't miss this time.

———— ◆ ————

The concrete hit her and everything was wrong. The world was a series of shuddering images, interspersed with a crushing weight on her chest that kept her from drawing air. The lights overhead burned like tiny suns in her eyes, blurring in and out of focus as the ocean raged in her ears.

And then the pain came.

She choked wetly and tasted blood as it filled her throat. Her hands slipped in pools of liquid, and Katherine appeared, blocking the lights and shouting without sound.

Magic enveloped her.

Uncomprehending, she stared at the woman as waves of energy coursed through her in rapid succession. Blazing heat raced over her chest, into her lungs, searing her flesh as it passed.

And she couldn't breathe.

She just couldn't breathe.

Everything was wrong.

The magic was tearing her apart.

And then the world went black.

———— ◆ ————

Ashe gasped as she opened her eyes. White lights glared overhead and the ground felt strange beneath her back.

The room was cold. Concrete. Windowless.

Panic hit her and frantically, she tried to rise. Pain lanced through her chest and then someone was beside her.

"No, your majesty," Nathaniel said, his hands pushing her gently back down. "Please, don't try to move."

Ragged breaths escaped her as she fought to make her mouth form the words she needed, but nothing was responding correctly and every choked sound was an agony.

He seemed to read the question in her eyes.

"You were shot," he told her, his matter-of-fact tone failing to fully disguise his tension. "But you are safe now."

Fear filtered into her gaze and desperately, she tried to force herself to speak.

"Please, your highness," he urged. "Don't. You'll be healed up soon. Katherine is coming back. She just couldn't do it all at once. Your…" He hesitated. "Your body couldn't handle it."

"Where?" she whispered, her voice raw.

"You're in the basement of one of Elias' safe houses. We brought you here once Katherine stabilized you enough to move."

Her eyes closed with relief.

On the far side of the room, the door swung open, admitting

Katherine. At the sight of the woman, Nathaniel stepped back.

"How are you feeling, your highness?" Katherine asked.

Ashe struggled to find an answer, uncertain what to say. She glanced to Nathaniel.

"She is having trouble speaking," he said quietly.

The woman nodded, her lips tightening. "I'm going to try a bit more healing," she told Ashe. "It may hurt. Just try to keep breathing."

Katherine studied her a heartbeat longer, and then carefully rested a hand on Ashe's chest.

Heat spread beneath her touch. Ashe's hands clenched the edges of the bed as the fire built higher. She gasped and then choked on the air, her body jerking as Katherine sent surge after surge of magic rushing through her. Nathaniel appeared, holding her down as tears leaked from her eyes.

And then the pain faded. The searing heat became warmth, became a breeze, became nothing. She squeezed her eyes shut as residual trembling shook her.

Katherine exhaled, the magic around her vanishing. Gently, Nathaniel released Ashe's shoulders.

"Water," Katherine ordered. He nodded, and strode for the door.

The woman watched him go, and then looked down at her. "If you will permit me, your highness."

Taking Ashe's silence as a response, she carefully pulled up the t-shirt and placed her fingertips on Ashe's chest, delicately examining the skin. A thread of magic shivered beneath her touch, disappearing almost instantly. The woman nodded to herself.

"Come on," she said, pulling the shirt back down.

Putting an arm around Ashe's shoulders, she helped her sit up. A dull ache throbbed in Ashe's chest as she moved, and she winced.

"Take it slow," Katherine admonished.

Jerkily, Ashe nodded. Bracing herself on her outstretched arms, she looked around.

She was on a table, its metal surface covered by layers of what appeared to be quilted mover's blankets. Beside her, a bank of gleaming steel refrigerators lined the wall, while a few cardboard boxes marked with food service labels were stacked in a corner.

Memories filtered in as she caught sight of her blurred reflection on the glistening refrigerator. Pain. Lights and no sound. People running.

She trembled.

Fire. Sebastian's words. Carter's crew. Her hands tightened again around the table's edge. The memories hurt. She could still see their faces. And because of her – because she'd trusted wizards when they'd taught her so much better – all of them were dead.

Anguish welled up, and brutally, she crushed it down. She wanted to believe Sebastian had been lying. That he hadn't killed Spider and the rest. But she'd heard the truth in his voice.

She'd seen it in his eyes.

Nathaniel returned with a glass of water. Right behind him followed Elias, whose face flickered with relief at the sight of her sitting up. He clasped a hand on his wife's shoulder, giving Katherine a grateful look.

Expressionlessly, Ashe took the water, drinking it slowly. As she lowered the glass, she could feel the others watching her.

"What happened?" she asked, forcing her voice to sound neutral. "Nathaniel said I was shot?"

Elias glanced to Katherine. "A human," he said. Ashe's brow furrowed at the words. "Somehow, he followed us and…"

Ashe set the glass on the table, studying the water.

"The bullet missed your heart," Katherine said when Elias fell silent. "For which you were extremely lucky. The man attempted to take additional shots, but by that point the guards had shielded the area."

Nathaniel didn't move, his gaze on the ground, but Ashe could see his jaw muscles jumping.

"He is not dead," Katherine continued, her tone making it clear the status was temporary. "As we concluded bringing him in for questioning would be a better option. The man was… deranged. Raging when the guards intercepted him. He had no difficulty seeing us, and appeared to be specifically targeting you." She paused. "If someone has enlisted humans as assassins in this war, we want to know."

Ashe didn't respond for a moment. "Has he shown any sign of magic?"

Elias made an awkward sound. "Your highness…"

She looked up at him.

"No," he amended. "So far, he just appears to be human."

She hesitated. "I want to see him."

"My lady, I don't think that's a very good idea," Katherine said. "You have barely healed and any stress–"

"I want to see him," Ashe repeated. She paused, resisting the urge to rub the aching space on her chest where the bullet had torn through. "If he's one of the Blood, I'll be ready this time."

Protests marked the faces of the wizards around her, but finally Elias sighed. "As you wish, your highness."

He motioned Nathaniel toward the door and then turned to help her off the makeshift bed.

"What is this place?" she asked as he eased her to the ground.

"It belongs to a friend of mine," Elias said. He caught sight of her expression and continued. "But don't worry, Darius won't find us. Even on the Council, we only trust each other so far – as I guess you figured out. Hideouts, escape plans and the like rarely get shared. And Joe's a good guy; he won't give us up to anyone who comes around – though there's almost no chance they'll ask him anyway."

She gave him a questioning look as she leaned her weight on him, but he didn't say more. The hall outside was narrow, barely affording them space as he helped her along, and the fluorescent strip lights flickered rapidly, making it difficult to watch the cinder-block walls for long. At the end of the corridor, a metal staircase led to the floor above, and near the base, a door waited with a guard by its side.

"I'm alright," Ashe said to Elias, trying to pull away as they reached the door.

"My lady, I–"

"Elias."

He hesitated, and then reluctantly lowered her arm from his shoulders. She winced as he stepped away, and quickly braced herself on the wall while her legs debated whether to hold her. The shakiness passed and taking a breath, she straightened and then nodded to the guard.

He pushed open the door. Letting her magic rise around her, she walked into the room.

And froze.

"Detective Harris?"

Chained to a chair with a pair of guards beside him, the man looked up from his study of the floor. A livid bruise marred his face beneath his disheveled hair, grown longer since last she'd seen him, and every trace of the compassion she remembered in his eyes was gone.

Only hate remained.

At the sight of her, denial surged across his face, followed swiftly by rage. Gritting his teeth, he shook his head. "No…" he growled. "How can you *still* be alive?"

"Do you know this man?" Elias asked her, alarmed.

Floundering, she struggled to drag herself from her shock. "He… he's a detective. From Utah. He…"

Tried to kill me.

She turned away. Hundreds of miles. Nearly half a year of running. And this man had found her. In the midst of all these guards, he'd almost taken her life.

"Is he human?" Elias asked her.

His voice pulled her from her thoughts, and she nodded jerkily. "I-I think so."

She blinked, working to regain her bearings. It didn't matter what he'd done. What could've happened. The bullet and the pain and the fact she could have died weren't relevant right now.

Straightening, she drew a breath, forcing herself to focus. She needed information.

And she could handle the look in his eyes.

"How did you find me, Detective?" she asked, turning back to him.

"I followed the dead," he answered coldly.

Nausea rippled through her core. She fought to keep her face expressionless.

"Her highness didn't kill those people, human," Elias said shortly. "Try again."

Harris' eyebrow twitched up and he scoffed. "*Highness?*" he repeated. His gaze flicked over Ashe, and then the dry humor melted back to loathing. "Figures."

Shaking his head, he continued. "It doesn't matter if you kill me too, you know. They're still going to find you. And they *will* stop you."

Her brow twitched down. She could feel the tension of the others in the room.

"Who?" she asked carefully.

He said nothing, dropping his gaze to the small drain set into the concrete floor. "What's it going to be?" he asked after a moment, almost contemplatively. "Gang killing? Maybe a drug deal gone wrong? Or are you just going to burn me alive like you tried with Scott?"

She trembled.

At his own words, his pensive expression faded. Jaw clenching, he closed his eyes, frustration twisting his face. "I had you," he whispered. "I…"

Breathing hard, he fell silent, and then visibly pushed the emotions aside. "Just get it over with."

She stared at him. "I'm not going to kill you," she said, her voice unsteady despite her efforts.

"So what? You hold me hostage? That's not going to save you. Brogan and Jamison won't negotiate with the likes of you. Not after everything you've done."

The words registered, but they were so deeply wrong, it took her a moment to remember how to speak. "Brogan…?" she repeated carefully.

A flicker of satisfaction moved over his face at the shock in her eyes.

"Brogan's alive?"

His expression was answer enough.

Turning sharply, she strode from the room, the pain throbbing through her chest nothing compared to the blood pounding in her ears. Baffled, Elias motioned swiftly for Nathaniel and the guards to watch Harris before he followed her.

"Your highness?" he called.

"You won't get away with this!" Harris shouted as the door slammed.

Her hands caught the cinder-block wall. Uncomprehending, she stared at the gray surface.

"Highness?" Elias reached out, touching her shoulder in concern.

Startled, she nearly set the hall aflame and he jerked back as the heat rippled from her. Gasping, she dug her fingers into the cinder blocks, fighting to stay in control.

"Ashe?" he tried.

She blinked, the familiarity breaking through where the idiotic titles never would.

"I'm sorry," Elias said as she looked over at him. "I just–"

She shook her head. "No. No, I told you… it's fine. I…"

"Who is Brogan?" he asked carefully when she trailed off.

"The man who killed my dad. And Carter."

Elias grimaced. "So Taliesin's using humans now."

"It wasn't *Taliesin*!" she shouted. Breathing hard, she stared at Elias. "Brogan's a Blood. The bastards who did all this were Bloods. It wasn't ever Taliesin."

She paused, hurt moving over her face as she looked back at the room. "And Detective Harris was working for them."

For a long moment, she watched the door, as though reading answers in the scratched metal. She'd been so terrified when they first met. So lost and confused. And he'd seemed compassionate. Pitying, almost. Like, on some level, he questioned whether she'd done the things they accused her of. Like, in some tiny way, he'd cared.

But he'd just set her up for them. Brought Brogan to the station. Expected that, as hurt and scared as she'd been, she would be easy prey.

Everybody always expected she'd be easy prey.

Slowly, she exhaled, burying the pain, and when she turned back to Elias, she saw him tense at the look in her eyes. "Gather who you can spare from guarding this place," she said. "And get a portal ready to take us downtown."

"Your highness, you can't go out there. You were just shot and I'm–"

"Do you serve the Queen of Merlin or not?" she snapped.

He blinked.

"I've been shot before," she continued more quietly. "Get together who you can spare."

Hesitating, he glanced to the door. "What about him?"

She followed his gaze. "Have Katherine find out what he knows. But don't kill him. We may need him later."

He bowed his head. "And your orders, highness?" he asked, weighing his words carefully. "What should I tell the guards?"

A smile crossed her face, dark and anything but warm.

"Tell them we're going hunting."

Chapter Eleven

The door to the upstairs storage room creaked back and one of his mother's interchangeable middle-aged cousins peeked his head through the opening. With a derisive snort, the man disappeared back into the hallway.

"Move," Cole hissed to Lily, who was feigning sleep at his side.

Scrambling from beneath the musty blankets, the little girl rushed to the door with Cole a step behind.

He'd barely slept all night. The Carnegeans watched them in shifts, and from their icy expressions, he couldn't discount the chance they'd try to take Lily from him the moment his eyes closed. Nearly as bad was the fact they never deviated from their fanatical commitment to security. He'd heard their footsteps pacing the corridor all night long, and gradually, he'd started to despair of ever getting out of the closet-like room.

And then this latest cousin appeared.

Sympathy clearly not a strong suit, Alfred hadn't given a damn when the cousin told him he wasn't feeling well. Striding off to attend to his own breakfast, Alfred left the man sitting in the corridor, shifting uncomfortably in his chair.

It'd only been a matter of time.

By the door, Cole paused, listening intently.

At the end of the hall, the bathroom door closed.

Slipping into the hallway and pulling Lily behind him, he eyed the bathroom as they raced past it on their way to the stairs. The cousin was groaning uncomfortably inside. Gripping Lily's hand tighter, Cole took the steps as fast as her shorter legs could keep up, and hit the first floor nearly at a run. Darting a glance around, he didn't spot anyone, though he could hear plates and silverware clinking in the distant dining room. Hurriedly, he started for the front door.

"Wait!" Lily hissed, tugging on his hand.

"What?"

Her brow furrowed. "The door feels wrong."

"Huh?" Heart racing, he scanned the oak door between glances to the rest of the house. "What? It's fine."

She shook her head, balking. "Check it."

Grimacing, he drew closer to the wood. "Lily, they're changing shifts out there. We've got to—"

Cole cut off at the sight of the thin wire running between the door and the frame. Cautiously, he reached his fingers toward it, ignoring Lily's squeak of incredulity.

Less than an inch from the wire, an ache twinged at the back of his skull. He cursed internally. Physical and magical alarms. Of course.

"Thanks," he told her quietly. "Come on."

Taking her hand again, he headed farther into the house. While he knew it was a long shot, the Carnegeans seemed more inclined to use the parlor's French doors. There was a chance they'd left them disarmed.

Now that he knew what to look for, he could see threads of alarms tracing each window he passed. No control panels marred the pristine eggshell walls, though upon brief reflection, he reckoned the Carnegeans either didn't need them or kept them safely hidden elsewhere.

He heard chairs scraping the dining room floor and his heart hit his throat. Pulling Lily behind him, he rushed through the parlor. All night he'd timed the wizards. They changed shifts every four hours. For a few brief moments, only the security cameras watched the yard, and if the two of them were quick, they might be able to reach the forest or the garage before whoever was watching the monitors could raise the alarm.

"What are you doing out of your room?"

Cole skidded to a halt at the sound of Florence's voice. Vehement cursing ran through his head, but he smothered it swiftly, trying to stay focused.

They weren't screwed yet. Not if he could keep them from being sent back upstairs.

"Are you *leaving*?" Florence continued, her tone becoming ominous.

Forcibly, he swallowed and then turned around, schooling his features into an expression of baffled surprise. "Leaving?" he repeated innocently.

"You little…" she growled. She nodded at him threateningly. "I'm getting your uncles. You're going back to your room and we're chaining you in there this time. I'll not have you jeopardizing–"

"No!" he protested, taking a step toward her and then stopping uncertainly. "It's not like that. I just…" His eyes darted around the room and he shrugged as though vaguely embarrassed. "It was just so hard to stay up there when…"

Florence hesitated. "When?"

His mouth worked as though trying to find the words, while his willpower worked to keep him from choking on them. At his side, Lily watched him unblinkingly.

"When all this is down here," he said. "I mean, I admit, I was really upset before. I said a lot of stupid things. I-I think I just didn't understand. But while we were up there and I started looking around, it just began sinking in, you know? This is everything no one ever told me. Everything…" He swallowed, pressing on. "I could be proud of. And for it to be only a few floors away, I just… I couldn't…" He dropped his gaze to the ground sheepishly.

"I needed to be down here," he finished. "I needed to know."

A heartbeat passed. Barely breathing, he risked a theatrically nervous glance at the old woman.

Motionless in the lofty archway, Florence watched him, her brow twitching in short, indecisive spasms. As he looked up, she blinked, struggling to bury the emotion on her face.

"Do you take me for a fool?" she asked, her harsh tone choked.

"It's not like that! They… they *kept* this from me. The truth, I mean. And with it finally so close…"

He gestured to the books helplessly.

Florence said nothing and then she cleared her throat primly. "And you brought the human down here because?"

Cole glanced to Lily. The little girl's gaze hadn't left him. His stomach churned. "I couldn't trust her to behave without me," he said, forcing the sentence out.

Another moment passed. Drawing a controlled breath, Florence turned to the books as though seeking focus there. Swiftly, Cole cast a look to the door.

The wizards were back. He wrestled down a scowl.

"Well," Florence tried with meticulous precision. "I suppose your curiosity is understandable, given your disadvantaged upbringing. It is logical that you would want to know about the more… respectable parts of your genealogy."

He drove a grateful look onto his face. "Th-thank you."

"But you should have spoken to your uncles," she continued, her tone becoming sharper. "Your desire to learn doesn't excuse leaving your room unsupervised, nor bringing *that* out among the antiquities."

She waved a hand at Lily.

"I'm really sorry," Cole made himself say.

"Still," Florence went on, almost as though speaking to herself. "We are forgiving by nature, and certainly not opposed to cripple education, within reason. Your disobedience can be attended to later. In the meantime, perhaps it would be permissible for you to have some material to study in your room. Provided you don't let *it* touch anything, of course."

Cole struggled not to crush Lily's fingers in his grip. He wasn't going to be able to keep this up much longer. "Of course," he agreed. "But, I just thought… I mean, if I was *really* careful… maybe we could stay here? It's just… all these books… I could learn so much."

Florence pinned him with a stare that didn't seem to want to end.

"Possibly," she allowed. "With supervision. Eventually. If you prove trustworthy with the books in your room."

"But what about the antiques? I can't take those with me and there's so–"

"Enough," Florence interrupted, her harsh tone returning.

He fought to keep from grimacing. There had to be a way to stay on this damn floor long enough for the wizards to change shifts again. Quickly, he looked to the yard, checking on their positions.

They'd all stopped moving, their attention fixed on something in the woods. Cole swallowed, praying it wasn't Ben. If he'd come looking for them, both the farmer and Lily were in serious trouble.

"But," Florence continued in a more conciliatory tone. "As long as you *are* down here, is there a particular artifact that elicited your curiosity?"

"Uh…" he faltered, the desperate look he gave the antiques this time becoming real.

"A thirst for education should be rewarded, Cole."

Cursing internally, he chose an item at random. "I was kind of wondering what that is." He gestured to a wooden staff resting upright in a corner of the glass case behind her.

Turning, Florence raised an eyebrow. "Truly?"

"Or whatever," he amended, glancing to the door again. A few wizards were heading for the trees. His pulse accelerating, Cole continued, "If there's something better to–"

"Quiet," she ordered casually. "I am merely intrigued you chose that particular relic. Of all our antiquities, it is arguably the least valuable kept on this floor."

"Yeah, well," he said distractedly, still watching the yard. "Figures I'd ask about that one, right?"

"Starting with the lesser valued artifacts will only give you a greater appreciation for the more valuable ones. Now, come."

She stepped over to the case and then waited impatiently for him to follow.

Tearing his gaze from the lawn, he reluctantly obeyed. Once he stood by her side, with Lily carefully out of the way, Florence turned the small brass knob and pulled open the door.

"Pay attention. The item we have here–" She pointed illustratively to the staff in case he'd somehow forgotten. "–is alleged to be the so-called 'Staff of Merlin'. Now, most testing indicates that it does indeed hail from that era, and given its apparent propensity for responding solely to members of the royal line, there is a reasonable amount of circumstantial evidence pointing to that identity. However, by noting the rather intriguing nature of its construction, we encounter a few discrepancies. Most significantly, we have the polished and yet almost vine-like character of the wood, with particularly irregular and organic terminations on both ends. There are very few staves originating in this era that possess such qualities, owing to the growing predilection for more refined items during that period. This leads us to conclude that Merlin – an indisputably refined wizard – would never have used such an outmoded accessory. Along that same vein, there are the wear marks, which can be seen at approximately the levels where one would hold this staff. This suggests repeated use by the owner and, as I've already described, *had* Merlin actually owned this, it is highly implausible that he would have used it with such frequency."

She gave him an amused look, as though sharing a joke.

"Uh, yeah," he agreed and then looked back to the yard when she turned to the staff again. The wizards hadn't calmed down. Two of them were on cell phones now. He felt like he was going to crawl out of his skin.

"So how could anyone hold such a silly theory, you ask?" Florence continued obliviously. "Well, there is the aforementioned peculiarity whereby it only reacts to those of Merlin's own family, and it does seem to possess the qualities of a supplementary device, created with the intent of increasing its wielder's powers. On this basis, some fringe historians posit that Merlin may have used such a thing in the binding, though the idea of a wizard of his caliber needing such an item is laughable. He was the premier wizard of his day, a distinction he certainly would not have received by using magical pick-me-ups. And while King Nicholas – the ruler prior to King Patrick; I'll be certain to send up genealogies for your study – and his predecessors acknowledged that it did increase their strength to an estimable degree, they certainly never felt the need to keep it close as some sort of security blanket."

Florence chuckled derisively. "Most historians worthy of note consider stories of Merlin *requiring* something of this nature to be roughly on par with eternal life spells and magical cripples." She laughed merrily and turned back to him. "Children's stories and fairytales. It's all very amusing, really. At least, to the educated community. I'm certain the canaille find such possibilities *fascinating*."

Silence fell as she finished, growing more awkward by the second. He made a noise more cough than chuckle and shifted uncomfortably. "Uh, right."

She gave him an approving smile. "Now," she concluded. "That is undoubtedly enough for you to digest in one day, so perhaps this would be a good time to return you to your room. Though–" She hesitated thoughtfully. "–I suppose sending a book or two with you couldn't hurt. If you feel ready…?"

Eyebrow raised, she waited for his answer.

"Um, sure," he said, using another uncertain look to cover a glance at the yard. Alfred was out there now. The man seemed to be reaming the guards for something.

Ignoring his hesitancy, Florence turned to the shelves. "Perhaps something easy to—"

Cole flinched hard as a crash from the kitchen brought her up short. Startled, Florence blinked at the sound of shattering glass.

"Louise!" she shouted. When no answer came, she darted a glance to Cole and made an impatient motion. "Stay here. Don't let the human touch anything."

Without waiting for a response, she rushed off, yelling for the other woman as she went.

Lily made a disgusted noise.

"Yeah," Cole agreed absently.

He looked back to the yard. Geoffrey was approaching from the forest. At his shout, Alfred left off berating the cousins and turned. The dark-eyed wizard held up a broken camera. Red-faced with rage, Alfred spun back to the others, motioning sharply for them to return to guard duty and then rolling his eyes as they rushed away.

Cole exhaled, his heartbeat slowing. Ben hadn't come looking, then. Or something else hadn't happened to jeopardize Lily's safety. Hopefully, anyway. Running a hand over his hair, he turned back to the parlor, wracking his brain for what to do. With the wizards back on duty, Florence determined to send them upstairs, and alarms on every damn window and door…

From the corner of his eye, he could see Lily regarding the room. Tossing a scathing glance to the kitchens, the little girl reached out, deliberately laying a fingertip on the staff.

White-blue light fluoresced between the twists of wood, casting sharp shadows from everything else in the case. Gasping, Lily jerked backwards.

The light vanished.

Cole stared as, wide-eyed, the little girl looked to him.

"I swear, that woman gets stupider every day," Florence announced as she strode back into the room. "How difficult is it to polish crystal? I mean, honestly?"

With an aggrieved sigh, she pushed the irritation from her expression. "Now, which book should we choose for you?"

Raising a narrow finger, she perused the shelves, conversing with herself quietly as she considered the options.

"Uh…" Cole said, tearing his gaze from Lily. "So the staff. It really only does anything for the, um, royal family?"

She glanced back at him suspiciously. "I told you that."

"No, yeah, I know," he recovered quickly. "I'm just surprised. I didn't know magic could do that."

Her suspicion fading, she nodded. "Wizards have been tying magic to one thing or another for millennia. In the staff's case, it would glow in the hands of the royal family, but remained inert for others. Quite theatrical, really," she added. "Another point to its disadvantage."

The parlor doors swung open and Geoffrey entered, only to come to a stop at the sight of Lily and Cole. "What are they doing down here?" he demanded of Florence.

"One of your dear cousins obviously let the boy and his pet slip past their guard," the woman replied, still examining the books. "I found him here, studying the artifacts."

Geoffrey's gaze slid glacially over to Cole. "Studying," he repeated flatly.

"Even cripples are capable of appreciating history, Geoffrey," Florence admonished with a pointed glance over her shoulder. "To the best of their ability, anyway."

Her son didn't answer, and with a sniff she returned to the books, only to make a pleased noise a moment later. "This should do nicely," she announced.

Turning, she presented Cole with a leather-bound book. Distractedly, he glanced down, catching sight of the words, 'A Merlin Primer: Being a History of True Wizardry' embossed in gold on the cover.

He felt nauseated.

"That should be a good starting point. This edition dates from the early eighteenth century, but we have three copies, so I'm willing to let you borrow it for a short time. But if I see so much as a scratch on that leather or a crease I don't recognize, we're restricting you to reproductions, understand?"

"Yeah," he managed, taking the book.

"I'll have someone bring you a genealogy of the royal family once I find one that won't be too difficult for you to understand. The more detailed accounts …" She shook her head pityingly.

Swallowing, he struggled to keep his gaze from straying back to Lily. "Sure."

Florence glanced to Geoffrey. "Would you mind escorting him back? Your aunt has mussed the cleaning again." She started to leave, and then caught herself. "Oh, and install some additional security measures around his room. He may well prove redeemable, given his desire to learn, but with a human in the house, we can't be too careful."

Geoffrey watched as she walked out of the parlor. "Move," he growled to Cole.

One hand clutching the ridiculous book and the other holding Lily, Cole gave a last glance to the wizards outside and then turned, trying not to swear as he headed back through the house with Geoffrey stalking his heels. Halfway to the fifth floor, they met the cousin rushing down toward them. At the sight of Geoffrey, the man paled.

"I-I just needed to use the–" the man started.

"Shut it," Geoffrey snapped. "I'll deal with you in a minute."

Awkwardly, the cousin let them pass, and Cole could feel the man's gaze on their backs as they continued up the stairway. At the storage room, Geoffrey stepped aside, eyeing them as they walked in.

"Stay," he snarled.

And then he slammed the door.

"Cole…" Lily started worriedly.

"Shh," he hissed. Crossing to the door, he leaned close, listening. Down the hall, Geoffrey was snarling at the cousin, his words mostly indistinguishable, though several shouted obscenities were abundantly clear.

Cole glanced back at the girl. Looking terribly small in the center of the crates, she watched him nervously, the deific painting of Merlin hanging behind her.

"Your dad's name was Patrick," he asked, fairly certain of the answer. "Wasn't it?"

She looked away.

Slowly, he exhaled and then walked the few steps back to the nearest crate, where he sank down. Giving a brief look to the book in his hands, he set it aside and motioned to the girl. She came over and sat next to him.

"It just keeps getting more complicated, doesn't it?" he said.

She nodded.

He glanced up as, on the other side of the door, someone began driving bolts into the frame. Part of their defense against having a human in the house, probably.

Cole closed his eyes.

"What happens now?" Lily asked.

He looked over. Uncertainty radiating from her, she didn't meet his eyes.

"We're still getting out of here," he said, actively ignoring the noises from the opposite side of the door.

Lily's brow furrowed, and he realized that wasn't what she'd been asking.

"Nothing's changed," he told her.

He put an arm around her shoulders. After a moment's hesitation, she leaned against his side.

"So how's it feel to find out you're royalty?" he asked in a feeble attempt at humor.

His weak smile died at the look she gave him. "Yeah," he agreed. "Same here."

A headache surged and then faded as they activated whatever alarms they'd placed on the doorframe. Lily shifted uncomfortably.

Cole didn't take his gaze from the door. Obstacles upon obstacles, and complicated didn't cover it. He had no weapons, and she was just a kid.

A kid with magic. A kid who might kill him if she lost control.

And yet, when the staff burst to life at her touch, there'd been nothing. No pain. Nothing but a vague sense of 'otherness' occurring, which he'd barely registered amid his shock.

He grimaced, cursing himself for even allowing thoughts like this in his head. She was eight years old. She'd die going up against these bastards. Their little display when he and Lily had first driven onto their property was more than enough of an object lesson in how they treated a perceived threat.

He pulled his gaze from the door. Something would change. He'd get them out of here. And he'd do it without using a little kid as a weapon.

Somehow.

———◆———

"Your highness?"

Ashe sighed, closing her eyes. The mid-afternoon sun streamed through the windows, unfettered by the curtains lying in heaps of moldy fabric on the floor, and lit upon the white outlines nearby. Flaking blood splatters dotted the shattered dishware and stained the grimy carpet brown. Bullet holes peppered the walls for good measure, piercing wallpaper that had long since surrendered its color to the years.

It was the third crime scene today. And except for the position of the outlines and the general décor, each one had been exactly the same.

She turned, expressionless, and strode past Elias as she left the room. Wordlessly, Nathaniel pulled the police tape aside, letting her pass.

The breeze felt good on her face, though she could sense the tension in the others as she stepped into the open. Darius' forces might see her. Or the inordinate amount of Taliesin roaming the area would finally spot them. They'd been avoiding both all day, taking portals from one part of the city to the next, hoping to stay a step ahead of everyone looking for them.

It was Elias' idea. Hiding. Running. And she knew he was aware that, on some level, she was just playing along.

She exhaled slowly and then glanced back as a group of teenage boys came out of the building door. Laughing and joking, they jogged down the steps, moving unconsciously around the girl standing in the center of the stairway.

Ashe watched them as they disappeared around the street corner. Not Blood then. Or humans trying to kill them.

Probably not, anyway.

As the heat around her faded, she ran a hand through her hair and turned back toward the door, though her gaze just caught on the sigils hidden in the graffiti on the building's side. A pang of guilt hit her. When she first spotted them, she hadn't recognized the names mixed in with the markers denoting the apartment as a hiding place, and now that she'd seen the inside, she hated the fact her lack of recognition made her grateful.

It didn't matter if she hadn't known the people who died here. Someone had.

With every attempt at casualness, she dropped her gaze away, hoping the wizards hadn't noticed her pause. They didn't know why she was choosing certain buildings over others, and though her unerring ability to find the abandoned crime scenes was leaving them blatantly skeptical, she was determined to keep them in the dark as long as she could.

Just in case.

"Where to?" Elias asked as he came down the stairs. "Somewhere out of sight, I hope?"

She pretended not to hear the annoyance in his voice, or see the disapproval behind Nathaniel's expressionless stare. The large man's stoic gaze at nothing should have sent the thin air running in fear, and the fact he knew she didn't care what the wizards thought right now just made the look more intense.

"Back up top."

"He'll be expecting that."

"Fine."

Elias scowled and then buried the expression with obvious difficulty. With a cursory nod, he turned to the doorway. A heartbeat later, she followed him through the portal, ignoring Nathaniel's impassive attempts at killing the air.

Wind tugged at her as she stepped onto the rooftop. A few yards away, a low concrete barrier separated the gritty surface of the roof from the sky. The sound of traffic rose from over twenty stories below, fading each time the breeze picked up speed.

Without pause, she crossed to the barrier and scanned the streets. By and large, the wizards stuck to nighttime hours when they wanted to move around; even for them, the darkness made it easier to hide. But the rule wasn't hard and fast, and while the sense of otherness around wizards was impossible to detect at this distance, spotting a person no one else seemed to see wasn't as difficult. Humans had a way of steering clear of her kind. To some degree, that avoidance was better than radar.

She tensed, her gaze locking on a man strolling down the street. Without breaking their conversation, two women stepped around him, barely seeming to notice he'd gone past. She started to call Elias, and then stopped. The man tripped on the smooth sidewalk and stumbled sideways, catching himself on a light pole. Waving his hand at the pavement, he launched into a tirade, while the two women looked back, their avoidance obviously intentional all along.

Closing her eyes, she sighed. Another homeless lunatic. Probably, anyway. She contemplated going back down to street level to check, but abandoned the idea as pointless. Of the few she'd seen, they'd all turned out to be human, and it wasn't like Elias' patience was going to last forever. Even among the wizards they'd spotted in the crowds, not a single one looked human when she and the others reached the ground.

Wherever the Blood were hiding, it certainly wasn't Croftsburg.

Opening her eyes, Ashe grimaced at the street. Katherine's questioning of Harris hadn't turned up anything beyond the admission that Brogan was alive. The detective didn't know where the wizard was, or what he would do now. The wizard's cohorts were also a mystery to Harris, as was nearly everything to do with the war. He didn't care about them or Taliesin. He just wanted to stop Ashley and anyone on her side.

As a hostage, the man was essentially useless, and as a human, Katherine believed he couldn't really testify to the 'Blood' even existing. They could still be just Taliesin wizards Ashe had mistaken for something else, or a creation by the same. And though no one said it, she knew that beneath the wizards' obedience lurked fears that she might actually be crazy, or else distraught with grief, which amounted to nearly the same thing.

She ignored Elias as he and Nathaniel walked up beside her, their tension clear. When it came to the Blood, they were playing along with her as much as she was with them. And the clock was ticking on how much longer they'd entertain their charade. With Darius after them and the Taliesin inexplicably everywhere, the others' tolerance of her endangering them all was swiftly fading.

"Your highness!" Elias hissed.

She looked up. On a rooftop two blocks away, a group of Taliesin wizards emerged from a stairwell door.

Swiftly, she dropped behind the concrete barrier, Elias and Nathaniel following suit. By the door, the other guards ducked away.

"How the hell are there so many of them?" she whispered to Elias.

"Because there are."

She glared. "That's not an answer." At his silence, her irritation grew. "I'm serious. The city is crawling with Taliesin. I thought this place was Merlin territory or something."

For a second, he didn't respond, but at her insistent expression, he frowned. "There's no such thing as Merlin territory," he said. "But yes, their numbers have been increasing in the city lately. And until now, we've done a pretty good job of making sure they don't know we're here."

The last was pointed, but as with everything else, she ignored the tone. "Why?"

"Because it's good strategy."

She gave him a flat look, but he returned the favor and pretended not to see it. "Are they still there?" he asked Nathaniel.

The man motioned to the guards.

Cautiously, one leaned out of the stairwell hutch. "Clear," he called.

Nathaniel stood, checking for himself before letting Ashe and Elias rise.

"That's not what I meant," she said, ignoring the twinge in her chest as she reached down to brush the rooftop grit from her jeans. "Why isn't there Merlin territory?"

"Because there are more of them than us," he said shortly. "There always have been."

Turning away, he directed the guards to scout the area surrounding the building.

Brow furrowing, she watched him briefly before returning her gaze to the street. Traffic was slow at this time of day and the people on the sidewalks still gave every sign of being human. As Nathaniel's footsteps moved off, she glanced back again.

"Elias," she called quietly.

Irritation still on his face, he looked over at her.

"Are we losing?"

He paused, the expression fading. For a moment, he said nothing, and then crossed to the barrier and rested his hands on the rough surface.

"We're doing the best we can," he said finally, watching the changing stoplights below.

She swallowed, unsure what to say.

"In the beginning, we tracked the Taliesin," he told her. "Made sure we knew who and where they were. But five hundred years is a long time. And we got lazy. Complacent, really. And they're making us pay for it."

He glanced over, seeing her expression.

"I don't mean that like it sounds," he said. "I'm not saying we should have tagged them like animals. Hell, we did that. We did all of it. Any stupid, vain atrocity you can think of in the name of keeping the 'Taliesin Threat' under control. And after a couple centuries or so, when that got to be too much work… we gave it up. Got bored. Wandered off to study magic while thumbing our noses at the losing team. But the losing team kept growing, and while we blithely enjoyed our unassailable supremacy, they surrounded us on all sides."

"You sound like you sympathize with them," she said, obscurely shocked.

He shook his head. "I don't sympathize with what they've become. Or what they're doing. Murder is murder, regardless of the justifications they give themselves. I mean, what did our children ever have to do with it? Or kids your age? They never asked for this. They've never been in a position to do anything but suffer from it either." He shook his head. "No, I don't pity Taliesin, and I'll damn well kill any of them that try to hurt you or any other Merlin at my side. But I get what started this, and how it's ended us up where we are."

She looked away. Cars pulled to a stop at the lights and then drove on. She didn't see them.

"Was that what my family was like?" she asked.

"No," he replied emphatically.

The answer was too quick. She glanced over, and watched as he turned away.

"Not recently," he amended reluctantly. "But politics are politics, your majesty. And five hundred years of bigotry and bad blood – on both sides – doesn't disappear overnight. King Nicholas tried. God knows, he tried. But, in all honesty, even with his reconciliation programs and attempts at dialogue, it ultimately came down to Taliesin wanting something your grandfather just wasn't sure he could give."

A moment passed and then Elias sighed.

"We should head back," he said.

"There are more places we need to check. We've barely touched the eastern side of town."

Frustration moved over his face. "How much farther are you going to push this?" he asked, keeping his voice low as he tossed a glance at the others. Several yards away and out of earshot, Nathaniel was conferring with the guards. "You haven't slept. You've barely eaten. And, in case you forgot, you nearly *died* twelve hours ago." He grimaced. "There are plenty of people who'd love to finish the job that human started, highness, and I'm not too interested in giving them the opportunity. We should leave town. The cripples aren't here anymore. And these Blood—"

"Don't say it," she warned.

"I wasn't going to. But Darius' people could be anywhere. And our luck in avoiding Taliesin can't last forever. I serve you, yes. I've done what you asked. But if we stick around here, out in the open like this, it's going to get you or someone else killed."

At her silence, he sighed. "If the Blood exist, there's as good a chance they'll be elsewhere as here. And a better chance the cripples will be."

She didn't answer, her eyes on the street below. He was right and she knew it. A handful of crime scenes and near misses proved it, no matter what she'd hoped to find.

Picking through the ruins left by the dead and their murderers wouldn't change what'd happened. It wouldn't bring anyone back.

Letting a breath out slowly, she nodded.

"Thank you," he said.

Quickly, he turned and ordered the guards to get ready to go.

Her hands on the barrier, she watched the people milling around beneath the buildings' shadows. School kids with backpacks on their shoulders and cell phones in their hands walked and texted simultaneously, while businessmen hurried to late afternoon meetings. Traffic was gradually picking up, joined by an increase in city busses depositing people on the street corners.

And every one of them looked human.

She felt the portal forming behind her and she sighed. Perhaps she could convince Elias to head south. Brogan and the others had followed her there; they might still be in the area.

"We're ready," Elias called.

She scanned the streets one last time, and then turned away from the view. Crossing the rooftop, she followed the others into the portal.

Landmarks appeared and disappeared in rapid succession, leaving her head spinning by the time they emerged through a white trellis archway on the fringe of a massive lawn. The smell of lilacs hit her in a cloud, emanating from carefully cultivated bushes all around them. She sneezed, and then winced at the twinge it sent through her chest.

Turning immediately, Elias began crafting the next portal to carry them closer to the suburb where Katherine and the others were hiding. Warily, the guards watched the enormous houses of the historic neighborhood, while on the porch of a Queen Anne nearby, a toy poodle began barking madly as it retreated toward the door.

Ashe grimaced and hurried into the portal to escape the high-pitched yapping.

Pigeons fled to the sky as the wizards stepped out of a picnic gazebo and into a park on the edge of the suburbs. In the distance, Ashe could see skyscrapers glinting in the late afternoon light, and several dozen yards away, a group of mothers chatted on benches while their children ran shrieking through the playground.

"Almost there," Elias said.

The others didn't answer. Ashe just closed her eyes, relieved to escape the noise and smog of the city. Taking a breath of comparatively fresh air, she waited for her head to clear.

"You sons of bitches, get away from me!"

Her eyes snapped open.

Two Merlin raced into the park, a few steps behind a man so lost beneath layers of coats, he could barely be seen. With sleeves flapping around his pumping arms, the man dashed across the grass, throwing panicked looks over his shoulder as he ran.

His hood fell back. An absence of magic registered on her.

Elias yelled at her as she took off.

On the playground, the mothers left their benches and gathered their children hastily, their attention locked on the crazy homeless man screaming at nothing. Ashe raced past them. Eyes widening at the sight of her, the man skidded to a halt, his feet sliding from beneath him to deposit him on the grass. Scrambling sideways, he tried frantically to keep simultaneous focus on the wizard in front of him and the wizards behind.

The ferals stopped. Their eyes ran over her contemptuously. "Well, fancy seeing you here," one said as the other glanced back at the guards running to catch up.

Instantly the wizards' magic rose, lashing out at her and the cripple. In rapid succession, it vanished. Derision gave way to shock on the men's faces, and then surrendered to horror as the magic of Nathaniel and the guards swept around her and struck them hard.

The two wizards toppled to the ground, their vacant eyes staring at the sky. Jogging past her, the guards approached them, nudging the bodies before dismissing them from attention. Coming up beside her, Nathaniel said nothing, though she could feel the displeasure radiating from him in waves.

Breathing hard, the cripple scrambled to his feet. Raising his hands defensively, he stared at them.

"We're not going to hurt you," Ashe said.

He didn't respond. Amid the dirt crusting his scruffy face, his gaze darted from one wizard to the next, seeking an opening.

She motioned for the others to move back. Coming to a stop nearby, Elias paused and then nodded to the guards. The cripple's eyes narrowed warily at the sight.

"I promise," Ashe continued. "We won't hurt you. We want your help."

The wariness melted into terror. "Oh, hell," the man swore, looking around in a panic.

"It's okay!"

"Hell it is," he protested, inching toward a space between two guards that was wider than the others. "I know that line. Everybody knows that line. They trust wizards. Then they end up dead. Well, not this cripple. Uh-uh."

She paused. "We're not–"

"Oh, pull the other one, girl," he retorted, his voice tremulous despite the forced bravado in his tone. "'Cause I'm *damn* sure it's got bells on."

Under his layers of coats, she could see the man shaking. His skin was bloodless beneath the dirt, and she couldn't tell if he was breathing anymore.

"It's not–"

His scoff spoke volumes.

She fell silent. Her gaze dropped to the dead ferals behind him.

Somehow, she'd just thought it would be that easy. Or at least hoped it would be. Everyone she'd known was dead and everything she'd had was gone, but she could still do something for the people who were left. Help them. Change their minds.

And somehow undo part of the damage Darius had done.

Feeling like an idiot as her stomach twisted inside, she nodded. "Right," she said quietly.

His brow drew down.

Distantly, she jerked her chin at the guards. "Step aside. Just… let him go."

He stared as the wizards moved back, creating a path. Darting forward, he made it a few feet before skidding to a stop, a renewed expression of dread flashing across his face.

"Oh, no way," he said emphatically. "You're just going to kill me when my back's turned. That's what wizards do. You think it's okay to say no to them and then…"

Making an illustrative noise, he shuffled from one foot to the other, trying to keep them all in view. "You just want me to think it's safe, because that'll make it more fun. Well, I'm not falling for that either."

"It's not like that," Ashe said.

The fearful certainty in his eyes grew.

She looked down, grimacing. "I want you to go so you can warn them. Every cripple still out there. Warn them never to trust a wizard." She paused, her gaze returning to the dead ferals. "No matter who that wizard says sent them."

Incredulity pushed through his panic. "W-what?" he sputtered. He hesitated, his brow furrowing with suspicion. "Who are you?"

"I'm the one who's actually trying to destroy the Blood." She jerked her chin at the ferals. "They're the ones who used my name to get my friends killed."

The sickened feeling grew and she turned away, walking back toward the gazebo.

"You're Ashe, aren't you?"

She glanced back. "Yeah."

"Well… what are you going to do?" he called as she started away again.

"What I said."

Nathaniel and Elias fell in beside her as the guards pulled back, their eyes still on the cripple standing in the middle of the empty park.

"Well, then… what if I did help you?" the man yelled.

She stopped. Looking back over her shoulder, she watched as he hesitantly started toward them. Eyeing the wizards around her, he came to a stop a few yards away.

"You'd let me kill them?" he asked, a hint of challenge in his tone. "Some of the Blood, I mean?"

Pausing a moment, she nodded. "Yeah."

Still watching the wizards, he edged closer. "You for real about this?"

She nodded again.

"Huh," he allowed. Inside his coats, he shifted in a loose approximation of a shrug. "And you'd really let me kill them?"

"We have to find them first."

The statement seemed to strike him as funny, and his lips pulled back, revealing yellowed teeth. The displeasure coming from Nathaniel was palpable, but she ignored it.

"What's your name?" she asked.

"Mud."

Her lip twitched. "Nice to meet you."

He gave an uneasy snort. "Yeah, right. So now what?"

Elias cleared his throat. "Can I talk to you for a second?" he asked under his breath.

Reluctance hit her, but she looked over at him, turning partly from the circle of wizards.

"You're not thinking of bringing him with us," Elias whispered. "Are you?"

She raised an eyebrow. "What's our other option? Leave him out here?"

He frowned. "No, we find a place for him to hide–"

"With no protection?"

"It's your protection I'm worried about."

"And having cripples with us is part of that. He can see Blood wizards, Elias. And if Detective Harris is any indication, they've graduated from wanting to capture me to wanting me dead, so…"

Frustration moved over his face. "I get that. But it doesn't mean I want someone who is possibly unstable hanging out in one of the few places we've got to hide you. What if he…?"

He trailed off, unwilling even to say it.

"What do you suggest?" she asked. "If the Blood get close to where we're staying and there's no one to see them…"

She glanced back at Mud. The man was scratching at something beneath his coats, while casting surreptitious looks to the wizards nearby.

"It'll be worse than this," she finished, trying not to grimace. "Trust me."

Elias followed her gaze. "What makes you think you can trust him?"

"Nothing. But we still need his help."

Reservations heavy in his expression, Elias regarded the cripple for another moment and then drew a breath.

"Then he's staying under guard," he said. "As is any other cripple we find. And they're not going near you unless you've got defenses against guns up and there are at least two other wizards in the room." He looked at her pointedly. "Agreed?"

She paused. More than she'd ever seen it, his expression was utterly intractable.

"Agreed."

"And we're still heading back to the hideout."

She looked away angrily, hating how perceptive he could be.

"I mean it, your highness. Just because we have a cripple with us doesn't mean these Blood wizards will suddenly show up. And it doesn't change the fact you need sleep. Hell, the guards do too. We've all been up for nearly two days straight."

She didn't answer. His face darkened.

"Fine," she surrendered bitingly.

"Good. Then I'll go secure us transportation."

Before she could speak, he turned, motioning sharply to the guards. "Search him," he snapped, and then strode toward the street.

"What's going on?" Mud called, eyeing one of the guards uneasily as they came close.

Her jaw tightening, Ashe watched Elias a moment longer and then glanced back. The guard prodded the misshapen lump of a man and then retreated, looking vaguely ill as he nodded.

Uneasiness moved through her, and she pushed it away.

"We're getting out of sight," she told him. "Care to join us?"

He shifted in what she could only assume was a shrug. "Okay."

Without another word, she turned and followed Elias, Mud coming shuffling after.

Chapter Twelve

———◆———

Turning on the leather seat of the SUV, Ashe glanced back, checking the location of the other car. Through the windshield, she could see Mud sitting squarely in the middle of the sedan's back seat, his head moving like a wind-up toy as it ticked back and forth between the wizards in front of him.

With a dry expression, she shifted back around, only to catch sight of a fluffy stuffed animal wedged by the trunk door. She grimaced. "You sure you'll be able to return the cars after we're done?"

"We'll put them somewhere the police can easily find," Elias said, as though he hadn't already told her twice.

She looked to the window, feeling vaguely embarrassed, though Nathaniel and the other two guards gave no sign of having heard.

Beneath the brilliant gold of the setting sun, the suburb rolled by. Storefronts glinted in the light and signs for fast food restaurants flickered to life between one blink and the next, while traffic rushed along, bringing commuters home.

Two police cars flew past, their lights wheeling.

Uncomfortably, Ashe looked away.

As the sun crept below the horizon, the vehicles turned, weaving into a parking lot. The mammoth sprawl of a shopping mall occupied the center of the concrete expanse, the radiant signs on its sides advertising the countless stores within. Outlying shops dotted the edges of the parking lot, their signs and sale banners dwarfed by the enormity of the building behind them.

Brow furrowing, she glanced to the others as Elias thumbed on his phone to make a call.

"We need to use the door," he said without preamble. A heartbeat later, he hung up and looked to the driver. "Around back."

The man nodded.

Circling the massive building, the vehicles headed for a restaurant on the furthest edge of the lot. Dense maple trees backed the building, obscuring the neighborhood beyond, though in the dimming light, the broad front windows gave a clear view of all the customers inside. Beneath the bright sign over the entrance, more people milled around, waiting for a table.

Her eyes narrowed as she read the cheerfully stylized sign. Joe's, Open Late. She hadn't seen the place they were staying; they'd taken a portal straight from the basement when they left this morning. But despite the food service boxes and refrigerators, she hadn't expected their hiding place to be somewhere quite so obviously popular.

Avoiding the busy restaurant parking lot, the driver steered them around to the rear of the building. By the back door, dumpsters sat within a corral of brick walls. Leaning on the enclosure, a busboy smoked a cigarette, his attention on the trees and the sky.

Continuing on, the driver waited till the dumpster's bulk was between them and the young man before pulling to a stop, the other vehicle right behind.

Elias glanced to her and then looked to the driver. "Somewhere easy to find," he told the man. "And make sure the police can't connect the cars to Joe."

The driver nodded.

Studying the building, Ashe climbed out. No windows covered this side of the restaurant, but the front and back entrances were the only ones she'd seen. She glanced over, biting her lip as Mud clambered from the sedan. If they kept Mud toward the center of their group, their magic might obscure him enough to distract the busboy. But it might not. And then she wasn't sure what they'd do.

"Come on," Elias said, breaking into her thoughts. Without looking back, he started for the restaurant door.

She glanced to Mud again, and then followed.

The kid didn't look over as they came near. Exhaling the smoke from his cigarette, he grimaced, shifting uncomfortably against the brick wall. Tensing, Ashe glanced to Mud. In the shadows of his hood, the man barely seemed to be breathing, his gaze locked on the busboy.

With a clang, the back door swung open. Heart pounding, Ashe looked to Elias as a large man strode from the building. Ruddy-faced with a splattered apron lashed around his middle, he was nearly the height of Nathaniel, though more than twice the girth. At the sight of the busboy, he froze and then turned a deeper shade of red.

"What the hell, Tommy?" he snapped. "If you're going to smoke, at least get your tail over by the trees where people can't see you!"

"Huh?" the boy sputtered.

"We've had complaints about people smoking back here. It carries through the air ducts. Stinks up the dining area. So from now on, you smoke by the trees, got it?"

"But no one told me about any–"

"You talking back to me?"

"No."

The man nodded, expecting the answer. "Good. Now get over there."

For a moment, the busboy eyed him up and down, as though trying to decide if the guy had suddenly lost his mind. When the man's expression became darker, the kid held up a hand defensively and then shrugged away from the brick wall to head for the trees. Shaking his head, the man watched him go.

"Sorry about that," he said, glancing to Elias.

Ashe blinked. Though he seemed utterly human, the man was nevertheless looking right at them. Shocked, she glanced back to Mud.

"Blood?" she mouthed.

The cripple looked startled and then shook his head hurriedly.

"Come on in," the man continued with a jerk of his chin toward the door. "I'll keep the others distracted while you get your friends downstairs."

Elias nodded and then followed him inside. Cautiously, Ashe trailed after them.

A wave of heat hit her as she came in, emanating from the kitchen ahead. Pots and dishware clanged in the massive sinks, enormous ovens poured out warmth, and everywhere she looked, people were hurrying around preparing food, picking up food, and depositing dishes still partly covered in food. Past the swinging doors, the dining area was full, and the noise of the restaurant pushed against the general clamor of the kitchen.

Striding on ahead, the large man walked to the entrance of the narrow back door hallway and then paused, surveying the frenetic hubbub like a ruler overlooking his kingdom. Through a sixth sense all their own, the cooks and waitresses seemed to perceive his presence without ever looking his way, and almost instantly, the pace of the kitchen accelerated.

From the corner of her eye, she saw Elias smile. She glanced to him questioningly, but he just turned to the small door beside the rear entrance. Nudging aside a few boxes with his foot, he pulled the door open and then headed down a metal stairway to the basement.

With a last wary look to the man by the kitchen, Ashe followed.

"What was that?" she asked as the door swung shut behind them. "How did he–"

"Long story," Elias said.

Her brow drew down, but he pretended not to notice as they reached the bottom of the steps.

Katherine emerged from the small room where they were keeping Harris. Wiping her hands as though to rid them of invisible dirt, the woman grimaced and then froze in mid-motion as she noticed their approach.

Carefully, she returned her hands to her sides. "Welcome back," she said. She paused as Mud came down the stairs. "Who is our guest?"

"He says his name is Mud," Elias said, his tone barely disguising what he thought of the statement.

Glowering beneath his hood, Mud muttered something unintelligible, and then blanched at a low noise from Nathaniel.

"I see," Katherine said neutrally, stepping to one side to allow the guards to pass.

"Have you found out anything from Harris?" Ashe asked before the cripple could make another comment.

Katherine sighed. "He remains obstinate." Her mouth tightened. "I could try to press him a little…"

"No," Ashe said, her voice sharper than she intended. She paused, regrouping. "No," she repeated more quietly.

"As you wish."

Mud looked between them. "Who?"

Katherine glanced to her husband. "I have a cot made up for you in the other room, your highness," she began carefully.

Ashe shook her head, trying to look reassuring. "I'm not tired. Listen, do you think a few of the others might be rested enough to–"

She cut off as Elias' expression hardened.

"Who's *in* there?" Mud demanded, stepping closer. "I mean it. I'm not hanging around if you've got bad guys behind every door. Seriously. You–"

"It's just a human," Ashe interrupted, forcing the dismissive words in the hope of getting the man to shut up.

"Who works for our enemies and shot her majesty," Elias said to her pointedly.

"You were *shot?*" Mud repeated to her.

"And I'm fine now," Ashe retorted, trying to ignore the little man. "Elias, I understand that the others need rest, okay? But I'm *fine*, and Mud being here is the first progress we've had all day. I'm not going to just–"

"We had an agreement."

"Things've changed."

"Not that."

"Listen, your queenness, if you were just shot, I mean…" Mud eyed her up and down as though shocked she was still standing. "I mean…”

Fury rising, she didn’t bother looking at him. “People are *dying* out there,” she said to Elias. “And now we can finally do something about it. We can’t afford to just sit here–”

“*You* can’t afford to have another assassin get lucky!” Elias snapped. Scowling, he reined himself in and continued more quietly. “And neither can we.”

She looked away.

“We had an agreement, your highness. Just a few hours of rest.” He paused. “Please.”

A heartbeat passed. From the corner of her eye, she could see Elias growing angrier.

“Fine.”

“Thank you.”

Not sure what to say, she turned, heading for the room where she’d woken up that morning. Nathaniel followed.

“How bad was she shot?” she heard Mud ask as she left.

No one answered him.

At a quiet noise from Nathaniel, she hesitated and then stepped to one side, letting him precede her into the room. In a corner, a sleeping bag lay open beneath a pile of pillows. Frustration still gnawing at her, she sank down cross-legged on the soft surface and propped an elbow on her knee. Rubbing her eyes briefly, she sighed, letting her forehead rest on her palm.

Exhaustion settled over her like a blanket, and after a heartbeat she jerked back, realizing she’d drifted off almost instantly. Grimacing more for Elias being right than anything, she shifted around on the sleeping bag and then paused, seeing Nathaniel still standing on the far side of the room.

"You're just going to stay there?" she asked.

He nodded once.

Uncomfortable, she glanced around the room.

"You really don't have to. I'm fine."

He said nothing, his gaze on the wall. Studying him a moment, she weighed her chances of getting him to leave.

"Right," she said.

Turning around on the blankets, she lay down with her back to the massive wizard and, after a second's hesitation, warily closed her eyes.

The room was dim when she opened them again.

Blinking, she rolled over. Nathaniel stood as she had left him, though the lights overhead were almost extinguished. The air was cool, and as she moved, she realized one of the quilted mover's blankets lay atop her.

She glanced at Nathaniel again. The man didn't look away from the wall.

Pushing the heavy blanket back, she climbed out of the sleeping bag and then rose to her feet.

"Thanks," she told him.

The man hesitated, and then bowed his head slightly, expressionless.

Pausing, she glanced from the wizard to the door, knowing the moment she moved he'd want to leave first. Reading her look instantly, he strode to the doorway and surveyed the area outside before nodding for her to follow.

At the end of the hall, a guard still stood watch outside the room holding Harris. "Where's Elias?" she asked, directing the question to him and Nathaniel equally.

"Upstairs," the guard replied.

She cast a look to the stairs skeptically, wondering why he was up there. With a distracted nod, she thanked the guard and then headed up to the kitchen.

Darkness greeted her at the top of the steps. Moving carefully around the boxes by the door, she walked into the shadowy kitchen, her shoes squeaking softly on the checkerboard tile. Stacks of pots and pans were tucked away in the shelving all around her, their metal reflecting the dim light coming through the small window in the dining area door. On the wall, a large clock showed the lateness of the time, and she grimaced, trying not to regret the extra hours of rest.

Nathaniel pushed open the swinging door and then held it for her. Dark red carpet deadened the sound of her footsteps as she walked into the room, and over the polished wood tables, most of the light fixtures were dark. From the walls, assorted pictures of everything from old sport teams to bizarrely painted animals gazed down on her, and in a corner, Elias sat with the man who'd met them outside earlier that day. Beneath the glow of a yellow-shaded lamp, the men were leaned back in their chairs, and Elias was shaking his head amusedly. A steaming plate of food sat between them, and on the wall above, the poster of a black-and-white science fiction movie hung, the characters pointing in horror at the plastic models of spaceships in the sky.

As the door swung closed, the men looked over. Grin broadening, the large man shifted his bulk out of his seat and rose to meet her. "Hey there," he said, sharing his friendly smile with her and Nathaniel both. "Name's Joe."

He extended a calloused hand. Mirroring Nathaniel's caution, she shook it carefully, her fingers lost in his massive palm. "Ashe," she answered.

"Nice to meet you. Are you hungry? Come have a seat."

Obeying his own direction, he started back toward the table.

"We need to get going," she said, directing the words mostly to Elias.

The wizard hesitated. "Joe just heated this up for us, your majesty. With your permission, it'll only take a moment to finish."

Hearing the message behind the words, she paused, and then glanced back as Nathaniel silently headed for a table near the windows to keep watch on the parking lot.

Burying her frustration, she walked over to join Elias.

"So…" Joe said as she sat down. He motioned welcomingly to the plate of breadsticks and cheese dip in the middle of the table. "Elias tells me you're queen to his folks?"

For all his friendliness, he didn't seem quite able to keep the skepticism from his voice. She paused in reaching for a piece of bread, casting a glance to Elias.

"Something like that," she answered, returning her attention to the food.

He grinned. "So you tell Mr. Wizard here what to do, eh?" he ribbed.

From the corner of her eye, she could see Elias carefully look down at the table. Uncomfortable, she said nothing.

"Ah," Joe said, smile fading awkwardly. Waffling for a moment, he took another bite of the bread and cheese. "So… cheese dip good?"

Wiping the corner of her mouth, Ashe nodded and then swallowed. "Yeah, thanks."

"Secret recipe," he said. Elias gave him a dry look and the man's grin returned. "Not really," he admitted. "It's just cheddar and cream with a few spices thrown in. You like it, I can always heat up more."

Uncertain what to say, she gave him another neutral smile. "Thanks," she said again.

He shrugged amicably.

A moment passed in silence.

"So…" she began.

"You're wondering how I can see you lot, right?" Joe filled in. He grinned. "Guess you all just make an impression on a man."

Brow drawing down, she glanced to Elias.

Reluctance flashed across the wizard's face. "Joe's daughter got caught in the crossfire a few years back," Elias explained.

She looked back at the large man in surprise. "Was she–"

"Danielle's fine," Elias said succinctly.

She glanced at him curiously. Leaning back in his seat, Joe scoffed as though the words were an understatement.

"So–" Ashe started.

Elias pushed away from the table. "How about I go see if Mud's finished up?" he offered, heading for the kitchen as he spoke.

"Tell him to lay off if he's not," Joe called. "Weird little guy was eating me out of business last I saw."

Lifting a hand in agreement, Elias disappeared through the door.

Ashe watched him go. "Why…?"

"He doesn't like to talk about what happened to Danni," Joe said. He cleared his throat. "I mean Danielle. Twelve going on twenty, my girl. Claims she's too grown up for daddy's nicknames."

She glanced back as he chuckled to himself.

"Not his fault," Joe said to her expression. "Just blames himself, I think. Hates that a kid got caught in this mess."

"What happened?"

"Eh," he said, shrugging expansively. "A couple of those Taliesin folks ambushed Elias and his lady. And Danielle and I were walking back from a movie. Been going every weekend since her mom died. Loves the romantic comedies, my girl. Puts a man to shame, being seen in them, but what am I going to do? So one minute we're walking along, and the next, my girl's bleeding like she's been hit by a firebomb."

Ashe swallowed, and Joe nodded. "I know, right?" he said. "So yeah. I'm standing there, my brain trying to make up all these explanations, but honestly, I've no idea what just happened. And meanwhile, there's my Danni, bleeding.

"Now, from what I've learned over the years, most of your kind just leave her, right? Collateral damage or whatever. But Katherine and Elias, they just pop out of nowhere, far as I can tell. He's bleeding and she's got murder in her eye, but he still grabs Danni and starts dragging her to the alley, while Katherine… well, she's making my head spin. Everything is. Can't really see her, can't tell what the hell's going on, but next thing I know, my girl's back on her feet, and those two are telling us to run like the devil's on our tail. Danni doesn't know what happened; she's just scared and wants to go home. But me… I know what I saw. My Danni was hurt. Now she's not. And these two? They just take off. Yell at us to run and then do it themselves. Like I'm supposed to forget what just happened.

"Well, I get Danni home, and she tosses her clothes in the laundry like she can't even see the blood. But me… like I said. I know what I saw. Leaves an impression on a man, watching someone you care about bleeding to death from something you can't explain."

Her gaze dropping to the table, Ashe said nothing.

"So yeah," Joe continued, lost in his story. "Danni doesn't remember. There's nothing on the news at all. But here I am, knowing damn well my girl was bleeding her poor little heart out not two hours before, and I've got nothing to prove it. My mind's trying to explain it, but…"

He grimaced, shaking his head.

"And then Katherine shows up. Just walks in from the living room like she's been there the whole time. Scared the daylights out of me, I'm telling you. Her too. Don't think she expected anyone to notice her stopping by."

Joe chuckled. "It's pretty rare, from what I understand. My kind seeing yours. Almost never happens, really. But when it comes to someone hurting my Danni, well… you better have more than magic up your sleeve to make me forget that. And Katherine, she'd snuck a peek at Danni's ID with the full intent of coming by to check on her after the dust had gone down. *Check* on her," he repeated. "Total stranger, Katherine was. And here she came, determined to make sure my girl was alright."

He shook his head again. "Danni was. Totally healed. Not a scratch on her. Because of them." He sighed. "So I have to thank them, right? But what do I have? Money? What good is that when my girl could've died? But when Katherine tells me what the hell's going on, well, then I see a way. Got this restaurant, right? And who's going to pay attention to a human in the middle of you all's war?" He grinned. "So we made a deal. And the rest, as they say, is history."

"I'm glad they could help her," Ashe said quietly, not knowing how else to respond.

Joe scoffed. "You and me both."

Oblivious to the awkward silence, he reached over, drawing

another breadstick from the plate. She looked away, her gaze moving over the walls without landing on any image in particular.

She hadn't known how to heal. Wasn't good at it even now. Five months ago, she hadn't even known what magic was. And Harris worked for the Blood. Maybe Malden had too.

Or maybe not.

Stomach twisting, she tried to push the memories away.

The kitchen door opened. Grateful for the interruption, she looked over as Elias returned, Mud trailing after him. Baggy coats still enveloped the man, making him look like a shuffling laundry pile. As he came closer to the light, however, she could see he'd made some effort to remove the dirt on his face, leaving scrubbed patches of paler skin amid the caked-on mess.

"What's going on?" Mud asked, a half-eaten sandwich in each hand.

"You leave me any food down there?" Joe replied.

Mud gave him a blank look, and the man snorted. Rising heavily to his feet, he shook his head and then glanced to Elias.

"Lock up if ya'll use the doors, eh?"

"Sure."

Still shaking his head, Joe headed back toward the kitchen, muttering about weird men being bad for business as he went.

"What was that about?" Mud asked, looking around nervously.

Shuffling sideways, he edged back from Nathaniel as the wizard left his surveillance of the parking lot and came over to the table.

"Nothing," Ashe said. She took a deep breath, trying to focus. "Mud, do you know of any other cripples hiding around here?"

Elias frowned.

"What?" she asked at his expression.

"We should leave town, your highness. We discussed this."

Her eyebrow twitched up. "After finding Mud here? What if there are others?"

"What if there aren't?"

"We still need to make sure. We'll need their help to find the Blood."

Elias looked away.

"So?" she prompted Mud.

Awkwardly, the cripple cast another glance to the kitchen and then gave a lopsided shrug. "Listen, your queenness. I risk my own life, alright? Not other's. I mean, folks don't seem to like me much, but I'm still not going to just volunteer them to get killed, okay?"

She couldn't believe what she was hearing. "We're trying to help them, Mud. The ferals are still out there."

"Yeah, well," he hemmed, shifting beneath his coats. "I mean…"

"And we're not going to force anyone to help us," Ashe pressed.

His mouth worked around again, as though struggling with a tough bit of food. "I don't know…"

"You're risking their lives by *not* telling us where they are."

"But how do I know that, huh?" Mud retorted defensively. "You've got your wizard guards haunting my every step, and just because you haven't killed me yet, doesn't mean–"

"*What?*"

"Well…"

Pushing to her feet, she shook her head incredulously. "Are the others ready to head back out?" she asked Elias.

"What're you doing?" Mud asked.

"Your majesty…" Elias started.

"*Are* they?"

Elias grimaced. "Yes."

"Good." She hesitated, her skin crawling at the necessity of stealing another car. "Then we'll hit the eastern side of town as soon as you find transportation."

With a resigned nod, Elias started back toward the kitchen.

Looking between them in shock, Mud shuffled backward. "So what? You're just going out there? But you don't even know if anybody else is in town. They could have left. Or–"

"Have they?" she asked.

"I dunno."

Fighting hard to keep her irritation in check, she took a breath, and then paused, watching the little man shift his weight from one foot to the other with an expression lost somewhere between defensiveness and bravado.

"Are you *scared*, Mud?" she asked.

Surprise flashed across his face, swiftly hidden. "No."

"You know you'll have half a dozen wizards around you if you go out there?"

Mud shrugged. "Just think it's safer if we stay here or whatever…"

At the kitchen door, Elias glanced back, giving them both a dry look. She ignored him.

"We're heading out either way," she told Mud. "But it'll go a lot better if you come too. And if you tell us what you know."

Unwillingness twisting around his face, Mud shrugged again. "Okay…"

"Are there other cripples around here?"

Mouth working reluctantly, he wouldn't meet her eyes. "I might've seen a few roaming the north side of town."

"What about anything more specific than that?" She cast an

oblique look to Nathaniel, uncomfortable. "You know, signs where they might be hiding or something?"

Mud's brow furrowed. "Signs?"

Ashe hesitated. "Or whatever."

He looked at her like she was crazy. "Didn't notice anybody putting up posters, if that's what you mean. I just spotted some folks with dogs over in this industrial area. Homeless-looking types. Might be cripples. Could just be humans." Defaulting to a shrug again, he glanced between her and Nathaniel. "I mean, hell if I know, right?"

"Okay," Ashe said. "What about the Blood? Any of them around?"

At this, he chuckled. "You kidding?"

Her eyebrow twitched up and he gave another snort of laughter.

"Your people been killing my kind off left and right, your queenness. The Blood'll be here. Trust me."

"But have you seen them?" she persisted, struggling not to react to the words.

"What? You think I've been looking?"

She mirrored a shrug at him. "I just think you have a better chance of spotting them than we do," she said, a hint of tension breaking through her voice.

He shifted his weight awkwardly. "Yeah, well…"

She waited.

"I haven't seen them," he admitted. "But they've got to be here. Like I said, you hung out the welcome sign when you killed off everyone who might notice they were around."

At Ashe's expression, Nathaniel made a low warning noise.

"I mean, not you *personally*," Mud backtracked. "Just, you know, wizards. I mean–"

"Yeah," Ashe cut in tightly. She glanced at Nathaniel. "North side of town?"

He nodded and then turned his laser gaze on Mud. "Move."

"Now, wait a sec. I didn't say I was going," the man protested. "I don't think any of us should just rush out and–"

At another noise from the wizard, he blanched and then retreated toward the kitchen.

Nathaniel's eyes flicked to her, concern showing through his stoic expression. She nodded. Taking a deep breath, she followed him from the room.

———— ◆ ————

"They're probably not even here anymore," Mud groused, watching the cars pull away. "This isn't a good idea."

Eyeing the industrial chaos, Ashe ignored him. Thin drizzle drifted down from the pitch black sky, coating everything. Blocky gray buildings lurked ahead, framed by metal girders and pipes like permanent scaffolding. Above the structures, lifeless smokestacks rose into the night to be lost in the rain, while past the torn chain-link fence behind her, a dead streetlamp gaped down on the street, casting no light.

"Where to?" she asked.

Mud grimaced, and then caught sight of Nathaniel and Elias behind her. From his expression, she could only imagine what their faces looked like, but he lifted an arm grudgingly, pointing deeper into the complex. "Down there."

"So lead the way," Nathaniel growled.

Horror flickered across the man's face.

"We'll be right behind you," Ashe said.

"I–" he started, and then cut off, swallowing hard. Casting furtive looks to the wizards, he shuffled toward the buildings.

She glanced back at Nathaniel. Expressionless, he bowed his head and then motioned for the other guards to fall in around her.

Deep shadows closed in as they entered the complex. Drawing slow breaths, Ashe scanned the darkness, unable to see if anything marked the walls. Despite walking carefully, gravel still crunched beneath their feet, the sound carrying through the susurrus of the rain. Around her, the others watched the girders and pipes, wary of an ambush.

She could feel her heart pounding. People with dogs, Mud had said. There wasn't a chance in hell Elias or Nathaniel would let her go on alone, but at the first hint of wizards, the dogs were bound to go berserk. And then, if the people ahead were cripples, things would really get tricky.

Swallowing, she concentrated on keeping just enough magic around herself to stop a bullet, hoping it wouldn't attract attention.

Gravel crunched ahead and she heard a dog growl. Breath catching, she glanced to the others, but they were already moving. Scrambling backward, Mud rushed for the space between two thick pipes, while the guards fell back. Following them, Ashe ducked through the entrance of a nearby building.

A heartbeat passed. Ignoring the quiet noise of displeasure from Nathaniel, she cautiously leaned her head around the doorframe, watching the opening at the end of the gravel stretch.

The footsteps came closer.

In the paler shadows ahead, a teenage boy stepped into view. The drizzle matted his unkempt red hair, and with a thin hand, he clutched the makeshift collar of the scruffy mutt at his side. For a long moment, he stared at the deep shadows between the buildings, barely moving.

Then he looked at the dog quizzically. Seeming uncertain, he turned and walked away.

Ashe exhaled. The kid was a cripple. So far, mostly good.

She glanced up at Nathaniel. The wizard watched the space left by the boy for a few more heartbeats, and then motioned for the guards hiding across from them to move. Edging out of the doorway, he paused, and then nodded for Ashe to follow.

They crept to the end of the row. A long span of gravel stretched away on either side, lined by more blocky buildings. Misting rain obscured the distance and only the glow of a security lamp gave any light.

Several yards away, the boy huddled inside the doorway of a building, his hand running over the dog's fur distractedly as he watched the darkness.

Nathaniel gave her a warning look, resting a hand briefly on her shoulder to keep her from moving. With quick gestures, he directed two of the guards to circle the building. On the other side of the gravel walkway, Mud shifted uncomfortably, clearly wanting to leave.

Minutes passed. The guards returned.

"Another kid watching around back," one whispered. "Three others sleeping inside. All cripples, but with no weapons we could see."

Nathaniel glanced to Elias, who scowled. Reaching over, Elias hauled Mud from the shadows.

"Go assure them we don't mean any harm," he ordered the man quietly.

"Don't you think we–"

"Now."

Shuffling reluctantly forward, Mud headed for the boy.

Elias looked to Nathaniel. The large man motioned for the guards to surround the building.

"Hey," Mud called to the kid.

Scrambling to his feet, the boy stared at him. Clenching the dog's collar with one hand, he held up the other defensively as he retreated deeper into the entryway, tugging the animal with him.

"Hey, wait a minute," Mud snapped, stopping in the middle of the gravel path. "I just said hi. You're acting like I'm a wizard or something."

The boy froze, the caution growing tenfold in his eyes.

"Oh, good grief," Mud grouched at the expression. "I'm not okay? I'm just here with some friends of mine. They told me to tell you they don't mean any harm. Oh, and they're going to want your help."

At her side, Ashe could hear Nathaniel make a nearly inaudible groan.

Alarm overwhelmed the caution in the boy's face and he back-tracked swiftly.

"What?" Mud called as the door slammed.

"Wonderful," Elias muttered.

She followed the two wizards out of the shadows.

"The kid wouldn't–" Mud started, gesturing helplessly as they approached.

Ignoring the man, they strode past him. Inside the building, they could hear the dog barking madly. Stepping in front of her, Nathaniel tried the handle, and then glanced back.

She grimaced and then nodded, not seeing another option. He shoved open the door, breaking the lock on the other side. Magic rising like a protective wall, Nathaniel led them into the building.

Panicked, the cripples were scrambling from their moth-eaten blankets. A dark-eyed young man was fumbling a handgun from beneath his coat, while behind him, another raced for the opposite door.

"Hey, wait!" Ashe called.

The gun went off. Bucking wildly with recoil, the weapon jerked from the young man's grasp and clattered to the concrete, while the bullet ricocheted from Nathaniel's defenses to vanish among the barrels on the building's upper level.

"We're not going to hurt you!" she tried.

Horrified, the young man stood paralyzed, his eyes darting from the wizards to the fallen gun, and then he dashed after his friends.

Successfully opening the rear exit, one of the kids rushed forward and then shrieked. Stumbling backward, he stared in horror as the other guards came in, the boy who'd been watching the rear door racing into the warehouse ahead of them. Claws skittering on the concrete, the dog bolted around the wizards and took off howling into the night.

"This is going well," Elias commented.

Ashe grimaced. "Come on."

The cripples backpedaled toward the center of the room, each of them trying to watch all the wizards at once. With Nathaniel a step ahead of her, she started toward them.

To a person, they were young. The oldest couldn't have been more than sixteen, and a boy toward the center of the group looked like he'd be stretching the truth to claim twelve. The one who'd guarded the front door stood clutching a girl with hair as red as his own, while the others cast frantic looks around, searching for alternate weapons.

She paused by the gun and then stooped to pick it up. As one, the cripples' eyes locked on her. For a heartbeat, she hesitated, and then sent the gun sliding across the concrete toward them.

Breathless, they watched her, and then the oldest-looking of the boys inched from the group toward the weapon. Extending a hand, he kept his eyes on her as he closed his fingers around the gun.

Her eyes narrowed. Red welts wrapped his wrists. Her gaze darted across the others. It was the same on each one she could see.

Sebastian killed two kids for escaping his custody. Others had fled too and at the time, the ferals hadn't located them.

A flicker of hope crept through her.

"I mean it," she said, returning her gaze to the young man and working to keep her voice calm. "We're not going to hurt you."

She heard shuffling footsteps behind her and she glanced back.

"Will you tell them?" she asked Mud.

Reluctance contorting his face, the man paused. "Okay, yeah, fine," he muttered. He ambled forward. "They're not going to hurt you," he called.

"Please do better than that," Elias suggested dryly, watching the boy with the gun retreat toward his friends. "The kids are about to have a heart attack."

Grimacing, Mud hesitated and then shuffled past them. "These wizards killed a freaking pair of ferals for me, alright?" he told the teenagers. "You can trust them."

He glanced back at Nathaniel and Elias, his eyes belying his own faith in the statement.

"So they're not going to kill you, okay?" he continued. "Not intentionally. They just want your help finding the damn Blood."

Any trace of color still present drained from the kids' faces. Near the center of the group, the smallest boy whimpered.

"No, seriously," Mud insisted. "These are the real ones who want to do that. Not the other bastards. And they'll let you kill them. I mean, the Blood. I mean, they'll let you kill the Blood." Flustered, he paused, and then tried for a reassuring smile. "That's good, right?"

Terrified silence answered him.

"Okay, I give up," Mud grumbled, turning and heading for the door.

Working to keep her frustration in check, Ashe watched him go and then glanced back at the kids. Elias was right. Whether they gained the cripples' help or not, the situation was precariously on the edge of becoming out of control. Another few moments and either the kids would pass out or that gun would go off.

And who knew where the ricochet would hit this time.

Her gaze flicked down to their wrists again.

"Elias," she said quietly. "How much cash do you have?"

"What?"

"How much?"

He hesitated, and then moved cautiously for his wallet. As a group, the kids tensed.

"About a hundred?" he answered, scanning the contents.

"Give it to me."

Carefully, she took the cash and then edged forward.

"We won't hurt you," she repeated. "But then… you've heard that line before, right?"

She jerked her chin toward the wrist of the young man holding the gun and watched his face tighten, confirming her words.

"I…" she began, wanting to apologize and then falling silent at the knowledge it wouldn't do any good. Their friends were dead because of what Sebastian and Darius had done. What she'd told the wizards.

Apologies wouldn't fix anything.

"We're not them," she amended. "We actually do want to fight the Blood. And if you don't want to help us… that's fine."

She laid the money on the ground.

"We're going to head outside. We'll leave the back door unwatched. If you want to help us, come find us out front. If you don't…" She backed away, leaving the cash. "Take the money. Get yourselves out of town. There's too many ferals around to keep hiding here forever."

She motioned for the other wizards to move away. Still clutching the gun, the young man watched them draw back at her command. His eyes narrowed suspiciously.

"Let's go," she said to Elias and Nathaniel, turning from the look in the boy's eyes.

Without waiting for a response, she walked out of the building. Leaving the kids huddled together in the center of the concrete floor, the guards filed from the room after her.

By a rusted garbage bin, Mud was sitting on a low cinder-block wall.

"So how'd it go?" he asked.

Ashe ignored him. Crossing to a point some distance away from the man, she hoisted herself onto the wall. Elias followed, stopping beside her to lean against the cinder blocks.

A moment slid past.

"Thanks for the money," she said quietly.

Elias shrugged. "Good cause."

She glanced down at him, but he was watching the door.

The minutes ticked by. Guards surrounded them, scanning the

area for threats. The rain continued to drizzle down, dampening any piece of her hair that had managed to dry while she was inside. Moisture clung to her skin and clothes, and she resisted the urge to let her magic drive it away.

No reason to scare the people in the building further.

"So when do we check if any of them are still there?" Elias asked.

She didn't answer.

"They're just kids, your majesty," he continued after a moment. "And if the Blood *are* real, then what we're asking…"

He paused, glancing up as though uncertain what to do with her age as well.

"Maybe it's better if they do leave," he finished uncomfortably.

Silent, she didn't look away from the door.

Time crept along. Drops of rain slid from her face. Still watching the door, she made no move to wipe them away.

"Come on, your highness," Elias said.

A heartbeat passed. Closing her eyes, she sighed.

"What'd you expect, your queenness?" Mud offered, making an attempt at sounding consoling. "They're children. You're Bloody Queen Ashe. They see things in black and white, and–"

She turned to him, her heart pounding.

His brow knit at her expression. "What?" he asked worriedly.

"What did you call me?" she whispered.

He blinked. "What did I… oh! Oh, no, no, no. *I* don't call you that. It's just… that's just… I mean, because of all the–"

"Shut up," Elias told him.

Mud glanced between her and the wizard apprehensively. "I don't call you that," he risked repeating, trying desperately to appear reassuring.

She looked away, her gaze running across the gravel as the title spun through her mind. On the wall, she could hear Mud shifting uncomfortably, and without even looking, she could feel the pressure of Elias' gaze.

Bloody Queen Ashe.

She closed her eyes.

"Your highness?" Elias said softly.

Not answering, she clenched her hands tighter around the wall's edge, letting the rough cinder blocks dig into her skin.

The sound of the door unlatching made her open her eyes.

From the shadowed entryway, the red-haired boy emerged. Clutching his arm, the girl followed. Watching the wizards, they edged away from the building out onto the gravel path.

Not taking her eyes from them, Ashe dropped down from the wall. Pushing away from the cinder blocks, Elias joined her, with Nathaniel a half-step behind.

"We want to help," the girl called timidly. Still clinging to the boy's side, she stopped as Ashe came closer.

"And the others?" Elias asked.

The girl hesitated. "They took off."

Ashe tried to stop her face from showing any reaction, and only partly succeeded. Swallowing uncomfortably, she kept her focus on the girl. Up close, the similarity between her and the boy was even more unmistakable.

"What's your name?" Ashe asked, working to keep her voice emotionless.

Nervously, the girl's gaze twitched over the wizards. "Crystal," she said. She nodded toward the boy. "Everybody just calls him Ghost."

She paused. "You're that queen, aren't you?"

Ashe hesitated, at a loss for what to say.

"Her highness, Queen Ashe of Merlin, lately betrayed by some of her Council," Elias supplied. "Yes."

"I just meant… you're the one who stayed with the Hunters… the one they said we could trust."

Feeling sick to her stomach, Ashe fought the urge to turn around and walk – or maybe even run – away.

"B-but you didn't know?" Crystal persisted, her gaze darting across the wizards as though expecting them to attack.

Not really trusting her voice, Ashe shook her head.

The girl looked at Ghost, meeting his gaze. Her eyebrows twitched up, and his drew down. With a tentative nod to him, she turned back to Ashe.

"We'll help," she said. "Both of us. We think… you could have killed us all in there. But you gave them money to get away instead. And you haven't gone after them. So maybe you're telling the truth, and maybe…"

She trailed off and then winced as Ghost gave her another insistent look, shaking her arm gently. "Maybe you could help us… me… too."

His brow drawing down, Elias glanced to Ashe. "With what?" he asked cautiously.

Crystal didn't respond. His mouth tightening, Ghost looked between the girl and the wizards, and then reached around her and drew up the edge of her dark shirt, exposing her stomach.

Elias swore under his breath. Ashe felt the tiny traces of expression still on her face melt into nothing.

Scraps of old t-shirts wrapped the girl's midsection, the bandages stained with blood. Past the edges of the worn fabric, the ragged tips of burns and countless shallow gashes could be seen, each of them ringed by the glossy sheen of swollen flesh.

"We couldn't go to a hospital," Crystal explained as Ghost lowered her shirt. "They were looking for us, and when they caught June and Case, we just…"

She swallowed. "Will you help us?"

Ashe looked at Elias.

Nathaniel cleared his throat. "Weapons," he warned succinctly.

For a moment, he met Ashe's gaze, and then he motioned to the others. The two cripples tensed as a guard came near. Barely breathing, they waited fearfully as the man gently patted them down.

With a nod, the guard stepped away.

Nathaniel bowed his head to her and then returned his gaze to the two kids.

"Can you?" Ashe asked Elias softly. "Without hurting her?"

He hesitated. "Katherine can try," he said, his voice equally low. "And even if she can't use magic, she'll still do something."

Ashe nodded. "We'll help in any way we can," she said to the girl. "I promise."

Crystal smiled nervously. "Thank you."

Nodding again distractedly, Ashe looked away. "Call the others," she told Elias. "Tell them to bring the cars."

Without waiting for a reply, she headed back for the road, eager to leave the reminders of what Darius and Sebastian had done behind.

———— ◆ ————

The kitchen door swung open.

Ashe didn't bother looking away from the coffee cup on the table in front of her. By her side, the first traces of dawn filtered beneath the thick curtains.

"Will the girl be alright?" she heard Elias ask.

Katherine sighed. "She'll be fine. I did what I could to prevent scaring, but the infection is gone."

"Those sick, twisted..." Elias muttered.

Her hands wrapped around the mug, Ashe watched the creamy liquid quivering inside. They'd been waiting for the better part of an hour, letting Katherine heal Crystal's wounds while Ghost hovered close by. Mud had taken the opportunity to find more food in Joe's refrigerators, while Nathaniel sat at a table behind her, surveying the brightening world beyond the edge of the restaurant curtains.

"We should go," she said to no one in particular.

Silence answered her, and she glanced up.

"The girl needs rest, your highness," Katherine said. "And quite frankly, that twin brother of hers could use some as well. He was hiding a few wounds of his own."

"Then we'll take Mud."

As if on cue, the kitchen door swung open and, his mouth and hands full of sandwich, Mud shuffled in with a guard on his heels.

Seeing everyone looking at him, he stopped cold. "What?" he asked around the mouthful.

"We're heading out again," Ashe said, pushing away from the table.

Swallowing forcibly, he blinked at her. "You sure? I mean, with the kid hurt, maybe we should just stay–"

"You don't need them to look for Blood wizards."

"Well, right. I mean, that's true. It's just... I'm pretty sure your folks here don't even believe the Blood exist, and that could be dangerous, so I'm just not certain I feel safe going out there with–"

He cut off as the kitchen door opened. Crystal and Ghost came in, each looking paler but more determined than before.

"I told you to get sleep," Katherine admonished. She gave a pointed glance to Ghost. "Both of you."

Crystal didn't meet her gaze. "We want to help."

Elias looked to his wife. "You should listen to her," he told Crystal gently.

"This is important," the girl said, shaking her head. "And we feel better. Really."

Not seeming convinced, Elias eyed them briefly and then grimaced. "She sounds like you," he said to Ashe.

Crystal looked to her in confusion.

Ashe ignored him. "Three teams then?" she asked Nathaniel. "Keep in touch by cell–" She glanced to Elias. "–provided you can get us some extras?"

He sighed, and then nodded.

"Well, if that's the case," Mud started. "Then I'm going with her queenness because–"

Ashe held up a hand, silencing him as Crystal made a small noise. "What?" she asked the girl.

Crystal hesitated. "Um…" She glanced to her brother. "He… Ghost doesn't, uh, talk to anybody but me. He won't. So we need to go together."

At the questioning looks, the girl grimaced reluctantly. "It's fine," she said, directing the words mostly to Katherine without meeting the woman's eyes. "It's not like that. He just… Mom and Dad were wizards, and when the Taliesin found us, they… I was hiding, but he tried to help and they…”

For a moment, she searched for words. “They made him watch.”

A heartbeat passed.

Ghost turned and left the room.

Crystal made a helpless gesture. “I’m sorry,” she said to them. “I shouldn’t have–”

She hurried after her brother.

“Well, guess they’re not coming then,” Mud interjected cheer-fully into the silence. “So it’s just one team… if we’re still going, that is.”

“Shut up,” Ashe said.

Ignoring his confused look, she headed after the two cripples.

Whispering together in a corner of the shadowy kitchen, Crystal and Ghost cut off as the door swung open. Defiance touched the young man’s face as he turned toward her, while Crystal just looked away.

Ashe paused, choosing her words.

“You can still see, can’t you?” she asked him, accusation in her tone.

His eyes narrowed.

“We could use your help.”

Hope showed on Crystal’s face as she glanced at her brother. After a moment, he nodded, still watching Ashe.

Turning, she walked out of the kitchen.

“Two teams,” Ashe said to the others. “And the twins come with me.”

“Hey, now!” Mud protested. “I already said–”

She looked to him flatly.

For less than a heartbeat, frustration showed through his beady eyes. "Fine," he muttered.

She glanced back as Crystal and Ghost emerged from the kitchen, and then returned her gaze to the others.

"So come on then," Ashe said. "Let's go."

Chapter Thirteen

Over the past five days, Cole had determined very few things. One was that he'd have to be Spider-Man for them to escape through the fifth floor window and reach the ground alive. The other was that 'paranoid' didn't even come close to describing the Carnegeans.

The wizards hadn't let them out for days, except to use the restroom under guard. Within an hour of depositing them back in the storage room, Geoffrey had replaced the solid wooden door with a screen, robbing them of the ability to even whisper without being heard. Whenever food arrived, two cousins watched while the third opened the screen, and both he and Lily had to stand in the far corner till the door was sealed again. The alarms around the doorway set his head to pounding if he came too close, making him suspect they were far stronger than any other guarding the house.

Whether or not Florence believed his interest in studying their hoard, Geoffrey and the others obviously thought it as likely as a pig taking flight. And though Cole pushed himself to look at the books they brought, trying to buy their belief with near-constant feigned interest, the wizards just scoffed and told him not to let the human touch the pages while he pretended to understand what they were giving him to read.

It was maddening. He couldn't speak to Lily and the cousins barely blinked anymore. To a person, the men were clearly too afraid of Geoffrey and Alfred's wrath to risk even looking away long enough for Cole to mouth a word to the girl.

Feeling in danger of losing his mind from sheer lack of ability to do anything else, he'd resorted to pacing their prison between chapters of the endless books, while Lily studied the paintings or stared out the window. He knew the Carnegeans would make a mistake eventually. The uncles would slip up; the cousins would get bored. Something would change.

Though, by this point, he'd started to wonder if that 'something' would just be him going completely insane.

Halfway through another circuit of the tiny cell, he stopped as Geoffrey's cursing carried along the hall. Outside the door, the two cousins straightened quickly, watching the man storm down the corridor to glare at Cole and Lily through the screen.

"You're wanted downstairs."

Cole didn't move. "Why?"

The derisive lip twitch that seemed to be Geoffrey's standard answer didn't materialize. Without a word, he opened the padlock securing the screen. A flicker of magic surrounded him, making Cole wince.

"Now."

Without taking his eyes from the man, Cole extended his hand to Lily, clasping it tightly before walking through the doorway. The two cousins led them away from the room, with Geoffrey striding behind.

At the parlor entrance, Magnus and Florence stood, the former in a posture of military parade rest and the latter with her white-knuckled fingers clasped as though to keep her from strangling him. Slowing warily, Cole glanced back. By the archway, Louise was peeking into the room, a look of barely restrained anticipation twisting around her face.

His grip on Lily's hand tightened. This could not be good.

"Check security," Geoffrey growled to the cousins. With a nod, the men disappeared into the recesses of the house.

"What's going on?" Cole asked cautiously.

"Who did you contact?" Magnus replied, his voice dangerously low.

Cole blinked. "What?"

"Stupid brat," Florence snapped. "'Who did you contact'? How hard a question is that?"

"I didn't–"

"Was it that farmer?" she interrupted, stalking toward him with her narrow finger pointed at his face. "Because I'm warning you–"

"I didn't contact anybody!" he protested, pushing Lily behind him as he backed away from the red-faced woman. "I don't know what you're talking about!"

"Right," Florence sneered. "And we're supposed to believe that the Taliesin wandering around with your photo have... what? No connection to you whatsoever?"

He froze. "What?"

The old woman's sneer widened and behind him, he heard Geoffrey scoff.

Magnus cleared his throat. "Bernhard witnessed no less than two separate groups quietly asking around about you this morning, while endeavoring to keep from being noticed by the populace at large."

"Taliesin?" he repeated.

"Do not make us ask again, Cole." Magnus pressed. "Who did you contact?"

Heart pounding, he shook his head. "No one. We've been locked upstairs, remember? You've been watching us day and night. We haven't been able to talk to each other, let alone anybody else."

"You sided with them, didn't you?" Florence said as though he hadn't spoken. "They killed your own mother and you sided with them to save your skin." Her lips twisted with revulsion. "You coward."

He stared at her as rage and incredulity tried to decide who got to come out first. "I *didn't–*"

"Enough," Florence snapped. "The truth was obviously too much to expect from you."

She motioned dismissively as she started from the room.

Swiftly, Geoffrey snagged Lily and threw her to the side. Ignoring the girl as she tumbled into the corner, the man stalked toward Cole, magic crackling around his hands.

"What the hell are you doing?" Cole demanded as he back-pedaled. "We didn't contact–"

"As the Taliesin are suddenly searching for you only miles from our location," Magnus interrupted calmly. "You obviously did. And the risk that presents simply cannot be tolerated."

Florence paused at the archway and glanced to her son. "Oh, and do be sure to leave the bodies somewhere *easy* for those miscreants to find. We need their attention dealt with quickly, after all."

Cole's eyes went wide and he retreated as Geoffrey continued toward him. His hands brushed a display table and, with a quick glance to it, he reached out, snagging the painted ceramic bowl on top.

Louise gasped, making Florence turn. The color vanished from the woman's face, while Magnus froze.

"Back off," Cole warned, holding the bowl up as he tried to watch them all at once. In the corner, Lily struggled to her feet. "We didn't do this. You're making a mistake."

Magic around his hands strengthening, Geoffrey's expression darkened hatefully.

"I'm warning–" Cole began.

Nothingness roared at him. Flinging himself to the side, Cole crashed to the ground as a glass case shattered behind where he'd been. Toppling from his hand, the bowl clattered away, cracking madly as it bounced across the floor and then disintegrating as it slammed into the wall.

Florence shrieked. Geoffrey's magic grew stronger.

Gritting his teeth against the pain, Cole shoved to his feet and grabbed the nearest object at hand. The ornamental vase smashed against the wall as Geoffrey sidestepped sharply.

"Run!" Cole shouted at Lily as he hurled another vase at the wizard. Staring, Lily didn't move, her back pressed against a glass case and her face white with terror.

Lightning crackled across the room, narrowly missing his head as Cole hit the ground. The cream-colored wall behind him turned black.

"What are you *doing*, Geoffrey?" Florence cried. "Outside, you stupid man! Magnus, do something!"

Cole scrambled up again. A book landed under his questing grasp and swiftly, he let it fly. Another followed, ripped from its display stand atop the desk. Twenty feet behind him, the parlor doors waited, though Lily was still paralyzed in the opposite corner of the large room. And Geoffrey was winding through the tables, heading straight for him.

Grabbing the display stand itself, he flung it at the man. "Lily, get out of–"

He registered the pain rushing him from the side, and then it was there, slamming into him, around him, through him, and there was nothing it didn't destroy. The ground came next, adding insult to agony, and then the world went white.

His skin was on fire. Muscle and bone screamed as if on the edge of being exposed to the air. Something gripped his shirt, hauling the pain that was his body up from the excruciating tile, and slowly, the white noise scream of the world resolved into color and sound.

Geoffrey smirked down at him. Past the man's shoulder, Magnus stood, regarding him expressionlessly. Cole turned his head, the movement torture, seeking out Lily on the far side of the room.

"Run…" he begged her, his voice barely a whisper.

The little girl looked around desperately, as though seeking a weapon too. He fought down another breath, trying to plead with her just to go while they were distracted with him.

Geoffrey jerked his grip on Cole's shirt, cutting off the words he'd wanted to say. With a gasp, Cole pulled his gaze back to the man, staring up as Geoffrey bent closer.

"I'll tell you something," Geoffrey said, his voice low. "Ordinarily, I'd just shoot one of your kind. I'm not interested in killing some pathetic cripple for power. And your grandfather held back to keep from doing the same. But–" He grinned humorlessly. "–you're special."

Magic rose, making Cole choke.

"This is for your father, boy."

The world became a hurricane of light.

Whiteness surrounded him, drowning everything in its glare. Winds shoved him over, rolling him with their force. Instinctively, Cole's arms wrapped around his head as Geoffrey's grip tore away and the smashing noises of innumerable heavy things breaking sounded nearby.

The wind vanished. Shaking, Cole lowered his arms.

Nothing was left. Bookshelves, artifacts, display cases and tables – they were all gone. The thick carpet beneath him had rolled in the blast, covering him mostly with its bulk. He pushed the weight of it away, and then blanched.

The room was on the other side of the room.

In a mountain of shattered wood and broken pottery, the bookshelves and displays were piled like flotsam on the far end of the parlor. Pockmarks from flying debris scored the empty walls and overhead, he could hear the groan of masonry and wood, interspersed with the hiss of shattered glass raining to the floor. Half-buried in the rubble, Magnus and Geoffrey stirred, their magic flickering visibly around them as they struggled to regain consciousness.

A small gasp carried through the wreckage and he turned.

Backed tightly into the corner, Lily stared at the destruction. In her bloodless hands, she clutched Merlin's staff, while blue-white light pulsed from between the twists of wood.

Another gasp escaped the girl as, unsteadily, Cole struggled to rise. Everything ached, though the pain was receding. Gritting his teeth, he shoved the rest of the way to his feet and then tottered briefly, fighting for balance.

"Lily," he said, pushing the word out. Swallowing, he started toward her. "Lily, look at me."

Trembling, the little girl turned her gaze to him. "I… I…"

Her gaze slid back to the room. He could see the panic beginning to bubble up.

"Lily," he said again, reaching out carefully. "You have to breathe. Look at me. Come on."

Cautiously, he wrapped his fingers around her wrist. The little girl tensed.

"I…"

"Come with me, Lily."

She didn't resist as he pulled her along. His arm wrapped around her shoulders, bringing her closer, and quivering, she rested her head on his side as he led her past the destruction.

Several yards away, Magnus groaned. Through the archway, Cole could see Florence stirring on the floor two rooms back. Behind the cover of a pockmarked wall, Louise sat blinking in dumbfounded shock, while by the splintered wreckage of the parlor doors, Geoffrey lay half-pinned beneath the vintage sofa.

And the man was still breathing, Cole realized. On some level, that almost seemed like a bad thing.

Pushing the thought away, he bent and tugged the man's keys and wallet from his pocket. Tossing another glance to the wizards, he pulled Lily with him as he stepped past the shattered doors and headed onto the patio.

Three cousins rounded the corner and, at the sight of the broken windows, they gasped. Their gazes swept the house, finding Lily and the glowing staff.

Electricity crackled up around them.

Lily's fear was faster.

Wind and light exploded outward, sending the men flying into the bushes on the far side of the lawn, while behind them, the walls of the house groaned.

Lily whimpered.

Cole blinked and swallowed hard. "Come on."

Tightening his grip on the girl, he hurried down the patio stairs and onto the grass. Around the corner, the brick carriage house of the garage stood. Two pristine sedans sat in front of it, parked like they were waiting for a camera crew. Releasing Lily just long enough to fumble with the key fob, Cole smashed down the unlock button.

The lights of the leftmost car flashed.

Making small noises of panic, Lily raced for the passenger door as he headed for the driver's side. Clambering in, the girl struggled with the staff and then finally wedged it between the seats with the base braced by her feet and her hands clasping it tightly.

Swinging into the cushy leather seat, Cole slammed the door and then searched frantically for the ignition before spotting a button on the dash. Muttering a curse, he mashed the button and then swore some more as, like an oblivious kitten, the sedan purred to life. With a grimace, he yanked the gearshift into drive and then crushed the pedal down. The engine roared, sending the car charging onto the gravel path.

Magnus stumbled from the house, his bleary eyes widening at the sight of the sedan. Magic surged around him. Gripping the steering wheel, Cole flattened the pedal farther into the floor.

Bark and pine showered the car as it sped between the trees.

Blind turns passed in rapid succession. The black metal gate surrendered to his frantic jab at the controller clipped to the visor, and as the fence pulled back, he raced the car through the gap onto the country road.

Drawing a breath for what felt like the first time in years, Cole loosened his chokehold on the wheel and glanced to the girl.

"You okay?"

She didn't answer.

"Lily?"

"Uh-huh."

At her tone, he looked over at her again.

"I-I barely let any out," she said, her voice inching toward hysteria. "I mean, I thought I could just scare them, but when he…" Her gaze dropped to the staff and then darted away. "I couldn't stop it. But it was just a bit…"

Unnerved, he didn't know what to say. In her hands, the staff still pulsed with light.

"Are you letting any out now?"

Her mouth tightened nervously as she looked at the staff. The glow faded till nothing but dead wood remained.

"I don't think so…"

Cole nodded, casting quick glances to her between navigating the rough back roads.

"It was just a bit," she repeated.

He couldn't read the tone. Somewhere between apology and fear, it contained plenty of shock too.

Which really just made two of them.

"Yeah, well," he said, attempting to sound calm. "Thanks. You did great."

She looked down. "Can we go back to Sue and Ben's now?" she

asked, her voice small.

He shook his head.

Desperation spread across her face. "Why?"

"It's not safe. That's the first place the Carnegeans will look."

"But…" she protested helplessly, "we have to warn them. What about those people they said were after us?"

"The Taliesin?"

She nodded.

"They won't bother Sue and Ben," he said, trying to sound certain.

"You don't know that."

Cole glanced over. She met his gaze insistently.

"I know that if the Taliesin come and we're there, Ben and Sue might get hurt. And if the Carnegeans come and we're there, my dear family will kill them just for possibly being a threat. That's what I know."

Pained, she looked away.

He grimaced, but there was nothing for it. Trying to bury his guilt, he glanced down at the dash.

An incredulous curse escaped him.

"What?" she cried, panicked.

"Nothing."

She glared.

"The car's almost out of gas."

Lily bit her lip.

"It's okay," he said. "We'll just stop for a second. They won't find us."

From the corner of his eye, he could see her shifting anxiously, looking unconvinced. He glanced at the rearview mirror.

Odds were even as to whether the Carnegeans would come after them. Lily had done quite a bit of damage, but if his grandparents' anger superseded their panic at the destruction, the two of them could be in trouble.

Checking the gas gauge again, he eased up on the pedal as he guided the car around another turn.

They'd stop for a moment. Just long enough to get the tank full. Then they'd get the hell out of Washington. It wouldn't be a problem.

Flexing his hands on the steering wheel, he cast another look to the rearview mirror, trying to make himself believe the words.

———— ♦ ————

"Come on… come on…" Lily urged softly, clutching his arm and the staff alike as she watched the numbers on the dial climb.

Gripping the pump handle, Cole said nothing. Despite the time of day, the tiny country gas station was bustling, and it made him nervous. They'd driven till the warning light on the dashboard had glowed for more miles than he could count and the car itself had started to feel heavy. He'd wanted to order the girl to stay inside when he finally spotted the gas station, though he'd known there wouldn't really have been any point.

She could see wizards. He couldn't. It was simple as that.

Barely breathing, he scanned the area again, trying to keep his face from the cameras on the main building. Cars were parked in nearly every space by the door, while by the parking lot entrance, a group of bikers leaned on their Harleys, smoking and watching the road as they waited for some of their number still inside. A family from Illinois pulled up at the pump next to him, obscuring his view of anything beyond their bumper-stickered minivan.

Cole turned away as the bikers looked toward him.

"Come on…" Lily continued.

He glanced at the dial. The pump couldn't have gone slower if it had been broken.

"You going hiking?"

Heart hitting his throat, Cole spun. On the other side of the pump, the driver of the minivan grinned at him before returning his gaze to Lily. A Cubs baseball cap shaded his eyes and a souvenir t-shirt for the North Cascades stretched across his belly.

"Eh?" the tourist persisted, bending to catch Lily's eye. In the van behind him, his children began arguing, their voices carrying through the open door. The man gave no sign of noticing the noise.

Clenching the staff tighter, Lily ducked behind Cole.

"She's pretty shy, huh?" the man asked, smiling as he straightened again.

"Something like that."

The pump clicked to a stop as the tank finally reached capacity. Attempting not to look anxious, Cole returned the nozzle to its slot.

"Nice talking to you," the tourist said cheerily.

Working his face into an approximation of a smile, Cole nodded as he pulled the girl around the vehicle toward the passenger side door.

"Where are we going to–"

Lily cut off with a whimper. He looked over as she slumped to the ground, a small dart protruding from the pale skin of her neck.

His gaze snapped from the girl to the gas station, while his body dropped to grab her. Across the parking lot, he saw the bikers rise from their motorcycles in alarm.

"Hey, she alright?" one called.

Ignoring them, he pulled the door handle and then scooped Lily and the staff from the concrete. Peering around the gas pump, the tourist stared.

"What happened?" the portly man sputtered.

A woman and a man emerged from either side of the minivan.

"Hello Cole," the woman said. "I wouldn't do that if I were you."

Her dark red lips curved into a polite smile as she tucked the tranquilizer gun back beneath the smooth lines of her jacket.

Cole froze. His gaze darted to the tourist and his kids as the two people calmly circled the gas pump and sedan. Crisp black suits with starched white shirts covered them both, and the woman's heels clicked sharply on the pavement.

And no one gave any sign of noticing them.

"Come with us," the woman said in the same courteous tone.

"Hey," the biker called, coming closer. Concern fought with intense confusion on his face. "Is the kid okay?"

"Tell them she's diabetic," the woman instructed.

Magic crackled around her hand in implicit warning when he didn't answer. He fought to keep from wincing, and watched her lips curve into another smile anyway.

"Now, Cole," she pressured. "Or she dies in your arms."

A second passed. The magic strengthened.

"She's diabetic," he called, not looking away from the wizard.

Appearing alarmed, the biker paused before glancing back toward his friends. "Hey, call the paramedics, okay? Kid's diabetic. And see what they got in the first aid kit inside."

"I think we have some juice," the tourist volunteered, hurrying back for his minivan.

The woman smiled again. "Now put the little human girl down and come with us."

"No."

"Do it, Cole," she warned pleasantly. "We'd hate to have to force the situation."

"Go to hell."

The woman gave the man a brief look.

"Fine," she said, razors edging her pleasant tone. "Keep the child. But move."

Gritting his teeth, he glanced around, desperate for a way to draw attention back to them.

The other wizard made a low growl. "We will not ask again."

Cole studied him. There was nothing in the man's eyes. Bugs probably qualified for more compassion than the little girl.

His face like stone, Cole hefted Lily and the staff higher in his arms, and started away from the car. Smiling slightly, the woman took the lead while her counterpart fell in behind.

Reflexive cursing ran through his head as they rounded the minivan. A black limousine sat by the curb, its length obscured by the bulk of the bumper-stickered vehicle. Arms crossed, the driver leaned on the hood, and his mouth curved at the sight of them. Shrugging away from the limo, the man crossed to the door and held it open as they approached.

"Welcome back," the driver said dryly.

The woman's hand on his shoulder pulled Cole up short. Amused expression unchanged, the driver stepped forward and patted him down swiftly, and then jerked his chin at the staff.

"Lose the stick."

Cole shook his head. "It's hers."

"I don't care."

"I'm not leaving it."

The woman made a small motion. The driver gave Cole a disgusted look. "Whatever. Get in."

Jaw muscles jumping, Cole lowered Lily into the vehicle and then climbed in after her. Shifting the little girl on the seat and pushing the staff back into the corner, he put himself between Lily and the wizards as they joined him inside.

With a dull thud, the limousine door shut, sealing off the noise of the gas station. Through the smoked windows, he could see the bikers looking around while, clutching a juice box, the tourist circled their sedan in bafflement.

The seats vibrated slightly as the engine turned over, and a moment later, the vehicle quivered as the driver put it into gear. Crossing her legs delicately, the woman regarded him with a hint of a smile as the limo returned to the country road. No expression dared come near the face of the man beside her.

Anger and frustration beat a throbbing duet in the back of his head as the gas station disappeared in the distance. Still eyeing the wizards, he eased over and tugged the dart from Lily's neck. A droplet of blood welled from the small wound, making his hand tremble with rage. Drawing a slow breath, he fought to keep his face from giving any sign.

"Here," the woman said, extending a tissue to him.

He didn't move.

"Oh, come now," she chided.

With careful control, he took the tissue and then wiped Lily's neck clean.

"Your concern is touching," the woman told him. At her side, the other wizard snorted.

Cole ignored them. Gently, he felt for the girl's pulse as he wracked his mind for ways to wake her. Between Lily and the staff, they just might stand a chance of getting out of here.

He struggled not to grimace, hating himself for the thought. One instance of the kid going nuclear and here he was, thinking of using her like a weapon all over again. It was sick. Stupid. There had to be a better plan.

It'd still really help to have her awake.

"You know," the woman offered conversationally. "She's going to be out for hours. The sedative is quite strong."

He said nothing. Resting his arm across the girl, he began gently rubbing her shoulder, hoping the minor contact would draw her back.

"Whatever tie you have to this little human," she continued. "You really ought to think of how much safer she'd be if you let us leave her somewhere. Considering our magic could accidentally hurt her and all."

His gaze flicked up to the woman. Smiling pleasantly, she raised an eyebrow at him.

"What do you want?" he asked quietly.

"Just your cooperation."

When he didn't respond, she sighed. "The Council wants to help you, Cole. They understand you're more aware of what's going on, though some of the intricacies might not be clear just yet. But they appreciate you're an adult, same as them. They'd like to work with you." She smiled again. "For all our benefit."

He glanced between her and the other wizard. In spite of himself, a humorless laugh slipped out.

"And how's that work? I don't listen, you kill me like you did my dad?" He paused. "The king of Taliesin?"

She hesitated and then her gaze dropped to her lap, a hint of ruefulness in her expression. "What happened with your father was regrettable, Cole. More than you can possibly know."

The cold laugh escaped again. He was having trouble stopping it, and wasn't sure he cared.

"Regrettable," he repeated. "What? Murdering him? Shooting my mother in front of me? You regret that?"

"We didn't kill your mother, you stupid boy," the other wizard interjected disgustedly.

Cole's gaze darted over to him.

"Your loving father took care of that. And as for Victor…" the man scoffed. "You think we whacked our own king, is that it?"

"Quinton," the woman warned. "The Council should be the ones–"

"Screw the Council, Vivian. Edmund's dead because this kid went off to find answers about mommy and daddy."

The woman's face took on an icy cast at the mention of the man who'd pretended to be Cole's counselor for years. Wordlessly, she turned away.

"We had no magic, moron," Quinton continued to him. "Nothing to defend ourselves against a bunch of Merlin who'd be out for blood if we dared kill any of their own. Kidnapping's one thing, but murder? We tranked your mom, same as your little human there. We just wanted to take you, not start a war. Honestly, you really think we'd risk what those Merlin would've done, just to make a point to your daddy?"

"And what point was that?" Cole asked quietly, watching the man.

"Not to go out of control," Quinton answered. "Though obviously, he didn't get the message. The man was a loose cannon. He wanted power and he'd do anything to get it. Victor assassinated the Merlin king and his whole damn family just to get his magic back, and when that was done, he went ahead and eliminated your mother simply because he didn't need her anymore. He only married her for information on Merlin, and probably only had you in the hope that mingling his bloodline with a Merlin's would break the spell." He gave a mocking laugh. "You should thank us for getting you out of there before he killed you too."

Barely breathing with the effort of not ripping the man's throat out, Cole shook his head. "Bullshit," he whispered.

Quinton scoffed. "Whatever, kid. Doesn't change what's true. Your dad murdered your mom, and the Merlin royal family to boot. He sided with insurrectionists hell-bent on overthrowing the Council, just to gain more power than he'd had to start. Your dad was a monster, boy. And he made himself and his buddies into something even worse when he killed the Merlin king."

Cole realized some hint of expression must have shown through, because the man paused. "Oh, you've seen them? Yeah, we don't spread that around much, you cripple's ability to somehow spot what your daddy made. What those insurrectionists became when they blew up the Merlin royal family on Christmas Eve. And before you think of scampering off to join the bastards who killed Ethel, Edmund and half our damn team in this past year alone, you ought to know that once your dad's buddies had their magic back, they decided they didn't really want a ruler after all. They got rid of Victor too. Big bloodbath, that was. Disgusting. And in the end, your daddy was toast."

"You're lying."

"You wish. We couldn't have gained shit from killing your mom, and even if we'd wanted to, we never had a chance to take out your dad. But you believe whatever you want."

He was shaking, though Cole was fairly certain his motionless body gave no sign. But tremors vibrated through his stomach while his mind spun. He'd known his dad. Victor had loved Clara. Loved Cole. If there was only one thing left in the world of which he was unequivocally certain, it was that his father would have moved earth, heaven and hell for his wife and son.

And as for the rest, there was no way… just no way at all…

His head felt like it was going to explode every time his heart beat.

"So why keep me around?" he asked, his voice still quiet. Controlled. Careful. Because this was garbage from beginning to end, and the minute Lily woke up, the bastards would regret every word.

His conscience whispered at the edge of his rage, but he shoved the noise of it away.

"Why do all this?" he finished, glancing illustratively to the limousine.

Quinton chuckled again. "Because unlike your daddy's friends, we're *not* monsters. Merlin and Taliesin, we've both got one bloodline with the ability to bind magic and recreate what was done five hundred years ago to your ancestors and mine. And guess who that trait belongs to? The royals. King Patrick, his lot, and you. Now your daddy's friends, they'd probably do God knows what to make a cripple like you share those genetics around. Maybe you'd get the chance to enjoy it. Or maybe they'd put you in a coma till they didn't need you anymore. They're not the nicest folks, after all, and they just want to get their hands on that power and keep it under their control. But us? We were more interested in giving you a life worth living. Family, friends, all that rot. And while you grew up in luxury, we risked our lives to keep your ass safe, hoping that if you turned out smart enough, you'd side with us when we brought you into the loop, rather than the folks who made your daddy into charcoal."

Silence fell over the car. With a glance to Quinton, Vivian leaned forward. "You saw what they did to Edmund, didn't you?"

His gaze snapped to her, his rage mounting higher at the faux concern in her voice. As though she knew that'd been hard, and actually cared.

"We're trying to protect you, Cole," she continued. "The Council. All of us. You've only seen the barest hints of what the Blood can do."

Unable to stand her tone, he looked away, and his gaze caught on Lily. Daughter of King Patrick. Last of the Merlin royal family.

The trembling grew stronger.

They were liars. Every day of his life they'd lied, starting from the moment they took him. Believing anything they said now would just distract him and make him a fool.

He closed his eyes, fighting to push everything from his mind but the goal of escape.

"We're here to keep you safe," Vivian said. "So cooperate with us. With the Council. Leave the girl and let us–"

"No."

The word slipped out before he could stop it, and it took everything he had to keep his expression controlled as he looked back at her.

"She stays with me."

Frustration tinged the woman's face as she glanced to Quinton.

The man had no such problem, and just rolled his eyes in disgust.

"I watched her family get killed," Cole said, spinning the tale without looking away from Vivian. "A couple of fighting wizards who didn't care who they hurt. I promised I'd take care of her." He paused, forcing himself to speak the words and stomach the lie, even if only for now. "So fine. I'll work with you. I'm not too interested in dealing with the folks who put Edmund through a car. But you make me a liar to this girl, and I'll make sure no one has a hope in hell of getting their hands on my bloodline. You understand me?"

"Oh, come on. You really expect us to believe you'd… what? Commit suicide?" Quinton sneered. "Over a human kid?"

Cole looked over, meeting the wizard's eyes. "Try me."

"Fine," Vivian interjected before Quinton could speak. She rested a manicured hand on the man's arm, stilling him. "Keep the girl." The woman smiled. "You'll see, Cole. We're not your enemies."

He couldn't answer. Somewhere between the truth he wanted to speak and the lie he needed to say, the images of the night his mother died rose like a wall too high to overcome.

Shaking, he turned away, his hand still rubbing Lily's shoulder.

The trees parted beyond the limousine's smoked windows, revealing the gravel stretch of a small airport. Steel shelters covered private planes at the distant end of the runway, and closer by, a concrete block of a building waited. A handful of vehicles peppered the unmarked parking lot, though their owners were nowhere to be seen. Several rusted vending machines stood sentry along the building's front wall, their faded paint still trying to shine in the morning light.

Bouncing over the rough terrain, the limo rounded the concrete building. Through the windows, Cole could see the shadowy forms of the people inside.

One of them turned as the limousine drove by. Cole tensed, his heart rate spiking.

"What?" Vivian asked.

Behind the cover of the smoked windows, Cole watched Keller study the limo, and then motion to his companions.

The limo continued on. Cole's gaze went to Lily, though his thoughts were elsewhere.

"Cole?"

He didn't answer. Two separate groups had been asking about him, Magnus had said. And obviously, one of them worked for the Blood. He began rubbing Lily's shoulder harder.

Vivian tapped on the divider between the back seats and the driver. The blackened window rolled away.

"Thomas," she said, her eyes still on Cole. "I think we have a problem."

She rocked slightly as the vehicle accelerated up onto the tarmac and then curved toward the far end of the runway. As they came to a stop, Vivian threw open the door, while Quinton reached toward Lily.

"Back off," Cole warned, the motion snapping him from his thoughts.

"Hurry up, then."

Cole watched the wizard clamber out. Wordlessly, he drew the staff closer and then awkwardly scooped it and Lily from the seat. A small jet waited outside the limousine, its engines already powering up. Without a word, Quinton snagged Cole's arm as he climbed out, pulling him toward the plane.

"Faster," the man growled.

Tugging away from him, Cole looked back at the building on the other end of the airstrip. He could see people running, while a car charged past them from the parking lot.

The Blood killed Lily's family, he reminded himself. And Taliesin killed his. But between the two groups…

Magic crackled around the wizard's hand. "Now," Quinton ordered, his gaze on the people rushing their way.

Grimacing, Cole shifted Lily in his grip and then headed for the plane as Thomas sped off in the limo.

Vivian looked up from buckling herself into the cramped quarters of the jet's interior as he came inside. Bent nearly double, Cole barely spared the woman a glance. He set Lily in a seat away from the wizards, and then lowered himself down next to her. Strapping in, he turned to the window.

The car was coming. Half a dozen men ran in its wake.

Quinton slammed the door. "Go!" he shouted at the pilots.

They didn't need the order. A shiver went through the plane as it started moving and then gravity pushed Cole deeper into his seat as the jet rapidly picked up speed. Outside, the car veered sharply, trying to cut them off.

The plane swept past the sedan and raced down the runway.

Cole turned away. The Taliesin were a known evil. At least more than the Blood right now. And Quinton's lies didn't matter. When Lily woke up, they'd get out of here.

He'd figure out what to do after that happened.

The plane shook and jumped, jerking from more than velocity. Pale-faced, Vivian watched the windows while in his seat, Quinton glared at the cockpit, visibly willing the pilots to go faster.

Cole ignored them all as he reached over, rubbing Lily's shoulder again. Boneless, the little girl slumped in the seat, one thin arm around the staff. Slow breaths rose and fell in her chest, their pace unchanged by the jostling around them.

Frustration and powerlessness swelled at the sight. Nearly half a year of running, and now this.

Closing his eyes, he cursed himself as he fought to calm down. He was a bastard for thinking it, for considering it. Magical powers or not, she was a kid, not a weapon. And he wouldn't be a monster. Not like the Blood, whoever they actually turned out to be. Not like the Carnegeans, with their casual cruelty in the name of history.

He glanced over as magic flared around Quinton's hands in response to a sharp lurch of the plane.

Not like them.

Shaking his head, Cole turned back to the window as, with a jolt, the jet left the ground and launched into the sky.

Chapter Fourteen

The cell phone buzzed on the mahogany console table, its sound like a large hornet in the quiet hotel suite.

"Yes?"

A moment went by. The call ended. Brogan's gaze slid to his employer. "The Taliesin have him," he said quietly.

There was no answer. His hands folded loosely and his leg crossed before him, the suit-clad man sat as he had for the past hour, watching the highway beyond the hotel window from the vantage point of a wood-framed desk chair.

"Keller questioned the human authorities at the airport," Brogan continued. "They're taking him to Croftsburg."

Silence followed his words. For his lack of reaction, the man could have been sleeping, though Brogan knew that was far from the case.

"Sir, you know they wouldn't take him to a city unless–"

"I know."

Brogan let the soft words end his own. After years of serving the king of Taliesin, he knew the man well. He could feel the orders coming.

"The Council is there," Jamison said, still watching the traffic. "They're going to use him to buy protection and then make him disappear. Again."

On the highway, cars flew along, racing each other for the exits. In the hallway, a maid's cart squeaked as it rolled by.

The chair creaked quietly as Jamison turned.

"Call everyone," he said, no trace of emotion in his tone. "Tear the city apart. Whatever it takes, Mason." He paused. "Before they hide him again."

Brogan nodded, but the motion was lost. Without another word, Jamison stood and left, the bedroom door shutting behind him.

Silence fell again. Thoughtfully, Brogan picked up his phone and then glanced back toward the other room.

Croftsburg. Despite the danger, he knew Jamison wouldn't stay behind. Not when they were closer to his son than they'd been in years. But protection wouldn't be hard to arrange, even on short notice. Their people had long since perfected ways of keeping their presence and any necessary violence far beneath both Merlin and Taliesin's radars.

Though there was Ashley to consider.

Idly, Brogan turned the phone over in his hand. Last word they'd received from Harris put the girl in the city. But that was days ago. Obviously, she could have relocated since then.

His gaze rose to the mirror above the console table.

Melted skin covered the left side of his face, and a milky eye stared out of the glistening mess. On half his head, his hair was shaved. On the other, nothing would ever grow again.

The corner of his twisted mouth pulled up in a smile as he thumbed on the phone.

———◆———

"So…" Crystal began with forced casualness as she picked up a piece of gravel from the rooftop. "Where're we headed?"

"South, I hope," Ashe said distractedly, her eyes on the boy creeping toward the edge of the office building. On either side, a pair of wizards shadowed his movements, their watchful gazes on the old business district around them.

As he neared the ledge, Ghost crouched low and then peered down at the street. Seconds passed and then he inched backwards, straightening only when several yards separated him from the open air.

He glanced to her and shook his head. Ashe sighed.

"Why south?" Crystal asked, tossing the rock aside as they rose from their places by the air conditioning units at the center of the roof.

"Because that's where the Blood were last time I saw them," Ashe answered, watching Nathaniel. Motioning her to stay back, the man left the cover of the massive units, his gaze sweeping the neighboring rooftops. Emerging from the opposite side of the air conditioners, two other guards did the same.

Silence followed her words. Ashe glanced back to see the twins sharing one of the countless enigmatic looks they seemed to possess.

"What?" she asked.

"It's nothing," Crystal said. "There was just this place down south we heard about. Like a colony of cripples or something."

Ashe paused. "The Abbey," she supplied, keeping her voice lower than she hoped Nathaniel could hear.

Crystal blinked in surprise. "Yeah, have you–"

"Do you know if it's still there?"

The girl hesitated, and then regret crept onto her face. Ashe's chest tightened. Stone-faced, she waited for the words.

"I'm sorry, I don't," Crystal said. "We never heard more than rumors in the first place."

Remembering how to breathe, Ashe turned away.

"But maybe we could check?" the girl continued. "Ghost and I always wanted to go if, you know, it was real and all. If you know where it is, maybe we could stop by?"

"Yeah, maybe," Ashe lied distantly, heading for Nathaniel as the wizard motioned her onward.

"So when are we leaving?" Crystal asked, following her across the gravel.

"Tonight. Unless something changes, anyway."

She ignored the silence behind her this time as she came up to the wizards. Checking around again, Nathaniel gestured for two of the guards to take the lead as they started across the rooftop.

For the past few days, they'd been searching for the Blood constantly, but despite the cripples' help, they hadn't found a single one. Merlin and Taliesin, on the other hand, were everywhere. Staying mostly out of sight, the Merlin seemed committed to quietly hunting her and, most likely, the cripples alike. Meanwhile, Taliesin had nearly reached the point of walking the streets openly, and their numbers seemed to increase with each passing hour.

It worried Elias. She wasn't sure what it did to Nathaniel.

On some level, she supposed she'd wanted to find the Blood in Croftsburg for the pure sake of dragging them back and proving to the Council once and for all that neither she nor Carter had been insane. And that Darius was a lying bastard. Seeing the looks on the councilmembers' faces might've been nice, though being able to stop simultaneously hiding from the wizards of Merlin, Taliesin and the Blood would have been lovely too. But they'd lingered in the city almost longer than Elias could stand, and even she could admit it was probably time to go.

Elias already had a trio of cars prepared, ever since the conclusion of yet another 'discussion' several days before. They'd leave Croftsburg after dark, heading in three separate directions, with the goal of meeting back up at a destination the other two drivers wouldn't know till Elias called them. She hoped she could convince him to head south without having to resort to playing queen on the matter. But given that finding the Blood was her priority, not his, she wasn't entirely sure.

The building came to an end, and like its neighbor they'd just left, the roof butted up against the old brick edifice next door. Without pause, she followed Nathaniel up the rusted ladder bolted to the adjacent building's side.

She grimaced as she crested the rooftop. The building overlooked an alley, which would force them to return to street level in order to cross. The whole point of searching along this stretch of shorter buildings was to give the twins the best chance of spotting the Blood wizards, but the surrounding rooftops and ambush possibilities left Nathaniel and the guards tense as hell, and descending through crowded offices and stores to reach the street just made it worse.

Crossing the asphalt expanse, she avoided the pools of standing water drying in the sun and then crouched dutifully away from the edge, knowing that approaching any closer would only annoy Nathaniel beyond measure. Moving ahead, Ghost and the guards inched toward the open air and checked the ground below.

A heartbeat passed. Ghost shook his head again.

Burying a grimace, she started toward the access hatch set into the roof.

A crash echoed up from the alley.

Turning sharply, Ashe hurried toward Ghost, barely noticing Nathaniel's angry look as she reached the edge.

The building door was open wide and a Taliesin wizard was scrambling up from the wet concrete. His hands and feet propelling him equally from the broken ground, he lunged toward the alley exit, but before he made it a step, magic burst through the doorway, striking him in the back and catapulting him into the opposite wall. Limply, he crashed to the ground and then weakly tried to rise, the fear on his face visible from the rooftop.

Another man emerged from the building.

Ghost gasped and backpedaled. Ashe froze, suddenly uncertain what to feel.

Nathaniel glanced between them and the man below. Incredulity fractured his stoicism, but he didn't waste any time in snagging her arm and yanking her out of sight.

She tugged away, glaring, and then crept back to the edge. Radiating displeasure, Nathaniel followed.

Though he appeared completely human, the man gave the ends of the alleyway a cursory glance and then stalked directly toward the wizard lying in a pool of drain pipe runoff. Frantically, the Taliesin tried to climb to his feet, magic flickering around him.

A swift jolt of electricity curtailed his effort. With a cry of pain, he crumpled to the concrete.

The Blood wizard spoke, his words unintelligible over the distance. Desperate contempt twisted the Taliesin's face. He spat a response.

For a heartbeat, the Blood wizard didn't move. And then magic slammed down.

The other wizard slumped dead to the ground. Ignoring the body, the Blood flicked a hand at the wall. Blue light curled across the bricks, tracing shimmering words.

Ashe stared, her confusion mounting.

The Blood wizard strode away.

Speechless, Ashe turned to Nathaniel, but the man appeared as lost as she felt. Swallowing hard, she looked back at the alley, watching the Blood disappear around the corner.

"Call Elias," she ordered.

Without another word, she headed for the access hatch.

The metal ladder rungs clattered beneath her feet as she descended the tunnel to the building interior. The roof access door squealed in protest as she shoved it open, but nothing in the hallway beyond stirred at the sound. Erratically patterned carpets softened her footsteps, and plastic sheeting draped the interiors of the offices along the hall.

Tossing her a heated glance, Nathaniel pushed by her, taking the lead. Gripping his cell, he passed information to Elias in terse statements while scanning the hall as though expecting more Blood wizards to burst from the plaster.

A doorway swung open behind them, a portal whirling to life in its frame.

Ashe spun, fire leaping around her hands, while protective barriers surged around the guards. Retreating, Crystal dug her fingers into Ghost's arm as they both cringed in pain.

Elias stepped out, his gaze already sweeping the hallway before he made it fully from the portal. Spotting them, he strode swiftly down the corridor.

"*What* happened?" he said to Nathaniel, as though asking the man to repeat himself.

Feeling every second between them and the Blood, Ashe turned, heading for the exit.

"Like I said," Nathaniel growled as he started after her. "We found one."

Her mind racing, Ashe ignored Elias' continued questions as she burst past the stairwell door. Cold cement surrounded her as she rushed for the first floor, and when she reached the landing, the open door to the alley made it easy to determine which way to go.

At her back, Nathaniel ordered her sharply to stay put and then shoved by her, giving her no chance to argue. Descending the short flight of steps to the alley, he checked either exit to the street and then scanned the rooftops.

Scowling, Ashe waited. Of its own accord, her gaze slid to the words on the wall.

Elias' brow drew down at the sight. "What the…"

"What is it?" Crystal asked behind them. "What happened?"

Ashe glanced back. The younger girl craned her neck, anxiously trying to see past the wizards.

"The Blood wrote 'Death to Taliesin'," Ashe said.

Crystal stared at her. Ashe's gaze flicked to Elias, but the bafflement on his face was answer enough. If any Merlin were working with the Blood, this was the first he'd learned of it.

"Where's Mud?" she asked.

"I sent him back," Elias said distractedly. "With the others. He wouldn't stop panicking at the idea of Blood wizards nearby."

He blinked in disbelief at his own statement, his gaze not leaving the iridescent words.

By the alleyway exit, Nathaniel motioned for them to follow. Without a word, Ashe headed out the door, leaving Elias to come behind.

Pedestrians ambled along the sidewalks and parked cars lined the road. Desperately, Ashe scanned the street, trying to find the Blood wizard amid the mess. Clutching Ghost's hand, Crystal came up and peeked around the edge of the brick building.

"There," the girl said, pointing.

For a heartbeat, Ashe couldn't see what the girl had spotted, and then the crowds parted. By a shop three blocks away, the Blood wizard turned and disappeared into another alley.

She started forward only to have Nathaniel grab her arm. Furiously, she tugged it away again.

"Taliesin," he whispered. "One block south."

Grimacing, she melted back against the alley wall. At her side, Nathaniel's hand flexed as he watched the street, waiting to strike.

A moment passed. It seemed like an eternity. She could almost feel the Blood wizard escaping.

Nathaniel checked around the corner. "All clear."

She followed him from the alley.

Three Taliesin rushed from behind a nearby building.

Her breath catching, Ashe froze. Without pause, the wizards dashed full speed across the intersection and down an adjacent street, running as though for their lives.

Brow drawing down, she looked to Nathaniel, but though he seemed cautious, the man just nodded in the direction the Blood had gone and then started walking. Drawing a breath and burying her confusion, Ashe followed.

At the mouth of the alley three blocks down the road, Nathaniel paused, glancing at her. Grudgingly, she fell back as he looked around the building's side. After a moment, he eased into the alley and then motioned for the others to follow, never taking his eyes from the narrow passageway.

Frustration surged as she came around the corner. The alley was as empty as she'd feared it'd be. Mouth tightening, she looked to Nathaniel and jerked her chin at the turn of the alleyway ahead. He nodded.

A shout rang out behind them.

From atop the building across the street, a Taliesin wizard plummeted toward the ground, his arms windmilling frantically as he fell. On the roof, another Taliesin stood, watching.

Crystal gasped and ducked her face into Ghost's shoulder as, with a sickening thud, the man hit the ground.

Pedestrians screamed. The wizard on the rooftop turned and walked away.

Ashe stared.

Nathaniel touched her arm, breaking her shock. Grimfaced, he gestured to the turn ahead. Swallowing hard, she nodded, determinedly ignoring the look he gave Elias and the guards.

Nothing moved in the next alley. Cautiously, they approached the opening to the street, and regret showed on Crystal's face after she peeked around the corner.

"I'm sorry," she said helplessly.

Ashe shook her head, disappointment rivaling the remnants of her alarm. "Not your fault," she said, watching the road. Apartments built into the husks of century-old buildings lined the road, with newly planted trees dotting the curbs. By the base of a stairway, small children played under the watchful eye of a young woman, while from another apartment, an old lady emerged, leading a fluffy dog by its bright pink leash.

Crystal didn't look comforted. "But he was the first one we'd–"

The sound of shattering glass carried through the open window of the building across the street.

Nathaniel shoved Ashe behind him. Mirroring the motion, Ghost pulled Crystal back protectively, his eyes locked on the window.

The crashing stopped. A heartbeat slid past.

A young Taliesin dashed out the apartment building door. Leaping from the steps to the ground, he stumbled and caught himself on the sidewalk before charging down the road.

The Blood wizard rushed out after him.

"Go!" Ashe cried.

Nathaniel motioned to the guards. The men took off, magic rising around them.

Trees and wrought iron stairways blurred as she chased them. Cars skidded to a stop as the wizards raced across the road and dogs barked madly as they passed. Up ahead, the young man ran for all he was worth, his arms and legs straining to give him more speed.

The Blood wizard never looked back.

Skidding around a corner, the young man darted between two apartment buildings. The Blood sprinted after him, barely pausing to catch an iron railing and whip himself around the turn.

Immediately the guards slowed, and Ashe stumbled to keep from rushing into them. A crash sounded between the buildings, and across the street, a couple with a stroller paused in confusion before shrugging and moving on.

"Stay back," Nathaniel ordered, pushing her aside as he came up and glanced around the corner.

He jerked back as another crash shuddered through the ground. Crackling violently, a burst of electricity shot out between the buildings and struck one of the young trees, killing it instantly.

"Take the Blood alive," Ashe whispered.

The look Nathaniel gave her made the conditional nature of his agreement abundantly clear.

They crept around the corner. The cobblestone path between the brick apartment buildings bisected the block through to the other side. Narrow windows faced the gentrified alley, with iron-railed porches extending from each. Leafy vines twined around the balconies even at ground level, providing cover as Ashe and the others inched closer.

The young man hadn't made it far. Pinned to the wall, he struggled in the grip of two much larger Taliesin. Livid red marks discolored his face, and one eye was swollen. A few feet away, the Blood stood, regarding him thoughtfully.

"It doesn't have to be like this, you know," the Blood said. "Just give us the information we want, and it'll be over."

"Screw you," the young man spat.

"We'll find your uncle, boy. Or someone else will tell us what we want to know. And then we'll have them, and you'll still be dead. So just give up. Tell me where to find the Taliesin Council, and I'll make it quick."

Behind the cover of the vines, Ashe glanced to Elias. Incredulity showed on his face as he stared at the group. With blatant deference, the two Taliesin waited for the commands of a man who appeared utterly human, while defiantly, the young man tried to hide his fear.

Cautiously, Ashe took her eyes from the Blood and looked back at Crystal and Ghost, jerking her chin at them. Swallowing, Ghost nodded and then pulled Crystal with him as he retreated behind the protection of the corner.

"Go to hell," the young man said.

Shaking his head, the Blood sighed. "Have it your way."

Electricity twisted around his fist. The young man recoiled, turning his face aside.

The Blood gasped as his own magic raced away from him and then back again. Crackling past him to strike his Taliesin companions, the electricity sent the wizards howling to the cobblestones. More magic followed, silencing their screams, and from behind the foliage, Nathaniel and the guards charged out.

Eyes wide, the young man looked from the Merlin to the Blood.

"Don't!" Ashe yelled.

Lightning arced from his hands. The Blood wizard crashed to the ground.

Shoving from the wall, the young man made a dash for the alley exit, only to skid to a stop as the guards cut him off. Turning sharply, he lunged in the opposite direction, but Nathaniel and Elias were there.

Magic flared and then vanished.

Terror overwhelmed the defiance in his eyes.

"W-what…" he stammered, his gaze darting across the men surrounding him.

"We're not here to hurt you," Ashe called, rising from behind the vines.

He barely gave her a glance. "Which one of you did that?"

No one answered.

"Dammit! Which one of you is the…" He trailed off, his gaze going to the two Taliesin. His brow twitched fitfully and then a trace of bravado crept onto his face. "Just do it then."

"Why are the Blood after you?" Ashe asked him.

He ignored her.

Elias grimaced. "She asked you a question, kid."

Still quivering despite his brave front, the young man scoffed. "So what? You Merlin bastards think I'll spill just because you've got a pretty girl asking the questions? Well, screw you."

Elias paused and then glanced to Nathaniel, his eyebrow twitching up.

"What? You the one in charge here?" the young man snapped at Nathaniel. "What're you waiting for?"

Nathaniel looked to Ashe and she could see the question in his eyes. She hesitated, and then bowed slightly.

With derision that was more forced than arrogant, the young man chuckled.

Face darkening, Nathaniel glanced to the guards. "Check the area. He could be stalling."

Two guards broke off, moving to either end of the alley. Warily, Ghost and Crystal peeked around the corner and then slowly approached.

"Yeah, that's what I thought," the young man sneered.

"What's your name, brat?" Nathaniel snapped.

"Fuck you."

"Charming," Elias retorted. "Speak to the king that way again and you'll wish we'd left you to the Blood wizard."

Magic twisted around Elias' fist and despite his bluster, the young man paled. His gaze darted between them.

"Luke," he allowed.

"Why are the Blood and Taliesin attacking each other?" Nathaniel asked.

"The what?"

Ashe's eyes narrowed. She glanced to Nathaniel and Elias.

A dry look flickered across Elias' face. "The man who nearly killed you," he elaborated.

"Bastard works for you," Luke said, adopting a dismissive tone. "You tell me."

Elias scoffed. "He had your Taliesin buddies kowtowing to him, kid. Try that answer again."

"And say what? You think I don't know he's working for you? Your girl tried to stop me from killing him, for pity's sake."

Ashe started to speak, and a sharp gesture from Nathaniel cut her off.

"She tried to stop you because we wanted information, you Taliesin pissant," he growled, striding toward Luke. The boy retreated till his heels bumped the brick wall. "We've been hunting his kind for longer than I care to tell you, and he was the first one we'd found. So yes, she didn't want you to kill him. And before you suggest that bastard worked for us again, I suggest you think long and hard about how exactly it will feel to have your own magic kill you."

Jaw clenched to keep it from shaking, Luke glared into the larger wizard's eyes.

"Why are your kind and Blood wizards attacking other Taliesin?" Elias asked.

Luke's gaze flicked over to him, taking on a derisive cast. "*I* don't know."

Irritation surged in her at his tone, but Nathaniel just took another step forward.

Struggling to hold onto his scorn, the young man pressed harder into the wall. "I swear, alright? I actually don't know. The bastards just cornered me and–"

"What was that about your uncle and the Council then?" Elias pressed.

Luke's face tightened, though he buried the fearful expression with lightning speed. "Hell if I know," he replied, his tone more dismissive than ever.

Ashe's brow drew down. The guy was barely breathing. His hands were braced on the brick wall, and he suddenly wouldn't look away from Elias, as though trying to convince the man by eye contact alone.

Suspicion crept up like rising floodwaters as the last few minutes played through her mind.

"Really." Elias said flatly. "You have no–"

"They want to kill your Council," she interrupted. "Don't they?"

Luke didn't answer, but she could see him trembling harder.

Her stomach twisted into a cold knot at the knowledge she'd guessed his fear right.

"And they want to blame it on us," she finished.

Nathaniel glanced back, and despite his lack of expression, she could see that the same thought was in his head as was in her own.

It'd be a slaughter. Even if the Taliesin Council knew what it was up against, the fight and its fallout would still go badly. Horribly. She wasn't sure there was strong enough a word. But the Blood would make it look like it'd been Merlin, same as they had with the bodies a few blocks away.

Her gaze dropped to the ground as implications spun through her head. The people of Taliesin would go mad for revenge. Her own people would retaliate to save themselves.

And the war would escalate till all the current bloodshed looked like nothing.

It was like a terrifying mirror of what happened eight years ago and the realization left her shaking. The story had always been that Taliesin's king butchered her family one cold Christmas Eve. He'd tracked them down and murdered them as vengeance for centuries of his people's magic being bound.

But the start of the war had been chaotic. Information was scarce and sketchy at best. No one had been entirely certain what'd happened.

And all signs had just pointed to Taliesin.

She wasn't certain she remembered how to breathe.

"You have to help us stop them," she said. "How do we find your Council?"

"Like I'm going to–"

"How do we find them!" she shouted.

He stared at her like she was deranged, and the tinge of contempt in his eyes grew stronger by the second. Her fingernails dug into her palms with the effort of not throwing his magic back in his face, and she couldn't stop herself from stalking toward him till Elias snagged her arm to hold her back.

With difficulty, she tore her gaze from him and looked to Nathaniel. "Your majesty?" she growled.

Nathaniel paused.

"Do you want the war to end?" he asked Luke.

The young man started to sneer.

"Before you open that mouth of yours," Elias interjected. "Think."

"If the Blood take out your Council, what do you think will happen?" Nathaniel said. "And what happens if they find your king too? So now you have a choice. You can keep being a smartass and let countless people die. Or you can shut the hell up and help us stop this war from reaching a level neither of our sides have seen."

Scornfully, Luke looked from one of them to the next, but as the seconds slid past, the derision cracked and began to fade.

"I don't know how to find the Council or the king," he said. At Elias' glare, his face took on an irritated cast. "I *don't*, okay? I swear."

Luke glanced between them again. "But," he allowed grudgingly, "I know someone who does."

* * *

"I'm just saying, Chuck is *not* going to be happy to see you." Luke stated as he opened the rusted alarm panel. Affixed to the alley-side wall of an aging brick building, the small box squealed at being disturbed.

Struggling to keep her hands from catching fire and her gaze from flicking yet again to the security camera above the door, Ashe said nothing. Though they'd only gone a few miles, it felt like they'd crossed half of Croftsburg with the idiotic young man, ducking through alleys and avoiding the endless streams of Taliesin suddenly hell-bent on killing each other. Behind her, the guards watched either end of the alley while a couple steps away, Nathaniel radiated enough impatient energy to power several city blocks.

Luke looked back and then grimaced when he saw his words had earned nothing but aggravated glares. Shaking his head, he returned to the number pad. Keys beeped discordantly beneath his fingers, and then a lock clunked within the metal door.

"Don't say I didn't warn you," he said, pulling the door open.

Fighting to keep from scowling, Ashe followed Nathaniel into the building.

A narrow hallway stretched ahead of them, at the end of which was the wildest conglomeration of furniture she'd ever seen. Victorian sofas pressed up against garish plastic armchairs, and crystal chandeliers dangled in front of posters made from the covers of magazines. Vases crowded every tabletop, along with lamps ranging from the ornate to the kitsch, while across the dusty front window, Good Old Days Antiques, By Appointment Only was stenciled in chipped paint.

Ignoring the mess, Luke stopped at a door to one side of the hall. The hinges squeaked as he yanked the tarnished knob, and a narrow staircase waited beyond, descending into pitch black darkness.

Reaching around the doorframe, he flipped a light switch and then cursed the cobwebs covering the surface. A dim bulb sputtered to life above the stairs as Luke headed down, and in plodding succession, other bulbs followed, lighting the basement hallway.

At the top of the steps, Nathaniel paused. Expressionless, he glanced back to Ashe and then farther to Elias.

"I'm coming with you," Ashe stated, reading the look in his eyes.

Without a word, he turned and walked down the stairs.

The concrete hall was silent but for the faint buzz of the old lights overhead. Doors lined the corridor, though most hung half off their hinges with broken furniture lurking in the shadows beyond. Unerringly, Luke continued to a door at the end of the hall and then pounded on the cracked wooden surface before heading in.

Ashe's brow furrowed. Resisting the urge to glance at the others, she followed the young man inside.

Leaning against the edge of a carved oak desk, an old man looked away from the headlines running across his flat panel television as Luke came into the room. On the green velvet desktop by his side, a bottle of brandy and a glass waited, their cut crystal edges catching the light of the candles burning atop the broad fireplace mantel on the opposite side of the room.

Above his sharp features and closely shaved goatee, the man's gray eyebrow twitched upward, though he gave no other sign of surprise. "You didn't expect me to be alarmed by over half a dozen Merlin, Lucas?"

"I typed the right code," Luke replied, a touch defensively.

The man ignored the response. As his unreadable gaze swept over them, he thumbed the mute button and then set down the remote control.

"So," he continued in the same dry tone as he stepped away from the desk. "To whom do I have the pleasure of speaking?"

Ashe glanced to Nathaniel. The large wizard's eyes narrowed as he weighed the situation.

"It's the king of Merlin and his bodyguards," Luke said into the pause, and she couldn't tell if his annoyance was intended for them or the old man. "I mean, I don't know who the kids are. That one tried to pretend she was their leader, and the others are cripples so…"

Ashe's face darkened at his tone, but she forced herself to keep silent as the old man's gaze flicked over her and then away. His lip twitched almost imperceptibly.

"The king of Merlin," he repeated to Nathaniel.

"And you are?" Nathaniel replied shortly.

The old man's lip twitched again. Turning, he crossed to an oak cabinet and pulled open the etched glass doors. Faint clinking sounded as he withdrew several crystal snifters.

"Charles Brentworth," he answered as he returned. "Formerly first in the line of authority on the Taliesin Council and… well, we never had regions quite like you." He gave Nathaniel an inscrutable smile. "A pleasure."

"We're looking for your Council."

The old man's expression took on a wry tinge as he poured brandy into the glasses. "I was going to ask the reason for your visit. I assumed, had you wished to kill me, you would have done so already."

Seething with impatience, Ashe glanced to Nathaniel, but he never took his eyes from the old man. "Where are they?"

"I haven't the foggiest idea," Brentworth replied calmly.

Nathaniel's gaze slid to Luke.

"What?" Luke protested. "Don't look at me."

"May I ask why you're searching for them? Beyond the obvious, that is."

Nathaniel returned his attention to Brentworth. "Blood wizards are hunting them."

Almost undetectably, the old man paused, and then his eyebrow lifted. "Who?"

Luke blanched as Nathaniel looked back to him.

"Listen… Uncle Charles…" the young man started, still watching Nathaniel.

"I apologize if Lucas wasted your time," Brentworth said. "But I simply don't think there's anything I can do to–"

"Oh, drop the act," Elias interrupted. "You've seen the news. All hell's breaking loose out there."

Brentworth regarded the television briefly. Homemade videos from amateur reporters played between bars of news station branding, showing scenes of police cordoning off another suicide.

"Well, we are in a war, my good fellow," the old man said with a hint of humored indulgence. "It does tend to ebb and flow."

Elias' eyebrows rose, and it was all Ashe could do to keep from exploding.

"Tell him," Nathaniel growled at Luke.

The young man faltered. "T-there really are these freaks, uncle. The bastard – sorry – I mean, the guy broke into my apartment. He looked human. But he nearly blew the whole place up."

Brentworth said nothing.

"He chased me down. Some Taliesin were working with him and they caught me. They wanted to know where the Council was, where you were, all of it. The guy was about to kill me, and then these Merlin showed up. The king here stole his magic, wiped them all out and then took mine too. But… the guy was real. I swear. He knew about you and the Council, and was damn, err, really determined to find you."

"So you led a collection of Merlin and a pair of young cripples to me instead?"

Luke shifted uncomfortably. "It wasn't like that…"

"And he took your magic?" Brentworth continued, glancing to Nathaniel.

"He still has it! Can't you tell?"

Pensively, Brentworth shook his head, and then looked away. His gaze drifted to the television.

Ashe felt like she was going to scream.

"Come on, Councilor," Elias urged, careful control in his tone. "They're murdering your people. They're blaming it on us, and your leaders are next. You do the math."

Silent, the old man watched as reporters cut to a press conference with the police chief. Even muted, the chief's emphatic denial of the fact he felt out of his depth was easy to read.

Brentworth sighed. "My apologies. My nephew is rather like a human, in his way. Only seeing what he expects to see."

His gaze flicked to her. "Your majesty."

Ashe froze.

"You have the look of your father about you," the old man explained.

Politely, he extended a snifter to Nathaniel, who regarded him and the glass with the impassivity of a wall. Unperturbed, Brentworth proffered additional glasses to Elias and the guards, and then nodded acquiescingly when they refused.

Ashe exhaled, regrouping. "Okay, so… where's your Council?"

"Safe," Brentworth replied, leaning against his desk again. "At least, one would hope they remain so. They've become rather adept at hiding, given that they've known the 'Blood' have been after them for quite some time."

"And?" she asked into the pause.

"And quite frankly, your highness, I'm not about to tell you more than that. You are, after all, our enemy."

He gave her a polite, but slightly condescending smile, and returned his attention to the news.

She stared, her self-control running a hard race with her temper and losing. "You've got to be kidding me."

Raising an eyebrow, he glanced back at her. "Why is that, exactly?"

"Because I'm trying to save your councilmembers' lives!"

"So you say," he said, his tone making clear his limited allowance for the possibility.

"And I'm trying to do that even if, *quite frankly*, they're not really my concern! I want the Blood dead, preferably before they make this damn war worse. That's it. So we can either do this now and stop them from murdering your Council and possibly your king, or we can wait and your leaders will die. Which would you prefer?"

He regarded her for a moment, and then his gaze flicked across Nathaniel and the others.

"But you see, your majesty," he told her quietly. "There really is no reason I should trust you. After all, you *are* Merlin."

"And you're Taliesin," she retorted. "And I really don't care."

The old man said nothing.

"Clock's ticking here, Councilor," Elias murmured.

Brentworth regarded him dryly and then looked away. His gaze landed on the television. An apartment burned on the screen.

The wryness melted slowly. He glanced back at Ashe, the barest hint of a considering look touching his face.

Her brow drew down warily.

"The Council is in Chaunessy Tower," Brentworth admitted. "Near the center of downtown. But," he added as Ashe looked to Nathaniel and Elias. "They will not take kindly to your showing up there. Not without an escort."

At her expression, he gave her a small smile. "So we can take a few of my cars."

Chapter Fifteen

"Cole?"

The little girl's brow wrinkled unhappily as the plane's landing jostled her. Eyes squeezed shut, she moved her arm as though it weighed a hundred pounds and tried to put her hand to her head.

"Shh," he said, watching her between glances to the wizards. By the cockpit, Vivian and Quinton were speaking in low voices to the pilots.

"What…" Lily started, but the question seemed to come with difficulty and she ran out of energy before the remainder could emerge.

"Everything's fine," he said quietly. "Just take it easy."

Lily wrinkled her brow again, not buying a word of it even in her stupor. He grimaced. It didn't matter. As lies went, it wasn't exactly convincing anyway.

"Taliesin wizards," he explained. "They drugged you and–"

He looked down as she slumped against his side. In slow rhythm, her chest rose and fell. Gently, he shook her shoulder.

The girl stirred slightly and then continued sleeping.

Cole sighed. She'd woken up. After hours of trying to bring her around, it was progress.

Vivian and Quinton returned from the cockpit, silently taking a window each to survey the airport. He glanced over as the plane began to turn. Large swaths of tarmac and countless blue and gold lights surrounded the private jet. Beyond the expanse of withered grass and painted concrete, a long chain-link fence topped with barbed wire hemmed them in.

The plane completed its turn, bringing a small hangar into view, past which lay the sprawl of a busy airport. As though set about by some giant child, massive jets dotted the space around the gleaming terminal, and people moved among the planes, their forms hardly bigger than toys themselves. Vans and luggage carts wove through the bustle, and as he watched, several of the larger vehicles turned and headed their way.

With a small jerk, the jet came to a stop. Wordlessly, Quinton rose and yanked the door handle as Vivian looked to Cole.

"Hurry," she ordered.

His eyes narrowed, but the woman was already leaving the plane. Scooping Lily and the staff from the seat, he inched his way through the tight quarters and then followed Vivian down the steps.

"Come on," she urged, striding toward the hangar.

Hesitating, he scanned the area. A small group of people emerged from a door on the hangar's side and hurried toward the plane, their attention clearly divided between the aircraft and the vans rushing their way.

He grimaced. Wizards then, and thus no help at all. Running was out as well, since nothing but grass and concrete surrounded them for several hundred yards. With an unconscious kid in his arms, there was no chance he'd get far.

Rage and frustration churning inside him, he tightened his grip on Lily and followed the woman.

Three silver sports cars waited in the hangar's shadow, all utterly identical down to their license plates and the partially open windows on their sides. Behind the wheel of each, a bulky wizard sat, baseball caps and dark sunglasses rendering them as identical as their cars.

"Move," Quinton growled.

"This way," Vivian said in a nicer tone, motioning tensely to the center vehicle.

His gaze went back to the airport. The vans were coming closer. Given the looks on the others' faces, there wasn't much question of who the drivers could be.

Cursing all wizards with the exception of Lily, he headed for the car.

The cramped back seat made it clear that comfort hadn't been forefront in the designers' minds when they put together the aerodynamic wisp of a car. With his knees almost squashed to his chest, the staff crushed lengthwise across his lap, and the little girl scrunched into the space beside him, he was fairly certain it would take the jaws of life to pry them both from the vehicle whenever they finally reached their destination.

Vivian barely spared him a glance as she swung into the car. "Go."

Gravity shoved him into the unforgiving seat as the driver slammed the pedal to the floor. Twisting awkwardly, Cole glanced through the back window and watched as the other cars sped in opposite directions. Hurriedly, the small ground crew was ushering the plane into the hangar while others were waiting to shut the doors.

Drawing a breath, he shifted back around, suddenly wishing that, even if Lily didn't wake up soon, he could've at least had a gun.

With a jolt that nearly drove his knees into his chin, the car leapt from the tarmac to the service road, and the driver cursed as the tires slid across the gravel before righting themselves. Bracing herself with one hand on the ceiling and the other on the dash, Vivian ignored him, her gaze locked on the airfield.

Her phone buzzed. Eyes still on the service road, she drew it out.

"Yes?" She paused, and then cursed, the words precise and vicious in her cultured tone. "Divert from your route in case they kept some alive."

She clicked the phone off and caught sight of the driver looking to her.

"First car's gone," she said succinctly.

The man's face darkened.

"Can you get down lower?" Vivian asked, glancing to Cole.

He stared at her, and then shifted on the cramped seat, succeeding in lowering himself a few more inches.

"Hang on," the driver called.

Vivian turned as the man released one hand from the steering wheel and extended it through the open window at his side. Pain spiked through Cole's skull and, up ahead, the gate in the airfield fence burst open. Gripping the wheel again, the driver hauled it around while the car left the gravel and bounded onto the country road. Snagging the back of Vivian's seat, Cole barely stopped himself from crashing into Lily as gravity tugged him sideways.

The little girl whimpered, her voice scarcely audible over the growl of the tires and the wind's roar.

Righting himself awkwardly, Cole glanced through the smoked

rear window. A blue sports car was visible in the distance.

And it was coming up fast.

"Um…" he started.

Vivian glanced back. Her eyes narrowed, tracking the vehicle. "Stephen…"

"I see them," the driver replied. He pressed the accelerator harder.

The blue car fell back briefly, and then began to match their speed.

Scowling, Stephen hit the brakes and the clutch. With his free hand, he downshifted while his other hand cranked the wheel around hard. The car whipped a tight turn onto another road, sending Cole crashing into Lily.

"Ow," Lily protested sleepily.

Extricating himself from the seat, Cole looked down, but the girl's eyes were still closed. "Lily," he said, trying to keep his voice low. He tossed a glance to the rear window.

The blue car fishtailed as it raced onto the road.

"Come on, Lily," Cole urged, shaking her shoulder.

Her brow furrowed in protest.

Vivian lifted her phone. "We've got company."

Cole shook the girl again. "You've got to wake up, kid. Come on."

"Head hurts…" Lily murmured.

"I'll get you something for it soon. But I need you to wake up now."

Her eyes opened slightly and then she cringed as if pained by the light. He reached over and shielded her eyes with a hand.

"Head… hurts…"

He grimaced. "Please, Lily."

She didn't answer.

Exhaling in frustration, he glanced to the window again. Country roads were surrendering rapidly to neighborhoods on the fringe of a city. Sapling trees and cookie-cutter houses blurred past, beyond which brief glimpses of parks and playgrounds could be seen. Stoplights in irrelevant colors zipped by as the car flew through intersections, bringing traffic to a screeching halt.

Block for block, the blue car kept pace.

"Where *are* they?" Stephen muttered.

"They said–" Vivian started.

A streak of silver raced across the intersection behind them. The sports car slammed into the blue vehicle, propelling it into a light pole.

Letting out a victorious whoop, Stephen whipped the car around a turn, leaving the accident behind. At his side, Vivian watched through the rear window, grimfaced.

Cole blinked and then turned back around in the cramped seat.

Streets sped by, one emptying into another as the car wove through the city. Stoplights flashed past, pointless and ignored, and neighborhoods became commercial districts, which transformed into towers of steel and stone.

Tires squealed behind them. From a blind intersection, a silver sports car barreled out, narrowly missing their bumper. Shattered windows marred its sides and its back was completely destroyed. Screeching around the turn, it careened wildly into the opposite lane and then took off after them.

"What the hell?" Stephen cried.

Vivian turned. "Those sons of…" Her glare snapped to Stephen. "Go!"

He didn't need the instruction. Crushing the pedal down, he sent the car charging into the dense traffic ahead.

Cole grabbed Lily, pulling the unconscious girl closer.

Through the intersection, twin city buses raced past in opposite directions, and the sports car lunged between them. Instantly, Stephen hauled on the wheel, veering the car down a narrow fork in the busy street. Tall buildings crowded in, cutting off the sunlight. Cole glanced back.

The other car was nowhere to be seen.

Lily stirred next to him and he turned. Brow furrowing, the girl struggled to lift her head, succeeding after a moment's effort.

"Cole…?"

"I'm here."

The furrows faded, though she didn't open her eyes.

Grimacing, he glanced up and then froze.

A silver sports car shot past an intersection a block away. Buildings brought his view up short, and then gave way again a heartbeat later.

The car was still there.

Swallowing hard, he looked down at Lily. "Hey, guys?" he called to the wizards.

They ignored him. Thumbing a button on her phone, Vivian tersely said, "Coming in fast," and then hung up.

Cole turned back to the window, watching the other car.

"Hang onto something!" Stephen yelled.

Before Cole had time to do more than register the words, the wizard crushed the brakes to the floor.

Lily tumbled forward with the staff, and Cole followed, his shoulder slamming into the metal supports beneath the thin seat cushions. Without pause, the vehicle cornered sharply, flinging him from the seat toward the door.

The ground sloped and magic rushed past in a crescendo of pain that faded as swiftly as it had come. Sunlight vanished and concrete walls appeared inches from the windows. The tires screeched as Stephen yanked the wheel around and hit the brakes again, the sound echoing impossibly loud. Shedding the last of its momentum, the car skidded and then lurched to a stop.

Vivian threw open her door. "Move!"

Glaring in her general direction, Cole pushed awkwardly away from the door. In a tangle between the seats and the floor, Lily groaned, her eyes fluttering open.

With a wince, he straightened and then froze as their surroundings came into view. People encircled the car, their lack of weapons and the dull ache in the back of his head practically broadcasting their status as wizards. Beyond them, concrete supports stretched from the floor to the ceiling of a massive underground parking garage. A few mismatched sedans provided cover for the wizards guarding the entrance slope, and along the walls, small cameras panned slowly back and forth like metronomes, watching everything.

In the midst of the wizards, Vivian barked rapid-fire instructions, her words muffled by the closed door. Fury on her face, the woman spun and yanked the door handle, nearly spilling Cole onto the concrete.

"Out!" she snapped.

Extracting himself from the seat, he drew the staff with him, noting with distant surprise that it appeared miraculously unharmed. As he reached for Lily, the woman made an irate noise.

Cole ignored her. "Come on, kid," he said, gripping the little girl's arm and helping her out of her wedged position.

Lily swayed as she reached her feet. "Where are we?" she asked, putting a hand to her tousled head as she blinked at the ground. "What happened?"

He glanced to Vivian, but the woman just gave him a dark look. "I said move," she snarled.

Putting her words to action, she gestured sharply to Stephen and then strode toward the elevator on the far side of the parking lot. Cole eyed the wizard as Stephen moved in behind him, cutting off any retreat toward the vehicle and wordlessly pressuring him to obey.

Grimacing, Cole put an arm around Lily's shoulder, guiding the little girl onward. Dizzily, she stumbled and then caught her balance on his side, her eyes locked on the concrete as though watching it roil beneath her.

"What happened?" she asked again.

He didn't answer. Up ahead, the elevator door pulled back, revealing a glistening chrome and wood-trimmed interior monitored by an array of tiny cameras all its own. By the opening, Vivian tapped her foot impatiently, her gaze on the exit from the garage.

"Cole?" Lily persisted.

His footsteps slowed. He could feel the wizards behind him, watching his every move. All around, the security cameras swept back and forth, covering every inch of the underground expanse.

He wasn't breathing. He wasn't sure he could anymore. Everything they'd gone through, and here they stood, watched by cameras and wizards, and squarely in the Council's hands.

And short of having an eight year old blow them all to hell and probably get herself killed, there wasn't a damn thing he could do about it.

He hated wizards. So much it hurt and the pain left him shaking.

They manipulated people, used people, lied and killed and didn't give a damn about people. But for Lily, every one of them were bastards, and if, a few floors up, he had the chance to do something about that, then maybe…

At his back, Stephen made a wordless growl. Cole closed his eyes. Maybe…

He wondered what his mom and dad would think of him now.

Drawing a breath, he opened his eyes and led Lily to the elevator. The door slid closed.

"What's going on?" the girl asked blearily.

"It's going to be okay," he said.

Lily winced as she looked up at him.

Her gaze caught on the wizards. The blood drained from her face.

"Lily," Cole said as the elevator began to climb. "It's going to be okay."

She stared at him. Watching her carefully, he handed her the staff.

"Just… hang onto that," he finished softly. "Alright?"

Trembling, she swallowed hard. Her gaze returned to the wizards and he could see the panic rising inside her.

"Hey," he said. "I promise."

She hesitated, and then nodded, clearly determined to trust his word. Resolutely, her grip on the staff tightened.

Cole looked back to the elevator door, watching his blurred reflection there.

He didn't want to be a monster.

But maybe he didn't have any choice.

━━━━◆━━━━

Behind the darkened windows of the limousine, Jamison glanced over as Brogan hung up the phone.

"They lost them near the fifteen hundred block of Midway Avenue, near Chaunessy Tower," Brogan said. "But they think there's a barrier hidden in the building walls."

Jamison's gaze slid to the man kneeled below. Sweat shone on the wizard's face, while blood dribbled past his lips to stain the floor.

"What other defenses are there?" Jamison asked softly.

Ragged gasps escaped the man, his unseeing gaze locked on the carpet.

Expressionless, Jamison sent the wizard's magic ripping back through his body, making the man thrash and scream. Ignoring the noise, Brogan turned in his seat and motioned the limousine driver onward.

"What other defenses?" Jamison repeated as the screams faded to whimpering.

"Each entrance…" the man whispered. "Twenty guards… dozen more… every level… security cameras… on the walls… alarms… on the outside doors…"

Tears slid from the man's closed eyes as he fell silent.

"Excellent," Jamison said. "And now…"

He lifted the man's cell phone from the seat. "Tell them to lower the barrier. You have a prisoner. And you're coming in."

———— ◆ ————

"How much farther?" Ashe asked tensely.

Brentworth sighed. "Just a few more minutes, your majesty," he said from the front passenger seat. "Though, as I have already explained, the Council's defenses are more than sufficient. I am certain they are fine."

Eyeing the back of the man's head, she fought the urge to snap at him. It was the same answer he'd given the past three times she'd asked.

She turned, checking the positions of the other vehicles. Two car lengths away, Elias and the twins followed in a dented Jeep that probably should have been put out of its misery a decade ago. Similarly, Luke and the other guards were another two lengths behind that, trailing in a tiny pipsqueak of a car that she marveled they could all fit inside. The retired councilmember apparently owned a dozen such vehicles, all registered under false names and stashed in nearby garages, just in case he'd ever needed them.

"And the king?" she asked, still watching the cars. "You're certain he's fine too?"

Silence answered her.

She turned back. "Councilman?"

"The king will not be an issue."

Her gaze met Nathaniel's briefly. "And why is that?"

Brentworth took a moment to respond. "Because there is a chance he has been dead for some time."

Ashe's eyebrows climbed. "What?"

"A 'chance'?" Nathaniel repeated.

"We were unable to recover a body. At least, not the full components of one. But what we found pointed to the king being dead, yes."

She paused, taking in the neutral tone with which he delivered the words. They could've been discussing missing pieces from a coffee table puzzle. "But you're not sure?"

He shook his head.

"And you haven't gone looking for him since?"

"We've looked your majesty," Brentworth assured her. "Trust me on that."

She glanced to Nathaniel incredulously. "So if your king isn't dead, then what's he doing? Why hasn't he come back?"

Brentworth paused. Carefully, he turned to her.

"Because, if he is not dead, then he remains the leader of the Blood."

Ashe froze. And then she blinked as her mind tried to play his words back again.

They didn't sound any less terrifying the second time around.

"Excuse me?" she heard herself ask in a tone far too calm to be real.

"Victor Jamison, king of Taliesin, betrayed us all, your highness. If he is not dead, then he is the one hunting the Taliesin Council. And the one who created those who call themselves the Blood."

She looked down. Her hands were far away and ever-so-bizarrely numb. She wanted to laugh for some reason. Chuckle at an impossibility that wasn't really funny at all.

The Taliesin king. And the winter night her family died. It'd all been true. Taliesin had killed them. He'd killed them. The Blood had killed them.

"Why?"

The word was raw. The calm tone was gone. Her mouth moved, but someone else was speaking now.

Silence answered. Her gaze snapped up to find Brentworth watching her, and at her expression, he sighed.

"Because he wanted power, your highness," he said, as though it was obvious.

She trembled. Nathaniel glanced to her warily.

"I would choose your words carefully, Councilor," he warned Brentworth. "And do not lie to her or I assure you, she will make it the last thing you ever do."

Brentworth's gaze went between them briefly. He inclined his head. "As you say."

For a long moment, he paused, weighing his words. A considering look flickered through his eyes.

"Taliesin is not like Merlin, your highness," he began delicately. "Contrary to your manner of government, our Council does not follow the rule of kings. We make a pretense of submission as a comfort to the people but, in actuality, our royalty are only figureheads. Icons for the purpose of morale. Nothing more."

She didn't respond. She wasn't certain she could have if she'd tried.

"Victor sought to change that. After his father passed away, he resisted the Council's efforts to mold him into the king our people needed him to be. He wanted more power. More control. He wasn't content to live as we had for nearly five centuries. And so there were... disagreements. The Council was forced to go to greater and greater lengths to keep him in line, but our efforts failed. And we had no idea how unstable he had become.

"The king wanted to break the spell. In his mind, restoring magic to himself was the only way to truly overcome the Council. And so, one snowy winter night, he did just that. With the aid of his supporters, he tracked down your family, slipped away from the bodyguards we'd assigned him, and then dressed as a delivery person and headed to your grandparents' home. Last minute Christmas gifts, I'm given to understand. And when your grandfather answered the door…" Brentworth sighed. "He shot him. A silenced weapon, I would assume. But he took Nicholas' blood, mixed it with his own and…"

Brentworth looked down. "The 'Blood', you see. It freed them. Or so they said. But the spell broke. Explosively."

Ashe's jaw tightened as she fought to keep the memories at bay. Oblivious, the old man turned his gaze to the window.

"Affiliation is a funny thing," he said contemplatively. "It damned us five hundred years ago. And eight years ago, it created something new. The spell was broken. The Merlin king and his family were killed, whether through the destruction of the spell or purely for revenge. And Victor and those with him… became something else.

"Utterly human in appearance, yet magically powerful like no wizard we had ever seen. His strength and that of his supporters dwarfed even the strongest of us, and we couldn't be certain what he would do. We had never been certain. Which is why, in our efforts at control, we'd finally hit upon something that we thought would make him see reason once and for all."

Brentworth glanced back at her. "We took his son. Had taken him, in fact, mere hours before Victor broke the spell. And when the king came for us, we suddenly found that, rather than negotiating for Victor to follow Council rule, we were bargaining for our lives with that of his child.

"It was objectionable," he admitted. "Some would say wrong. But the boy was a half-Merlin cripple and his mother wound up slaughtered by Victor's hand not twelve hours later. In light of the evidence, one can only assume the boy would have died too. Our actions, however unpleasant, saved the child's life.

"Victor disappeared almost immediately after. The Council put the boy in hiding and then followed suit. And in a few weeks, we received word that his supporters had turned on him. With their magic back, they suddenly had little use for obeying a king."

He paused. "It was convenient. Plausible. But terribly convenient. The Blood have continued hunting the Council through the intervening years, an effort which could be prompted by a desire to take over Taliesin, or which could be Victor still trying to reclaim his son. And so you see, we say 'most likely dead'. But we cannot be sure."

Mouth tightening, he fell silent, and then looked back up at her. "For what it is worth, I am sorry about what happened to your family. I will not insult you by saying I'm displeased to have our magic back. But the method by which it was returned was… deeply unfortunate."

Ashe regarded him. The considering look still tinged his gaze, though he nodded to her in acknowledgement of his words.

She turned away. Outside the car windows, skyscrapers swept by. She barely noticed.

The Taliesin king had killed them. Because of a stupid Taliesin power struggle, he'd wiped her family from the face of the earth. In the fallout, hundreds, maybe thousands had died. Children. Families. People he'd never met, who might've even agreed with him if he'd ever taken the time to ask.

But instead, he'd just killed them all.

Memory teased at the edge of her mind. Harris said Brogan and Jamison.

So that answered one question. Victor Jamison, the king of Taliesin who'd orchestrated the murder of her whole family, was still very much alive.

"How much farther?" she asked quietly, her voice foreign to her own ears.

From the corner of her eye, she could see Brentworth glance to Nathaniel. "Another few blocks," the old man replied. "We're almost there."

She nodded.

"Your highness?" Nathaniel asked.

Ashe didn't answer, watching the buildings go by.

She wondered if he'd be there, at Chaunessy with the Council, or if he'd stay in hiding. If he did show up, he'd almost certainly try to take the magic of anyone who attempted to fight him, assuming he knew how. Which meant she'd have to get to him first. Before he could do to her or any of her people what she wanted to do to him.

Her gaze tracked toward Brentworth, the reason for the look in his eyes finally falling into place.

He wanted her to fight their king. Stop their king. As the only other person with the ability to bind magic, she stood the best chance. And if she died in the process… well, she was a Merlin. And the last of their ostensible nobility, an institution he disliked anyway. Her death would probably just be 'deeply unfortunate' too.

She felt cold, though she wasn't entirely certain why. The blood just seemed frozen within her and the air left icicles on her lungs. It was strange.

The car came to a stop at the curb. Across the wide sidewalk, mirrored doors waited in the side of a building so high it blocked the sun.

"Your majesty?" Nathaniel asked quietly as Brentworth stepped from the car. "Are you alright?"

She drew a breath, her gaze still on the sheer glass walls, and carefully, she set the memories and the history aside. They didn't matter. It wasn't like the truth or Brentworth's plotting changed her plans anyway.

The other cars pulled up behind them. Nervousness radiating from them, the twins climbed from the Jeep, Elias following a heartbeat later.

"Your highness?" Nathaniel asked again.

She glanced to him, and paid no attention to the way the concern strengthened in his eyes.

"Oh, yeah," she answered calmly. "I'm fine."

Chapter Sixteen

ole closed his eyes as the glistening ebony doors swung
ponderously open. Magic permeated the air. He could
feel Lily tremble as she picked up on it, and her quivering
only served to worsen his already pounding headache.

Of course the Council surrounded themselves with magic. The
wizard bastards couldn't get enough of it.

Fighting back a scowl, Cole kept Lily behind him as he followed
Vivian through the doors. He'd tried to shield the girl from view for
the last few minutes, as they'd passed level upon level of checkpoints
on the way to this floor. It had been a fool's errand, given the sheer
number of guards and cameras surrounding them, but there was
nothing for it. As with everything else, it was just the best he could
do.

At his back, Lily shivered, whether from fear or the icy air, he
couldn't tell. Dim light emanated from frosted glass sconces lining
the walls and glistened on the black marble floor, though it barely
lessened the shadows pressing down from the distant ceiling. Up
ahead, a ten-foot-high wall ringed the space, and behind the top

ledge, anonymous silhouetted figures sat in high-backed chairs and gazed down on the spotlighted center of the room like manifestations of a conspiracy theorist's nightmare.

Cole's lip twitched humorlessly, disgust moving through him again.

Tense decorum on her face, Vivian took a breath before stepping into the spotlight and then motioning him to follow. Cole didn't move. Irritation cracked her demure expression as the woman glared at him askance, while behind him, Stephen growled a quiet warning.

"Fine," Cole muttered.

Satisfaction showed in the wizards' eyes, but he ignored it. Keeping Lily as hidden as possible, he moved forward, the blazing light overhead further disguising the figures above. Instantly burying their frustration behind masks of propriety, Vivian and Stephen bowed to the Council, though grimaces twitched the wizards' faces a heartbeat later when he didn't do the same. Reaching over, the woman grasped his arm and tugged it in sharp-nailed encouragement.

He pulled away, damned if he was going to pay obeisance to his own kidnappers.

"Hello Cole."

His gaze snapped to the figure at the center of the Council.

"Who's your friend?" the deep voice asked.

Vivian grabbed the girl while Stephen snagged his arms from behind. Jerking in the man's grasp, Cole fought to break his hold, succeeding only in sending pain shooting through his shoulders. Desperately, Lily clung to him, but the woman was too strong and with a vicious yank, she ripped the child away and sent her stumbling into the light.

Silent, the Council watched the exchange, saying nothing as Lily rushed back toward Cole and ran into Vivian instead. Spinning the girl around, the woman pinned Lily's arms, immobilizing the child for the Council and giving no sign she noticed Cole struggling behind her.

"He calls her Lily," Vivian told them.

Magic strengthened around the room. Internally, Cole swore.

"Hey!" he snapped, trying to pull their attention back to him. "I'm not here to talk to you about some kid!"

"How long has Merlin been working with the Blood, Cole?" the voice asked.

Ice hit his veins. "What? Merlin? Who said anything about–"

"How long have they been turning their royal children into monsters?"

"I don't know what you're–"

"The staff. The 'human' girl," the voice continued implacably. "Princess Lily. She looks like the Merlin king. She has a weapon from their golden age. How long have you sided with them without our knowing, Cole? What did they offer you?"

Terrified, Lily twisted in the woman's grasp, her panicked gaze finding Cole. Faint glints of light leaked from the staff in her hands.

"You'll find it was a mistake to conspire with them," the voice said.

The magic in the room surged.

Cole yanked against Stephen's grip. "She's not–"

A door flung open at the far end of the councilors' seats. A short figure rushed in, making a beeline for the center of the row and paying no attention to the seething weight of magic hovering in the air.

The figure whispered to the central councilmember, who instantly rose.

"Security breach!" the councilor barked. He gestured sharply to Vivian and Stephen. "Take them to the service tunnel! The rest of you, escape routes! Now!"

Stephen and Vivian didn't waste a second. Wrenching Cole around, the wizard muscled him toward the side of the room, with Vivian bringing Lily behind. Along the ledge, the councilors headed for the exit the smaller figure had used, while on the wall beneath the elevated seats, Stephen shoved one of the tall ebony panels, revealing a door to a blindingly white room.

Cries of confused alarm rang out. Frozen for a moment, a few councilors recovered themselves enough to bang on the locked door while others spun, abandoning the exit for the stairs nearby.

With a snarl, Stephen flung Cole around the doorway and into the white room. Scrambling up to his knees, Cole barely had time to turn before the wizard sent Lily stumbling after him. Grabbing her to stop her from hitting the ground, he winced as she clung to him, the staff squashed awkwardly between them.

He looked up from her tousled head. Through the massive window set to one side of the door, he could see the whole of the chamber, though from the opposite side, he'd been certain the space the window occupied had been nothing but wall. Councilors were running down the stairs and rushing toward them across the marble floor, while by the doorway, Stephen motioned for them to hurry. Across the room, Vivian punched a code into a keypad on the wall and then cursed vehemently when the numbers remained stolidly red.

The door to the Council chamber exploded.

Ballistic chunks of wood and metal ripped through the center of the room, tearing down the councilors as it passed. The percussion drove the surviving wizards to the ground and left debris tumbling in its wake.

Stephen gasped, frozen by the sight of the wreckage and the writhing bodies within, and then he slammed the door. Eyes wide, he looked to Vivian. The woman was staring through the blood-splattered window in horror.

"Move!" he shouted.

The order broke her paralysis, and she whirled back to the wall, jabbing codes into the unresponsive panel with hysterical ferocity.

Shaking, Cole climbed the rest of the way to his feet, his gaze locked on the window and the bodies on the opposite side. In his arms, Lily began to turn, and he gripped her tighter, halting the little girl's motion.

"Don't," he said.

Barely breathing, he watched the councilors. The survivors were trying to rise. Dust filled the room like smoke, obscuring the wizards on the far side, and the bright spotlight swung like a pendulum, revealing and then hiding the bodies on the floor.

Through the dust, a man stumbled into the room. Crashing to his knees on the marble, he stared at the bodies and then slowly began rocking back and forth, clutching his stomach with burnt and blistered arms.

Cole swallowed hard, barely recognizing Quinton through the blood covering him.

"Those sons of…" Stephen whispered.

Vivian turned at the words. A choked gasp escaped her and tears welled in her eyes. She spun back to the panel.

Still rocking, Quinton looked up, his gaze drifting over the chamber and then stopping on the window as though looking into the eyes of everyone inside the white room.

"Can he…?" Cole started.

"No," Stephen said, his tone more cautious than confident. "This is an observation room for council aides. No one can see or hear anything from that– oh, hell."

More wizards rushed into the chamber. Jabbing the keypad harder, Vivian whimpered and didn't turn around. With methodical precision, the wizards swept the space, kicking over bodies and heading for the outer edges of the room.

"The door, Viv," Stephen prompted, his gaze on the wizards. "Get the damn door."

"It won't–" the woman replied, choking on her tears. "All the overrides aren't–"

Stephen tossed a sharp glance back. "Keep it together or take my place over here."

The woman swallowed and shook her head, trying to focus. "No. No, I can get it."

Growling a wordless encouragement, Stephen returned his attention to the other room.

Cole ignored them. At the outer reaches of the chamber, the wizards turned from their surveillance to form a perimeter, giving no sign they could hear the cries of the injured or Quinton's sobs. Rigidly, they drew themselves to attention, their formality breaking only for the anticipatory grins he could see hovering around their lips.

He shivered, suddenly wanting to join Vivian on the opposite side of the room.

Two figures strode into the Council chamber, dust curling around them as they moved. Silhouetted by the dim light, they appeared as little more than shadows.

Then the swinging spotlight caught them.

And everything became perfectly still.

Beneath the garish illumination, Victor Jamison paused, the light overhead nothing compared to the glow of Blood magic on his skin. His gaze dropped contemplatively to a quivering wizard splayed on the marble and swiftly, the scarred giant beside him kicked the wounded man over.

"Hello Terrence," Victor said.

Cole's gaze snapped from his father to the walls and back as the sound of Victor's voice carried with crystalline clarity through the small room.

"It's been a long time."

On the floor, the wizard coughed, blood seeping from countless shrapnel wounds. Weakly, he tried to drag himself away and failed.

"Where is my son?"

Cole choked on his own air.

At the wizard's silence, a thread of electricity whipped down, slicing the man's chest to the bone.

"Where is my son?" Victor repeated in the same calm, controlled tone.

"You won't... he's gone... you can't kill us..."

Victor regarded the gasping councilor. His face could have been made of ice.

And then his hand rose.

"That won't work this time."

Lightning lit the room.

Cringing from the blinding flashes, Cole heard Stephen curse as screams filled the Council chamber. Her face buried in his side, Lily's grip spasmed tighter. As the lightning faded, Cole straightened, one hand still averting Lily's gaze.

Smoke clouded the air beyond the window. Within the ring of silently observing wizards, the councilors' bodies lay scattered, their corpses reduced to smoldering bones and blackened flesh. Huddled at Jamison's heels, Quinton stared around him, his mouth working like a fish on dry land.

And then he began to scream.

The giant lifted an eyebrow. Expressionless, Victor turned away.

Magic cracked down. Like a marionette robbed of its strings, Quinton hit the ground and didn't move again.

Victor glanced back at the giant. "Cole's here. Find him."

The giant nodded and then strode for the door, motioning for a few wizards to follow. Ignoring them, Victor looked down at the charred bones. A heartbeat passed before his gaze rose to the remainder of the room.

Cole stared, his thoughts spinning circles down into insensibility. His dad was alive. He hadn't been shot. He hadn't died because of the Council. He hadn't died from the Blood wizards. His father…

Led them.

Was one of them.

His father…

A gasp escaped him. He couldn't breathe. Couldn't…

Vivian let out a cry as the keypad turned green. Reeling, Cole looked to her briefly before the sight of his father drew his gaze back again. Victor still stood there, the bodies around him. The bodies of the councilmembers he'd killed.

Cole had wanted them dead too.

He'd wanted…

Shivers struck him and they wouldn't stop. In his arms, Lily began to squirm. She needed air. He was crushing her against him.

Gasping again, he released the girl, blinking at her in dumbstruck shock as she began to turn. Cole's hands moved of their own accord, blocking her view.

His father led the Blood.

His father was looking for him.

All these years, he'd never stopped. And the Blood who'd killed Edmund Vaughn had just… they'd really just…

Murdered Ashley. And Patrick. And every family member Lily had.

He couldn't breathe.

The door locks released. "Dammit, come on!" Vivian shouted.

Stephen grabbed his arm, yanking him from the window. The motion jarred him and instinctively, he fought back.

"Leave him!" the woman yelled.

"Insurance!" Stephen snapped.

"Cole!"

Lily's frightened cry startled him. Twisting in the wizard's grasp, he looked down, realizing she'd been thrown to the ground in the struggle.

She was staring up at him. At the blood on the window. At the smoke curling beyond.

He drove an elbow into Stephen's midsection. Choking, the wizard released his grip and staggered backward, regaining his footing a moment later with a pained glare.

Ignoring him, Cole reached down to the little girl. "Close your eyes," he said.

Scooping her and the staff into his arms, he stood and looked back through the blood-splattered glass.

His father…

He...

Gripping Lily tightly, Cole stumbled away from the window and ran from the room.

———◆———

"Breathe, your highness," Elias murmured.

In the center of the marble lobby, Ashe flicked her gaze to him before pinning it back on the infuriating young aide behind the front desk of Chaunessy Tower.

She drew a slow breath. "I am."

He hesitated, and then returned his attention to the guards and security cameras lining the walls. "Just checking."

"Sir, I told you," the young man repeated to Brentworth tiredly. "I've been watching the monitors all morning. Everything is fine. And if the Council *was* in this building somewhere, which I won't confirm they are, I can assure you, they'd be completely fine too. The only threat right now is these... people... you felt compelled to bring here."

"And *I* am telling *you*," Brentworth replied, his cultured voice coming perilously close to a growl. "I am well aware that the Council is here. I am also well aware of what these people are. And I am ordering you to stand aside and let them speak to the leaders of Taliesin, or so help me, I will personally–"

A dryly amused look flickered across the aide's face. At his uncle's side, Luke blanched and looked away.

"Do you have *any* idea who I am, young man?" Brentworth snapped.

The amused expression increased. "No, sir, to be honest, I don't.

But with all due respect, it doesn't matter. There is no way a bunch of Merlin scum are ever going to be allowed near–"

"Enough," Brentworth interrupted, his patience finally giving out. "You will call your superiors and tell them that Councilman Brentworth is here."

"I will not–"

"*Now.*"

The aide paused. Drawing a breath, he tossed a glance to the black-clad guards arrayed along the walls, and then forced his face into a semblance of a smile.

"Very well," he said tightly.

As the young man picked up the phone, Brentworth turned. Expressionless, Ashe met his gaze. He tried to give her a politely reassuring look, and when it failed, he sighed and looked back at the aide.

With ostentatious patience, the young man dialed a number and waited. Gritting her teeth, Ashe focused on the guards. Standing at military attention against the marble walls, the bulky wizards bore every resemblance to standard human security guards, down to the brass badges on their chests and the firearms strapped at precise angles on their sides. For every single second of the minutes Brentworth had been arguing with the aide, the Taliesin had watched them, the implicit threat in their eyes easy to read. All around her, Nathaniel and his own contingent had been returning the favor, leaving the tension in the cavernous lobby nearly enough to set the air on fire. A suggestion of magic hovered around both groups, as though to remind their opposing number with whom they were dealing, and the result left Crystal and Ghost wincing.

And yet, aside from the tension in the room, everything was

disconcertingly still. The soft whir of the air conditioners could be heard from time to time, chilling the already refrigerated atmosphere. Sunlight streamed past the two-story high windows behind them, and through the dense glass, no whisper of traffic could be heard.

Compared to the firestorm they'd all known they could have been walking into, the silence was eerie. And a bit disturbing.

"Yes, that's what I said, sir," the aide repeated into the phone. "Seven Merlin and two cripples. They want to speak to the Council and–" He cut off, obviously interrupted. "Six men and one girl. Yes, sir. Just a boy and a girl. They– no, I don't think so. Well, Councilman Brentworth led them to the front door. Councilman *Brentworth*, sir. No, sir, I'm fairly certain he's not. He– Their names? I didn't ask but…" The aide paused and Ashe glanced back to see him studying them all. "Yes…" he allowed. "It's possible. But there's only the– oh. Are you sure you–" He cut off, blanching. "Yes, sir. Right away, sir. I–"

The aide paused, and then set down the phone. He cleared his throat. "One of my superiors would like to meet in the conference room."

Brentworth snorted.

Jaw tightening, the aide pretended not to hear. "This way, please," he said, gesturing to the far end of the lobby and then casting a swift look to the guards. Six of them stepped away from the wall.

With a glance to Elias, Ashe followed Nathaniel, with Ghost coming a step behind. Startling at the sudden motion, Crystal pulled herself from her surveillance of the street and hurried after them.

"Anything?" Ashe asked softly.

Ghost shook his head, and Crystal worriedly echoed the motion.

Taking a slow breath, Ashe returned her focus to the guards. The Taliesin strode ahead of them, while behind her, the aide followed with a few of the Merlin acting as a buffer between the unhappy young man and their queen. Ahead, the lobby narrowed between two marble walls lined with the reflective doors of elevators. Another door waited at the end of the corridor, and above its wooden surface, brass letters hung, denoting the space beyond as the central conference room.

A Taliesin pushed open the door and stepped aside. As the other Taliesin headed in, Nathaniel glanced back at her.

Without a word, she waited a moment with Crystal and Ghost, letting the large wizard and Brentworth precede her.

Gray soundproofing boards hung on equally gray walls around the windowless expanse. Folding tables rested against the rightmost wall and a tall stack of metal chairs teetered precariously beside them. A presentation screen hung on the far side of the room, flanked by twin doors of pale wood and, in the center of the colorless carpet, a Taliesin wizard stood speaking into his cell phone while two additional guards waited like statues by his side.

Stirring the stale air with their motion, the lobby guards started toward the man while the aide turned and walked back to his desk, letting the doors swing closed behind him.

"My apologies for the confusion, Councilor," the man called as they approached. Sliding his phone into the pocket of his sport jacket, he ignored the lobby guards as they joined the other Taliesin around him. "Our desk staff can be rather obstinate at times."

A meticulously diplomatic smile presented itself to the Merlin and Brentworth.

"Now," the man continued. "What was it you wished to discuss?"

The Taliesin struck as one.

Ashe's defenses buckled and the air raced from her lungs as she slammed to the ground. Gasping, she rolled to her feet, her magic rushing back up around her.

Crystal lay on the floor next to her, staring emptily toward the ceiling. Unsteadily, Ghost pushed up from the carpet at her side.

His gaze came to rest on his sister. He shivered once.

And then he began to scream.

Ashe stumbled back as the boy lunged up and rushed toward the Taliesin.

Magic tore through the air, spinning him as it passed. Meeting her eyes with a last look of horror, Ghost crashed boneless to the ground.

She couldn't breathe.

People were shouting. But half the Merlin guards lay dead. His face bloody, Nathaniel struggled to rise a few yards away, while Elias was nowhere to be seen. Brentworth was under attack by three Taliesin and Luke lay crumpled by a wall.

The door on the far side of the room burst open. More Taliesin flooded through.

One of them spotted her. Instinctively, she strengthened her defenses and before his magic reached her, it was already gone. The Taliesin tumbled backward, carried by his own attack turned against him.

A man with a graying ponytail strode through the doorway, a blonde woman coming a step behind.

They looked human.

And then their magic struck her.

———— ◆ ————

The walls hurt. Magic radiated from them.

Gasping with pain, Cole gripped Lily as they raced down the hall on Stephen and Vivian's heels. The ground shook beneath them, the product of explosions he could hardly hear, but overwhelmingly feel.

By an elevator door, Vivian skidded to a stop. With panicked intensity, she jabbed the call button repeatedly, cursing through gritted teeth till the door slid back, revealing the dull metallic interior of a service elevator.

"Get in!" the woman snapped, putting her words to action by rushing inside.

The ground rocked again. Someone was blowing up the world nearby.

Not waiting to see if he followed, Vivian smacked the elevator controls. Growling, Stephen grabbed Cole's arm and hauled him and Lily through the opening.

The door slid closed. The elevator slid down.

Everything lurched and the door buckled inward. Lily shrieked, her arms tightening around Cole's neck enough to choke him. Swearing, Stephen braced himself on the wall, and Cole winced as the wizard's magic pressed on the air.

The elevator kept moving.

"A-are we good?" Vivian asked, eyeing the ceiling.

Stephen didn't respond, his gaze locked on the digital readout above the door and his mouth moving silently to urge the decreasing numbers along.

Distractedly, Cole loosened Lily's grip and moved her arm down to his shoulders.

"Sorry," the little girl whispered.

He couldn't answer. He could barely think, and the cause was only partly the magic pulsing through the air.

An explosion sounded in the distance below. The elevator shivered.

The numbers kept counting down.

Several floors down, magic reverberated through the shaft and the elevator rocked.

Stephen cursed, watching the glowing numbers.

Lily's arms clenched around him. Inching to one side, Cole pressed his back to the cold metal wall.

The numbers became single digits. The glowing buttons on the wall ticked toward the ground level.

Magic shredded the elevator ceiling.

And the world became weightless.

Emergency brakes howled and then the ground arrived. Metal screamed and glass shattered. Support beams and cables scythed down, carrying the lights with them. Cole crashed to the ground as the floor and the walls crumpled.

The lights flickered overhead, sending off sparks. Broken glass fell from him as he pushed up on an aching arm. Beneath him, the little girl groaned.

"Lily?" he gasped, shoving away from her.

"What happened?" she whimpered.

Cole didn't answer, running his gaze over her. She seemed okay.

He remembered how to breathe.

Blinking in the fitful light, he looked up from the girl to what was left of the elevator.

He wished he hadn't.

Stephen was dead. That was certain. No one could survive what that support beam had done. A few feet away, Vivian was braced against the wall, her gaze locked on the dead wizard and her mouth working silently.

Swallowing hard, he returned his gaze to Lily, noting the splatters of Stephen's blood covering his own arms. Forcing himself to breathe, he grabbed the staff with a shaking hand, and then wrapped his other arm around the girl.

"Keep your eyes closed," he told her. "Hang onto me."

Unquestioning, Lily reached up and clung to him again. Taking another breath, he adjusted his grip on her and then struggled to his feet.

The elevator door was ajar and the building floor was several feet above the uneven ground beneath him. Dim lights shone past the opening and as he stood, explosions rocked the area beyond.

He tried not to swear, uncertainty hitting him. But there was nothing else to do. Swallowing again, he glanced to Vivian. The woman gave no sign of seeing him. Unsteadily, he inched toward the door and then peered cautiously through the gap.

Footsteps rushed past. Gasping, he jerked away and plastered himself against the elevator controls.

While most of the footsteps continued on, some slowed. Approached. And stopped inches from the dislodged doors.

Breathless, Cole pressed farther back against the buckled metal, his grip on Lily tightening.

Beyond the opening, he heard a man chuckle. At the sound, a woman murmured a response, her words too low to hear.

A burst of utterly painless magic sliced across the elevator, pinning Vivian to the wall. Electricity tangled over the woman and she spasmed, her head cracking over and over into the metal handrail.

The magic faded. Vivian crashed to the ground.

And then the footsteps walked away.

Cole couldn't move. Air made its necessity known to his lungs, and after a moment, he gasped, and then choked as the shaking started.

Closing his eyes, he turned his face away, trying to pretend he hadn't just seen what he'd seen. Ordering himself to stop shaking, he turned his head to the door and opened his eyes, watching for the slightest hints of motion, but none came. After the eternal span of a few heartbeats, he made himself step away from the wall and ease toward the door.

The hallway looked empty.

He drew another breath. "Keep your eyes closed," he whispered to Lily.

The little girl didn't answer. He glanced over. Below her coal black waves, her skin was bloodlessly pale. He shuddered, wishing them anywhere but here. The kid had to have heard everything, even if she hadn't seen a bit of it.

"Good girl," he told her.

Forcing himself to stay steady, he shifted Lily around and then hoisted her onto the ledge. Carefully, he set the staff at her side before pulling himself up onto the cold tile floor.

"Here," he said, pushing the staff into her hands.

"Can I open my eyes?" she whispered.

Glancing to the elevator, he pulled her farther down the hall. "Yeah."

Blinking, she eyed the dim corridor.

"What do we–" she started.

Six men rushed around the corner, running in the same direction the others had gone and bringing a migraine's worth of magic with them. Cole stumbled back, pushing Lily behind him, while with widening eyes, the wizards slowed.

"Wait," one said. "Are you—"

Lily screamed. Cole spun.

She was staring at the bodies in the elevator. Swiftly, he grabbed her and pulled her away. Panicked, she turned to him, and then her eyes went to the wizards.

They started forward.

Her magic obliterated the hall.

Shaking, Cole straightened and opened his eyes. The walls were missing, he noted. Some of them, anyway. Through the hole where the end of the corridor had been, he could see an alley. Dust poured from what was left of the ceiling and suddenly, he couldn't hear the sounds of other explosions anymore.

His gaze moved to the wizards. With difficulty, he swallowed.

Lily whimpered. He turned back. Paralyzed, she clutched the staff in both hands, her gaze locked on the tile.

"Everything's fine," he told her, his voice less steady than he would have liked. "Just… close your eyes."

Trembling, the girl obeyed.

Bending down, he scooped her up again and then shifted her around to keep the staff from being pinned between them. He glanced to the direction the others had gone. A pile of debris blocked the end of the hall, beyond which he couldn't see a thing. Drawing a breath, he headed for the alley.

They'd flown, most of them. Past remnants of plaster, he could see a few of the wizards on the far sides of the newly revealed rooms. Others had hit the metal struts and supports within the walls. Hard.

He drew a breath, unable to turn from the sight of what Lily's magic had done.

The wizards had been wearing badges and guns. They looked like security guards. He wondered whose side they'd been on, and then he pushed the thought away.

At the corridor's end, another body lay slumped and tumbled in a position too awkward to be survived. Through the broken wall beside the wizard, the sounds of traffic filtered.

Carefully, Cole stepped around the body and then paused.

Swallowing dryly, he returned his gaze to the dead wizard and the weapon clasped at his side. Before he could question the thought, Cole shifted the girl around and then tugged the gun from its holster.

Slowly, he exhaled. It wasn't much, but…

He glanced to Lily, uncertain of the thoughts now clamoring deep inside. He was fairly certain his conscience was among them.

Tightening his grip on the gun, he headed for the alleyway.

Chapter Seventeen

The wave of magic slammed into her and then came the wall. Pain shot through her as she crashed into the drywall and the support beams. Her defenses shuddered and her vision exploded into stars as she hit the ground.

Gasping, Ashe scrambled for her feet.

Magic shot past her toward the Blood wizards.

She spun. Half a dozen corpses behind him, Elias strode between her and the Blood and struck out again.

The ponytailed man smiled, his shields barely rippling from the attack, while behind him, the blonde-haired woman sent her magic racing toward the councilman.

Frantically, Ashe intercepted it. The magic rushed around Elias and flowed into her, burning like acid and making her cry out at its strength. Gasping, she flung it back at the Blood.

As his shields buckled, the man's eyes went wide.

"Grab the girl!" he shouted.

A battering ram of nothingness mowed down the Taliesin as they ran at her. Bruised and bleeding, Nathaniel shoved an attacking wizard from his path and struck again, sending the surviving Taliesin flying.

"Get her out of here!" Nathaniel yelled.

Elias rushed toward her.

The wall behind the Blood wizards exploded.

Ashe whirled, ducking instinctively as the blast flung her to the ground. Debris strafed the air as the walls disintegrated and the tortured ceiling collapsed with a roar. Steel and plaster crashed down on the center of the conference room.

Shaking with shock, she pulled her arm from her head. Bracing herself with one hand on the remnants of the wall, she stumbled to her feet.

She could see the lobby. Shredded drywall hung between the twisted girders in front of her, and the door had become kindling. In the room beyond, the marble floors and walls were intact, though the enormous windows hadn't survived the blast. The guards were dazed and struggling to rise, and behind the remains of his desk, the aide moved weakly.

Barely breathing, she slid her gaze to the room behind her.

The ceiling was gone. Most of the level above had come down in its fall. A mountain of rebar, steel and concrete now lay behind her, separating her from whatever was left of the conference room.

Her trembling grew stronger. If she'd been a few feet closer…

"Elias!" she shouted. She rushed toward the mess, her eyes sweeping it in horror as her mind emphatically denied any possibility he lay beneath. "Elias!"

"Your highness!"

Relief hit her at the sound of the councilman's voice. "Here!" she called.

Magic slammed the pile of ruins. She gasped, stumbling back as the blast sent debris cascading down around her.

"Elias!" she yelled.

Another blast followed. From the opposite side of the rubble, she could hear people shouting.

"Elias!"

No one answered.

Her gaze raked the mountain separating her from the councilman, and she grabbed at the first handhold she could see.

"Your highness, get out of here!" Elias shouted.

She froze. "I'm not–"

Magic drove another minor avalanche down.

"Now!"

On the other side of the debris, she could hear him calling orders as magic burned the air. Others yelled, their words unintelligible, and his voice merged with the noise as he left the tumbled mess behind.

Breathless and torn, she stared at the wreckage for a heartbeat and then shoved away. Sliding down through the rubble, she scrambled to her feet and then took off.

Lobby guards rushed to intercept her as she dashed through the remnants of the door. The nearest stumbled in shock, and then his magic drove them all back to the ground.

She didn't stop running.

Broken glass crunched beneath her as she reached the street and she skidded, looking around frantically. Each direction was the same. Brentworth's cars were gone and it wasn't like she had keys for them anyway. Gulping down air, she darted right, racing down the sidewalk and praying for a doorframe deep enough to hold a portal.

Not that she was close enough to reach Joe's easily. Or knew anywhere else to hide.

Panic surged and she fought to crush it down. Where to go wasn't the issue and neither was the distance to Joe's. She just needed to be somewhere, anywhere, without wizards long enough to call Elias or Nathaniel. Then they'd all get out of here. And they'd all be fine.

Clinging to the thought, she cast a hurried glance around.

Her feet stopped before her mind caught up with them and the world tilted, her balance thrown.

A gasp escaped her as reality shifted. Spun. Erased itself and started over again because at the end of the alley beside her, the impossible had just become real and nothing else mattered at all.

And then she was running.

Fear in her eyes, Lily looked back at the sound of footsteps racing across the concrete. Light glimmered from the wooden staff in her hand, and by the girl's side, Cole turned.

Horror rippled across his face. His hand swung up, holding a gun.

Shock hit her before the bullets left the weapon, and then her magic was there. Ricocheting from her defenses, the bullets pelted the brick and steel while the gun went flying from his grasp.

Cole thrust Lily behind him and shouted for her to run.

Ashe's heart hit her throat. The girl was stumbling away. Gasping, she started to yell Lily's name.

Cole slammed into her.

Concrete met her and drove the breath from her lungs. Instinctively, she shoved him away, scrambling to reach her feet before Lily disappeared. Magic rushed through her, begging to be released as he grabbed her again and threw her to the ground.

"Wait!" Lily yelled.

Cole froze. Confusedly, he glanced to the little girl.

Trembling, Lily approached. "Ashley?" she whispered.

Cole's gaze slid back to her, incredulity painted across his face. He stared, his brow twitching down in shock, and then he backed up, grabbing Lily with one hand as he stood.

Shaking, Ashe rose.

"Ashley?" Lily repeated, desperate hope in her voice.

A rough breath escaped Ashe and in a single step, she crossed the distance between them and grabbed the girl, enveloping her in her arms.

Time slowed. Stopped. Made everything in the stupid, horrible world somehow almost alright again.

"How did you…" she heard Cole ask.

And then reality returned.

Footsteps pounded up to the alley. Magic crackled through the air, racing toward them.

Panic hitting her, Ashe spun, her defenses shuddering as the energy punched them. At the alleyway entrance, the four guards struck a second time, their magic rippling from her shields as Lily shrieked in fear.

The guards flew into the road and didn't move again. Breathing hard, Ashe lowered her arm and looked back at Cole and the little girl.

"We have to go," she said.

She paused. We. The simple word registered and hysterical joy almost overrode the adrenaline racing through her veins. Roughly, she drew a breath, struggling to stay focused.

Cole stared at her. Lily stared at the guards. Moving mechanically, Cole reached out and pulled the little girl around so she couldn't see the bodies.

"Yeah," he agreed reflexively.

Swallowing down her residual panic, Ashe glanced to the alley. The guards lay in one direction, and there might be others coming behind them. At the opposite end, the alleyway split around two blind corners, but one of the resulting paths led away from Chaunessy.

It would have to do.

"Come on," she said, shifting her grip down to Lily's hand. Her gaze caught on the wooden staff in the little girl's other fist.

Her brow drew down, memory fluttering at the edge of reach, and then the insistent drum of adrenaline drove it away. There wasn't time. The Blood could be coming. Taliesin. Anyone.

Clutching Lily's hand, she headed for the turn. Beyond the edge of the building, the alley was empty, and when she came to the far end of the next stretch, an equally empty corridor of concrete and brick waited. Heart pounding, Ashe kept going, tugging out her cell as she moved.

She hesitated, clutching the phone. Elias could be dead. Captured. Her eyes flicked to Lily, panic gripping her again, and she cursed never having come up with code phrases the way Carter had done.

But it was too late now.

She thumbed the speed dial.

"Where are you?" Elias snapped upon answering. "Are you okay?"

"Yeah. You?"

"Great," he said tersely. "The Taliesin are dead but the Blood escaped. Now where the hell are you?"

She trembled, trying not to envision the Blood around the next corner. "Alleyway. About two blocks north of Chaunessy."

"We just reached Brentworth's. Can you get there?"

Ashe's gaze flicked toward Cole. "Not exactly."

"What? Why?"

"Just get here, Elias. Please."

He paused. "On my way."

The phone went dead. A moment passed, and then a portal spun inside a doorway near the end of the alley.

Cole swore. With a shriek, Lily skidded and then yanked Ashe's hand as she tried to retreat.

Elias rushed from the portal, Nathaniel on his heels, and they both looked terrible. One of the councilman's sleeves was soaked in blood and a roughly healed gash covered half his forehead. Nathaniel had fared worse, with thickly dried blood on his face and arms, and burn marks scoring his clothes.

"Are you alright?" Elias demanded as he spotted her. His gaze flicked to the others as he strode closer, and his brow drew down.

Ashe tugged Lily back to her side. "It's okay," she told the girl. "They're friends."

The little girl swallowed hard, clearly doubting the words.

Ashe's gaze returned to the wizards. "Elias. Nathaniel. Meet Cole and…" She hesitated, trembling. "Lily."

Incredulous, Elias looked between them.

"We need a car," Ashe finished.

Blinking, Elias regrouped. "Done." He clasped a hand to Nathaniel's shoulder and then headed for the alley exit.

Ashe turned to Nathaniel. "You alright?"

Silent, he nodded and then raised an eyebrow at her. She echoed the nod.

"The others?"

His pause was answer enough.

She looked away. Her gaze fell on Lily. Wide-eyed, the little girl was staring at Nathaniel in horror.

"It's okay," Ashe repeated. She glanced to Cole. Distrust was blatant on his face. "I told you. Nathaniel's a friend."

The distrust barely faded.

At the end of the alley, Elias pulled up in a sedan.

"Come on," Ashe said, pushing Cole's reaction away.

Nathaniel hesitated and she could see the desire to search Cole and possibly even Lily written on his face. Visibly, Cole tensed.

"It's alright," she said to Nathaniel. "He's the one who saved us when the Blood killed my dad."

Nathaniel's gaze went from her to the pair and back again. Briefly, his eyes narrowed and then he turned, taking the lead as though nothing had happened. Tightening her grip on Lily, Ashe started after him.

A moment passed before she heard Cole follow.

Scanning the street, Ashe opened the door and motioned Lily inside. Cars zipped past the intersection several hundred feet away. The sound of sirens was conspicuously absent and along the pavement, pedestrians strolled blithely on.

Cole paused on the opposite side of the sedan, casting an unreadable glance to her and Nathaniel. His mouth tightened, and then he got into the car.

Over the top of the vehicle, Nathaniel caught her eye.

She buried a grimace and slid in after Lily, not knowing what to say.

Elias glanced at her in the rearview mirror as the door closed. "Joe's?" he suggested, his tone only half-questioning.

She nodded, taking up Lily's hand again and gripping it in both her own. "As fast as you can."

A familiar wry grin tugged his lips, the expression marred with blood, and then gravity pushed her deep into the seat as the sedan surged forward.

By one of the many gaping holes in the conference room walls, Brogan paused. Wires dangled overhead, sparking fitfully. Rebar protruded from shattered concrete and occasionally, small bits of debris pattered down on the destroyed floor.

It would take a tremendous amount of repair, assuming Jamison decided to stay.

Dismissing the damage from his mind, he continued into the room.

"What happened?" he called.

Simeon grimaced as he looked up from the corpse by his feet. His normally neat ponytail was disheveled and dust covered his clothes. A few yards away, Isabella glanced over. A large splash of blood, obviously not her own, marred the eggshell white of her knee-length coat, though her pale blonde hair was smooth as ever. On her cold face, the lack of expression was even more pronounced than usual.

He'd rarely seen her so furious.

"Merlin queen," Simeon stated succinctly. "She got away."

Brogan paused. His gaze snapped between them.

"Any survivors?" he asked, his voice betraying nothing.

Isabella's eyes narrowed slightly. He raised a brow at her in response and the woman looked away.

"No useful ones," Simeon supplied, glaring at them both before he caught himself. Swiping a sweaty strand of hair from his face, he turned the glare on the bodies. "And most of our side is dead as well, thanks to her guards and whatever the hell happened back there."

The man gestured abstractedly toward the remnants of the far wall.

In Brogan's pocket, his phone buzzed. He drew it out and listened briefly to the wizard on the other end.

He returned the phone to his pocket.

"It doesn't matter," he told them.

Isabella looked back at him, a flicker of incredulity in her ice blue eyes.

"Why?" Simeon demanded, not bothering to hide his own surprise.

A humored expression touched his face. "Because we know where they're going to be."

———◆———

Harris didn't look up at the sound of the lock turning, knowing there was no point. Throughout however long he'd been handcuffed to a chair in this hellhole, the questions had never changed, and he'd grown tired of them. Hours or days or years before, he'd fastened his gaze on a slight discoloration on the concrete floor of his cell, and now it was all he bothered to see.

Because he'd almost had her. Almost killed her. He'd come so close, only to fail, and the thought tortured him more than anything the damn wizards would do, once they got done playing nice and finally resorted to using pain to make him answer their incessant questions.

Assuming they didn't just give up and kill him first.

The door swung open, and then shut again a moment later.

"Well, aren't you a sorry sight?"

Despite himself, the unfamiliar voice drew his gaze up even as the words made his blood boil. He didn't recognize the man in front of him, though he was fairly certain he knew all the wizards Ashley kept around. And the little bastard certainly didn't have any room to talk. Layers of moldering coats covered him and his face looked like it'd been shaved by a weed whacker.

"Who're you?" Harris growled.

Ignoring the question, the little man shuffled around him. "I mean, *damn*," he continued, coming to a stop behind the chair.

"I asked you a question," Harris said, twisting to see the little man.

The man snorted. "Like you care."

On Harris' wrists, the handcuffs shifted and then clattered to the floor.

Alarmed, he rose to his feet.

Days of motionlessness made themselves felt and he nearly crumpled to the ground. Stumbling, he caught himself on the cinder-block wall.

"What's going on?"

"Damn, you just don't quit," the man replied as he returned to the door. When Harris didn't follow, he glanced back, an irritated look on his face. "Mud, okay? The name's Mud. Now can we get going? They don't want you left behind and we don't exactly have a lot of time."

"They?"

"The Blood."

"You work for Jamison?"

At this, the man snorted again. "Yeah, right. I work for me. Always have, always will. Jamison's just the best game in town right now, and I'm not stupid. I want to survive, I side with the big dogs. Simple as that. Now, come on."

He started for the door.

Harris didn't move. "Are you a wizard?" he asked, barely feeling his own incredulity at the word anymore.

"Like hell," the man scoffed, turning back. "I'm the same as you, buddy. Honest guy caught in their war, though I was born on their side. Call me a cripple, wizards do, and they can go to hell for it. Now, really, unless you want us both dead, I suggest you let me get us out of here before Brogan shows up and blows this place to kingdom come."

Harris' eyebrows rose.

"Well, you called, didn't you?" Mud said as though it was obvious. "Told them where she was, back before the bitch survived being shot. Good job, by the way. Between you and me, wish it'd worked."

He flashed a yellow grin. "But yeah, you called, we came, I damn near got caught by ferals but it all turned up roses because hey, here I am, here you are, and now here we go."

Mud headed for the door.

"What about the wizards?" Harris pushed away from the wall and started after him, his pace slowed by his tingling legs.

"Guards are dead," Mud said over his shoulder as he pulled open the door.

Harris stared as the man checked the hall. "All of them?" he asked, unable to keep the incredulity out of his voice.

Mud glanced back. "The ones that count, anyway," he said defensively. "Others are upstairs, the oblivious freaks. Took me a bit to get away from the guy that bastard Elias set on me, but some Blood across town got 'em all spooked now. Jerk wasn't paying as much attention to yours truly as he should've been." He chuckled. "But yeah, called Jamison's group first chance I got, and now they're coming to wipe out these lemmings and set a trap to bring her in." Mud grinned. "He's got a plan for Bloody Queen Ashe and oh, there ain't no way it's gonna be pretty."

Still grinning, the little man shuffled into the hall. Warily, Harris followed, glancing in both directions before leaving the room. His gaze caught on the guard propped up over the stairway banister.

Small caliber bullet wound to the chest, he noted. Probably from close range.

He looked at Mud.

The man's grin took on a dark edge and he drew a silenced weapon from the folds of his coats. "Bullets'll kill a wizard if they don't know they're coming, my friend," he said. "And I got about a million ways to hide a gun."

Harris didn't answer. The man seemed to read his thoughts anyway.

"Oh, give it time, Detective," he chided, clapping Harris on the shoulder. "We'll kill her yet."

Chuckling, the little man scurried up the stairs.

Harris eyed the body briefly and then followed. The door at the top of the stairway opened into a short hall. At the end, a restaurant kitchen glistened, though the place was mostly empty with only a few cooks and waitresses moving about. One of them headed into the dining area, pushing past the swinging door with a bin of napkin-wrapped silverware in her arms, and through the opening, he could see additional waitresses bustling around, while a hostess busily straightened her post by the entrance. Only one other person occupied the room, seated in a booth against the far wall, and Harris paled at the sight of her. The harpy with the gold glasses didn't turn, however; her gaze was locked on the windows and the front door.

Ducking back, he looked to Mud with a grimace, but the little man ignored the expression. Anticipation glinted in his beady eyes, and Harris' brow drew down at the sight.

The back door opened. A man strode in, passing them with a derisive glance. In the dining area, the harpy gave a shout and an explosion reverberated through the room, bringing screaming on its heels.

"Time to go," Mud announced cheerfully.

The little man darted for the exit. Across the kitchen, the harpy burst through the swinging door, two men chasing her.

Shoving off the doorframe, Harris raced out of the restaurant as all hell broke loose behind him.

———— ◆ ————

The sedan flew through another intersection, barreling past the red lights and the traffic, and besides Lily, none of the people in the car with him batted an eye.

Struggling to keep from being obvious, Cole glanced askance at Ashley for what felt like the hundredth time. Black tendrils of hair fell around her face and blended with the jacket covering her, and her dark eyes swept the streets with a predatory gleam, as though daring the world to attack. Seated on the opposite side of Lily, she clutched the little girl's hand, readjusting her fingers every couple seconds as if to reassure herself the child was real.

He hadn't recognized her. It wasn't the new look, or the dust covering her, or the dried blood from the scratches on her face that she didn't even seem to notice. It wasn't that he'd only seen her for a few minutes all those months before; the wild car ride and its results were firmly etched in his mind. It wasn't any of those things.

Up ahead, the blood-covered linebacker she'd called Nathaniel shifted in his seat and Ashley's gaze snapped toward the man instantly. A heartbeat went by. The wizard shook his head. Ashley looked back out the window, her fingers continually gripping and re-gripping Lily's hand.

It was that she was so different. And when he'd seen her barreling down that alleyway, he hadn't for a moment considered it was the same girl he'd given up for dead in a forest fire nearly half a year before. The thought hadn't even occurred to him. And as for the rest of it…

His gaze dropped to Lily's hand resting lightly in his own.

She didn't glow like the little girl, but she damn sure was a wizard. And a formidable one, if the migraine from hell he'd gotten from her brief display of power was any indication. But he'd bet the Summers' farm she hadn't been able to do any of that back when they first met. At least, he was fairly sure. Maybe.

But now she killed people. Without hesitation, without hardly doing more than registering they were there. She'd just eliminated those four wizards in a heartbeat, and then moved on as though it was nothing.

Yet, it wasn't like the wizards hadn't been out to hurt them too. And given the chance, he would've tried to stop them as well. It was just… just…

Unable to keep the grimace from his face, he turned back to the window.

His dad. And Ashley being alive. And the Blood. And being back with a bunch of Merlin all over again. It was too much. Just too much.

And he had no idea what he was going to do now.

———•◆•———

Ashe tensed as a man on the sidewalk glanced toward the road. Raising a hand, he called a greeting to a lady on the other side of the street.

And then their car shot past him, with leaves and paper fluttering madly in its wake.

Up ahead, a yellow car flew through a stoplight to a chorus of horns and shouting pedestrians. Her chest constricted all over again, and then the intersection was behind them and the yellow car was gone.

Crystal's dead eyes rose before her, followed instantly by the memory of Ghost screaming.

Jaw clenched, Ashe trembled. She couldn't think about them right now. About what'd happened or how many more were dead behind her. She couldn't handle it and she had to stay focused because, if she let it, the fear would run away with her and she'd be useless. Paralyzed. She couldn't risk that.

Not again.

At a crosswalk, a woman looked their way. Ashe's gaze snapped over, magic twisting beneath her skin, ready to strike.

The woman hesitated, a distracted expression coming onto her face. Turning back, she glanced to the shops behind her as though trying to figure out if she'd forgotten something.

Their car raced past. Expression fading, the woman shook her head and then briskly crossed the street.

Shivering, Ashe forced herself to breathe.

Lily's hand moved in her own and her gaze flicked down. The girl's skin was darker. Tan in the way it got after hours in the summer sun. She'd been outside somewhere. And there was a knick like a paper cut on her ring finger. She always got those when working on her crafts.

Joy and fear surged again and Ashe swallowed hard, tearing her gaze away and fastening it on the street. She couldn't let herself look at Lily for too long. The sight just made her want to crumble and cry, and she couldn't afford that. The emotions. The distractions.

And the questions.

Lily looked human. Completely. No hint of a Merlin aura touched the girl, and she didn't feel like a cripple. Cole was. Ashe could tell that easily. But from Lily, there was just… nothing.

Ashe watched a couple glance toward the road and then continue on their way. She pulled another breath into her lungs.

Her sister wasn't like the Blood. She wasn't and she couldn't be. The lack of what surrounded other wizards didn't matter. It just meant Lily was different. Special.

Lily had always been special.

But she had magic. Or something. Ashe's gaze darted to the staff propped between Cole and the girl. There'd been light inside that when she'd first seen Lily holding it, although the wood was inert now. But the staff was familiar. Important somehow, though the memory kept flitting out of reach. It'd been in a book, one of the countless books, but beyond that she couldn't seem to grasp it.

Fighting a scowl, she ordered herself to stay focused. She'd ask them about the staff later. Hell, she'd ask them about everything later, from Cole's reason for saving them in the first place to where the two of them had been all these months. They'd talk when there was time. When people weren't trying to kill them at least once an hour.

She didn't want to think about what she'd do if they couldn't.

Taking another breath, she shifted as the car whipped around a turn. The skyscrapers of downtown were gone and somehow in the past few minutes, trees and houses had appeared. Foliage obscured the sky and the aging homes crowded one another to the exclusion of any grass between. Squirrels raced for safety as the car shot by, and on the sidewalk, a young man walking his dog suddenly scrambled for control as the animal tried to flee.

Something dark flashed beyond the trees.

Ashe's brow furrowed. The car hugged another turn and she bent in her seat, looking past Lily and Cole as her gaze tried to pierce the thick cover of leaves.

"What is it?" Cole asked.

She didn't answer.

The trees parted.

Ashe's blood went cold. "Elias…"

She saw him glance back and then follow her gaze to the window. For a moment, he looked confused, his attention darting between the road and the horizon.

And then his breath caught. The car accelerated and jumped the curb in attempt to round the corner faster. In her seat, Lily whimpered, her grip tightening on Ashe's fingers, and as they left the neighborhood, the trees gave way to afford them full view of the horizon.

Ashe pulled Lily's hand closer.

In the distance, black smoke poured into the afternoon sky. By the sides of the road, people had stopped, watching the billowing clouds.

The car flew past them all.

At top speed, the sedan crested a hill, bringing the mall into view. Flashing lights ringed the parking lot and scattered crowds waited on the sidewalks, held back by barricades. Beyond the massive building, flames roared, stark against the backdrop of trees.

"Councilman," Nathaniel said, his eyes on the fire.

Elias didn't answer.

His face darkening, Nathaniel looked over. "Elias!"

The man's gaze flicked in his direction.

"The Blood could still be there," Nathaniel finished more quietly.

Another moment passed. Elias' gaze darted to Ashe in the rearview mirror.

She felt sick at the look in his eyes.

He slammed on the brakes. The car fishtailed and then skidded to a stop several blocks from the flames. Trembling, Elias eased his hands from the wheel and looked to Nathaniel.

"Where else can we go?" the large wizard suggested carefully.

Elias let out a breath and then nodded. "Outside town," he said, his voice rough. "We have another safe house that the Council doesn't–"

He cut off as his phone buzzed. Hurriedly, he yanked it from his pocket and thumbed it on.

Another breath escaped him. "I saw. Where is she?" A moment passed. "Thank you," he said sincerely and then hung up the phone.

The engine roared as he smashed the pedal to the ground.

"Katherine's safe," Elias told them. "She's at Joe's house."

Nathaniel said nothing. His gaze slid back to Ashe, the caution in his eyes mirroring her own.

The sedan raced down the road. Bright new stores became fading older ones, and then the commercial district vanished behind a wall of greenery as Elias sent the car flying down a side street. Stout ranch homes surrounded them, each evenly spaced house looking a million miles from the parking lots only a few hundred yards away.

"Who's Katherine?" Lily whispered.

Ashe glanced down, trying to ignore the somersaults her stomach turned at the sight of the girl. "His wife," she said quietly.

Lily's brow knit worriedly and she leaned her head against her sister's arm. Swallowing, Ashe struggled not to tremble at the feeling of her there.

Spinning the wheel, Elias whipped the car into the driveway of a brick two-story house. Hitting the brakes, he barely waited for the sedan to come to a stop before throwing the gearshift into park and then shoving open the door.

Nathaniel made a growl of displeasure. Glancing back, he gave Ashe a pointed look and then followed Elias from the car.

Jaw tightening, Ashe eyed their surroundings. Flowering bushes only half-heartedly tamed crowded the house, blocking the view of the backyard and creeping up to obscure the first floor windows as well. The brick box of a garage sat at the end of the drive, encircled by its own wreath of greenery.

A door slammed. Katherine rushed from the backyard, her hair disheveled and a guard on her heels. "Are you alright?" she demanded, her sharp gaze sweeping the two men and the car before returning to Elias. "What happened to you?"

"We're fine," Elias replied, embracing her. "Are you okay?"

The guard's gaze went to Nathaniel. "All clear, sir. The daughter's still at school so the house is empty."

Nathaniel nodded and then looked back at Ashe. She climbed from the car, drawing Lily after her.

"Gavin and I are fine," Katherine said with a nod toward the guard. "The others…"

Her mouth tightened and she looked away. Her gaze caught on Lily and Cole. "Who…?"

Elias hesitated. "We should get inside."

Katherine eyed him briefly and then nodded. She started toward the house, smoothing her brown curls as she went.

Glancing to the guard, Nathaniel jerked his head toward the car. Gavin went to move the vehicle.

The back door opened into a large kitchen. Dishes were piled high in one side of the sink, though the countertops were sparkling clean. White and blue patterned linoleum reflected light from the window above the kitchen sink and squeaked beneath their shoes as they came inside. Heading for the sink, Elias snagged a few paper towels from their dispenser and then flipped on the faucet to wash the blood from his face and arms.

"What happened?" Ashe said as the back door shut.

Her expression still tight, Katherine leaned against the counter, her hands braced behind her. "Mud," she said precisely.

Ashe's brow drew down. From the corner of her eye, she could see Cole look between them confusedly.

"I saw him," Katherine continued. "He helped the human escape. And I can only assume that he contacted the Blood too. He seemed fully aware that they were coming, and the guards in the basement–" She grimaced again. "–never came upstairs."

Ashe dropped her gaze to the tile. Burying her reactions was getting harder, though she didn't know what she'd do anyway.

Except scream.

The woman glanced to the window as Gavin shut the garage door, hiding their vehicle inside. "The Blood knew we were at Joe's. They had already killed Derek out back before they ever came in the front door, and with Ethan and Wes downstairs dead as well… we barely made it out."

Katherine looked over as Elias motioned for Nathaniel to take his place by the sink. "Joe saved us," she continued. "He flung a vat of oil on one of them after they followed me into the kitchen. Another struck back, Gavin defended, the oil caught fire…"

She drew a breath. "Joe yelled at us to come here and then he ran. I presume, since you knew how to find us, that he is still alive, and that the Blood left him alone after we were gone."

The back door opened and Gavin came inside. With a brief motion, Nathaniel ordered him toward the rest of the house. The man nodded and then disappeared down the hall.

"And now it's your turn," Katherine said, directing the words mostly to her husband.

Elias hesitated. "The twins are dead, Kat. And Joshua and the others are too."

The woman was silent for a moment. "I was afraid you were going to say that."

"I'm sorry."

She nodded tightly. "How did it happen?" she asked, her tone edging toward clinical.

"Ambush."

"The Blood have taken over Taliesin," Ashe supplied distantly.

Katherine's eyebrows rose. "What?"

"We don't know for sure that they–" Elias started.

"Yes, we do," Ashe countered, her heart starting to pound. "You really think they'd be *that* calm and have *that* strong a hold on Chaunessy if they hadn't already killed the people hiding there?"

Elias grimaced.

"The Blood are making it look like we did this," Ashe told Katherine. "And the Taliesin king controls them. Our best guess is, now that the Council's gone, he plans to blame their deaths on us and call for the Taliesin people to retaliate."

Lily's brow furrowed in confusion and then she looked from Ashe to Cole, the expression taking on an edge of concern. The young man turned away. Around the room, the wizards were silent, scenarios playing out behind their eyes.

"What do you want to do, your majesty?" Katherine asked quietly.

At the title, Cole glanced toward her and Ashe looked away, trying to ignore the twinge of old discomfort revived by the strange look in his eyes.

She caught sight of Lily's hand in her own. The air slipped from her.

They couldn't hope it'd take Jamison long to consolidate his hold on Taliesin. Nor to find out where the Merlin were hiding. With the tactics they'd seen on the streets not an hour before, the Blood and their wizard allies would have the factory's location in no time. And then…

No one would believe what they were up against. And while a few hundred angry wizards were probably more than sufficient match for the Blood, she couldn't think the Blood would be stupid enough to just go and get themselves wiped out by taking on the Merlin piecemeal. They'd have a plan. A strategy. They'd neutralized all of Chaunessy Tower, and the Taliesin guards, at least, had known what they were fighting.

She closed her eyes. So many innocents would be killed. Children. Families displaced by the war. They thought she was crazy and it didn't really matter, but she'd spent the better part of the past few months trying to find a way to save them. Even if they did think she was insane, she couldn't just leave them to die.

Though Darius and the Council would probably try to keep her from even getting in the factory door. And that was putting it mildly.

But anyone she sent in her place stood even less of a chance. The first mention of the Blood and Darius would have them locked up so tight, they'd still be in a cell when Jamison's people found them. And anyone she took with her would be a target.

Lily leaned her head against her side. With her free hand, she ran her fingers across Ashe's forearm as if to soothe the conflict twisting in her older sister. Heart pounding at the small contact, Ashe glanced down at the girl again.

She couldn't just leave Lily here. She wouldn't. Something could happen to the girl, even if she didn't really know what. Anything. Something that maybe she could prevent, even if it was just by being there. Even if it meant taking the hit instead of the girl.

And she didn't want to bring Lily to the factory. Darius wanted a puppet queen and he'd do anything to force her to become one. Regardless of who it hurt. Regardless of who it killed.

"Your majesty?" Katherine prompted.

Ashe looked up, her gaze running over the others in the room. There weren't enough guards in the world to keep Lily safe. All these Merlin and even Cole… they weren't enough. Nothing was.

Roughly, she made herself draw a breath. There wasn't any choice. There was never any choice. She couldn't leave the girl. And she couldn't let hundreds of people die.

"We have to go back to the factory," Ashe said.

Silence greeted the words.

"Are you insane?" Elias blurted.

"Excuse me?"

He reddened. "I'm sorry, your majesty. It's just–"

"You know what Darius will try to do to you if you go back, your highness," Katherine filled in. "And what he will try to do to us as well."

"I know what the Blood will do if nobody at the factory knows they're coming," Ashe said. "The Taliesin Council can't have been their only targets. They'll go after our people too." She paused. "I really don't want us to be the only Merlin left in this city by the end of the day."

Katherine looked down.

"How quickly can you get a second car?" Ashe asked, glancing from Elias to Nathaniel.

The large wizard hesitated.

"This is suicide, your highness!" Elias protested. "And if that's what you order, then fine. So be it. But–"

"I'm not ordering suicide! But we have to tell them–"

"Then let me go," Nathaniel cut in. "I will tell them."

"And when Darius tries to stop you? He'll lock you up, and that's the best case scenario. He won't get that far with me." She fought to keep her gaze from dropping to Lily. "He doesn't have hostages he can threaten this time."

"The couple hundred people hiding there ring a bell?" Elias

snapped. "The man is *insane*, your majesty. We didn't break you out of his custody just for you to trot back to it again!"

She stared at him, eyebrows climbing. Scowling, Elias turned away.

"We cannot continue risking you like this, your highness," Nathaniel said more quietly.

"And what do you suggest?" Ashe said, tearing her gaze from Elias. "Send them a text message and run for the hills? You won't get past the door, Nathaniel."

His face became stone. She turned away, hating herself for letting her anger answer him.

"What about your sister?" Elias argued. By her husband's side, Katherine looked between him and Lily in alarm. "This puts her in danger too."

Ashe glanced to him. "She stays with me."

"Sister?" Katherine said, looking at the little girl. Lily shifted, uncomfortable under the scrutiny. "She's…?"

"Yeah," Ashe said flatly.

"But–"

"She stays with me," she repeated, desperate to keep the focus from turning to Lily's strange appearance. "And the rest of you do too. Everyone sticks together, we go warn all the innocents who'll otherwise get killed, and if Darius tries to stop us… we handle him." Her heart pounding, she met Elias' eyes. "You know I'm right about this."

Elias looked away.

"So how soon till you have another car?" Ashe asked Nathaniel again.

The wizard watched her and she struggled not to drop her gaze from his eyes. "A few–"

He cut off as tires grumbled on the gravel drive. Striding across the room, he motioned her away from the window.

"Who is it?" Katherine asked, her attention torn between Lily and Nathaniel.

"Joe," Nathaniel said after a moment. "He appears to be alone."

"He's back from the restaurant already?"

"It would seem so," Nathaniel answered as the back door swung open.

His attention on his key in the lock, Joe got halfway through the door before spotting them. He came to a stop, his gaze running over them all. "You folks look like hell."

Elias scoffed. "You seen a mirror, Joe?" he replied, jerking his chin to the man's soot-covered clothes and bandaged arms.

Chuckling, Joe came the rest of the way inside, shutting the door behind him. "Not sure I want to."

He tossed his keys onto the counter and then caught sight of Nathaniel by the window. "It's okay, big guy. Nobody followed me. Told the police I needed to run home to get my insurance info. Took the longest route I could think of, and I didn't see anyone behind me."

Nathaniel appeared scarcely reassured. Lifting his phone, he called Gavin to check on the status of the house and then summoned the guard back to the kitchen.

Shrugging equitably, Joe looked over at Ashe. "You alright?"

"Yeah," she said, and then her gaze went to Elias. "But we should go."

The councilman sighed.

"Hope it's not on my account," Joe said.

"No," Elias told him, shoving away from the counter. "We're just giving the people who want us dead another shot. You know, for old times' sake."

Ashe eyed the councilman, but he didn't look her way. Pulling open the back door, Elias strode outside.

"Let me look at that," Katherine said, starting toward Joe.

"Nah, it's alright. Cops see me all healed up, they're going to have some interesting questions."

The woman's lips tightened, but she left his arm alone.

A moment went by. "Anybody want something to drink?" Joe offered.

No one answered. Uncomfortable, the man hesitated and then went to the refrigerator. He pulled out a can of soda and then opened it with an expression that made it clear he wished the contents were much stronger.

Taking a breath, Ashe looked away, trying to calm down. Her gaze caught on Cole. Standing by the back door, he was studying them all, his eyes flicking to Lily from time to time.

Ashe's brow drew down, uneasiness moving through her, and instinctively, her arm went around Lily, pulling the girl closer.

Cole blinked, his gaze twitching to meet hers. Muscles moved beneath the skin of his jaw and then he looked away.

Elias pulled up outside in a blue sedan.

"That was fast," Joe commented.

Katherine gave him a small smile and headed for the back door. Motioning to Gavin, Nathaniel sent the guard ahead and then glanced to Ashe, waiting.

Pulling her gaze from Cole, Ashe tried not to scowl at herself. She was on edge and just needed to calm down. Cole wasn't a threat. He'd rescued them from the Blood, for pity's sake, and obviously kept Lily safe ever since. Everything was fine. As much as it could be, anyway.

Drawing a breath, she drove the tension from her expression and ordered herself to focus, determinedly ignoring the fact she couldn't have pried her arm from Lily's shoulder if she'd tried. Pushing away from the counter, she started toward the back door and then paused, her conscience catching her.

"Joe?"

He looked to her curiously.

"I, um… I'm sorry about your restaurant."

The man smiled. "Danni's worth a thousand of them."

She tried to mirror his expression and failed miserably. Nodding awkwardly, she headed for the door.

"Hey, Ashe?" Joe called.

She glanced back.

Seeming uncomfortable, he hesitated, and then crossed the distance to the back door.

"Listen, they told me what happened before you first showed up at my place, and well…" He shrugged. "Just take care of yourself out there, alright? Like to see you all back under better circumstances someday."

She nodded again, though the motion felt like a lie. They'd all do what they could. And anyone who hurt Lily wouldn't survive the mistake. She couldn't promise anything beyond that.

Wordlessly, she walked out the door. In the garage, Gavin was waiting with the other car.

"Ashe?" Lily asked.

She glanced down to see the little girl looking up at her.

"He called you Ashe," Lily said, a touch of accusation in her tone.

"I…"

Hesitating, she caught sight of Cole studying her as though unsure what to make of what he saw.

"I go by that now," she finished uncomfortably.

Lily's expression became vaguely hurt.

Ashe grimaced. "I'm sorry. It's just…" Her mouth tightened as she tried to put it all into words. "Everything fell apart, Lil. Everything. And I just… I didn't want to lose the last thing I had of you. The last thing that felt real."

She paused and then bent to catch the little girl's eye.

"Is that okay?"

Biting her lip, Lily said nothing for a moment, and then she nodded. "Yeah, I think so."

"Thank you."

Lily nodded again.

Exhaling, Ashe straightened.

Cole was still watching her. The look on his face hadn't changed.

Tightening her grip on Lily's hand, Ashe pulled the little girl with her as she headed for the car.

Chapter Eighteen

The vehicles crested the rise and the roar of the tires faded as the sedan slowed. On the opposite side of Lily, Cole raised an eyebrow as the factory came into view.

"This," he said, "is where the Merlin Council is hiding?"

Ashe glanced over, her brow drawing down at his tone. "Yeah. Why?"

His gaze went to her briefly before returning to the decrepit building. "Nothing. It's just… different."

She watched him a moment longer, trying to judge the meaning behind the words.

The sedan drove down the hill, following the other car to the gate. A dozen wizards lined the fence, watching the vehicles roll closer. Nathaniel pulled to a stop and tossed a quick look to her in the rearview mirror.

"Don't let your guard down," he ordered.

The command was unnecessary, but she nodded anyway.

His gaze flicked to Katherine in the passenger seat and then he pushed open the door. From the car ahead, Elias emerged as well.

Checking Nathaniel's position by the sedan, the councilman nodded and then approached the gate.

Ashe swallowed dryly as Elias called to the guards, his words unintelligible over the distance. One of the guards responded, and she could see Elias' anger at the man's words. He snapped back, the guard paused, and then ostentatiously consented to draw out his phone and call someone else.

Moments crawled past. The guard hung up and then grinned. Nearly inaudibly, Katherine muttered something, her disgust clear even if the words were not. With a sharp motion to the others, the guard stepped away from the gate.

The barrier flickered. Cole's eyes narrowed, whether from pain or caution, Ashe couldn't tell, and he twitched slightly as though surprised. Moving to the sides of the road, the guards waited as the gate rolled away.

Elias turned and walked back toward his vehicle. In the passenger seat, Katherine tensed, barely breathing. By the driver's side, Nathaniel stood motionless, his gaze locked on the guards.

The councilman sank back into the car and shut the door. With a small growl, the engine turned over. Still watching the guards, Nathaniel returned to the driver's seat and put the sedan into gear.

Ashe's gaze slid to the guards as the cars crept past the gates.

Of the dozen men, only a few met her eyes. Contempt twisted their faces, making her blood boil. The lead guard let out a chuckle, equal parts disgust and satisfaction in the noise.

The rest wouldn't look at her. Eyes on the ground, they let the cars pass with expressions as still as stone.

Warehouses closed in. On the rooftops, more guards watched, motionless as the vehicles moved by. In the rearview mirror, Nathaniel studied the men as the barrier flickered and strengthened, sealing them all inside.

Near the opposite end of the parking lot, the sedans stopped. Drawing a breath, Nathaniel opened the door while, on the other side of the car, Katherine did the same.

Ashe looked down at Lily, trying to ignore the nervous twisting in her stomach. "Just stay near me," she told the girl quietly.

Lily nodded.

Echoing the motion, she pulled Lily with her as she left the car.

Broken concrete crunched beneath their feet as they walked toward the entrance. Wind swept around them, stirring the weeds and, up ahead, the rooftops showed no sign of security.

The factory door swung wide. Ahead of her, Nathaniel and Elias came to a stop, their magic strengthening simultaneously. Two dozen guards emerged from the building and fanned out immediately, surrounding them.

"Nice welcoming party," Elias murmured.

Nathaniel snorted, his gaze tracking the guards.

Ashe pulled Lily closer, ready to strip the magic from the first one stupid enough to attack.

From the circle, the man nearest the door stepped forward. "The regent has consented to grant you an audience," he said coldly. "You will follow us."

"The regent." Elias repeated flatly.

Eyes narrowing, the man turned and headed back inside. The other guards stepped closer, tightening their circle.

Jaw muscles jumping, Nathaniel glanced to her and then started forward. Silent, she followed.

The quiet beyond the entrance was eerie. The din of the factory was all but gone, replaced by a hush that made her skin crawl. In front and behind, the guards marched, pressing her and the others onward with their presence alone.

Light from the factory floor cut through the shadows and when she turned the corner, she felt Lily tense. Wizards were everywhere.

And every single one was waiting for them.

A narrow path cut through the crush of Merlin, leading to the distant stairs. The walkways hosted more watchers, though at the opposite end of the gallery, the crowds stopped. Only a few people stood on the stretch of walkway on the far wall, and even over the distance, she recognized them immediately.

Air slid from her. She'd wondered how it all went after she left. Now she knew.

Along the path between the masses, the guards strode. Without a word being spoken, the crowd pulled back to distance itself from them. She glanced around, trying to read faces, and then abandoned it as useless.

They'd think what they wanted. She was just here to give them a chance.

With military precision, the guards stopped at the base of the steps. The lead guard bowed deeply to the man atop the staircase, and then turned to Ashe and the others, dark threats in his eyes.

She ignored him, her gaze on the men above.

"And so the prodigal queen returns," Darius called down serenely. "Again."

From the top of the steps, he regarded her, a small smile touching his lips. Smooth lines of a gray suit covered him, with silver threads twisting through the fibers to glisten in the light. The remaining councilors waited against the wall and, while contempt showed on the faces of some, others just dropped their gazes to the floor.

But one of them had another expression altogether. Across the factory floor, he'd seemed to be standing so straight at Darius' right hand. But closer, she could see the truth in his eyes.

Cornelius looked like a man in whom something had died.

"Are you willing to let us help you at last?" Darius asked her.

She pulled her gaze from Cornelius. The calm on Darius' face didn't waver and she looked away before anger could get the better of her.

"I'm here to warn you," she called to the crowd. "The Blood have taken over Taliesin. They've killed the Council and they're going to blame the deaths on Merlin. You need to evacuate before the Taliesin find out where you've been hiding and come here for revenge."

Cornelius' eyes closed, pain flickering over his face.

"Oh, highness," Darius sighed, and the pitying edge in his voice could have made the air bleed. "Please. First surrender and now this? Do you care nothing for what this does to your people?"

"I never ordered surrender, Darius," she snapped. "And I'm trying to save their lives."

He shook his head sorrowfully. "Perhaps, if you will only let us separate you from these influences that have so clouded your mind–"

"The queen isn't mad," Elias cut in. "The Blood are real and they–"

"*Mister* de Vila," Darius interrupted. "How dare you? As if secretly encouraging our poor queen in her delusions wasn't enough, you would advertise the crime that forced us to remove you from your position by saying these things before witnesses as well?"

"Crime?" Elias retorted. "You want to talk *crime*, you sick bastard? We saw what you and Sebastian–"

"You've already been found guilty, Mister de Vila. Do not try to twist your case–"

"Enough!" Ashe yelled. Breathing hard, she turned from Darius toward the crowd. "This man is lying to you! He wants you to think Taliesin is the only threat, when the truth is there are wizards out there who make Taliesin look like nothing! You have to evacuate before–"

"Highness!"

She looked back. Cornelius stared down at her, his expression as close to begging as she'd ever seen him come.

"Please," he said more quietly.

Darius glanced to him. For less than an eye blink, his mouth twitched toward a contemptuous smile.

And then the expression disappeared back into pity.

"Oh, your majesty," Darius said. "These 'invisible' wizards aren't real. And they're not controlling Taliesin. Trust us, your highness. We investigated it thoroughly and the cripples did as well. They finally admitted they'd never found evidence of what your dear friend, the 'Hunter', Josiah Carter claimed. So please. Let go of these delusions and allow us–"

"They are real."

Ashe blinked and looked down. Lily was eyeing Darius as though uncertain of what she was seeing, but not sure she liked it.

"What's wrong with you?" the little girl asked. "Ashley's not crazy. She's just trying to save everybody from the monsters who killed our dad."

Darius' eyebrow rose. His expression flickered toward humor before swiftly settling into a concerned cast.

"Is this 'Lily', your majesty? Your sister whom Taliesin killed? Oh, your highness, I beg you. Send this poor little human girl home. Allow us to get you the help you need."

Sighing heavily, Darius shook his head as if he'd exhausted all he could think to do. At the motion, Lily started forward, but Ashe's grip held her back.

"The Blood exist and they're coming, Darius," she said. "The Taliesin Council is dead, and once the Blood have a hold on their people, they'll be after us too. Whether you accept it or not."

She looked back at the crowd. "We're leaving Croftsburg. Any of you who choose to believe me can follow us–"

"That is enough!" Darius interrupted. "Queen or no, you do not have the right to frighten our people into panicked flight, or to jeopardize their safety with your delusions. I will not allow your–"

The sky quivered.

As though he could see past the ceiling to the barrier surrounding the factory, Darius looked up and everyone else did as well. Murmurs of confusion rose around the room.

"Oh hell," Ashe whispered.

The background of magic in the air shuddered again. Harder.

"Elias!" she yelled. "Portal!"

"No!" Darius shouted. "She's trying to drive you beyond the factory's protection! Guards! Grab her!"

The nearest man's magic vanished and he barely had time to gasp before the ring of guards was blown to the floor. People stumbled back, horrified.

"Elias, now!" Ashe snapped. "Everyone, get out of here! The shield's coming down!"

"She's lying!" Darius bellowed. "No one can breach our–"

The barrier shattered.

"Run!" Ashe shouted.

Doors around the factory blew open at the pressure of portals forming inside them. People racing toward the exits tried to stop only to be shoved forward by others coming behind.

Magic scythed through the crowd as Taliesin wizards poured into the room. Ashe spun, grabbing Lily and ducking fast as energy sliced the air over her head.

Chaos took hold.

The circle of guards disintegrated as the crowd tried to escape in every direction at once. Screams filled the air and people tumbled into her, knocking her hard to the side and making it all she could do to hang onto Lily. Through the mass, she saw Cole stagger as wizards crashed into him, and then he was gone. Nathaniel flung another wizard away in effort to reach her, and then three more smashed into him and she lost him to the crowd. Blasts of energy ripped through the roof, sending concrete and steel raining down to the sound of more screaming. Magic pounded her shields from behind, sending her stumbling. Clutching Lily with all her might, she looked back, searching for the attacker.

On the walkway, Darius was shouting. Cornelius was nowhere to be seen. The other councilors were running and some of them had already reached the stairway.

Darius' hand lifted toward her, magic crackling madly around his fingertips.

In the conference room doorway, a portal swirled and the pony-tailed man and his blonde companion stepped out. Darius turned, his eyes going wide.

The woman's lips curled into a smile.

Ashe gasped, spinning away with Lily as blood splattered the wall.

Cornelius slammed into her back. "Move!" he ordered, grabbing her and Lily under his arms and propelling them with him into the crowd.

People fell back as Cornelius' magic tore them down. She couldn't tell if they were Merlin or Taliesin, and he didn't seem to care. His grip dug into her as he strode through the chaos, carving a path to a destination only he seemed to know.

She caught sight of Cole behind a chunk of concrete from the roof. Eyes wide, he spotted them and lunged from the cover. Energy shot through the air behind him, slicing across the space where he'd been and wizards tumbled into his path, thrown by battles all their own. Cornelius turned toward him, preparing to strike.

"Don't!" Ashe yelled.

Diverting his attack, Cornelius cut down a Taliesin coming their way. Barely sparing the young man a glance, Cornelius pushed Ashe and Lily onward, leaving Cole to fall in behind.

Another explosion shredded through the roof, sending beams slamming down on the crowd. Whipping them around, Cornelius shielded them as metal strafed out from the impact, and then he shoved them sideways, sending her tumbling with Lily into the shelter of tented slabs of concrete. Spinning, he grabbed Cole's arm, hurling the young man after them.

"Stay down!" Cornelius ordered.

Magic tore the air near his head and the wizard ducked back swiftly, cursing.

"Are you okay?" Cole asked Lily, shouting to be heard.

The little girl nodded. He looked up at Ashe.

"Plan?" he called.

Ashe turned back to the chaos, not sure what to say. The concrete shelter kept the three of them from view for the moment, but the protection couldn't last forever. Through the gaps in the debris, she could see people running for cover or cowering behind the same as magic seared the air. The far wall of the factory was already in flames and the ceiling was a shattered wreck waiting to come down. The air pressure dropped as portals flared, delivering more Taliesin or allowing frantic Merlin to escape. She flinched as a body tumbled past the gap in the shelter, charred and screaming, and somewhere nearby, she could hear a child bawling for its mother.

Trembling shook her. She couldn't stop this. She didn't know what to do.

By the edge of the concrete, Cornelius struck out at something she couldn't see and then stepped back. Nathaniel rushed around his side, skidding to a stop in the shelter of the debris.

"Your majesty," he started, relief in his eyes.

"Cover!" Cornelius barked.

The large wizard turned instantly, taking Cornelius' place. Breathing hard, Cornelius dropped back.

His gaze caught on the staff pulsing with light in Lily's hands. "What the…?"

Swiftly, he sank down beside the little girl, looking from the staff to her as though seeing the child for the first time.

"We need to go!" Nathaniel shouted over his shoulder, and impacts shook the shelter as though to emphasize his words.

"What is it?" Ashe asked Cornelius.

He tore his gaze from the girl. "I think… the Staff of Merlin."

Ashe blinked, the fragment of memory finally clicking into place. She looked to Lily.

Pale and shaking, the girl nodded.

A breath escaped her. She'd only seen a handful of stories. Scraps of legends, really. And while not one of them agreed on whether the staff helped Merlin bind Taliesin, the amount of strength it reputedly gave wizards of his line was another matter entirely.

"Where did you–" she started.

Nathaniel swore and ducked back as magic struck the concrete shelter, sending dust and pebbles raining down.

She shook her head, dropping the question. It didn't matter and there wasn't time. Swallowing hard, she looked back at her sister. Reading her expression, Lily bit her lip, the fear in her eyes strengthening, and then hesitantly she held out the length of wood.

"Your majesty, you don't know if–" Cornelius began.

Ashe wrapped her hand around the staff.

Her eyes went wide. Like a shadow fleeing the sun, the dark void limiting the strength of her magic rushed away. In a heartbeat, the boundary of her power became nothing more than a black line on the horizon, irrelevant and too distant to matter at all. Shivers ran over her as magic coursed from her into the staff and back again, as charged as lightning, as expansive as the sea.

And all of it utterly awaiting her command.

Carefully, her fingers closed tighter around the twisted wood. Her gaze rose to the chaos beyond their shelter as the blue-white light in the staff deepened to fiery red.

"Guard Lily," she told Cornelius and Cole.

In her hand, the staff burst into flame.

"And stay behind me."

She shoved to her feet and strode past Nathaniel before the large wizard could react. Outside the shelter, three Taliesin rushed toward her, magic flaring around them.

The first one's magic vanished. She still couldn't reach the energy in the others. Gasping as the realization hit her, she regrouped swiftly and struck out at them.

Her magic leveled the Taliesin for fifty feet around.

She kept moving.

More Taliesin came. Stripping magic from the closest, she threw it at them all, barely noticing as they fell. Others rushed her, some from each side, and they screamed as her magic mowed them down. Nathaniel and Cornelius shouted behind her, calling for the Merlin to run their way, and she looked back, burning the Taliesin who tried to intervene.

Fire pulsed from the staff, growing stronger and stronger, and the air around her rippled with the heat. At her glance, the flames snaked between the Merlin to tear down the Taliesin coming their way.

And she strode onward.

Elias and Katherine were behind her now, along with families clutching their children and wounded hanging onto life. On the wall ahead, she could see a doorway still clear despite the walkway fallen on either side and, if any Taliesin hid nearby, they remained out of sight. Turning, she looked to Elias and jerked her head at the door.

"Get them out of here!" she yelled.

He rushed past, and she could feel the air pressure plummet as magic spun to life in the doorway.

People flooded by her, but she paid no attention. Smoke poured through the shattered ceiling, veiling the distance but not disguising it entirely, and across the warzone the factory had become, she could see the Taliesin regrouping. The blonde-haired Blood was still standing, the man with the ponytail at her side, and in a doorway near them both, a portal began to form.

Her heart pounding in rhythm to the seconds slipping by, she adjusted her grip on the staff and let her shields grow stronger.

"Your majesty!"

At the sound of Elias' voice, she glanced back.

"Go!" he shouted at her.

She looked at the portal and then saw Lily. Clinging to Cole, the girl shook her head at Cornelius as he tried to pull her away.

Elias followed her gaze. "I'll get him out of here," he yelled. "Just go!"

Magic ripped through the air behind her, smashing hard into her shields and she stumbled. By the wall, she saw Cornelius' eyes go wide. She turned, and her blood went cold.

On the other side of the factory, Brogan stood by a portal. Another man emerged behind him, his cold gaze sweeping the wreckage and then catching on the Merlin by the far wall.

Magic roared to life around him, dragging at hers and stronger than Brogan's had ever been.

"Go!" Ashe cried.

Cornelius grabbed Lily and disappeared into the darkness. Elias vanished with Katherine in tow.

Cole froze, his eyes on the Blood with a look somewhere between loss and horror.

Ashe raced at him, drawing everything she had through the staff. In the air behind her, she could feel the strike coming, and as she flung herself at the young man, she poured her magic into the strongest shield she could form.

She slammed into Cole, wrapped the shield around them both, and yanked him with her into the portal.

———— ◆ ————

Blackness. The air screamed with magic, buffeting her shields and howling with rage. She couldn't feel Cole in her grip and every flash of light was like a physical blow. Her magic fragmented around her, shredded by the forces whirling through the portal and disintegrating with each heartbeat.

And then she was through.

Grass slipping beneath her feet, she stumbled to a stop and looked around frantically as the magic surrounding her died.

Cole stared at her.

"You…" he began, and then swallowed again, his face bloodlessly white. "What…"

She gasped, relief hitting her almost as hard as the portal had. Struggling to breathe, she choked on a smile and closed her eyes, trying to stay standing. Swallowing hard, she blinked and then looked up at the place where they now stood.

Dozens of Merlin were staring at them.

Scattered around a grassy lawn, the wizards said nothing. Wounded lay among them, shadowed by massive oak trees. Tending to them with the portly nurse Ermengarde hovering nearby, Katherine cast glances at her, while Elias, Gavin and Nathaniel stood several feet away, their faces stunned.

"Are you alright?" Elias asked, looking between her and Cole.

She didn't answer, scanning the crowd as panic started to rise.

"Ashley?"

She turned at the sound of the little girl's voice. From the wooden steps of a dilapidated mobile home, Lily leapt the distance to the ground and dashed toward her. Still seated on the stairway, Cornelius hesitated before starting to rise.

The girl skidded to a stop, staring at Ashe's hands with her eyes widening in alarm.

Ashe looked down.

Black as charcoal, the staff lay lifeless in her grip. Carefully, her fingers shifted position, easing from the charred wood.

The staff crumbled to dust.

Her brow furrowed as her gaze rose to Elias.

"Too much," Cornelius said.

She looked over at him. A few yards away, he had stopped, as though unwilling or unable to bring himself closer. Caution in their eyes, Nathaniel and Elias watched him, making certain he stayed that way.

Cornelius' gaze moved between her and Cole. "To shield a cripple through a portal," he said, and his brow rose and fell before he looked away.

"What?" Cole said, his voice still rough with shock.

She hesitated. "Portals, um, kill… people like you."

Cole blinked and then looked back. She followed his gaze. The front wall of the shed behind them was blackened. The doorway itself had shattered, its fragments littering the grass.

"Oh," he said.

Covering her discomfort, she turned away.

"Are you okay?" Elias repeated.

Ashe nodded.

"What was that?" he asked.

She looked down at the dust in her palm and then carefully let it fall to the ground.

"The Staff of Merlin," she told him, watching the cinders coat the grass.

Silence fell.

"What do we do now?" Lily asked.

Ashe pulled her gaze from the dust. Around her, the other wizards were gathering closer, and in the distance, the skyline of Croftsburg was fading into the twilight.

She drew a breath. "We run."

Epilogue

———◆———

He was in a taxi, and that in itself was bizarre. For someone who'd just survived yet another wizard battle, the normalcy of a cab ride was ludicrously surreal.

"Thanks, buddy," Mud said cheerfully to the driver as they pulled to a stop.

The cab driver regarded the little man in the rearview mirror and said nothing, clearly just waiting for Mud and his silent companion to let him get on to less smelly fares.

Shoving open the door, Mud clambered from the car and then waited impatiently on the curb. "Well?" he scoffed. "Pay the guy."

Halfway out of the seat, Harris paused. Beyond his residual incredulity for the sheer state of his own life, he felt a flicker of annoyance at the little man. Grimacing, he pulled out his wallet and then passed a few bills through the grate.

"Sorry," he said to the cab driver, though he couldn't quite put his finger on what for. Mud, maybe. Or the world.

Without another word, he climbed from the taxi. The driver pulled away, disappearing back into traffic almost immediately.

"On we go," Mud announced.

Shuffling eagerly across the pavement, the laundry lump waddled off.

Harris hesitated.

The sidewalk had seen a better day, but it looked stellar compared to the building it ran beside. Shattered glass glittered like diamonds beneath the remnants of two-story windows and crunched under the feet of passersby. In the lobby, a row of bodies lay against one marble wall, covered with what could only be curtains taken from elsewhere inside. The front desk had been pulverized, as had the far wall, and through the mess, a few people moved, as though searching for where to begin in the odious task of cleaning up the destruction.

And on the street, pedestrians strolled past as though they couldn't see any of it at all.

Numbly, he followed, his feet crunching across the glass as he crossed the threshold of what had been a window. Up ahead, Mud bounced along, ogling the bodies and shuddering sensationally at the ruined walls.

Harris looked back. On the sidewalk, a hotdog vendor rolled by, barely noticing as his cart jostled over the debris. A young couple followed, holding hands and smiling as they crossed the street.

We're so blind, he thought. *We just see what we want to see, believe what we want to believe, and ignore whatever doesn't fit in our world.*

Even when the truth is right in front of our eyes.

"You coming?" Mud called.

For a moment, Harris didn't move. His brow furrowed distantly, discomfort stirring in him as he watched the ordinary people walking along the pavement.

And then he turned, following the little man deeper into the building as he struggled to leave the troubling thought behind.

412

Want to know what happens next?

Read Wildfire

Book Three of the Kindling Trilogy

Available Now

Loved the book?

If you've enjoyed Ignite, please consider leaving a review on Amazon.com, Goodreads.com, and other book-related sites.

Hear about all the new releases!

Join Skye Malone's mailing list at

www.skyemalone.com/mailinglist

Other titles

The Awakened Fate Series

The Touch Me Series

The Kindling Trilogy

About the author

Skye Malone is a fantasy and paranormal romance author, which means she spends most of her time not-quite-convinced that the magical things she imagines couldn't actually exist.

A Midwestern girl who migrated to the Pacific Northwest, she dreams of traveling the world — though in the meantime she'll take any story that whisks her off to a place where the fantastic lives inside the everyday. She loves strong and passionate characters, complex villains, and satisfying endings that stay with you long after the book is closed. An inveterate writer, she can't go a day without getting her hands on a keyboard and can usually be found typing away while she listens to all the adventures unfolding in her head.

Connect with Skye

Website: www.skyemalone.com
Twitter: www.twitter.com/Skye_Malone
Facebook: www.facebook.com/authorskyemalone
Instagram: www.instagram.com/authorskyemalone

Acknowledgements

I am so grateful to the many people in my life who have supported me in the creation of this series.

To all of my friends and family, thank you for your encouragement and your belief in me throughout the years.

To Neil Peterson, thank you for beta-reading again. Your comments and thoughts, as always, are so appreciated.

To Mary Ann and Keri, thank you for your support, your faith in me, and for reading, re-reading, and spot checking random scenes when requested.

To Avery, thank you for just about everything, since I don't know where to begin or end with that list.